"With heartwarming family drama, well-wrought tension, faith, and sparkling banter between reunited childhood friends, Michelle Griep's *Of Silver and Secrets* is sure to delight fans of archaeological adventure and historical romance. Includes a fun visit with characters from Michelle's previous book *Of Gold and Shadows*. Recommended!"

> Julie Klassen, bestselling author of the ON DEVONSHIRE SHORES series, on *Of Silver and Secrets*

"Beautifully written. *Of Silver and Secrets* may be my favorite of Michelle Griep's books. She immerses her readers in Victorian England, where you'll meet Eva and her sweet sister; Bram and his quirky, forgetful uncle; and rotten-to-the-core villains. Add in a twist you won't see coming, and you've got an unforgettable historical romance."

> Ane Mulligan, author of the award-winning *By the Sweet Gum*, on *Of Silver and Secrets*

"Michelle Griep once again dazzles with her trademark twist of mystery, intrigue, and romance. Duty-bound Eva Inman clashes with charming-yet-stubborn archaeologist Bram Webb, and the sparks fly. Add in a forgetful uncle, a precocious sister, and a man with a vendetta, and *Of Silver and Secrets* provides the perfect recipe for a tale that leaves you guessing each moment and tugs the heart."

> Tara Johnson, author of *To Speak His Name*, on *Of Silver and Secrets*

"*Of Silver and Secrets* is one of those novels you throw yourself into and never want to leave. The heroine is humanly relatable, the hero roguishly dashing, and the plot so intriguing and fresh, I didn't want it to end. Throw in a heart-throbbing romance, a search for the Holy Grail, and a group of fascinating characters, all expertly woven by the fabulous pen of one of my favorite authors, and you have yet another Michelle Griep masterpiece."

MaryLu Tyndall, author of the award-winning LEGACY OF THE KING'S PIRATES series, on *Of Silver and Secrets*

"[A] high-octane historical . . . Griep keeps the suspense sky-high throughout. . . . Readers won't be able to put this down."

Publishers Weekly on *Of Gold and Shadows*

"Griep delivers a romp that will leave a grin on readers' faces, especially those interested in archaeology."

Library Journal on *Of Gold and Shadows*

OF
SILVER
AND
SECRETS

Books by Michelle Griep

From Bethany House Publishers

TIME'S LOST TREASURES
Of Gold and Shadows
Of Silver and Secrets

OF
SILVER
AND
SECRETS

MICHELLE GRIEP

BETHANYHOUSE
a division of Baker Publishing Group
Minneapolis, Minnesota

© 2025 by Michelle Griep

Published by Bethany House Publishers
Minneapolis, Minnesota
BethanyHouse.com

Bethany House Publishers is a division of
Baker Publishing Group, Grand Rapids, Michigan

Printed in the United States of America

Library of Congress Cataloging-in-Publication Data
Names: Griep, Michelle, author.
Title: Of silver and secrets / Michelle Griep.
Description: Minneapolis, Minnesota : Bethany House, a division of Baker
    Publishing Group, 2025. | Series: Time's Lost Treasures ; 2 | Includes
    bibliographical references.
Identifiers: LCCN 2024041942 | ISBN 9780764242571 (paperback) | ISBN
    9780764245046 (casebound) | ISBN 9781493450817 (ebook)
Subjects: LCGFT: Christian fiction. | Romance fiction. | Novels.
Classification: LCC PS3607.R528 O37 2025 | DDC 813.6—dc23/
    eng/20240329
LC record available at https://lccn.loc.gov/2024041942

Scripture quotations are from the King James Version of the Bible.

This is a work of historical reconstruction; the appearances of certain historical figures are therefore inevitable. All other characters, however, are products of the author's imagination, and any resemblance to actual persons, living or dead, is coincidental.

Cover image by Lee Avison / Arcangel; cover design by Dan Thornberg, Design Source Creative Services

Published in association with Books & Such Literary Management, BooksAnd Such.com.

Baker Publishing Group publications use paper produced from sustainable forestry practices and postconsumer waste whenever possible.

25 26 27 28 29 30 31   7 6 5 4 3 2 1

To Ami Vose.
Your smile is missed by so many, dear one.

And as always,
to the One you are smiling with
right now.

1

Royston, England
October 1889

The end of Eva's world started with a window she never should have left open. A small neglect, yet twelve years later, one that had culminated in a leaky roof, a ledger that refused to balance, and a blind sister. Not to mention her dead mother—for Eva wouldn't. She kept that memory locked tightly in a closet.

Hefting a great sigh, she set down her pen, trying to ignore the incessant *plip-plip-plip* of raindrops collecting in a nearby bucket. Inman Manor may have a long list of needs to fill, but at least she did not need to worry about their water supply.

She picked up her father's silver letter opener, taking a moment to admire the scrollwork on the handle, then slit the next missive on the pile. Thankfully this one wasn't a bill but a note from her friend Lottie, bemoaning the fact she'd not seen Eva in ages and would Eva please consider coming to the harvest ball on Saturday. A lifetime ago she would have. She'd have bought a new gown and ribbons for her hair, maybe even splurged on a pair of silk slippers. She'd dance with the young men and laugh with the ladies. Oh, what a dream she'd lived in.

She wrote a short, yet pleasant, refusal. Lottie would understand. Hopefully. Eva sealed the note and set it in the post bin. In her haste, her elbow caught on the bottle of ink. Black liquid spilled on the desktop and crawled up the fabric of her sleeve like a disease. Bother!

Grabbing a rag, she blotted up the mess on the desk, then did what she could to dab away the stain on her gown. So much ruin. A sigh leached out of her. It was the best she could do.

She sank heavily onto the chair, pressing her fingertips against her eyes, wishing she weren't the one who must hold everything together. And yet here she was, sitting in Papa's office, at Papa's desk, filling Papa's shoes.

Oh, Papa.

It had to be nigh on a year ago since the riding accident that horrid grey morn. But her father's commands hung heavy on the air as if he had just spoken them. *"Take care of your sister. Always. And the house, don't lose it."* Expected commands. Promises she easily gave and had every intention of keeping. But it was his final words that haunted her the most.

"Blackwood. Beware of Blackwoodssss . . . hissss."

A statement unfinished. A warning she had yet to decipher, for in the twelve months since, she still hadn't figured out why she ought not trust the Reverend Mr. Blackwood.

"Are you unwell, miss?"

She swiveled in her seat at the steward's voice. How had she missed the thud of Sinclair's boots on the office floorboards? Yet there he stood, water dripping from the brim of his hat, adding to the cadence of the *plip-plip-plipping* in the corner bucket. He was a sinewy man with an incongruent softness of cheek, as if the sugar biscuits the cook, Mrs. Pottinger, slipped him now and then were never swallowed but stayed bunched up right there beneath the skin. Would that change now that there were no more coins for sugar?

"I am fine." She tapped the ledger, ignoring the jagged edges of her bitten fingernails. It was a slovenly habit, one she'd picked up over the past year, but she had bigger concerns to master first. "Our budget, however, is ailing. Do you have a moment? I should like to speak with you about an idea to increase our income."

"I was just stopping by for the supply list, miss, but I have time to hear you out." He pulled off his hat, the crow's-feet at the corners of his eyes a mix of hardship and laughter. "What's on your mind?"

She pulled the list he wanted from atop a stack of papers, quickly penned an addition, then held it out. "As long as you're going into Royston, would you stop by Mavers Feed and pick up enough winter wheat for ten acres? I know it's not much, but every bit will help."

He slanted her a skeptical look. "I thought the budget was strained."

"It is." So much so that she'd nearly considered fluttering her eyelashes at any man of means in Royston, for marrying into money ought to be easier than grabbing pennies out of thin air. Another great sigh leached out of her. "But I pawned my locket for extra funds. If God wills, no one shall purchase it, and I'll buy it back when the wheat is harvested next summer."

A frown tugged down his brow. "I hate to see you suffer such hardship, miss."

So did she, and yet there was nothing for it. Perhaps this was what came of buried secrets. "Thank you, Sinclair," she murmured.

"I can do that, miss, but . . ." He tucked away the note, rainwater collecting in a pool at his feet. "Where is this seed to go? The fields are already sown."

"Which is why I'd like you to speak with Tom. As soon as this rain lets up"—she glanced out the window, the leaden skies giving no hint of relenting—"have him begin work on the fallow plot near the northwest corner of the estate. If we can get that wheat in before a hard freeze, next season we'll increase our yield."

"Mmm." An ominous grumble rumbled deep in Sinclair's throat. "I don't think so, miss. You know it's not right."

She pulled her shawl tightly to her neck to hide her frustration. "You cannot negate the fact that eighty extra bushels—one hundred if God smiles upon us—will bring in extra money."

"I don't fault your mathematics, miss."

"Then what do you fault?"

He fiddled with his derby, inching it about in a circle, the veins on the backs of his hands sticking farther out with each twist. "It's not wise to turn earth that ought not be disturbed. You know this."

She snorted, wholly unladylike yet completely unstoppable. "Don't tell me you believe such poppycock. I should have ordered this done earlier."

"It's not called the cursed acres for no reason, miss."

"Look around you, Sinclair." She swept her hand through the air, knocking her shawl aslant. "The house is falling down about our shoulders. The Inman estate is already cursed. Besides, that tale is from centuries ago. I'm sure any truth to the legend has expired by now."

"'When the land is left alone, in peace the curse is overthrown.'"

As if on cue, a low drone of thunder added a sinister tone to the ancient words. A shiver spidered down Eva's spine—one that annoyed more than frightened. She faced the steward with a lift to her chin. "Be that as it may, the account numbers leave me no choice. That ground must produce, despite traditions—or superstitions. And even then we'll barely get by."

"I don't like it, miss." He blew out a long breath. "But I'll do as you ask."

"Thank you, Sinclair. I know it's not been easy on you since my father died. It's not been easy for any of us. I pray we will soon see better days."

"Your words to God's ear, miss." He clapped on his hat. "And may the good Lord grant us a speedy answer. Good day."

"Good day." Her words blended with the chime of the wall clock. Eleven already? Where had the morning flown? She closed the ledger cover, weary of trying to balance numbers that refused to be wrangled into any sort of common sense.

Leaving the office, she wound her way through the back corridor, passing by the open kitchen door. The mouthwatering aroma of baking bread pinched her empty stomach. Thin soup and toast for dinner again, yet she was grateful for it. Why her father had kept the abysmal state of their finances such a secret was beyond her. After managing the books this past year, she still couldn't account for how he'd kept things going, save for the odd earnings he'd labeled as sundries. She'd sure like some of those sundry payments now—payments that had dried up after his death. Apparently he'd had some unknown source of sporadic income to keep the manor running, not enough, though, to provide her with a new gown for the Guy Fawkes festival. If only he had explained instead of hiding their money woes. If only she had not pushed him so hard on the matter. For if they'd not quarreled, he wouldn't have taken out his fury on such a hard ride.

And he'd still be here today.

She sighed as she threaded her way to the front of the house. No sense obsessing about monetary matters now. She simply must trust God to provide, and the devil be drawn and quartered. La! What a thought, but even so, a wry smile twitched her lips.

"There you are!" Penelope Inman whirled from where she'd been pacing in the entry hall.

Eva smirked. The girl had the ears of a dormouse.

"Aren't you eager today." Closing in on her sister, Eva straightened the girl's collar.

"You're late." Penny flinched away, waving her copy of *Little Women* in the air. "I'm dying to find out what happens now that Marmee cut her hair. Do you think Jo will cut hers? Why, I was of half a mind this morning to do away with my own."

"I'm glad you didn't, poppet. I happen to like this head of yours as it is." Bending, Eva planted a light kiss atop her sister's crown. "It is a far more respectable colour than the wildfire burning atop mine."

"Then perhaps we should clip off yours."

"Perhaps we should," she murmured, then added under her breath, "it might bring in a coin or two."

"What's that?" Penny cocked her head, a single dark wave falling over her brow.

"Nothing." She grabbed the book from her sister's grasp. "Let's find out what is happening in the March home, shall we?"

Penny spun toward the drawing room, a folk song on her lips and her skirts swishing around her legs, which didn't slow her in the least. She marched off, completely unhindered by her lack of sight, as the front bell rang.

"Be there in a moment, poppet. I'll save Dixon a few steps." Eva set the book on the entry table before pulling open the front door.

A round fellow smelling of lilies and sausage stood on the front stoop. Rain droplets dripped from his hat brim onto his moustache—which was a curled affair, the sides neatly swirled into downward circles at the sides of a stern set of lips. His direct gaze was no merrier, and she got the impression he summed her up with as much pleasure as she had this morning's ledger.

Even so, Eva managed an amiable smile. "How may I help you, sir?"

"I should like a word with the man of the house." He sniffed, his bulbous nose bobbing. One fat raindrop fell to the ground.

"There is no man. I am Eva Inman, mistress of the Inman estate, and you are?"

"Mr. Buckle, tax collector from the Royston Assessment Office. I'm paying a courtesy call to all the homes in the area, reminding owners that taxes are due by December thirteenth." He held out an envelope that may have been crisp at one time but was now damp and wilted. "Oh, and there's been a slight surcharge added. Rates have gone up. Good day."

He dipped his head as she broke the seal. Of all the inconvenient times for a tax increase!

And then her jaw dropped as she glanced at the formal missive.

"Hold on there, Mr. Buckle." She dashed down the stairs, chasing the man to his horse in the rain. "There's nearly a fifty-pound difference here." She shoved the horrid document against his chest, blinking away the moisture collecting on her eyelashes.

He retreated, palms in the air, water dripping from his elbows. "As I said, miss, rates have gone up. If you take issue with the amount—which I can only surmise that you do—you'll have to direct your inquiries to the appeals board, not to me."

"Very well. I will." She lifted her chin, refusing to show cowardice though it cost her a face full of raindrops. "When do they next meet?"

"In January." He swung up into the saddle, leather creaking.

"But that's after the deadline!"

"So it is. Walk on." He clicked his tongue.

Leaving her standing agape. In the rain. Alone. Again.

Would God never smile upon her?

2

TRINITY COLLEGE, CAMBRIDGE

There were two things Bram Webb couldn't stand. No, make that three. A cheaply made cigar tasting of green tobacco. Spiders. And, worst of all, sitting around waiting for an execution—especially when it was his own neck that would feel the bite of a noose. Irritated beyond measure, he cracked his knuckles, garnering several frowns from the Faculty Misconduct Review Board. The six suits behind the long table at the front of the room couldn't look more forbidding if they tried.

Yet their expressions were child's play compared to the cancerous scowl he was sure to receive from ol' Grimwinkle—if the man ever arrived. For the third time since Bram and his uncle had taken their seats, he flipped open the lid of his silver pocket watch, then frowned. This meeting should have started a quarter of an hour ago. Where was the department head? Was his tardiness some sort of ploy to increase anxiety?

Leaning aside, Bram whispered for his uncle's ears alone. "What do you suppose I've done this time? And why have they dragged you into this?"

Uncle shrugged, wafting an earthy smell of dirt and greenery, and no wonder. The only time Uncle Pendleton wasn't tending his extensive collection of potted ferns was when occupied by a dig or teaching. "You know Grimwinkle. That man will stab at me any chance he gets, and driving a knife into your side is as good as drawing my blood."

As if conjured by the mention of his name, a long-legged stork of a man stalked in, his ridiculous shoes clacking on the tile. Wooden clogs, of all things! Professor Algernon Grimwinkle ought to have been born a preening peacock, so fastidious was he about his appearance. Herringbone during the winter months. A pastel suitcoat for spring. Paisley in the summer, and for autumn he adorned himself in rust-and-gold plaid. Every man rose as he approached the center chair. And though Bram despised giving this popinjay such recognition, he stood out of respect for the man's position of head of the Trinity College history department.

Fabric rustled as Grimwinkle made a great show of enshrining himself in his seat. Once everyone else sat as well—save for Bram and his uncle—Grimwinkle peered down the length of the long table. "Are you ready, Mr. Clem?"

The department secretary blinked, his eyes no bigger than two drops of indigo ink on the broad canvas of his face. He dipped his pen with gusto. "Yes, sir."

"Very good." Grimwinkle smacked a gavel against the tabletop, the sharp report of it causing everyone to flinch. "This disciplinary meeting is called to order. We are convened today to address a matter of utmost importance—one concerning the integrity and reputation of this hallowed institution. If the charges brought forth are found to be substantiated, there will be severe and immediate consequences for the involved party. Is that quite clear?"

Bram resisted the urge to tug at his collar, desperately running through all the possible infractions he might've committed. There'd been that incident with the pith helmet, but how was he to have known the thing belonged to the headmaster? He should've questioned the student who'd brought it in before using it as a prop to demonstrate improper excavation techniques. The helmet had been no match against the pointy end of a steel trowel.

Toga Tuesdays might have been a bad idea as well, especially since he'd allowed the students to go to the pub in such immodest array.

Or perhaps it might've been the Roman banquet that'd caused this meeting of the pinch-faced misconduct board. The wine had flowed too freely, leaving the library quite a mess. In hindsight, he ought to have used a different area, but it was one of the few rooms for which he possessed a key.

He rubbed the back of his neck. Indeed, any one of these offenses was foolish and perhaps ill-timed, but none were grounds for *severe and immediate consequences.*

"Before proceeding," Grimwinkle continued, "I would like to remind everyone that all conversation in this room is not only binding but confidential. From here on out, be advised to keep this in mind." His gaze lingered on Bram.

Pah. As if he'd wish to breathe a word of whatever humiliation he was about to suffer.

"Mr. Clem." Grimwinkle eyed the secretary. "Kindly outline the nature of the charges if you will."

Bram stiffened.

Here it came.

Clem riffled through a folder and pulled out a single document. "The first complaint alleges that an archaeological excavation—dated March through August of 1887—was performed on university property without obtaining a duly required permit. Such an unauthorized action is in violation of code A31–72."

Bram glowered. Of all the petty indictments! "That dig was two years ago," he huffed, "and you're just looking into it now?

What a bogus waste of time, dragging us in here for such a minor infraction."

Grimwinkle's gavel cracked on the tabletop. "Mr. Webb! You were not yet addressed, and I will thank you to hold your tongue until called upon. I should first like to hear from the senior member of your team." The department head's malignant gaze drifted from him to his uncle. "Now then, what have you to say about such a dereliction of academic duty?"

Bram's uncle swiped up his satchel and, with a loud click, opened the latch. Surely his uncle hadn't been carrying around a two-year-old permit, had he?

After an excessive amount of pawing through papers, his uncle snapped the bag shut and planted it at his feet, having accomplished exactly nothing. "There you have it."

Bram tensed. His uncle made no sense whatsoever, which was exactly what he'd been trying to conceal the past year or two.

Grimwinkle's brow bunched as he looked from the satchel to his uncle. "Have what?"

The six other men behind the table wore the same wrinkled brow of confusion as Grimwinkle. A few whispered behind raised hands.

Uncle Pendleton merely adjusted the spectacles on the bridge of his nose. "I don't appear to have that paperwork."

"I didn't expect you would." A satisfied smile rippled across Grimwinkle's thin lips. "Therefore, Professor, you are hereby found guilty of—"

"Guilt?" His uncle flourished his hand in the air. "Nothing of the sort. I deferred the acquisition of a permit to my nephew." He slapped Bram on the back, knocking him off-kilter. "So all is well."

Bram sucked in a breath. Uncle Pendleton had never asked him to file any paperwork.

"Well, Professor Webb?" Grimwinkle's dark eyes narrowed on him. "Can you produce verification of a permit application?"

Blast. What to do? Take the fall—once again—for a slip of his uncle's mind or refute what the man had just told the entire history faculty? Granted, this charge was far less serious than the last time, when he'd been indicted for theft of an artifact, but that didn't make the accusation any less bitter.

He cleared his throat, thinking fast. "That, em, paperwork must've gotten lost in the shuffle. We all know how it is with the longnecks in administration. No offense, Mr. Clem."

Clem shifted on his seat, the wooden chair creaking in protest. "None taken, Professor Webb."

Grimwinkle toyed with the gavel. "An insufficient excuse, Professor. That being the case, as a disciplinary action, you are hereby placed on academic probation until the end of the term. I will personally take over your classes for the rest of the year, and during this time, I suggest you rethink not only this oversight but all your recent displays of questionable judgment."

"Now see here!" Bram squared his shoulders, ready for battle. "That dig, while admittedly not yielding any artifacts of real value, gave the students hands-on experience, training them in the techniques of relic recovery right here in our own backyard. It was my ingenuity that saved the college hundreds of pounds in travel and other sundry expenses. You cannot suspend me for what was clearly beneficial to the school."

"I can and I am. Now then, Mr. Clem, on to the next allegation."

Bram's hands clenched into fists as the secretary once again rose.

"The second complaint asserts that false and improper classroom instruction has been committed in violation of code A31–17. Furthermore, said teaching is indicative of a mind in decline, which is in direct opposition to the standards of excellence required for this institution."

What a load of claptrap. Bram stifled a snort. His methods were innovative, not false and improper!

Uncle Pendleton hitched his thumbs in his lapels, puffing out his chest. "My nephew has done no such thing, Professor Grimwinkle."

"The accusation is against you, sir." Grimwinkle aimed the end of the gavel at his uncle as if he might fire off a shot. "You are the one charged with spouting nonsense in the classroom. Your theory positing a supposed settlement hereabouts of a Roman intellectual and spiritual refuge is nothing but the meanderings of forty years of wishful thinking. You've been warned before to stop teaching such make-believe nonsense until evidence is presented." Grimwinkle leaned forward, teeth bared like the wolf he was. "There is no such evidence, and yet I have it on good authority that you lectured last Thursday on the fabled settlement of Caelum Academia as if it were a real place."

"Caelum Academia *is* real!" Uncle jammed his forefinger and thumb in the air, holding them a breath apart. "I'm this close to finding it, and you know it."

"I admit no such thing. There never has been—nor I suspect will there ever be—proof of this mythical Roman refuge for persecuted Christians and artisans. Yours is the mind that is slipping, not mine!"

Grimwinkle's sharp words sliced through the air, cutting holes in the thin screen Bram had desperately constructed to hide his uncle's increasingly erratic behaviour. Whispers swirled amongst the men flanking the department head.

Uncle Pendleton rose to his toes, impervious to the accusation. "You're just jealous because you'll be toppled from your department throne when I find the Holy Grail."

The committee gasped in unison.

Grimwinkle tossed down his gavel as he threw back his head, laughter shaking the plaid fabric at his shoulders.

Bram clenched his fists all the tighter. Everyone had their quirks of faith. Silly beliefs such as fairies or leprechauns—or that the Queen was secretly bald and only wore wigs. But most knew not to speak of such things aloud. Apparently his uncle hadn't gotten that memorandum.

"The Holy Grail itself? You see, gentlemen?" Grimwinkle's belly laughs turned to a mere chuckle. "We all know the grail is nothing but a literary and historical subject for mere speculation, not a tangible item to be acquired. Need I say more to make my case against the intellectual capacity of this man?"

With a swift, furious grasp, Uncle Pendleton swiped up his satchel and rummaged in it like a mad man.

"Steady on, Uncle." Bram squeezed his arm, then stepped forward, a moot—yet unstoppable—attempt to shield his uncle. "Professor Grimwinkle and other esteemed members of the board, clearly there's been some sort of misunderstanding here. Like myself, my uncle teaches nothing but classic yet innovative archaeological techniques and solid Roman history. Even so, I am certain this entire matter can be easily corrected by a simple change in my uncle's curriculum. Surely that's all that need be done."

A feral light glinted in Grimwinkle's dark eyes. "With such a tarnished career as yours, Professor Webb, I am astonished by your boldness to suggest how we go about our business here today. I am the one who will decide what needs to be done, and that is immediate termination. All in agreement, say aye."

"Termination! Don't be absurd." Bram paced in front of the long table, clasping his hands behind his back to keep from flailing them in the air. "Members of the board, I beg you to consider the consequences of Professor Grimwinkle's harsh penalty. My uncle has dedicated his life to the pursuit of knowledge and has been a loyal Trinity servant for decades. To cast him aside now, with only two terms left before his retirement, would be a grave injustice. It would not only be a blot on his legacy but rob him of the pension he's worked so hard for over the years."

Bram paused, searching the faces of those who held his uncle's fate in their hands. "And so I implore this venerated committee to carefully consider the weight of your decision. This is not simply about one man's career. It's about a lifetime of dedication to the pursuit of knowledge and a desire to pass that intellectual wealth on to the next generation. I ask that each of you let reason and fairness guide your judgment."

His uncle dashed up beside him and slapped down a portfolio of papers in front of Grimwinkle. "Take a look at this. Are these documents the sign of a slipped mind? I dare you to find one fault—*one*—and if you do, I shall resign this instant."

"Is that so?" Grimwinkle smiled as he picked up the packet. "I look forward to this. Take a seat, gentlemen, while my colleagues and I read over these papers."

Bram's shoulders sank as they returned to the smaller table—or the isle of indictment, as he often thought of it. He'd suffered here far too many times to count. Sitting on his hands was the only action that kept him from planting his face in his palms.

Oh, Uncle, what have you done?

After a few deep breaths, he whispered to his uncle, "What did you give him?"

Uncle Pendleton leaned back in his chair, folding his arms over his potbelly. "The first part of my *Treatise of Caelum Academia*. My finest piece of writing if I do say so myself."

"Silence!" Grimwinkle glowered as he passed along one of the papers.

Bram folded his arms, working hard to contain a scowl. Here he was again, waiting for an execution, though this time it was his uncle who would swing. Seconds, minutes, what might very well be hours ticked by, though he couldn't confirm it. In the mood Grimwinkle was in, sliding out his cherished pocket watch just might get him terminated as well.

So there was nothing to do but sit there and sweat as the men digested his uncle's writings. Would to God it all made sense. But with every raised brow, each huff of astonishment, and not just a few murmurs of disbelief, Bram's hope flagged.

An eternity later, Grimwinkle handed off the last page, then frowned at Uncle Pendleton. "Impressive work, Professor, yet incomplete. Is there more?"

Uncle met his gaze. "Not yet."

"Then I'm afraid, sir, your theory of a refuge for Roman Christians is null and void until—as I said earlier—evidence is presented. I warned you before when you lost your lecture notes for the annual fall seminar that I would suffer no more negligent behaviour from you, and I meant it. I'm afraid in this instance there can be no other resolution besides immediate termination, and so, gentlemen, once again I ask for your vote. All in agreement say—"

No! This couldn't be happening. Not to the man he owed everything. He'd always known there'd been rivalry between Grimwinkle and his uncle, but not to this degree. Bram shot to his feet. "You will have your evidence by the end of the term."

Grimwinkle's finely manicured eyebrows lifted to the ceiling. "You're going to unearth the Holy Grail—something that's been sought after for millennia—in a mere ten weeks? You're as mad as your uncle."

"Even so"—Bram jutted his jaw—"one way or another, my uncle and I will prove that Caelum Academia is real."

Hushed voices droned so low that Bram couldn't make out a word. But at least the board was talking amongst themselves instead of rendering an immediate decision. That had to be good, didn't it? He closed his eyes.

Please, God, make it so.

After a lengthy round of ominous discussion, Grimwinkle folded his hands atop the table and gave them an evil eye only a demon could be proud of. "A decision has been reached."

Tension hung thick as an October fog.

For a long moment, Grimwinkle said nothing, no doubt

enjoying this cat-and-mouse game, then he opened his thin lips. "This board shall reconvene on December thirteenth, at which point irrefutable confirmation will be presented by Professors Webb and Pendleton authenticating the existence of Caelum Academia, the supposed refuge of Roman Christians and artisans. If no such evidence is provided, Professor Pendleton will be deemed unfit as an instructor of excellence in the classroom and immediately dismissed. Is that clear?"

Before Bram could say anything, Uncle Pendleton's voice rang out loud and clear. "Not only do we understand but we heartily embrace the challenge."

"Then this meeting is adjourned until the end of Michaelmas Term." Grimwinkle banged the cursed gavel louder than ever.

Bram flinched, gut twisting. How in the world was he going to find the remains of a settlement that more than likely never existed . . . all while keeping his uncle's increasing bouts of senility a secret?

3

A lot could happen in three days. Or not. No golden-egg-laying goose had waddled through Eva's front door, nor had some long-lost relative gone to glory and left her with a sizeable inheritance. Worse, the numbers in the ledger still refused to yield anything but a warning—and a dire one at that, with the added fifty pounds she must raise by mid-December. Hence, the sole reason she stood in the drawing room this morning with a sharp-nosed widow circling her mother's beloved writing desk. Mrs. Muggins had been dissecting the antique bureau for the better part of half an hour now with nothing better to say about it than an occasional flat-lipped *humph*.

Eva smoothed imaginary creases from her skirts, giving her something to do other than bite her nails while waiting. "As I'm sure you've noticed after such diligent examination, Mrs. Muggins, you'll not find a writing desk of higher quality at such a fair price as this one."

The woman humphed again while rubbing her thumb furiously on one corner. "I cannot abide blemishes."

Eva studied the wood at the indicated spot. Glossy wax reflected her face. "I don't see any damage there."

"I was merely pointing out a fact, Miss Inman."

"Of course." She forced a smile. "However, I assure you this desk is in impeccable condition, for it has had nothing but the utmost care. My mother was particular about such things."

"Mmm." She eyed Eva with all the admiration she might give a crust of dried manure on her shoe. "I must say it is rather callous of you to part with a sentimental heirloom that is part of your family legacy."

Her stomach tightened. The woman could have no idea how much selling this desk wrenched her heart. She pressed her features into a benevolent smile. "This beloved piece of furniture is dear to me, which is why I feel your home is the perfect sanctuary for it. I know you will shower nothing but tender affection upon such a valuable keepsake."

Mrs. Muggins pressed her hands to her belly as if digesting a compliment was a distress. Probably was. Not many in Royston favored her with so much as a good-day, so sour was the elderly woman. Eva wouldn't have willingly singled her out if the widow didn't possess such a sizeable bank account.

Without further ado, Mrs. Muggins went back to examining every nook and cranny of the desk.

Eva retreated several steps. She'd rather be spending her time helping those in need with the Royston Relief Society than hawking a family treasure to a tight-knuckled purse clutcher, but there was no time for that interest anymore. If she didn't start setting away money for that tax bill now, she'd never have enough to pay it.

Another ten minutes ticked by. At this rate, her sister would be tromping in here with her book, which could cause Mrs. Muggins to flee. The woman barely had patience for adults, let alone for a precocious twelve-year-old. Surely there had to be some tactic she could use to force the widow's hand. . . . "Now that I dwell on the matter," she drawled at length, "I suppose Mrs. Grandbloom's sitting room would make as fine a haven for this desk as your front room."

"Mrs. Grandbloom! Tsk. That will never do." Mrs. Muggins wagged a gnarly finger in the air. "The woman has cats. Cats!"

It was more of a hiss than an accusation.

Perfect. Clearly the idea ruffled the woman. "True, but she also has a husband who dotes on her, and she has admired this piece before."

"Humph. The woman is spoiled, if you ask me."

"And yet she might offer more than what I'm asking." Eva paused to let that sink in. "Yes, now that I think on it, I could get more money if I—"

"Nonsense! Have your man deliver the desk to my home tomorrow, and I shall send the payment with him."

"I don't know." She ran a finger along the front length of the desktop. "Mrs. Grandbloom might pay quite handsomely and—"

"I'll add on a gratuity for prompt service. Good day, Miss Inman." Mrs. Muggins whirled so fast, the feather atop her hat flapped in protest.

"Good day, Mrs. Muggins," Eva called to the woman's retreating skirt. Once the rustling fabric was fully out of sight and sound, she collapsed onto the sofa, an inordinately large grin stretching her jaw. The battle had been fierce, but what a victory!

Not two breaths later, Sinclair's boots clunked into the room.

"Sorry to bother you, miss, but I think you're going to want to see this." He held out something small and grey. A stone?

She crossed the room and retrieved the thing from him, surprised that it was nothing of the sort. Oh, the metal ring was as dirty as a stone picked from the soil, but as she licked her finger and rubbed at the piece with the pad of her thumb, the filth gave way, revealing a tarnished silver band with an engraving of a fish on the front. She glanced up at the steward. "Where did you get this?"

"From Tom. He's been finding all sorts of scraps while plowing that plot o' land. This one, though"—he pointed at the ring—"could be of value."

"Perhaps that land isn't cursed after all, eh?" She smirked.

Dixon sailed in then. Though lacking in stature, the white-haired housekeeper was an unsinkable frigate, going about her duties as if the Inman household were fully staffed instead of having only a maid and a cook to manage. "Reverend Blackwood is here to see you, miss."

Just when things were starting to look up with the sale of the desk and a potentially valuable relic in her hand, the dour clergyman had to call. She stifled a sigh. "Very good. Show him in."

Sinclair clapped on his hat with a dip to his head. "I'll leave you to your company, miss."

"Thank you, Sinclair. Oh, and would you see that my mother's desk is delivered to Mrs. Muggins's home tomorrow? Ten o'clock sharp, for she has all the patience of a gnat."

"You're being generous, miss." He chuckled. "But, yes, I'll see it's done."

Eva absently rubbed the ring as the steward exited. She'd never been completely comfortable in the rector's presence even before her father's deathbed warning. There had been a few Sundays when she'd considered attending a different church, but it seemed wrong to break with generations of Inman family tradition all for the sake of a severe clergyman. Besides, it wasn't as if he singled her out with his cold ways. Mr. Blackwood was terse with everyone and had been ever since she could remember.

He stalked into the room on silent steps, dressed head to toe in grey, which added to the impression that he'd recently crawled from one of the graves in the churchyard. The only colourful thing about the man was the intense blue of his eyes—and that was no improvement. His gaze cleaved one's spirit from the bone.

She dipped a proper curtsey. "Good morning, Mr. Blackwood."

"Miss Inman." He gave a sharp nod.

"Please have a seat. May I offer you some tea?"

Please say no. Please don't stay.

"None needed. I shan't stay long."

She breathed freely, but only for a moment. The longer he stood there staring at her, the more she fiddled with the ring. "Did you have a matter you wish to discuss with me, Mr. Blackwood?"

"I believe the matter has been resolved without any discussion whatsoever. I came to see for myself if you were alive and well, being that your pew has remained empty these past two weeks." His aquiline nose bunched. "My sister is worried about you."

His sister? As shepherd of the parish flock, ought he not have been concerned? She slid the ring on and off her index finger, composing a less snappish response.

"It is kind of Mrs. Mortimer to have noticed my absence, though she needn't suffer any anguish on my account. The truth is that Penelope suffered a cough the Sunday before last, and more recently our only horse to pull the pony cart got into the hemlock and came down with a case of colic. I fully anticipate, though, that my sister and I shall make this week's Sunday service."

"Hmm. And yet neither of those occurrences directly affected you." He lifted his nose. "Neglecting the gathering of the saints is no small thing. The consequence of such abandon not only reduces the church rates but hinders your spiritual health."

Hah! Church rates indeed. There wasn't a single rain bucket catching leaks beneath the roof of All Saints Church. Nor did the rectory suffer in any way. She forced a smile. "I shall take that into consideration."

"Very good. But I am curious, Miss Inman, what is it you're so preoccupied with this morning?" His gaze shot to her hands.

Her fingers froze. How many times had she scolded Penny not to fidget when entertaining a guest?

"It is nothing of consequence, sir. Just something my farm-hand unearthed out in the field."

He held out his hand, palm up, the lift of a single brow commanding her to pass it over. Which she did. One ought not to refuse a man of God such a simple request. So why the anxious twist to her belly?

"Hmm." The sound rumbled in his throat as he studied the tarnished ring. "Very interesting. Where was he digging?"

"The back corner of the estate. Why do you ask?"

"Clearly this is a historic find, possibly even church related."

"I assure you my man only did as I asked. He wouldn't have ventured to plow on any property other than my own."

His blue eyes skewered her. "I implied no wrongdoing, Miss Inman."

Oh dear. She'd gone and indicted a clergyman. Perhaps missing services truly had impacted her more than she realized. "I beg your pardon, Mr. Blackwood." But then just as quickly, she jerked up her chin. "What do you mean, church related?"

He held up the ring, observing it with one narrowed eye. "I cannot be sure, of course, but this engraved fish, while admittedly much more ornate than I've ever seen, might be an ichthys."

"A what?"

"Ichthys. The Greek word for *fish*. It is claimed Christians used the inobtrusive symbol to silently identify one another at a time believers faced persecution by the Roman Empire. Though what it would be doing buried in your farmland is anyone's guess."

Now that was interesting. She paced a tight circle on the rug, each step adding to her excitement. If that ring was of historical significance, it just might bring in the funds she needed. This could be an answer to prayer!

She stopped in front of Mr. Blackwood, disregarding her usual caution about the man. "Might you have a connection with anyone who would be interested in purchasing that ring?"

A frown darkened his face. "How can you sell an item if you don't know what price to collect?"

"Point taken." Selling the ring might not be as easy as she'd thought. She held out her hand. "Thank you, Mr. Blackwood. I appreciate your insights."

"I am happy to help, Miss Inman. I shall get this appraised for you." He pocketed the ring and wheeled about. In two long strides he was at the door.

Eva scurried after him, and though it was not proper or probably even holy, she sidestepped the man and planted her body directly in his path. Clergyman or not, there was no way she'd let him take what might be a valuable antiquity from this house. "While I appreciate the offer, I should like my ring back now, Mr. Blackwood, and will trouble you no further."

The cut of his jaw was a diamond, hardened at her deterrence. "I thought to save you the trip to Cambridge, what with your colicky horse."

He may as well have given his whole explanation in Greek, so little did she comprehend it. "Why would I be going to Cambridge?"

"You will need an expert's opinion on whether this ring is of Roman origin. The history professors at Trinity College are unmatched in their scholarship. It is not proper or seemly for you to travel such a distance alone. I shall accompany you. Does tomorrow suit?"

Pah! She'd sooner travel three hours seated next to the Grim Reaper. "That won't be necessary. My steward's been meaning to visit his brother there anyway, and I'm sure he'll be glad for the diversion from his work. Our pony is also quite well now and will likely enjoy such a jaunt. All that being said, you may return the ring."

Once again she held out her hand.

And once again he ignored it, holding the bit of silver up to squint at it.

"Mr. Blackwood. The ring, please." It took all her willpower to keep her tone pleasant.

"Hmm? Oh. Of course, Miss Inman." He lowered the ring to within an inch of her palm, his unsettling gaze boring into her soul before he dropped it. "But be mindful of the past you've unearthed. More often than not, things are buried for a reason."

4

Wherefore fain would I sit out in my heart
That I might see the marvel of the Grail;
But ever I dread me that I be not worthy.

Bram smirked as he tossed back a mouthful of cider. Sitting in a pub stinking of sour ale and sweat probably didn't make him quite the worthy soul Sir Thomas Malory had written about four centuries ago . . . which didn't bode well for him to see "the marvel of the Grail" anytime soon. If ever. Apparently only a man who was brave of heart, stalwart in spirit, and had led a life of valorous purity would unearth that sacred relic. He was sufficient in the brave and stalwart departments, but after his delinquent younger years, the life of purity was out of the question.

He heaved a sigh while toying with his now-empty mug. At least he didn't have to produce the grail itself, just the settlement of Caelum Academia, which wasn't as stringent a requirement. Unfortunately, after three days of scouring every word in his uncle's leather-bound journal—the last half of which made no sense—he couldn't pinpoint where the settlement might be, though from what he'd pieced together, it could be somewhere around Royston.

A place he'd hoped to never see again.

"There he is!"

The shout was followed by three strapping young men jostling onto the bench across from him. Foam sloshed over the sides of their tankards.

Jonathan Barker, the usual spokesman of the trio, slapped the table with his hand. "We've been looking all over for you, sir."

"And so you find me." Bram saluted them with his mug.

"You've got to come back to the classroom. Grimwinkle's killing us!" Barker tugged at an imaginary noose, emphasizing his claim.

"Come now." Bram chuckled. "It can't be all that bad."

Charles Wimble, a tall fellow with tousled dark hair, grimaced. "We've had three exams in as many days—and I've failed every blasted one of them."

"Please, Prof," the lad next to him joined in. "We're close to a mutiny."

"Hear, hear!" The three clacked their tankards together, then drained them dry.

Bram couldn't help but grin. It was gratifying, this show of allegiance from his undergrads. "I appreciate your vote of confidence, men. Truly. But I'm afraid I've a task to complete before I can return."

"Then let us help you." Barker swiped the back of his hand across his mouth, wiping away the frothy remains and knocking his tie further askew. "We'll speed up the process."

The other two nodded vehemently. "Aye."

"I shall take that into consideration, gentlemen, should the need arise. Until then, there's nothing for you to do but lash yourselves down and weather the storm, eh? No mutinies allowed on pain of death." He eyed all three. "Understood?"

Barker nodded and rested one elbow on the table. "But only because you ask it, sir. Were it up to us, we'd keelhaul ol' Gruff Grim and not be the sorrier for it."

"Then it is a very good thing it is not up to you fellows." Or to him. Ever since he'd trudged out of that misconduct meeting, it had been a struggle to push aside wicked thoughts of what he'd like to do to Grimwinkle. "Now, off with you. I'm sure you must study for tomorrow's exam." He waggled his eyebrows.

Wimble moaned. "I cannot fail again."

"I suppose I can spare an extra fifteen minutes tomorrow in my office. Why don't you stop by before class and show me what ol' Gruff Grim will be quizzing you on?"

The young man's face lightened considerably. "You're the best, Professor Webb! See you then."

The students bumped their way off the bench, ribbing each other like overgrown pups. Which they were.

Bram leaned his head against the back of the tall bench, feeling inordinately old. What did he have to show for his life? Hardly more than that trio of young men. All his former classmates were married, many of them with children. Even his old friend Price, who had sworn off women, had married last year. And what did he have to go home to every night? A rented room in the fellows' house, which was more of a monastic cell than a home, and a growing collection of lonely nights.

He scrubbed his face, weary—which was new. Usually he grabbed life by the neck and gave it a good shake. What was wrong with him? Bah! He needed a change, that's what. A new venture and possibly someone to share it with.

And that was another new thought. He'd had plenty of women take interest in him in the past, but none he'd given a second thought to. Settling down always seemed like a weight that would pin him in place, stifle the very air he breathed. But now? For some unexplainable reason—though he highly suspected it was his recent twenty-seventh birthday—things were different. Or maybe his perspective had changed. Whatever the reason, matrimony with the right woman didn't seem so bad anymore.

He yanked out his silver pocket watch, thumb poised to click the latch, when Uncle Pendleton sloshed into the opposite seat looking like a shipwrecked sailor. Water darkened his coat, matted his silvery hair, and dotted the lenses on his spectacles.

"Uncle! You're soaked to the skin, and it's not even raining." Bram flew off his bench and wrapped his coat around his uncle's shoulders. Wheeling about, he hailed the nearest server with a wave of his hand. "Miss! A hot toddy right away, please."

Uncle Pendleton laughed merrily. "I'm not at death's door, nephew, though I won't turn down that drink."

Frowning, Bram resumed his seat. "What happened?"

His uncle sniffled while producing a limp handkerchief as soaked as he was. "Apparently the Willow Bridge is under repair."

"Yes, it has been for some time now." He handed over his own handkerchief. "Surely you didn't try to cross it? Oh, Uncle." He groaned. "You did, didn't you? Sweet mercy. Are you hurt?"

"None of it. These old bones are stronger than you think." He honked into the cloth and offered it back, to which Bram held up his palm. He may soon be destitute if he didn't find that forgotten Roman settlement, but for now he could provide his uncle with a dry handkerchief.

An apron-clad young miss arrived with a steaming stoneware mug. Uncle Pendleton wrapped both hands around it. "Thank you. Oh, and a hearty bowl of beef and ale stew as well."

"Right away, sir."

His uncle winked at Bram as he held up his cup. "This ought to do the trick."

Bram gave him a few moments to relish the warm brew, all the while trying to shove down the rising concern for his uncle's mental state. Several memoranda had been sent to faculty and students detailing the slow progress on the pedestrian bridge. Either Uncle hadn't read them or—more likely—had forgotten about the warnings. Was his uncle becoming more absent-minded, or was Bram simply noticing it more?

"Stop looking at me like I'm a doddering old fool." Uncle Pendleton set down his empty cup. "Judging by the rut worn into the bank I climbed up, I'm not the only one who's made the mistake."

"Maybe so, but I insist on hiring a cab to take you home as soon as you've eaten."

"Don't tell me our roles are reversing so soon." His uncle arched a brow. "It wasn't so very long ago I was the one seeing you home from the pub."

A snort ripped out of Bram. "For a very different reason."

"True." A serious gleam flashed in his uncle's eyes. "I'm glad you've mended your ways. Your mother would have been proud, God rest her."

Bram's gut clenched. Much to his regret, he hadn't given the woman any reason to be proud of him when she was alive.

Then again, she hadn't been the picture of virtue herself.

The server returned with a bowl of stew, the meaty scent almost making Bram wish he'd ordered one of his own.

"Thank you, my dear." Uncle spared her a smile while picking up his spoon.

Bram waited for him to enjoy several mouthfuls before sliding the journal to the middle of the table. "About these notes." He stabbed the cover with his finger. "The last half of this journal makes no sense whatsoever."

"What's that you say?" Stew suddenly forgotten, his uncle grabbed the worn book and paged through. The longer he looked, the more a slow grin grew until he exchanged the journal for his spoon again. "Oh yes, now I remember."

As if that explained anything.

Bram waved the book in the air. "Care to expound on that?"

Uncle Pendleton shoveled in one more large bite before pushing away his bowl and leaning across the table. His voice lowered to a whisper. "It's not meant to make sense."

"Then why waste the ink on such gibberish?"

"Have I taught you nothing at all?" Uncle puffed out his cheeks with a great blast of air. "Surely you remember the origin of the bad blood between me and Grimwinkle?"

"Yes, yes. He claimed the credit on a dig for which you should have gotten commendation, earning him the head department chair instead of you. But I fail to see what that has to do with your journal."

"He never would have gotten that commendation had he not stolen my notes and written the article that made him look like a genius."

Bram blinked. This was news. "Why have you never told me that?"

"I just did." Uncle humphed.

"Why did you not press charges against him?"

"Wouldn't have done any good. It was his word against mine, and he had powerful backers in the department at the time. At any rate, it taught me a good lesson." He thumped his hand on the journal. "Never put all your eggs in one basket, and for those that you do, be sure a few of them are cracked. The information on the final pages is for the express purpose of throwing off anyone who might try to use these notes for nefarious reasons."

Aha. Now there was a ray of light in this dimly lit little pub. "So you're saying the rest of the notes are in another notebook, yes?"

"I am."

"Thank heaven. Then let's be on our way." He grabbed the book while scooting off the bench. "I'll pick up the rest of your notes when we stop at your house."

"Splendid idea except . . ."

He wheeled around to face his uncle. "Except what?"

Uncle's chin tucked sheepishly. "I can't seem to remember where I put them."

5

Eva gloried in the route from Royston to Cambridge. All along the way trees disrobed like blushing brides, shedding their reds and oranges into colourful swirls on each side of the road. The sweet scent of cherry tobacco puffing out of Sinclair's pipe had made for a pleasant accompaniment as well. A good start for what she hoped would be a profitable outing.

Cambridge itself was a charming town despite the crowds. Carriage wheels clattered along the cobblestones, pedestrians darting about like water striders skimming a pond. And such clamor! Hawkers barked about their candied apples and hot sausages, competing loudly with the ring of bicycle bells and street musicians. Such lively activity was exhilarating.

Shortly after Sinclair turned the pony cart onto a quieter lane, the hallowed halls of Trinity College came into view. Eventually he pulled on the reins. "Easy now, Dusty."

As the faithful old horse slowed to a stop in front of the entrance, the steward hopped down and rounded the carriage. "Here we are, miss." He held up his hand, helping her from her perch. "My offer yet stands. I'll gladly wait while you conduct your business."

She brushed wrinkles from her traveling coat. "I don't want you to miss out on one minute of your brother's company. I'll meet you at the Golden Lion as planned. I'm sure you'll have plenty to discuss until I return. Besides, in this glorious weather, I relish a stroll. I may even stop at Heffer's bookshop on the way. You know I don't mind getting lost in there for an hour."

His lips twisted into a wry grin. "Knowing you, it will be two or three, miss. *If* I can get you out the door even after that."

"I'm not promising anything." She returned his smile as she tucked away some strands blown from the refuge of her bonnet.

"Very well, miss." Sinclair tipped his hat. "Until then."

Gathering her hem, Eva climbed the college's front steps, then paused as the gateway opened to a vast quadrangle. Gothic-style buildings lined the courtyard. Cloistered walkways hemmed the edges. Students dashed to their classes or clustered in groups on the lawn, their academic gowns billowing about in the autumn breeze. Where to go?

"May I help you, miss?" A man with the college insignia embroidered on his collar approached.

"Yes, please. I'm looking for the history department. Could you direct me?"

"Of course, miss." The porter angled his head, indicating for her to step out of the flow of foot traffic. "This stretch of lawn is the Great Court. You'll be wanting Nevile's Court, just through that gateway on the west side. See it?"

She followed the length of his blue sleeve, spying a smaller yet as ornate entryway. "I do."

"Very good. Once you pass through, you'll take the cloister walk on your right, which will lead you to the building you're wanting. You can't miss it. The entrance has a bronze plaque with the word *History* on it."

"Thank you very much."

"My pleasure, miss. Enjoy your visit to Trinity College."

She set off at a brisk pace and found the place easily enough, for the porter's directions had been very thorough. The front desk clerk, however, wasn't nearly as helpful—though perhaps he might've been if he was at his station. Her stomach rumbled, and she pressed her hand against it. It was lunch hour, after all, which likely accounted for his absence. What an ill-timed arrival.

Pulling off her gloves, she glanced at a wooden bench, debating if she ought to wait it out or go looking for a professor. If the front of the building had a placard, ought not the instructors' offices bear markings as well? There were two corridors to choose from, plus a stairway straight ahead. It seemed most logical that a teacher's office ought to be easily accessed by students, so she discarded the stairs idea just as a jolly chuckle pulled her attention to the passage on her left.

A tall young man with dark hair swung out of an open door, laughing, his scholarly robe open at the front and flapping behind him with each long stride.

"Excuse me." Clutching her gloves, she boldly approached him. "I'm wondering if you might point me in the right direction?"

"Perhaps, but it'll have to be quick, miss, or I'll be late for an exam." He shifted the thick books in his arms. "What is it you're looking for?"

"I have an item I wish to authenticate. It might have some church history and is possibly of Roman origin."

"Roman? Why, that's easy enough. One of the most knowledgeable professors I know happens to be in his office now. I just came from there." He tipped his head over his shoulder. "First room on the right."

"Thank you." She bypassed him with a grateful smile, then rapped on the frame of the open door.

"Pardon me, but I wonder if I might have a moment of your time, Professor?" She spoke to a broad set of shoulders, for the man stood with his back to her, tucking papers into a file.

He held up a finger. "One moment, please."

She studied him while he worked. He was in desperate need of a haircut. His shaggy locks, the colour of watered-down Darjeeling, feathered raggedly against his collar. The hem of his suitcoat sported fraying threads and his trousers were more wrinkled than her traveling coat. Obviously his work held sway over his appearance. Still, a seed of respect for him took root, for she never could abide a milksop gent, tossed to-and-fro by the whims of fashion and popular opinion.

"Now then," he said as he turned. "How may I help—"

His jaw dropped.

So did hers.

Time stopped. Sound. Motion. Everything ground to a halt.

"Eva?"

A cascade of emotions poured like ice water over her head. Disbelief. Anger. Heartbreak and longing.

But most of all the gut-punching feeling of abandonment. Bram had been the first in a string of people to leave her, and she would *not* risk that happening again.

She spun on her heel and stalked away with long strides. She'd rather lose the family estate than speak with Bram Webb.

God was definitely not smiling upon her today.

It wasn't every day a ghost from the past knocked at his door. Thank God for such mercies as that! But this red-haired spirit? The very sight of her conjured a myriad of memories. Eva Inman, the girl who had always been around, trailing him with wide, admiring eyes. Such adoration had softened his heart toward her and had fostered a protective instinct—leastwise as protective as a bubbleheaded lad could be. Seeing her now, transformed into a captivating woman, brought a wave of unexpected emotions.

Bram bolted around the desk.

"Wait!" He overtook Eva, stopping in front of her to block her path. "What are you doing here?"

Her jaw tightened—and what a fine jaw it was. He'd never imagined the formerly gawky-limbed Eva Inman could grow into such an entrancing vision. Oh, her long nose might not fit conventional beauty ideals, yet that feature lent her an air of regal grace. Her mouth, far too wide to be considered a dainty rosebud, held a magnetic allure. She was an October morn, this woman, with hair of fire and the threat of bluster in her pale blue eyes.

"I am seeking an opinion." She lifted her chin. "But not yours."

Oof. That stung. "And yet you came to my office."

A bitter laugh spouted out of her. "Trust me, I didn't realize it belonged to you."

"Ah, carrying a grudge, are you?" His grin grew. "So you do still think of me even after all these years."

"I don't give you a thought, Bram Webb. Ever. Step aside, please."

He plowed his fingers through his hair, thoroughly intrigued and more chagrined than he cared to admit. It wasn't as if such a response wasn't warranted. He'd been a hellion in his younger days . . . and admittedly, even now had his moments, may God forgive him. "It's been twelve years, Eva. I was a thoughtless young lad then, looking for attention in all the wrong ways. I never meant to hurt you."

"Yet because of you, I nearly died of fever."

He shook his head, thoroughly confused. He'd done many things he wasn't proud of, but making a girl nearly three years his junior ill? "What are you going on about?"

"Don't play the innocent with me." Tossing back her shoulders, she strangled the life out of a pair of gloves. "You left town right after leading me into that abandoned barn."

"Yes, the very next day as I recall. But I had no choice in the matter. My mother sent me away. And I fail to see how taking you to see a litter of kittens—which I thought was a kindness—could nearly have been the death of you."

"It wasn't the kittens. It was the scratch from the mother cat you scared into a frenzy." She shoved up her sleeve. "I owe this to you."

An angleworm of a scar crawled across the finely veined skin just above her wrist . . . an injury of his own making. His heart wrenched. What a careless, callous boy he'd been. "Eva, I'm sorry." He reached for her, then thought the better of it and pulled back. "I had no idea. Please do not hold the sins of a foolish lad against the man who stands in front of you now."

"I tried to find you, you know," she said, her voice softening. "I begged your mother to tell me where you'd gone, but she refused to give me any information. Said a girl like me wouldn't understand and to run home to my mother. She was right. I didn't understand." Eva pushed her sleeve back over her wrist, her gaze now more wary than a cornered fox. "I could never understand why you left without a word, breaking our friendship without so much as a good-bye. So my forgiveness you may have, but my trust? Well, that is a bridge that could use some mending."

His gut twisted. He'd never meant to hurt her so deeply, and yet truly he'd had no choice in the matter. A sigh drained out of him. "Fair enough. At least return to my office and tell me why you've come."

She didn't move a whit, just stared with an inscrutable gleam in her eye.

"There's not a single cat in there. I vow it." He slapped his hand to his heart.

The slight quiver of a smile rippled across her lips. "Are you truly a professor of Roman history?"

"I am." Thanks to God's grace and Uncle Pendleton, though she needn't know that.

"Very well." She whirled, marching off before he could so much as blink.

He scurried after her, surprised to see she'd already taken a chair in front of his desk, the timid lass he'd grown up with nowhere in sight. How had the girl who'd feared her own shadow come by such confidence? He took his own seat, inordinately curious. "Why the sudden interest in the Roman Empire?"

"This." She rummaged in her pocket, then produced a silver ring.

The moment he held it up to the lamp on his desktop, he knew this bit of silver was something special. "Remarkable craftsmanship," he muttered as he turned the relic one way and another. "Exquisite engraving. Definitely an exceptional piece of history. Late for the era, third century, maybe second—but that's just a guess. The use of silver was a widespread practice during this period, particularly for artisans. Early Christian symbolism, perhaps, signifying faith during a time of persecution."

The more he examined the ring, the more his pulse thrummed. This was a find! At length, he cocked his head at Eva. "Who did you purchase this from?"

"I didn't. It was found on my land."

Her land? He fingered the ring, flipping it over and over. "Are you speaking of your family's estate outside of Royston?"

"Just as I said."

Interesting. He'd expected her to be married by now. Then again, his uncle had expected as much out of him. He looked at her—truly looked—and saw weariness shadowing her eyes, belying the determined set of her shoulders. "So you are still living at home?"

"I am. I have been in mourning for the past year."

Hmm. He'd heard her mother had died long ago, and being she now said the land was hers . . . "Your father?" he surmised.

"Yes." She lifted her chin defiantly, but he also saw a flicker of pain—a pain she clearly tried hard to conceal.

"I am sorry to hear it." He kept his tone respectful. The loss of a parent was a wound that never truly healed. Still, that didn't account for her not getting married before her father had died. It seemed an odd omission for a woman of her standing, especially one as captivating as she had become.

But that was none of his business.

Her gaze drifted to the relic in his grasp. "So what might I sell that for?"

A strangled oath rumbled in his throat, and he tugged at his collar. Why must everyone be so quick to make a coin off antiquities? He'd liked her much better when he thought she was merely wishing to date the thing. He set the relic down, the clack of the metal against the wood mirroring his unease. "Most people don't realize that value is not always measured in coin. This ring"—he tapped the silver—"holds a worth that transcends time. It is a symbol of perseverance, faith, and survival against all odds. Putting it on the open market would be to undersell its intrinsic value."

"I didn't come here for a lecture, Professor Webb." She jerked on a glove rather forcefully, the fabric stretching thin over her knuckles. "I came here for a price suggestion. If you cannot provide one, then please refer me to someone who can."

"I see." He sighed. Clearly she was not to be persuaded of any other course—and though he disagreed with her wishing to sell the piece, he couldn't help but admire her determination. "Can you tell me exactly where on the estate it was uncovered?"

She yanked on the other glove. "The cursed acres."

"You don't say." He pressed his lips tight to keep from smirking. His friend Edmund Price had suffered through a supposed curse just last year—one that turned out to be completely manmade. The folklore surrounding Eva's land was likely instigated simply to keep people away from the area . . . though to what end?

He held the ring up between them, studying the ancient

craftmanship. The piece fairly winked in the light, hinting at secrets that may be linked to it still lying undiscovered beneath the dirt. Generally, where there was one buried artifact, more were to be found.

"What if . . ." he mused. "What if this relic isn't the only one there? What if this is more than a forgotten ancient ring and could be the key to understanding secrets buried long ago?"

She rose, impatience flattening her mouth to a straight line. "Can you value the piece, or can you not?"

Stubborn woman. "Of course I can, but not precisely off the top of my head. I'd have to compare it to other recent sales of similar artifacts, which involves a bit of record digging if you wish an accurate valuation."

"Good. Then do so and let me know as soon as possible. Thank you, Mr. Webb." She held out her hand. "Though I should like a receipt for leaving the item here with you."

He set the ring down, hard-pressed to know if he was more irritated by her abrupt manner, her resolve to sell a piece of history as if it were nothing more spectacular than a loaf of bread, or her lack of trust. Whatever the reason, there was no doubt whatsoever that Eva Inman had grown to know her own mind. He dipped the tip of his pen into the inkwell.

"If I find you to be trustworthy," she spoke while he wrote, "I will bring you more items my farmhand digs up, though I don't suppose you're interested in the broken bits of pottery and whatnot he's already unearthed."

"So there is more!" A large splotch of ink bled onto the page as he flung down the pen. Could that ring have belonged to a Christian refugee hiding from the long arm of a Roman emperor? Perhaps his uncle's theory of just such a refuge in that area was more than a senile old man's wandering mind. Maybe he didn't need to find the still-missing notebook. This discovery by Eva's farmhand might be a more accurate suggestion as to the location of Caelum Academia than any notes his uncle might've penned. Dare he hope? It seemed too good to be true, yet did God not work in mysterious ways? Such perfect timing did seem to bear His fingerprints.

Eva eyed him. "He has found other items, but the ring is the only thing of worth."

"He must stop." Bram shot to his feet. "You must order him to stop digging!"

"What on earth for? I need the income—I mean, it's none of your affair, really." Colour bloomed on her cheeks.

"A plow could destroy that whole area. Let me do an archaeological survey. Immediately. I can leave tomorrow."

She laughed, the sound as merry as a summer morn. "You jest."

"I've never been more serious."

Instantly she sobered, her gaze measuring him in ways he could only guess. "No. That land is to be sown with winter wheat. I cannot allow it."

"And yet if you do, I might find relics of more worth than that ring you brought in. You could add to your bank account beyond your wildest dreams."

Her gaze shot to the relic on his desk, lips pinching tightly for a moment. "Why should I trust you again, Bram Webb?"

He folded his arms. A lot of time had passed between them, but he wanted—needed—a look at that site . . . and that warranted the biggest gamble of his life. As a girl, she'd mooned after him—when she wasn't annoyed with him. Might she still in some small corner of her heart harbour that juvenile infatuation?

He met her steely gaze with one of his own. "Why should you trust me? Because, Eva Inman, though you'll never admit it, you were once in love with me, and I suspect, deep down, you may still be."

6

Rogue. Scoundrel! Eva had never loved any gent, least of all Bram Webb, and for him to have bluntly told her such a thing in his office made her blood boil. Infuriating man! Apparently he hadn't outgrown his arrogance. Were she not so desperate to dig up money, she'd not now be standing at the edge of the cursed acres, nibbling on her thumbnail while he conferred with three students in the middle of the churned-up field. Would he be able to manage this crew?

And even more maddening, just as when she'd been a young girl, she found it impossible to pull her gaze away from him. He stood with his hat in one hand, allowing his hair to run as wild as his adventurous spirit. Stubble lined his jaw, flaunting societal norms—as did his garments. His scuffed boots needed a stiff brush to revive the leather, and he wore the same fray-hemmed coat she'd seen him in yesterday. There was not one thing traditionally handsome about him, what with a scar on his cheek and a point to his chin, but he attracted attention all the same. The passion with which he spoke to the young men, his verve as he gestured his hand through the air, these marked a man who cared fervently about scholarship, which—though she hated to confess it—was a change for the better.

A rock skittered next to the hem of her skirt, and she turned. Sinclair strode her way, chuckling at something Bram's uncle must've said, for that fellow grinned beside him with a twinkle in his eyes. Though she'd not heard the comment, she smiled as well. Regius Professor Pendleton's merriment was contagious merely by virtue of being within ten feet of him. She'd only known the man for the better part of an hour now, but already she considered him a long-lost family member . . . even if he was Bram's relative. Which had been surprising. In all their younger years, Bram had never once mentioned having an uncle.

The man on the other side of Professor Pendleton was a completely different story—a gothic one, judging by his dark eyes and thin lips pinched like a clamshell. Did this Professor Grimwinkle never smile? Though, to be charitable, he might be so put out because of the amount of soil caking the bottom of his absurd wooden clogs. What a coxcomb. As much as she was loath to admit it, she was glad Bram and his uncle led the dig instead of this man.

"There's a lot of potential here, Miss Inman." Bram's uncle flung out his arms as he approached, sunshine glinting off his spectacles. "My team and I are grateful to have the opportunity to explore what might very well be the greatest archaeological discovery of the ages!"

Professor Grimwinkle frowned as he vigorously brushed dust from his sleeves. "That is a bit presumptuous."

Eva toyed with the stick she'd been holding. Clearly there was disagreement about the validity of the dig. Had she made the right choice to allow them here instead of planting the seed? "I hope it turns out to be profitable for us all."

"Oh, my dear." Bram's uncle laughed at the blue sky, genuine delight rumbling out of him. "Unearthing the Holy Grail will be more lucrative than you can possibly imagine." He squeezed her arm lightly. "Just think of not only the historical significance but the religious as well."

Professor Grimwinkle snorted.

Eva angled her head. "You cannot be serious. Why would such a renowned artifact be found in the middle of a common English field?"

"It's got to be somewhere, doesn't it?" Bram's uncle winked.

Ahh. So that's where Bram's impish sense of humor originated. A gust of wind blew in, and she clapped her hand to her bonnet as she turned to the steward. "Well, Sinclair, I should think such a discovery would end the absurd legend of this plot of land being cursed, don't you?"

"I have to admit, miss"—he picked up a rock and pitched it onto a nearby pile—"we've met with no bad luck thus far."

"Because there is no such thing as luck. God alone is sovereign." She lifted her chin.

Yet if that was true, then why didn't God simply bring her a fish with a coin in its mouth to pay the taxes? He'd done so for Peter. Then again, Peter was a saint—and she bore the responsibility of two deaths on her hands. Was it any wonder God had abandoned her to her own means?

"Well said, Miss Inman." Professor Pendleton pulled off his spectacles and tucked them into the top pocket of his waistcoat. "Now that I've had a good look around, I think I can speak for the rest of the men when I say we'd like to get started straightaway. There are several hours' worth of daylight remaining and setting up always takes longer than one expects. However, after rummaging in the wagon bed, it appears I've forgotten my field bag. Must've left it in your front hall. Would you mind if your steward here runs me back to the house in the pony trap? Unless you'd like to accompany me, that is. With my girth"—he patted his ample belly—"I don't think all three of us will fit on the seat, and I'd hate to take the wagon with the excavation tools."

"Sinclair is a better horseman than I. He'll get you there

and back faster than I could, so I suggest you hang on to your hat, Professor."

"Ho ho! Thanks for the warning." He snugged his bowler tighter as he strode away, his silvery hair eaten up by the brown felt.

Another gust of wind flew in, taking Professor Grimwinkle's hat for a ride. Grumbling, he dashed after it while Eva poked at the dirt with her stick. Was there truly more treasure here? All she found were tufts of overturned turf, rocks, and a rather malnourished earthworm writhing from her inadvertent jab. Holy Grail indeed. A smile lifted her lips. Bram's uncle was quite the jester.

"I didn't know you had an interest in archaeology." Bram's deep voice reached her a moment before the tips of his worn boots appeared in her line of vision. "We could use such a lovely addition to our team."

Lovely? Hah. Her nose was too long, her mouth too wide, and no true beauty sported such atrocious red hair. Dropping her stick, she rose and dusted her hands. "Sorry to disappoint, but digging for buried treasure is not my calling."

Professor Grimwinkle returned, his hat jammed so tightly on his head that it puckered his brow. He fixed his dark gaze on Bram. "Archaeology is certainly not for everyone. Some men just don't know when to quit."

Bram's jaw hardened, yet he said nothing. Why such tension? Did Professor Grimwinkle share her doubts about Bram's abilities?

She attempted a laugh. "Well, I am sure I would never begin to understand all the facets of excavating for antiquities, but it appears Professor Webb has his students under control."

Indeed, the young men were already unloading tools from the big wagon.

"Mmm. One can only hope. Now, if you will pardon me, I should like one of those students to drive me back to the manor.

I have some business to take care of in town." Without so much as a good-day, Professor Grimwinkle stalked off.

Rude man!

Eva's gaze shot to Bram to gauge his response to such an affront.

A vein stood out on his neck, then vanished as he turned to her. "So what is it, then?"

"What is what?" She scrunched her nose, thoroughly confused.

"Your calling. You said digging for buried treasure isn't it, so what is?"

What a question. She'd been sure of an answer once, a lifetime ago it seemed. She'd never felt more fulfilled than when volunteering with the Royston Relief Society. Helping those in need. Creating beauty from ashes when disaster struck those less fortunate. Now if she wasn't careful, she and her sister would *be* the less fortunate. "I am a landowner, Mr. Webb, and that is no small career."

"True, but I have no doubt you'll make a success of it. And call me Bram. We are friends from childhood, are we not?" He winked just like his uncle. "Come. Would you like to see what we've already found?"

She licked her lips to keep from smirking. "You've hardly been here half an hour."

"Is that all?" He pulled out a silver pocket watch and arched a brow at the time. "You're right. I suppose I am just that good, milady." He folded into a regal bow, sweeping one arm high up behind him, just as he'd done that time he'd tried to convince her and her friends he was a magician, only the rabbit he'd pulled from a hat hadn't been his. When Mrs. Muggins found out he'd borrowed one of her hares, she'd whacked him with a broom.

Eva smiled at the memory. "Found the Holy Grail already, did you? Your uncle is certain it's here."

Bram's wind-reddened cheeks drained of colour. Odd, that.

She'd expected a snappy retort, not a silent offering of his upturned palm.

"The terrain is treacherous now that it's been plowed," he said simply.

Hiking her skirt to her ankles, she bypassed him. "I have walked this land all my life, Professor. I certainly don't need your help."

She marched ahead, stepping over mounds of turf and hopping across furrows gouged by the plow. Despite her sister's pleading to come along, it was a good thing she'd held firm. Penny managed the house and yard like any agile twelve-year-old, but she'd surely have taken a tumble on this rough dirt—and the image of Penny crashing face first squeezed her heart.

A harsh puff of wind caught the scarf she'd tucked around her neck, the long tail of it flying off like a naughty sparrow. She reached for the fabric—just as her toe caught on a rock. Flailing, she pitched forward.

A strong arm wrapped around her waist, righting her world, shoring her up against a solid torso.

Bram's.

She whirled away. Bad idea. Once again, she teetered on the uneven ground.

And once again, Bram grabbed hold of her, a mix of concern and amusement sparking in his eyes. They stood so closely, his breath feathered against her brow, and she inhaled his scent of rich tobacco and dampened soil. No, not soil. Something greener. Fresher. Moss, perhaps?

"As I said." He angled his head to a playful tilt. "Treacherous."

The land? Or the way her heart thudded against her ribs?

Capturing her hand, he firmly planted her fingers in the crook of his arm, then set off, whistling a cheery tune. Several times she nearly pulled away—and she would have, were she not so absurdly mesmerized by the feel of his muscles riding beneath her touch. This man was no gangly-limbed youth anymore. She'd been right to be cautious of him.

But now she must also be wary of herself.

"Mr. Barker," Bram called. "The Samian specimen, if you please."

A towheaded young man with enough curls to make a debutante jealous broke away from the other two students—one of whom she recognized from yesterday in the college corridor. Mr. Barker handed over a dirty piece of broken pottery.

Bram held it up as if it were the Queen's tiara. "Behold."

"That's what you wished to show me?" Eva frowned. "My farmhand has a whole bucket of those bits by now."

"It's not a mere *bit*, Eva. See these floral motifs mingled with these geometric designs?" He brushed his thumb over the chunk of clay. Dirt flaked off, revealing a glossy red finish. "This is from the first or second century, possibly early third. Such pottery was crafted by Roman artisans. There's treasure beneath this soil." He grinned, the boyish show of pleasure almost as infectious as his uncle's good humor. "I have a good feeling about this."

"Well, hold on to that feeling, Professor." She winked as saucily as he and his uncle. "For it may change when you see where you'll be lodging."

He'd stayed in questionable quarters before. Seedy inns. Shabby boardinghouses. One time in Tunisia, he'd slept in a hut made of hundreds of barrel staves lashed together. All had been palaces compared to the ramshackle workmen's cottage on the Inman estate. Cottage, huh? More like a shoebox of spiders. Bram took a long drag of his cigar, grateful his uncle had granted him a reprieve from sweeping out the place. Judging by the hoots of laughter from inside the weathered walls, though, his students were having a cracking good time.

He blew one last puff of smoke, then ground out the butt with the toe of his shoe. After a quick readjustment of the lantern wick, he picked up his uncle's notes lying beside him on the bench. While he'd have preferred his uncle had found that missing journal of his, at least the man had given a valiant effort to recreate what he'd felt were the most important leads. This rough sketch of Uncle Pendleton's layout for Caelum Academia might not prove to be a solid fact, but at least it gave him an idea of how to proceed tomorrow. If the ground was pliable enough, they might—

He jerked up his head, listening hard. He could've sworn he'd heard someone approaching. From what he could see, the windows of the manor house were nothing but dark shadows. Perhaps on the front side, though, the sitting room was still lit. Even so, Eva would not venture out to pay him a visit, and neither the steward nor the farmhand had such light steps.

Setting aside the journal, he rose on silent feet. Much to his shame, he knew a thing or two about stealth. He crept the short length of the front of the cottage, then peered around the side. Hardly eight feet from him stood a young girl on tiptoe, ear pressed against the window glass. His lips twisted. With walls as thin as this cottage's, she truly needn't go to so much trouble to eavesdrop.

"You know," he murmured, "if you stepped on that crate next to you, you could probably hear a lot better, though you'd get more of an earful if you simply knocked on the door and asked to come in."

The girl whirled. "You scared the life from me! Who are you, and how did you creep back here so quietly?"

"Professor Bram Webb at your service, and I have years of experience sneaking away from my mother." He stepped closer, examining the sprite. Dark tendrils escaped from a coiled braid at the back of her head, but other than hair colour, her wide mouth and long nose matched Eva's. Why, dye those locks brownish red and he'd be transported back to a time when Eva had looked at him with admiration instead of indifference. Why had she not told him about the girl?

"Does your sister know you're out here?" he asked.

"What makes you think I have a sister?"

Now that was interesting, not so much her evasive maneuver but the fact that she didn't look him in the face. "Because you're much like Eva Inman when she was a girl."

"I am?" Her fingers flew to her face, exploring the contours of her cheekbones and jaw.

He dared another step closer, then sucked in a breath. Her gaze hadn't met his because she hadn't known where his eyes were, for the girl was clearly blind. "What are you doing out here?"

Her nose bunched all rabbity, a few solid sniffs blending with the laughter from inside the cottage. "You smell of cigars."

"Good thing I was downwind of you, then, or you'd have run off the second I rounded the corner."

"Dixon says tobacco is a filthy habit." She lifted her nose in the same pert manner Eva had used on him earlier that day. "I agree with her."

Saucy little pixie. He grinned. "Then you and Dixon will be happy to know I have none left, though I do wonder what Dixon might say about you stealing off into the night on your own. Do you wish to continue our conversation here like the wild beasts we both are, or shall we pretend to be civilized and retire to the bench I recently departed?"

"Humph. My sister was right."

"About?" He could only imagine what Eva might've said.

"You do talk a lot. Though that could be to my advantage since I have some questions for you. Come along, then." The girl marched past him, her hand only reaching out once to determine the end of the building.

He followed, marveling at the girl's lack of inhibition in

speech and in movement. He sank next to her on the bench, taking a moment to settle the lantern on the ground. Not that the light would matter to her, but an inadvertent jostle could send it tumbling. "So what would you like to know?"

"Everything. What is it like to be an archaeologist? Does the dirt smell differently as you're about to uncover something? When you first hold a relic that's been buried for centuries, can you feel a connection to the last fingers that held it? Can you practically taste a long-forgotten meal just by handling an unearthed bowl?"

He chuckled. "Those are big questions. Such an inquisitive mind rivals some of my best students. I daresay you have a bright future ahead of you."

"I have a lot of time to think." She shrugged.

"Well, well. You may look like your sister, but you're surely not as timid."

"Eva?" She laughed, girlish and bright. "My sister is far too much of a take-charge and mind-your-manners sort of person."

Bram shifted on the hard bench. "She wasn't always like that," he murmured. Might things have been different between him and Eva now if he'd stayed in Royston? Would she trust him more if he'd never left? Hah! It was a good thing he had gone. If he'd remained any longer in this town he'd have either killed Trestwell or Trestwell would have done him in.

The girl leaned toward him, and he caught the faint scent of ginger drops on her breath. "What was she like?"

Memories surfaced like bubbles on a pond. Eva running down a hill with her long braid bobbing against her back, frightened of the toad he'd shown her. Or the time she'd burst into tears when one of the other boys had called her a rusty-topped bean pole. He'd tried to comfort her by sharing a biscuit he'd pilfered from the baker's cart, but the treat had turned to crumbs in his pocket. And then there was the great snake-in-the-sack debacle. He never should have given it to her as a gift. She didn't speak for a whole week—to anyone.

Bram rubbed his knuckles along his jaw. Now that he thought on it, yes, she had been a bit melodramatic for a child, but not without cause. "You'd better ask her."

The girl's lips pursed into a pout, but only for a second. "And you? What were you like?"

He smirked. Remembering Eva's past was painful enough. There was no way he'd voice what an awful lad he'd been. "You'd better ask her about that too."

She kicked her toe against the gravel, clearly displeased. "I think you're very secretive, just like her. But no matter what my sister says"—her toe stopped, and she lifted her face toward him—"I've decided I like you."

"Is that so? Well, you're not so bad yourself, Miss Inman."

"You can call me Penny. But not poppet. Only my sister gets that privilege." She stood and offered her hand. "Good night, Professor Webb."

"And you may call me Bram but not badger." He gave her a hearty shake.

"Badger?"

"It's what your sister used to call me. Good night, Penny."

With a song on her lips, she strode toward the house, sure of every step as she sang. Which left him to wonder. If Eva hadn't bothered to mention her sister, being the delight that Penny was, what else was she not telling him?

7

Monday mornings were hard enough without hosting a stark-faced rector and his overly effervescent sister. My, what a pair they made. Enough to tire a saint. Eva poured tea while Mrs. Mortimer blathered on about the thick rope of pearls she'd recently purchased. The woman's podgy fingers danced over the necklace while her brother shot her a gangrenous look at such a display of worldliness.

Blocking Mr. Blackwood's view, Eva handed him a cup lest they all be forced to entertain a sermon. "Here you are, Mr. Blackwood. Haven't we had fine weather of late? How long do you suppose it will last?"

"As long as God allows, I should think." He sipped his tea.

Eva breathed relief as she served his sister. Of necessity, Mrs. Mortimer perched on the edge of a chair. She wouldn't fit between the arms of it otherwise. The woman was grand of girth and even grander in appetite, the gleam in her eyes hungry as she gazed at the simple plate of toast circles lightly smeared with jam. Despite being a widow, she laughed at life, her plump cheeks ever rosy, her great bosom always jiggling. She was a blazing sun compared to her brother's eternal midnight.

But she was also a whirlwind. Her inexhaustible vigor and incessant chatter never failed to overwhelm even the heartiest of souls.

Eva offered her the plate.

"What an unusual idea to serve toast. Very simple—yet delicious, no doubt." Mrs. Mortimer immediately plucked two small circles. Any other woman would have snubbed such a common refreshment. By the time Eva poured her own tea, Mrs. Mortimer had already finished them both off and had her head tipped back, draining her cup.

"I was so relieved to see you at services yesterday morning, Miss Inman." The woman reached for another piece of toast. "And your darling sister as well. Will she be joining us this morning?"

Eva blew the steam off her brew. "I had thought she might, but she wasn't in her room. It appears she's off on an adventure."

"But the child is blind!" Mrs. Mortimer fanned her face with a lacy handkerchief. "Does that not concern you?"

It did. Every time she couldn't account for her sister's whereabouts, worry moved in and unpacked its trunks for a good long visit. It took all her willpower to force a pleasant smile. "I am certain Penny will return by eleven, which is our usual reading hour. She never misses it."

Mr. Blackwood set his half-drunk cup on the table, his uneaten toast taunting Mrs. Mortimer.

"Such waste, brother." She leaned forward to pinch the treat.

He blocked her hand. "Gluttony is a sin, sister." His glower drifted toward Eva. "And what did you find out about the ring on your visit to Cambridge, Miss Inman?"

It was a harmless enough question, but the intensity in his gaze was already sifting her answer, though she had yet to speak a word. She fortified herself with a sip of stout Assam. "It turns out the relic is of historical value. There is a small team of archaeologists currently in my field who are hoping to discover larger items of greater worth."

The rector's thick brows gathered into a thundercloud. "I hope I need not warn you about false hopes or greed. It is our duty as Christians to rely solely upon the grace and mercies of God."

How dare he assume she wasn't depending upon God? Ever since she'd been a child this man had used harsh and authoritarian methods. His sermons and teachings, filled with brimstone and fire, had scared her at the time. Now his insinuations just made her angry. Eva set down her teacup, porcelain rattling. "I have no doubt you would never allow a sheep of yours to stray onto such a delinquent path."

"Just so." A flicker of approval—so faint she almost missed it—flashed in his gaze. "And yet you mention a team of archaeologists. Who are they?"

"There is Regius Professor Sebastian Pendleton, Professor Bram Webb, and three of Mr. Webb's students, making a total of five men on the job."

"Webb?" The reverend rolled the name around his mouth like a bite of rancid meat. "I seem to recall something associated with that name."

She recalled far too much about the man. Oh, what a foolish girl she'd been, secretly pining after a silly boy three years her senior. "I am not surprised you may have heard of him. He is quite knowledgeable about Roman antiquities and, I am told, a professor of some renown."

"Well," Mrs. Mortimer cut in, "I for one pray there shall be many treasures unearthed, for I know it cannot be easy for you to care for this home and your sister." The woman tsked with a little shake of her head. "And all on your own. I shudder to think of your burden."

So did she. "As the reverend says, I must rely upon God." And while he may have meant that as a spiritually cutting remark, she meant it in earnest.

"Miss Inman . . ." Setting her own cup aside, Mrs. Mortimer went back to fingering her pearls. "I wonder if I may be so bold as to make a suggestion."

Oh dear. Eva ran her palms along the cool fabric of her skirt, smoothing out imaginary wrinkles. The one thing the rector's sister could expound upon for hours was beauty—the need for it, how to maintain it, and above all, Eva's lack in that department. She ought to know, for she'd suffered the woman's lengthy discourses on more than one occasion. So it took every ounce of her willpower to force a pleasant tone. "I am all ears, Mrs. Mortimer."

"Very good." The lady inhaled deeply, her bosom threatening to spill out like overstuffed cushions. "As you know from our time together at the relief society, I delight in works of charity. Through my vast connections, I found a suitable placement as a jeweler's apprentice for the Widow Kitman's lame-legged son. Then there was the cleft-lip girl belonging to the Novaks. You know, the immigrant family who live in the old Hoffman place just outside of town? I daresay the girl is happy enough to be working in a fine home as a scullery maid. And let's not forget little deaf Lucy. Poor soul—though not so poor anymore. Working as a junior seamstress earns her a fair penny, sure enough."

"No one can call into question your compassion and generosity, Mrs. Mortimer."

"Tread carefully, sister. Flattery is a deceitful poison, one that goes down smoothly yet festers into a canker in the soul." While the warning was clearly directed at Mrs. Mortimer, the rector aimed his scowl at Eva.

"Of course, brother." Mrs. Mortimer laughed heartily, the tight curls on her brow dancing along with her merriment. "But as I was saying, I have a suggestion for Miss Inman to consider." She turned to Eva. "As a means to alleviate any sort of strain on your financial situation, I would be more than happy to sponsor young Miss Inman to attend a notable school for the blind that I am associated with in London."

Eva's heart tightened in her chest. "London! But that's so far away."

"She must leave home sometime, my dear. Surely you're not thinking of keeping her under your care indefinitely? Why, I daresay placing your sister elsewhere will free you up to find a suitable match for yourself." The lace handkerchief flew out again, this time employed at dabbing the corners of Mrs. Mortimer's eyes. "It's a lonely world without a man, take it from one who knows."

But she wasn't lonely. Not with Penny around. Eva had cared for her little sister since the day of her birth—and promised her father she'd always do so. Besides, her strong-willed poppet got on as well as girls with normal vision and was cheerful as any with a song perpetually ready on her lips. No, sending Penny away was out of the question. She'd already failed her parents. She would not abandon her sister.

Eva squared her shoulders, facing Mrs. Mortimer head-on. "I am sure you have nothing but the best intentions at heart, and I do appreciate the offer, but I don't see a need for such a gesture. Thank you anyway."

Mr. Blackwood rose like a bat in a night sky, towering over her with a downward turn to his thin lips. "God's ways are not our ways, Miss Inman. Do not be so rash as to refuse what might very well be providence. I suggest you commit the matter to prayer before such a hasty rejection."

Eva stood, unwilling to allow him such intimidation. "I shall consider your words, Mr. Blackwood."

"Of course you shall. My brother is right, as usual." Mrs. Mortimer chuckled as she rose, a cloud of violet toilette water wafting about her. "Do think on it, my dear. I shouldn't like to take no as an answer."

Eva assembled what she hoped was a smile and not a grimace. As much as she didn't wish to, she set the offer on a shelf in the corner of her mind—for if she failed to pay the taxes and lost the house, she wouldn't have a choice but to accept. There were no other relatives to care for Penny, or herself, for that matter. Her trusted friend Lottie yet lived beneath her parents' roof, and the walls of that house were practically bulging at the seams. No one in Royston that was suitable could take on a blind twelve-year-old. She nibbled on her index finger.

Was this offer from Mrs. Mortimer a providence of God?

There was nothing more glorious than sifting through dirt on a brisk October morn. The sun on his shoulders. The wind in his hair. Bram hefted another shovelful of soil onto the screen, smirking as he did so. If ol' Grimwinkle were here to witness such an unorthodox method—the screen Bram had fashioned being far too wide for conventional filtering—the man would no doubt blister them all with a fiery lecture. Thankfully, Uncle Pendleton was open to innovations. Employing a smaller sieve was far too time consuming at this stage. And time was the one luxury they didn't have, not if they hoped to find evidence this was Caelum Academia before the deadline.

"Hey, Professor! Over here." Jonathan Barker waved at him from across the field. "Look what I've found."

Bram chunked the tip of the shovel into the ground, standing the tool upright before setting off. Beyond Barker, Charles Wimble and Nathaniel Hammet dropped their trowels and advanced on him as well.

"Let's see what you've got." Bram crouched next to Barker, the other students already huddled near him.

"Right there."

Sure enough, what appeared to be a nozzle or some sort

of spout poked from the soil where the young man had been digging.

Bram pulled out a metal rod he kept looped to his belt and poked tentatively around the area. Whenever the tip met with resistance, he eased it out. Eventually, he outlined the shape of the item, then held out his palm. "A trowel please, Mr. Barker."

The curly-headed young man handed over the tool, and with a few precise gouges into the dirt, Bram unloosed a chunk of pottery with globs of dirt clinging to it. Removing a stiff brush from his pocket, he knocked off most of them, revealing an ancient oil lamp.

"Well, well. This is quite a find. Looks like this is the area we need to focus on." Rising, he eyed the other men. "Take care the deeper you go, fellows. If there was indeed a settlement of some sort here—which is very likely—then you're bound to hit a foundation. And that will be a key discovery."

"We're on it, Professor!"

Bram grinned at his students' enthusiasm while trudging toward the tent at the edge of the field. Were he in their shoes, he'd be just as animated. Working on a dig was a far better prospect than sitting through Grimwinkle's dull monologues.

He ducked beneath the canvas roof, bypassing a table with the other antiquities they'd unearthed thus far. All were shards or fragments, mere hints of an ancient habitation, not bad for only two days' work but could've been better if Grimwinkle had allowed him more students. He was thankful for the three fellows he had been able to snag, but with more hands the work would go faster.

Bram set the lamp on the old desk Eva's steward had rummaged up for them. "Our first whole relic, Uncle."

"You don't say!" Uncle Pendleton whipped out a magnifying glass. "Yes, yes. Very good! End of the second century. Definitely of Roman origin. Amazing it is in one piece. Now . . ."

He set down the magnifier and fingered about on the tabletop, shoving aside papers and making quite a mess of things.

Bram stopped his hand. "Perhaps I can help. What are you looking for?"

"My cleaning kit. Ah, here we are." Completely bypassing the desktop, Uncle Pendleton grabbed a small bag sitting near his feet. Opening the clasp, he poked about inside with one finger. "But it appears my bottle of cleaning solution must've fallen out in the wagon."

Bram swiped up a rag, then carefully retrieved the lamp. "I'll go clean it, then wrap the piece up and leave it on the wagon seat. You can show it to Miss Inman when you ride back for your afternoon break."

His uncle scowled. "Pah! I'm no nursling who needs a nap."

True, but if the man didn't rest his mind periodically, his memory lapses grew worse. "Of course you aren't. I was merely hoping you'd make the drive to the house and show this piece to Miss Inman so I wouldn't have to. You know, give her some tangible evidence we are making progress."

"Oh. Well, in that case, I suppose I shall finish up logging these field notes and ride over there. Off with you, then." He ruffled his fingers in the air.

Bram retreated into the sunshine, a tiny bit ashamed he'd used such manipulation. Still, it was a necessary evil, what with Uncle Pendleton's current state of fluctuating cognizance . . . though admittedly the old fellow had seemed better the past few days. Now that Bram thought on it, he hadn't noticed as many mental slips of late. Dare he hope things may be leveling off?

Nestling the little lamp tightly against his chest, he picked his way across the uneven ground to the wagon. He set the relic carefully in the back corner of the bed, then retrieved a burlap sack and began digging about for an amber bottle. The first thing he pulled out was an empty canteen. Apparently Wimble hadn't thought to fill it, so he set that next to the relic and dug some more. This time he pulled out a broken-handled trowel, which would do none of them any good until he fixed it. And he'd never remember to do so if it remained in the bag. He pitched it toward the front of the wagon and—

"Ow!"

He jerked his head toward the muffled cry. The stained canvas lumped in one corner moved slightly. On silent feet, he rounded the wagon bed and yanked the covering into the air, allowing it to billow to the ground at his back. Two brown eyes looked his way, not quite finding his face.

"Lurking about again, are you?" He folded his arms. Penny Inman may be a dark-haired version of Eva, but that was where comparison stopped. Eva never would have been so bold to have stowed away on a wagon full of men. "What were you hoping to accomplish tucked beneath a tarpaulin like that?"

She sat upright, picking pieces of straw from her hair. "I wasn't planning on staying beneath it all day."

"Then what were you planning?"

"I wanted to hear what it sounded like on a dig site."

Which reminded him entirely too much of himself at that age. "Is your interest in archaeology so very keen, then?"

"It is. And I know you found something." She scrambled to the side. "What is it?"

He smiled at her eagerness. The little sprite was a kindred spirit. "Would you like to see?"

She nodded vigorously.

"Then scoot yourself to the edge, and I'll meet you there." He retraced his steps to the back and pulled the lamp from the corner, then waited for Penny to dangle her legs over the open gate. Gently, he set the relic in her upturned hands. "I should warn you this hasn't been properly cleaned yet so you will get dirty."

"Pish! I don't mind in the least." She explored the surface and as far as her slender fingers would reach inside. Closing her eyes, she lifted the relic to her nose and inhaled deeply several times, as if the past were a scent she might remember. She bowed over the ancient oil lamp like a prayer, pressing it against her cheek, tendrils of her hair flying to the heavens. His own heart squeezed in response. Were he an artist, he'd capture this passion for all to experience the holy innocence of the moment.

"Thank you," she whispered, then her eyes flashed open. Carefully, she held it out for his retrieval. "And do be careful of that small crack on the inside of the spout. Any more pressure could break it into pieces."

He angled the lamp so sunlight could climb down the spout. Sure enough, a whisper of a hairline marred the inside. "Good catch." He pulled the rag from his pocket and began wrapping the little lamp. The piece would be better served by cleaning it back at the manor than out here in the elements. "Did you notice any other blemishes?"

One of her feet swung back and forth, the hem of her skirt swishing with the movement. "No. But holding it made me feel sad and kind of empty inside."

He frowned. Such an incongruous answer compared to the bliss on her face a moment ago. "Why?"

"I can't have been the only girl to have ever held that piece in my hands. And does anyone remember that other girl now? She's gone. Never to feel this same wind on her cheeks." She lifted her face to the breeze. "I ache for her."

He stiffened, unsure what to do with such unbridled depth of feeling. Yet here he was, the sole recipient of a young girl's tender emotions.

And he had no idea how to respond.

Clutching the lamp in one hand, he rubbed the back of his neck with the other. Part of him admired her willingness to be so transparent, even longed to be genuine himself, but that would never do. He'd learned at a young age such a vulnerability could be turned against him. No. This world was a cold place, filled with ruthless men. The only way to survive was with a grin and a cheeky remark. And though it had never really bothered him before, somehow, here with this blind girl on a fallow field, he felt as empty inside as Penny.

But he couldn't very well tell a child that. He'd be hanged if he told anyone.

"You're wrong, you know." He tousled her hair.

"About what?"

"That other girl isn't forgotten. You remembered her, and now so have I. One of the best things about archaeology is that it honours the past."

A smile brightened her serious face. "Yes, I suppose you're right."

"I usually am." He reached for her arm. "Come. Let's get you back to the house, and this time you can ride up on the seat with my uncle."

"Oh, please, can't I stay? I'm already out here so there's no sense in you wasting time to drive me back. I can be of help. I know it!"

He grinned. It was astounding, really, how sightless eyes could turn all puppy and pleading. "I don't know. Won't your sister worry about you?"

"She won't even know I'm gone." She tossed back her loose braid. "She was entertaining visitors when I left."

Absently, he ran his finger along the lamp's spout, debating what to do with the girl. Naturally she'd be no help whatsoever out in the field, and yet she had proved valuable in pointing out a hairline crack he'd not noticed. And as she'd said, she was already out here. Perhaps he could give her something to do, especially since Uncle Pendleton would be away from the dig for a few hours.

"All right, then." He grabbed her by the arms, helping her to the ground. "I shall set you up in the tent, where we've accumulated several relics already and will likely add more today.

You can use that heightened sense of touch of yours to examine the items and identify any peculiarities such as the crack you discovered in this lamp. Then you may dictate your findings to one of my students. How does that sound?"

She bounced on her toes. "Like a cracking good time!"

"Right then, let's have at it." After planting the lamp on the wagon seat, he guided her back to the tent, where his three students had gathered near his uncle, passing around a large jug of water.

Bram set Penny squarely in front of him. "Men, meet our new assistant for the day, Miss Penny Inman."

8

Eva could hardly blame Penny for missing out on tea with the reverend and his sister. Had she an excuse, she would have skipped out on it as well. But then Penny hadn't appeared for reading hour, which was alarming. Though to be fair, the girl might've gotten preoccupied with the new litter of kittens in the barn. Yet now, seated across from Penny's empty chair for lunch, worry crept in to nettle the corners of Eva's mind. Monday was potato soup day. Penny's favorite. Surely she'd arrive winded and rosy cheeked from some grand adventure any minute.

Holding to that hope, Eva dawdled with slow bites, listening hard for the trill of a song to come waltzing through the door. Perhaps her sister was simply running late for some obscure girlish reason . . . and yet by the time her spoon scraped the bottom of the bowl, there was still no sign of Penny.

Odd, that.

She nibbled the nail of her index finger. It was an inescapable fact that girls would be girls. She herself had missed a meal or two in her day, running off with Lottie or chasing after Bram, for yes, though she hated to confess such an inappropriate action, the truth was that she had.

But this was different. Though admittedly she felt a bit abandoned by her sister, she couldn't help but worry about Penny's absence. What if she'd had an accident? Tripped over a rug and bumped her head? It was always hard not to jump to conclusions when it came to her sister, for she dearly wished to protect the girl from any sort of harm. Yet stifling Penny was just as hurtful.

Balling up her napkin, Eva wandered to the kitchen. Mrs. Pottinger was always grateful for help with kneading, especially since she'd taken on the feeding of five strapping men. After Eva had worked out her frustrations on several mountains of dough, Penny still hadn't turned up.

Was her little sister merely coddling a sulky mood? She was getting to that age where such dispositions became more frequent. Eva headed up to Penny's room, trying to recall if she'd said anything that might've set her sister off.

"Penny?" She rapped on the door, and when no answer came, she tried the knob. Inside, the rosebud-sprigged counterpane lay serene and smooth with no sign of a pouting girl curled beneath. The window seat—a favorite perch—was empty as well. Nothing seemed out of place, save for the open wardrobe. Eva advanced, glancing inside the hulking piece of furniture, and then her heart really did stutter.

Penny's coat and bonnet were gone.

All the worry she'd been stiff-arming since Mrs. Mortimer had first questioned Penny's whereabouts rushed in like a mongrel horde. She pressed a fist to her belly, sick with concern. Had she said anything to Penny that might've caused her to run off?

Oh, poppet! Where are you?

Eva sped to her own bedroom, vainly trying to outpace the horrid memory of another such instance a year ago when she'd quarreled with Papa, and he'd stormed off. . . .

It had been strange seeing her father laid out on the kitchen table like that, his forehead gashed, blood flowing. But that wasn't the worst of it. The right side of his chest sank unnaturally where the horse's hooves had caught him, making every breath a wheeze—when he could catch one. Mostly he struggled for air. Eva had held his hand in a tight grip, heart breaking with a loss she wasn't ready to own.

Yet the strangest thing of all had been when he rallied, ordering everyone except her from the room. His pale blue eyes burned with an eerie intensity as she leaned over him, and she knew it was now or never to reveal her secret.

"Papa, I must tell you—"

"No. No time." He struggled to suck in air. "I'm sorry, Eva. So sorry. I never should have—" He grimaced, the muscles on his neck standing out like cords.

"Papa, don't talk. Just listen. I—"

He grabbed her hand. "Take care of your sister. Always. And the house, don't—" He convulsed with a gasp. "Don't lose it."

She kissed his knuckles, her tears falling freely. "Yes, Papa."

"Promise!" he rasped.

"I vow it. I will not fail you. Not again. I love you." Her throat closed then. Tightly. Forbidding her own breaths to pass. He could have no idea how sorely she'd failed him in the past, which was a poison she'd swallowed for far too long. "Papa, please, before it is too late, I must ask your forgiveness because I was the one who—"

"Blackwood," he hissed, his eyes bloodred. His lips grey-blue. "Beware of Blackwoodsssss . . . hissss."

His words degraded into a death rattle, a sound not meant for the ears of the living.

And then he was gone, the bulwark of her life, leaving her broken, scared, scarred. Abandoned. Just as her mother had done. And Eva had no one to blame but herself.

She shrugged her arms into her coat sleeves, shoving away the memory, then snatched her bonnet and dashed out the door. She was not going through that again. She would not lose Penny because of her failings too. God may see fit to send trials her way for her own wrongdoings, but Penny didn't deserve to suffer. Fiddling with her hat ribbons, Eva called for Dixon while trotting down the stairs.

"Yes, miss?" The housekeeper sailed into the front hall just as Eva stepped foot on the landing. "Where are you off to in such a hurry?"

"To find my sister." Eva pulled her gloves from her pocket. "Penny's been absent all morning and half the afternoon. Would you please search the ground floor and have Mary do the same on the first? Tell her to also nip into the attic, though I don't know why Penny would possibly go there. And let Mrs. Pottinger know to keep an eye out for her as well."

"Absolutely." Clenching her apron, Dixon took a step closer, worry pinching her face. "Though I do wonder, miss, if we ought to send for a constable? While the girl is given to ambling about the yard, it's not like Miss Penny to be gone for so long."

Eva tamped the fear that prompted her to agree. "Not yet. We ought to first conduct our own search. For all we know, she may have fallen asleep in the hayloft or climbed an orchard tree and can't get down." She shivered at the thought. Penny may be a fearless little imp, but, oh, how Eva hated heights. "And let's not forget the new litter of kittens. I'll alert Tom in the barn and get Sinclair to poke about the apple trees. After that, I'll walk the road a bit, see if she may have gone for a stroll and met with some sort of mishap. I'm sure she'll turn up." She squeezed Dixon's arm, as much to encourage the older woman as herself.

"Very good, miss. We shall hope for the best."

Indeed, she would. To do otherwise would be her undoing. She'd promised Papa to care for the girl. She should have kept a better eye on her sister. If something happened to Penny, it would be her fault.

And she truly would be all alone.

Once outside, she tugged on her gloves while rounding the house to the backyard—just as a wagon lumbered to a halt.

Professor Pendleton perched on the driver's seat, setting the brake. If he'd been out and about, perhaps he'd seen Penny.

Please, God, let him say he's seen her. Smile upon me just this once.

"Professor Pendleton," she said as she approached. "I wonder if—"

"Ah, Miss Inman. Though my spectacles are in an atrocious state at the moment, you are just the person I was hoping to see."

"I wish I could say the same. Oh my!" Her fingers flew to her mouth as her words hit her ears. How rude he must think her. "Please don't take offense at my careless sentiment, sir. It *is* lovely to see you as well, but the truth is, I was hoping to spy my sister."

"Yes! The young Miss Inman." Yanking off his spectacles, he huffed on the glass, then buffed out a smear. "Delightful girl."

"She is, and I'm wondering if you may have—"

He held up a finger. "Sorry to interrupt, my dear, but if I don't say what I must now, there's a good chance I might forget." He collected a cloth-wrapped bundle and handed it down to her. "As you see, we are earning our keep already. Have a look."

Hope blended with her worry as she unwrapped the fabric.

Then quickly faded.

The relic he'd seemed so proud to show her was nothing but a small, dirty pot of clay with a handle and spout. "It's, em, well, it appears to be a lamp."

"Brilliant!" Holding his spectacles to the sky, he examined the glass, then went back to buffing. "You are spot-on, Miss Inman."

She rewrapped the tiny bundle, offering it back. "Is it valuable?"

He parked the spectacles on the bridge of his nose and collected the relic. "Indeed it is. Finding this little gem proves we are excavating in the right place."

"I meant monetarily."

"Hmm." Setting the package on the seat, he climbed down, then reclaimed it. "I suppose a museum would purchase this piece of history, wouldn't they? Though there is a hairline crack on the spout, and I'm not certain the finish will hold up to cleaning. Even so, I'd say perhaps it ought to fetch five pounds due to its age." He cradled the lamp like a babe in arms. "Is there a museum in Royston? I hadn't heard of one."

"No, not yet, but there has been talk of starting a new one."

"Capital! They might take an interest in our dig." Behind his glasses, his dark eyes twinkled.

"I suppose I could mention it next time I'm in town, but for now, I really must be off. My sister has gone missing, you see, and I'm hoping to—"

"Oh! I nearly forgot. That was the other thing I wished to talk to you about."

"Penny? You've seen her?"

"Indeed. My nephew told me to relay to you he's acquired a new assistant for the day—your sister." He chuckled merrily. "Apparently the girl stowed away in our wagon this morn. At any rate, she's having the time of her life, and you can rest assured Bram will take excellent care of her until she returns with the team for dinner."

Oh, that girl! Penny's antics would be the death of her. Eva glanced past the barn toward the fields, as if by some supernatural act the girl could see the glower on her face. Any number of dangers were a possibility for a foolish girl venturing out alone, especially one with sightless eyes. She could've easily been hurt or accidentally left behind.

Or worse.

"There now, Miss Inman. Don't fret." Professor Pendleton patted her shoulder. "Miss Penny is ensconced at a desk beneath the tent, happily inspecting some recent finds, and when she's not singing to herself, she's dictating what her gifted sense of touch can detect. Truly, Bram couldn't have found a more perfect task for the girl."

The tension in Eva's neck eased—not completely, but at least somewhat—and she smiled at the old fellow. Penny was safe and accounted for, and that was what truly mattered. "I appreciate your nephew's kindness, and yours. My sister can be a bit of a wild card at times."

Then again, so could Bram.

Could she truly trust him to know how to keep Penny safe?

Bram guided the horses along the last stretch of road to the house. Behind him, the three students boasted about who was the better field hand. Beside him, his uncle praised Penny's performance in the work tent, telling her what a fine student she'd been and how she might excel at a school for the blind he knew of in London. The rhythmic clip-clopping of hooves added to the pleasing chatter, and a smile eased across Bram's lips. All was right in the world. In fact, it was days like this he wondered why he should ever again set foot inside a stuffy classroom reeking of sweaty young men. The grand weather, how well the team had meshed, and all their spectacular finds had added up to a smashing day.

Yet when he drove into the yard, all that contentment was crushed, ground into the gravel with each heavy-footed pace of a woman in a brown coat gripping a lantern—

And marching his way.

He set the brake as Eva approached, her pale blue eyes sparking in the moonlight.

"I should like a word with you, Professor Webb." She spit out his name as she would a mouthful of soured milk, then looked past him to Penny. "And I will speak with you, sister, before you retire."

Next to him, Penny whispered, "She's angry."

"I should say so," he whispered back. "How about if you and my uncle hop down to see if Mrs. Pottinger has any dinner left? You must be famished. I know the rest of the men are."

"I am." Penny grinned, then impetuously threw her arms around him. "Thank you for such a fun day. Same time tomorrow?"

He didn't dare glance back at Eva as he endured the embrace. He didn't need to. He could feel her icy gaze boring into him, her wrath hitting him between the shoulder blades like grapeshot.

"Maybe not tomorrow, young Miss Inman." He tousled her wind-blown hair. With the girl's aptitude, she truly ought to be out at the dig again. He would do everything he could to encourage the girl's natural appetite to learn, even if it meant facing Eva's wrath. Penny ought not be squelched by the world around her. After all, he knew how harsh that world could be. "You did a bang-up job today, Penny, and I suspect it won't be long before your services are needed once again. Now off with you."

"Come along, Miss Penny." Uncle Pendleton guided the girl down. "If I don't collect that dinner basket for the men, I could have a riot on my hands."

"Don't wait on me, Uncle. I'll catch up with you and the fellows shortly." Hopefully, anyway. Eva might kill him in cold blood with the mood she was apparently in.

"We'll gather after dinner, men," Bram called over his shoulder, then jumped down from the seat, his boots landing with a harsh crunch. Before Eva could fire her first shot, he held up his hands in surrender. "You needn't say anything. I apologize for not getting Penny back sooner. She was completely swept up in the moment. We all were. And I think you'll understand why when I tell you—"

"What I understand, Professor Webb, is that it is half past seven. Do you seriously think a young girl ought to be in the company of five grown men until well after dark?"

One of the horses snorted—which he seconded, thoroughly frustrated. He'd apologized! What more did the woman want? "I would never let harm come to your sister. She was with me the entire time, not with some stranger. You know me."

"I do know you, which only adds to my concern. You are all action and hang the consequences! Any number of things could've happened to her out in that field." Her nostrils flared, her cheeks flaming redder. "I was worried about her, Bram. *I* am the one responsible for her care, not you. You had no right to keep my sister out so late."

He sighed. She did have a point. Penny wasn't one of his students—but that didn't stop him from being a teacher, and she had learned so much today. The light in the girl's eyes had been hungry. "Listen, Eva, your sister is not a bird to be caged. Like you, she owns a brilliant mind, one that needs to be fed. There are schools for the blind where she would thrive. Have you ever considered sending her to such an institution?"

Anguish rippled across her face, eventually hardening into a determined jut of her jaw. "I have been teaching Penny myself, and thus far she is not beyond what I know. I realize she will have special needs, such as learning Braille, but I intend to learn it right along with her."

"I did not mean to insult you. I merely wish to see Penny spread her wings a bit, fly like the bird she is. At the very least, please consider allowing her to come back out to the dig. I promise I shall keep better track of time in the future."

Moonlight draped over her shoulders, which visibly lowered. "I . . . I will consider it. Thank you." She turned away.

With a light touch to her arm, Bram pulled her back. "Hold on. You've had your say with me, and that's fine, but please don't be as harsh on the girl. Penny had a wonderful day. Do not ruin it."

She slipped from his hold, the lantern in her hand swinging wildly. "My sister should not have hidden away in your wagon like that. She needs to understand the seriousness of her rash actions."

"But she's just a girl, prone to following the whims of her heart, not convention. I seem to remember you following me around like a little lamb when you were that age, and yet you appear to have turned out just fine." More than fine, truth be told, with the way her skin glowed in the spare light, her loosened red hair gleaming. There was no denying her earthy appeal.

Eva flattened her lips. "I only mean to save Penny from the same scars I endured."

Hah! There was far more behind that statement than she let on. "You mean you wish to save her from me, is that it?" He flung out his hands, cracking his forearm against the wagon but so be it. "Am I such a monster to you?"

She lifted her face, her blue eyes searching his, like she was looking for answers to questions he couldn't begin to understand. The type of stare he'd give anything to hide from. Yet instinctively he knew not to turn away or allow some glib remark to slip out. So he stood deathly still in the October night, bearing the awful weight of her scrutiny.

And dreading what she might say next.

At length, she sighed, her warm breath puffing a small cloud into the cold air. "No, I do not think you are a monster."

The tension in his jaw eased, yet whatever wounds he'd unintentionally inflicted had to be drained completely before healing could take place. "Look, Eva, I am sorry for the sins of my youth. I acted recklessly, clearly causing you pain at times and leaving you with a bad taste in your mouth where I am concerned. But that was twelve years ago. I've grown up since then. What will it take for you to trust me?"

Her gaze dropped as if the answer might be found written in the scuff marks on the toes of her shoes. She clutched the lantern with both hands in front of her. Was this such a difficult question?

Eventually she lifted her head. "If only I could be sure you weren't keeping secrets from me."

His brows shot to the rafters. What suspicions did she harbour behind that pretty face of hers? "Why would I keep secrets from you?"

"Because you did all those years ago. You must have known you would be leaving Royston, yet you never breathed a word of it to me. You never told me where you went or why. You never even said good-bye. How can I trust you when I don't know if you will do the same again?"

"Is that all? Eva, I promise I won't leave you without a good-bye this time. Believe me, I would not have done so all those years ago if I'd had a choice in the matter—which I did not. Not even I knew I was leaving at the time, but that is a discussion for another time. Please, give me a chance, won't you?" He flashed the most disarming smile he could muster.

And when a small smile whispered across her lips, satisfaction made him grin all the more.

She lifted her nose in the air. "Very well, badger. I will try. We shall leave the past behind us, where it belongs."

"Thank you, but we can leave that nickname in the past as well, if you don't mind." He winked as he grabbed the lantern from her hands. "Follow me."

Her footsteps lagged behind his. "Where are we going?"

"Not far." He set the light on the back end of the wagon. Pulling a canvas sack to the edge, he groped inside for a small wrapped parcel. What a find this had been! He peeled away the cloth and held out the relic.

Eva's nose crinkled. "What is it?"

He set the pendant in her hand. Granted, the trinket didn't look like much now, but it surely would once polished. He pointed to each part as he spoke. "This thin gold sheet holds a cylindrical bead that's pierced through longitudinally. You can't see it in the evening's shadows, but that bead is made of a stunning azure glass. Attached to the bottom are two golden loops that each connect to a pearl. Either some woman wore this as a pendant or she's missing an earring, for we only found the one."

After a hard look at the bauble in her hand, Eva's gaze drifted to his face. "Is it valuable?"

"Very much." He grinned. "I thought you might like to see the fruits of our labour."

"Your uncle showed me the oil lamp earlier today, so I have no doubt on the matter."

"See? You're trusting me already."

She laughed, a delightful sound after such seriousness. "I suppose time will tell, Professor." She offered back the pendant. "And with that, I bid you good night."

She collected the lamp, leaving him with the moonlight as his sole companion. No, that wasn't quite true. He was also accompanied by a foreign urge to be a man she could trust, one she could confide in, depend upon, lean against.

But did that mean he must tell her all his secrets?

9

She really didn't want to do this. Not one little bit. The closer Eva drew to Tattleton's Pawn and Jams, the more her steps lagged. She tugged the drawstring of her reticule tighter around the handle of the letter opener that didn't quite fit inside her silk pouch. She'd already pledged her personal valuables and now was down to soliciting whatever else she could find that would bring in money. But parting with her father's favorite desk ornament stabbed deeply. Not that Mr. Tattleton would care. He was too busy making a profit off other people's misfortunes and his wife's homemade preserves. A shop of such heartbreak ought to be somber, not displaying brightly labeled confectionery spreads the moment a person walked in the door.

Jam. Of all things!

Ahead, a street vendor haggled with a woman in a ridiculous hat over the price of apples. The ostrich feathers on her bonnet wisped about like furry little arms. A good distraction, that. Eva couldn't help but take advantage of the opportunity, for as much as she'd like to purchase a newspaper, she couldn't spare a coin.

With the man's back turned toward her, she picked up a copy of the *Royston Gazette* and quickly paged through to the employment adverts. It never hurt to keep her options open, especially if worse came to worse. It'd been a week now since Bram had proudly shown her the Roman pendant. It truly was a beauty after he'd cleaned it up, and yet neither he nor his crew had found much of anything else since. Not that such lack was entirely their fault. The work tent had collapsed in the middle of the night, creating quite a mess and tearing the roof. Repairing the canvas and putting things to rights had taken a good day. Bram never did figure out why the thing had collapsed. Probably a freak wind burst, despite the mild weather they'd been enjoying. Unfortunately, the event had started Sinclair going on again about disturbing the cursed acres. At least it gave her an excuse to keep Penny away from the dig site the next couple of days before her conscience caught up to her again about giving her sister new challenges and experiences. On the other hand, the event had preoccupied her time in helping patch the canvas roof, taking her away from Penny—and her sister had been most vocal about her displeasure on that.

She scanned down the newspaper columns, looking for a governess or teaching position. She could do either. Ah, what about a lady's companion? She narrowed her eyes on the small type declaring a need for a lady of good standing—which she was—who loved to read—which she did—and who wouldn't mind if—

"That'll be two pence, miss."

She glanced up at a pointy-nosed weasel of a man, the ostrich hat woman already walking away behind him with a bright red apple clasped in her hand.

Eva set down the paper immediately. "Oh, I'm not purchasing a newspaper. Good day."

Bypassing the man, whose face had settled into a dangerous glower, she set off at a good clip. She didn't get very far when the door to the greengrocer's opened. Crisp leaves swirled in an eddy on the pavement as yellow skirts emerged. Charlotte Channing. Eva couldn't help but smile. Lottie was a sunbeam of a woman on a grey day such as this. Her bright blue eyes, her golden ringlets hanging in perfect spirals from beneath her bonnet, even the flash of Lottie's grin never failed to lift Eva's spirits.

"How lovely to see you in town, my friend! Seems like you never grace the streets of Royston anymore, other than on Sundays." Lottie shifted a basket of carrots to peck a friendly kiss on Eva's cheek.

Eva breathed in Lottie's lingering perfume, a sudden craving for marzipan biscuits rumbling in her stomach. Her friend smelled good enough to eat. "I had a few errands to see to. How is your mother?"

"Still abed, grumbling about her ankle. With the way she's going on, you'd think she'd been trampled by a herd of elephants instead of taking a simple tumble over Freddie's toy soldiers. She ought to perform on Drury Lane with such dramatics." Lottie huffed. "And now she's set on creating a Guy Fawkes effigy that will go down in history instead of burning up in a fire for a horde of rowdy children. So it's off to the rag shop for me. Would you like to come along?"

Eva mentally tallied up the days until November fifth, then pursed her lips. "But Guy Fawkes Day isn't for at least a fortnight."

"That's the same thing I said. But you know my mother." Lottie struck a regal pose, one hand in the air, her voice rising an octave to match Mrs. Channing's notoriously shrill tone. "One must start early to ensure perfection, Charlotte."

They both laughed at the parody, garnering them a stern look from a passing duo of black-coated men.

Lottie grabbed Eva's hands, giving them a little shake. "You will be there this year, won't you? I missed you dearly last time, though I know it couldn't be helped, what with your father's death and all." She squeezed Eva's fingers before letting go. "Oh, do say you'll come—you and Penny both!"

"You must know I'd love to spend the evening with you, but I cannot promise anything." A pang of melancholy twinged her heart. Before Father had died, she'd enjoyed such frivolities as a bonfire or gala. Though she still had yet to account for where he'd gotten such irregular influxes of money for the gowns she used to purchase for those events.

Lottie pinched her cheek lightheartedly. "I won't take no for an answer, and you know I mean it."

She surely did. Lottie was a kitten after a saucer of cream, unwilling to let anything get in her way once her mind was set on something. And she could hiss just as vehemently when riled.

"There you are, Miss Inman," a jolly voice called down the pavement.

They turned to see a potted fern bobbing straight for them, clutched in a man's arms just above a potbelly.

"Who's that?" Lottie whispered. "And why is he carrying such a large plant?"

"That is Professor—oomph." She reflexively flung her arms around the brass pot as Bram's uncle handed over the greenery.

"Isn't it a lovely specimen?" He fluffed some of the fronds as he spoke. "It's an adiantum, lusher than I'd expect it to be with the poor care it was receiving in the bookstore. Criminals. Relegating this beauty to a dusty old corner smelling of camphor. Camphor! What's this world coming to when a bookseller doesn't employ the requisite scents of ink and binding glue?"

Eva blew one of the fronds from her face. "I thought you came into town to inquire at the historical society office?"

"Historical society?" He rubbed his jawline a few times before snapping his fingers. "Capital idea, my dear! Enjoy your fern. Good day, miss." He tipped his hat at Charlotte and strolled off.

"Don't forget to meet me at the market square so we can ride home together, Professor," Eva called after him. While absent-mindedness was a common trait of an academic, this man took it to a whole new level. Hopefully it was nothing more serious than that.

Without slowing a step, he waggled his fingers in the air.

Lottie arched a brow. "Don't tell me that man is living in your house, Eva. Who is he? And why did he not stay long enough for a proper introduction?"

Eva shifted the fern to one hip, cradling it like an overgrown babe. "He's a bit, em, unconventional. He *and* his crew are staying in the old labourers' quarters, not in the house."

Lottie's curls fairly quivered at this news. "A crew? What sort? Do tell."

"I suppose I should have explained myself better. Professors Pendleton and Webb have come from Trinity College to dig in the back field on my property. Turns out there are some Roman antiquities buried beneath that fallow ground. They brought some students along and have found several relics."

"Webb. Webb?" Lottie tasted the name several times, her tongue darting over her lips. "Any relation to the divine fellow we grew up with?"

Eva's cheeks heated. For the past week, she'd been trying to stay away from the man, and physically, she'd done a good job of it. Yet despite that, her mind had kept injudicious company with him. The night he'd apologized for his past behaviour, he'd been so genuine, so . . . She bit her lip. Though she could hardly believe it, he'd seemed vulnerable, at least for a minute, which was quite the stark contrast to the carefree and mischievous boy she remembered. His candid remorse had done something strange to her heart, and she found herself stealing glances in his direction, watching his every move whenever she chanced to be in his vicinity, a certain amount of respect growing for the man he'd become.

But she couldn't very well tell Lottie such a thing. Her friend would have them married off by Sunday.

Once again, she shifted the big fern, this time holding it in front of her like a shield. "I wouldn't say he was divine."

Lottie poohed her words with a wave of her fingers. "Come now. Every girl had a crush on the dashing Bram Webb. You most of all, as I recall. Is he one of the professors you've hired?"

"I didn't hire him. He volunteered to lead the excavation."

"So it is him!" Lottie fairly squealed as the grocer's door opened once again.

A stoop-shouldered matron shot her an ulcerous look. "Such an outburst in public. Take a care, young lady, to put a guard on that imprudent tongue of yours."

"Yes, madam." Lottie dipped her head in penance, yet behind the gloved fingers covering her mouth, Eva saw a smile flash.

Once the lady strode far enough down the pavement, they both laughed—and how good it felt to be so lighthearted. Once the giggles were over, though, Eva tugged her friend farther away from the shop door to avoid further censures.

Lottie reset her hat, which had been knocked askew. "Is he as handsome as he used to be?"

"I can't really be the judge of that, beauty being in the eye of the beholder and all. But if you like a piratey sort of fellow who more often than not forgets to shave his whiskers, then I suppose you could say he's handsome." She would, which surprised even her.

"Well, it's settled, then. You must bring Mr. Webb to the Guy Fawkes bonfire so I can judge for myself."

"I didn't say I was attending."

"Oh yes, you will"—Lottie pushed a finger in Eva's shoulder—"or I'll have my impish little brother lead the procession right to your doorstep."

"You wouldn't."

"You know I must always get my way, Eva dear."

Eva sighed. Though Lottie would never admit it, she was

as dogged as her mother. "Fine. I'll invite him, but I cannot guarantee he will accept."

"You're the dandiest." Her friend beamed. "Until then!"

Stepping around her, Lottie strode away, taking all her sunshine with her.

Eva trudged in the opposite direction, toward Tattleton's Pawn and Jams. The fern bumped against her hip, making her cross, but deep down she knew that wasn't the true reason for her irritation. Oh, why had she allowed herself to get duped into asking Bram Webb to escort her to Bonfire Night?

Now she had two things she really didn't want to do.

Bram had always been a night owl, a trait acquired from his mother. In more ways than one, she hadn't been like other women, a fact that undisputedly came with benefits. She wasn't always breathing down his neck to go to bed. She didn't care if he made noise at an ungodly hour. Frequent complaints spouted from their neighbour, Mrs. Hempstone, however, especially that time he'd tried to make a diamond from coal dust and gunpowder. What an explosion. He'd blown a sizeable hole in the kitchen wall, nearly taking out Mrs. Hempstone's cat in the process. But his mother hadn't noticed because she wasn't home. Most evenings she wasn't, which left him to his own imaginative devices. His childhood had been a young lad's dream, and yet, such freedom had come with a price tag. Namely shame.

And if Eva was to discover the truth about the circumstances of his birth . . . well, their growing friendship would face significant strain. A lady of her standing would likely struggle with societal expectations and the potential scandal it could bring to associate with him.

Rubbing his eyes, Bram leaned back in his chair in the Inman breakfast-room-turned-makeshift-antiquity-studio. Coming back to Royston had exposed memories he'd thought he'd folded neatly away.

Light footsteps padded into the room, followed by Eva's soft voice. "Am I catching you at a bad moment?"

He removed his pocket watch and snapped open the lid. What a curious time for her to seek him out. She'd been avoiding him the better part of the past week. Tucking away his watch, he arched a brow at her. "It's nearly midnight. What's gotten you out of bed? No, that's not true, is it?" He narrowed his eyes on her lithe form still garbed in her serviceable blue day dress. "You've not been to bed yet."

"I was . . . reading. Yes. That's it. You know I like to read." Absently, she picked up a shard of a clay pot, suddenly interested in examining its jagged edges. "But if this is awful timing, I shall go back to my book."

A playful grin lifted one side of his mouth. "It is never awful timing to be visited by a lovely lady."

"Come now, we both know I am no beauty." She set the shard down and faced him. "You need not pretend otherwise."

He gaped. "Who on earth ever gave you the idea you are not beautiful?"

"'Big mouth, long nose, Eva Inman has no beaux.'" Her terrible words singsonged like a shiver in the night. "That's what Richard Trestwell always said."

Bram's hands curled into fists as he rose. Of course it had been Trestwell. "I knew the cully owned a foul mouth, but I never knew he said such a rotten thing about you. Why would you allow lies from a muckle-headed urchin to shade your own view of yourself?"

"They are not lies, as you can see for yourself." She circled her hand in front of her face.

He grabbed her wrist. Blast that Trestwell for planting such a wicked falsehood so deeply into her soul. "What I see, Eva Inman, are lips capable of great smiles, bright enough to light my day—or night, as the case may be. And that nose of yours is noble. Regal, even. Had I a diamond coronet in my pocket, I wouldn't hesitate to crown you queen here and now. You are a striking woman, crafted in God's image, and are not defined by the cruel words of a callous boy. You are—and ever will be—a beauty in my eyes. Do not doubt it."

Like a spooked filly, her chest rose and fell deeply, her nostrils flaring on the inhale. He could only guess at what might be going through her mind, but he hoped—and prayed—the genuine truths he offered would somehow heal the wounds inflicted by that infernal Richard Trestwell. Blasted jackanapes. If he ever saw that devil again, he'd pop him a good one on the jaw.

"Well." Eva pulled away. "I suppose you ought to be allowed to have your own opinion, and . . . I thank you for it."

"My pleasure." He grinned. "So would you like to see what I have been working on?"

She nodded.

He led her to the end of the canvas-covered table. "I have just been cleaning these coins. See the brass tokens?" He poked his finger into the mix, separating the pieces farther apart. "Those are sestertii, the silver are denarii, and there is even a single gold aureus right here." He picked up the most valuable coin.

Bending close, she examined it. "Is that a good find?"

"Very. This selection of currency shows whoever lived on your land had at least one person of means in residence." He set the coin down as Eva sidestepped to the next item, her understated scent of newly mown hay lingering in the air. He appreciated she didn't douse herself in lemon verbena or violet witch hazel, as was all the rage of late. Her tastes were simpler, an attribute he could respect.

"Let me guess." She ran a light touch along the side of a long-necked vessel. "A water pitcher?"

"Close. That amphora was used for wine."

Doubt swam in her pale blue eyes. "How do you know it was not used for water?"

"There is residue inside." Retrieving a metal pick with a hook at the end, he gently scraped the interior ceramic wall. A tiny fleck of brownish-red sat on the tip, and he held it up. "See?"

"Mmm," she murmured as she studied the speck . . . *really* studied it. Did she see the same connections he made when examining such a peek into the past? Was she pondering this tangible link to a forgotten moment in time, a celebration perhaps, when love and laughter had echoed in an ancient Roman dwelling? Every find, no matter how minor, was a bridge to hearts that had beat, lungs that had breathed, so many lifetimes ago.

Eva peered up at him. "It makes one wonder, does it not?"

"It surely does." He smiled, chest warming that she shared—at least in part—in his passion. "But the best find of all is this."

He beckoned her with a crook of his finger to the opposite end of the table. "This may seem insignificant"—he waved his hand over a sizeable mosaic chunk—"but the motif in this piece of flooring is important."

She bent closely, sweeping back a loose wave of red hair in the process. "It looks like . . . Is this design part of an anchor?"

"It is."

A wrinkle creased her brow. "We are nowhere near the sea. I should think the artisan would have incorporated something more fitting for the area, such as wheat fronds or ivy leaves."

"A valid train of thought, yet the symbol itself has nothing to do with this geographical location. The anchor was used as a key Christian symbol during the time of Roman persecution."

"But . . ." Her gaze drifted back to the mosaic. "I thought that fish on the ring was what they used? Or maybe even a cross."

"Not back then. Think about it; if you are a first-century Christian hiding from crucifixion, would a cross be a comforting icon? I do not think so. No, you would need something more uplifting to remind you to stay strong when facing death

94

by lions or being set ablaze as a human torch for one of Nero's garden parties."

Her nose scrunched. "Like hope?"

"Very good." He smiled. "Yet even more, you would need faith to believe God saw your trials, cared about them, cared about *you*. A fish emblem is not going to remind you of the solid rock in which your faith is rooted. One of my favorite verses is in Hebrews. 'Which hope we have as an anchor of the soul, both sure and stedfast, and which entereth into that within the veil.' Jesus is that hope. Jesus alone is our anchor."

"Why, I . . . I never thought of things that way. I mean, that trials are good in that they increase faith and are not necessarily a punishment. I guess I have always thought of hard times as a sort of penance, but that wouldn't be so if—as you say—God cares about them . . . about me. I—" Her lips parted with an audible intake of air, as if some great revelation had taken root. Slowly, she shook her head. "I had no idea you were such a theologian, Bram Webb."

He laughed aloud. "I have been accused of many things but never that."

She grinned in return. "Well, whatever the case, it is plain to see you take your faith seriously, which is quite a change from the wild boy I once knew."

"That is because I did not have any faith all those years ago. That came later when I went to live with my uncle. Housing beneath the same roof as a man who takes the Bible seriously has a way of speaking to a hungry heart. At any rate, it is probably a good thing I have tamed a bit, or those historical society members would be frightened off in a heartbeat." He winked as he reached for a cloth to cover the mosaic.

"What do you mean? What members?"

He smoothed the wrinkles on the canvas before draping the cloth over the mosaic. "Several board members are coming around noon on Friday. Did my uncle not tell you?"

"No, he did not."

Bram stifled a sigh. Of course Uncle hadn't. Would the man even remember he'd invited them to view the dig? He shrugged, defying the tension ripping through him. "Must have slipped his mind."

"I am afraid you will have to reschedule." Eva tugged at the hems of her sleeves, lamplight brushing over a furrow in her brow. "I am not prepared to host a luncheon."

Women. Always taking things a step too far when it came to societal expectations. "No meal is required. They're coming to see the antiquities and the dig, not to eat a bowl of tomato bisque."

She tapped her finger to her lip, looking as if she might take a bite on her nail. "Are you sure they are not expecting more?"

"If they are, I shall catch a chicken with my teeth and roast it over a fire for them."

She didn't laugh. Didn't smile. Just tap-tap-tapped at her lip.

Clearly she was chasing some rabbit down a hole in her head. An inordinate amount of fuss over the prospect of a few men wishing to examine some relics. Why such tension over a no-frills sort of entertainment?

Then again . . . Lacing his fingers, he cracked his knuckles. This house needed repair in several spots. Eva and her sister wore somewhat-faded gowns. And every evening he and the men returned to the same fare of soup and bread. Granted, the soup changed, but nothing more substantial was ever served. Either Eva was frugal to a fault, or her money trouble was more than she admitted.

And he'd bet on the latter, judging by that quiver to her lower lip.

"Look, Eva." He put all his effort into spooling out his words in a soothing tone. "If there is anything you need to talk about, I am a good listening ear."

She inhaled deeply, visibly pulling herself together. "Thank you, but there is no need. I look forward to hearing what the historical society has to say about these pieces."

"Probably a lot of oohs and ahhs."

Once again she didn't smile in the least. She merely turned away and scrutinized part of a stone tablet, which of course was absurd. Even if she could read Latin, most of the letters were destroyed.

He carefully pushed the piece aside. "Why did you come here tonight? Why did you seek me out?"

"I, em, I was going to ask you . . ." A lump traveled her throat as she swallowed audibly. "Well, it was not anything important, and it is getting late. Good night." She whirled, the hem of her skirt whapping against his ankles.

Bram folded his arms, his gaze following her out the door, all the while wondering what *un*important reason had driven her to this room in the dead of night.

10

Four days. How absurd. By now she should have invited Bram to the Guy Fawkes bonfire, yet she hadn't. She'd tried, several times, but the words didn't make it past her lips. Eva tipped the watering can, draining liquid into the outlandishly large fern in the sitting room. Why the sudden shyness around a man she'd known practically all her life?

She set the watering can on the mat near the baseboard and took to pacing a circular route. Late-morning sunshine bled through the windows, easing her foul mood somewhat. Another mild October day, which would be a boon for the historical society members who were due to arrive soon. Perhaps after they left she could steal a moment with Bram. *Yes, that's it.* A quick invitation and they'd both go about their day. Nothing could be easier.

But even so, she pressed her fingers against her belly. What in the world was wrong with her? It was only a silly bonfire. She was overthinking the matter, that's what, and all because of eleven wonderful words.

"You are—and ever will be—a beauty in my eyes."

She stopped dead in her tracks. Naturally she had no right

to believe such foolishness, but it had been kind of Bram to say such a thing, kinder still to voice it without a smirk or hint of jesting to his tone. Despite all his boyish pranks of long ago, it appeared he wished nothing more than to be a good friend. She sucked in a little breath. That was it! They were, after all, friends. Inviting him to a bonfire wasn't some kind of romantic gesture. She'd simply say there were Guy Fawkes festivities in Royston and he could ride along with her if he liked. His crew, too, if they wished. Simple. Innocuous.

Perfect.

Relieved, she strolled to the large mirror above the mantel and tucked some stray hairs into her chignon. Usually she would be reading to Penny right now, but thankfully her sister had been amenable to listening to *Little Women* earlier than normal—as long as Eva would drive her over for a visit with her friend Amelia after service on Sunday. The little bargainer. Her sister had also started pestering her about attending a school for the blind as suggested to her by Professors Pendleton and Bram, but that wasn't something Eva would barter for. Not quite yet, anyway. Penny was only twelve. Surely waiting another year or two wouldn't hurt, when she could hopefully send her sister to school by her own funding rather than relying on the charity of Mrs. Mortimer.

Eva nibbled on her nail. This pestering by her sister was to be expected, though, in light of all the time Eva had been spending at the dig site and with Bram in the evenings. Guilt niggled at the back of her mind. She'd promised to take care of Penny, to be there for her, but lately her thoughts were elsewhere—namely on a grey-eyed man with a ready smile. She recalled the disappointed look in Penny's eyes yesterday when she'd declined an invitation to play the piano together in order that she might discuss with Bram the price he thought that amphora might bring in.

Bah! How could she balance it all? She winced as she bit too near the quick of her nail. Penny had accused her of neglect recently, a sharp reminder her little poppet was growing up and becoming more perceptive. Eva had tried to make Penny understand the importance of this dig, the significance of the discoveries, but her sister had merely turned away, her sightless eyes shining with tears no words from Eva could wipe away.

And then there was Bram. His insistence that Penny needed more education than Eva could provide made her bristle. He had no idea of the depth of her responsibilities.

Sighing, she pressed her hands to her cheeks. She had to find a way to keep Penny close while allowing the girl the freedom to grow. But how? How could she be everywhere, do everything, without cracking under the pressure?

The front bell rang. Though it was only several members from the historical society, Eva pinched her cheeks for colour. The Inman estate might be falling down around her ears, but she didn't have to look decrepit.

By the time she made it to the front hall, Dixon and Mary were already collecting the hats of two men and wraps of two women. *Women? Oh, that's right.* She'd forgotten Mrs. White was a board member. But since when had Lottie taken an interest in history? Then again, one could never pin down the merry whims of Charlotte Channing.

Stepping forward, Eva curved her lips into her best hostess smile. "Welcome to the Inman estate, ladies and gentlemen. The professors are waiting for you in our breakfast-room-turned-workspace at the back of the house before we head out to the tent at the dig site, so follow me, if you will."

She led them down a stretch of corridor, mortified by the loose plaster hanging in spots overhead. Another thing to fix once funding came in. She paused by the workroom door, angling so everyone might pass.

Mrs. White patted her on the arm while she swept by in a cloud of Bulgarian rose and ambergris. "Thank you, Miss Inman."

"My pleasure, Mrs. White."

The two gentlemen followed her, one short, the other valiantly trying to hide a shiny bald spot with wispy strings of overlong hair. Both dipped their heads as they passed. "Miss Inman," they said in unison.

"Mr. Toffit, Mr. Hamby, happy to have you."

The sweet scent of marzipan came next, but before Lottie could cross the threshold, Eva blocked her path. "What are you doing here?" she whispered. "You are not on the board."

Lottie grinned as she rose to her toes, peeking past Eva's shoulder. "Mrs. White visited Mother yesterday and said she was coming here to see some relics. I merely asked to tag along."

"Since when are you interested in ancient Roman artifacts?" Eva followed Lottie's line of vision. "Aha. You are not. You just wanted to see Professor Webb for yourself."

Lottie lowered to flat feet, a twinkle in her eyes. "Maybe I simply wished to see one of my dearest friends."

Mmm. Right. "I thought you were too busy making a Guy Fawkes effigy for your mother?"

"I am, but that's a whole week and a half away. Besides, I told Mother I was sure to get some inspiration looking at your fine artifacts." She leaned sideways, once again peering at Bram. "And I am feeling very inspired at the moment. You were right, you know. He does have a piratey flair. Very dashing, and more than intriguing. Do you think he'll remember me?"

"I would imagine he has other things on his mind at the moment."

"Let's find out." Lottie looped her arm through Eva's, turning her about as she marched into the room.

"Maybe we should wait. Let him chat with the historical society first."

"Nonsense." Lottie headed straight toward the cluster of board members and professors. "You must learn to grab hold of an opportunity." She stopped next to Bram and loudly cleared her throat.

Five pairs of eyes swung their way.

Lottie beamed.

Eva barely managed a sheepish smile. Most often she adored her vivacious friend. This wasn't one of those moments. "Pardon me, Professor Webb, Professor Pendleton. I should like to introduce my friend Miss Channing. She is not part of the historical society but has recently taken a keen interest in certain things related to academics."

Or more like a certain professor.

Bram's uncle collected Lottie's hand and bowed over it. "Lovely to meet you, Miss Channing."

"Yes, enchanted," Bram echoed at his side.

"I say!" Mr. Toffit called from where he'd wandered farther down the table. "This amphora is in near-perfect condition. First century or second?"

"Pardon us, ladies. Duty calls." Professor Pendleton ushered Bram away.

Lottie turned to her, lower lip pouty. "He didn't remember me."

"Like I said, Lottie, he has other things on his mind right now. Give him some time." Eva squeezed her arm. "As long as you are here, would you like to see what they have unearthed? They really have discovered some interesting items."

With a last longing look at Bram, Lottie brightened. "That would be lovely. What have you got?"

"I am no expert, but I have learned a little." Eva led her to the mosaic. "This is part of some flooring or maybe a decorative bit of wall."

Lottie eyed the artifact. "The colours are so brilliant I can hardly believe this was buried in your back field."

"The professors are adept with their cleaning methods. See the pattern here?" Eva pointed toward the anchor. "Early Christians used an anchor as a symbol of encouragement. I did a little reading on it in one of my father's books and discovered it was also the royal emblem of Seleucus the First, one of the leaders after Alexander the Great. Supposedly he chose the design because he had a birthmark in the shape of an anchor."

"Well, well, you are the scholar! Nicely done, Miss Inman." Bram drew alongside her, admiration thick in his voice. "Or another explanation could be from when the emperor Trajan banished the fourth pope, Saint Clement. When Clement converted the people there, Trajan ordered his death by tying him to an anchor and drowning him in the sea. It is said the water receded afterward that his body might be buried by angels in a marble mausoleum. Not a very believable tale, but one that inspired the persecuted Church at the time."

Lottie grinned, no longer interested in the coloured tiles on the table. "Neither can your scholarship be denied, Professor. Though, yes, Eva is brilliant. She's always got her nose in a book. Surely you remember that from when we were young?"

"I do." His gaze drifted to Lottie. "I am sorry, but did you say *we*? Have we met before?"

"We have." Lottie fairly bounced on her toes. "My full name is Charlotte Channing, but when we were young, everyone called me Lottie. Eva still does."

"Ah yes. Forgive me for forgetting."

"Oh, no need to apologize." Lottie giggled. "We all change over the years. You certainly have."

"In a good way, I hope."

Lottie leaned toward him. "In the best way."

Eva rolled her eyes. If she didn't break this up now, there was no telling how much more Lottie would gush about Bram's attributes. Lightly, she rested her hand on her friend's arm. "We should let the professor get back to the society members."

"I suppose so." Lottie sighed. "But I will see you at the bonfire, Professor, and we can catch up then."

Eva stiffened.

Bram angled his head. "What bonfire?"

"Oh"—Lottie didn't miss a beat—"I should have spoken more clearly. The bonfire at the Guy Fawkes festival Eva invited you to."

You mean the bonfire I should have invited him to.

Lottie's gaze bounced between them. "Eva, you did invite the professor, didn't you?"

The same sunshine that had warmed her in the sitting room now angled through the window like a brash aunt come to point out her shortcomings. "I . . . did not. I mean, I did not have the chance yet."

"I see," Lottie drawled, and with her next breath, she flashed a bright grin at Bram. "Then allow me to extend the invitation, Professor Webb. I'd be delighted to see you in Royston on the fifth."

"I think that can be arranged, Miss Channing. Now if you will excuse me, I really should be getting back to business." He left them with his trademark wink.

Eva deflated. At least she didn't have to torture herself about how to ask him anymore.

Lottie nudged her with her shoulder. "I thought you were going to ask him."

"I . . . tried. It just never seemed like the right time."

"Then it is a fortuitous thing I came along today, hmm? So how about you dazzle me with more information about these items? That bauble over there is so pretty in the sunshine." Lottie ambled toward the pendant.

Eva followed. *Fortuitous* wasn't quite the description she'd use. More like slightly irritating, for it had been uncomfortable witnessing Lottie flirt with Bram. Not that Eva had any claim on the man, nor did she intend to have any, but still . . .

Why the sudden rebellion of the morning tea in her belly?

Though two sides of the field tent flaps were rolled open, it was still a bit stuffy with so many bodies milling about, particularly when one of those bodies had apparently been dipped in rose and ambergris. Bram fought the urge to sneeze as he waited for Mr. Toffit to finish scrutinizing a set of first-century iron chisels he'd recently finished cleaning—which had been no small feat considering several of the excavation implements had been broken the other day. When he'd pulled up to the dig on Tuesday morn, he'd accidentally rolled the wagon wheels over an assortment of scattered tools. The students had no idea how the items had gotten there, and he believed them, but when he'd questioned his uncle, well, the old fellow had dithered a bit before spouting a denial. Either the cursed-acres lore had caused the mishap, or his uncle's forgetfulness might be turning into a liability.

Across the tent, Eva's friend Miss Channing flashed him a smile. Honestly, he didn't remember much about her, but one thing was crystal clear: The woman was interested in him. Was Eva? His gaze drifted to where she stood next to Miss Channing, chatting with his uncle. Sunlight haloed her head, burnishing her hair to an autumn glow and painting her face in honeyed light. She didn't so much as slip him a side-eye, so taken was she with whatever his uncle said. Bram rubbed his knuckles along his jaw. It was hard to say what she thought of him with her mixed signals, sometimes friendly, other times cool.

"What are all these bottles and jars, Professor Webb?" Mr. Toffit waved his hand over the analysis set at the back of the table. "This looks more like a chemistry laboratory than a dig site."

"So I have been told." And warned against by Grimwinkle. The man fussed about the potential harm that could be inflicted upon a relic, but if he'd have taken an hour or two for deep discussion with the chair of the science faculty as Bram had done, then Grimwinkle would know what a baseless concern he held.

Bram held up an amber bottle in a ray of sunshine. "I find that by employing chemical analysis, I can achieve a more comprehensive interpretation of the past, connecting artifacts to specific practices or trade routes. In this case, I've not identified any linkage between this settlement to the Roman road between London and Cambridge, which means the people who settled here—who were clearly of Roman origin—were either horribly lost or they didn't wish to be found. I am hoping for the latter, as the settlement we are looking for would have purposely kept a distance from other Romans who might persecute them for their faith."

Now if he could just find something definitive to mark this as Caelum Academia, for a mere Roman village would do nothing to vindicate his uncle—and every day spent here meant one day not spent finding the colony they so desperately needed to prove existed to Grimwinkle. He needed to find something, a wax tablet, a fragment of a codex, or, by a great act of God's mercy, a preserved scroll. Something—*anything*—to prove this was Caelum Academia.

"Professor Webb." Mrs. White gestured to two large canvases he'd pinned to a tent wall. "About these drawings?"

"If you will excuse me, Mr. Toffit." He dipped his head at the short fellow and crossed the now-flattened grass to the side wall.

"Not much to look at, are they, Mrs. White?" He grinned as he stationed himself next to her and Mr. Hamby. "And yet these line sketches are invaluable. These are stratigraphic drawings, illustrating the layers and relationships between different deposits, which is crucial for understanding the chronological sequence of artifacts and features we find."

Mr. Hamby's lower lip stuck out. "Impressive."

"More like helpful, I would say."

"Professor Webb," Miss Channing called. "Are those young men out there your students?"

He couldn't have planned a better transition. "They are, and I have no doubt they would love to show us what they are currently working on. Shall we join them?"

As if on cue, Uncle Pendleton crooked both his arms for Eva and Miss Channing. "Allow me to lead you out, ladies."

Mr. Hamby accompanied Mrs. White, though he did notice the man turn his head aside to breathe lest he suffocate in her cloud of perfume.

Which left him and Mr. Toffit alone. Bram stepped toward the open flap and swept out his hand. "After you, sir."

Mr. Toffit held his ground, one finger up in the air. "A word first, Professor, if you don't mind."

"Not at all." He doubled back to the table. "Have you more questions about chemical analysis? I can assure you the compounds I use are all safe for delicate antiquities."

Mr. Toffit sniffed, his pencil-thin moustache crinkling into more of a wave than a straight line. "Actually, I have some inquiries that are more personal in nature."

Bram tensed. Blast. What had the man heard of him? "Ask away."

"I am wondering how beholden you are to Trinity College."

Huh. Of all the turns of conversation, he hadn't seen that one coming. "Quite frankly"—he cracked his knuckles—"I know nothing else. Trinity is where I was educated and have worked ever since."

"Would you ever consider leaving?"

He hadn't until Grimwinkle's latest witch-hunt. And now with his uncle retiring next spring. "Perhaps, if the timing and opportunity were right."

"I must say I am impressed with what you and Professor Pendleton have accomplished here in such a short time. You show a great passion for the preservation of the past. Does that passion extend beyond Roman antiquities?"

Bram picked up one of the cleaning brushes, running his thumb over the bristles. "I enjoy interacting and being of help to my colleagues who work with a span of cultures and eras, from ancient Greece to Egypt, even to the Mayan and Incan peoples. So yes, while Rome is my first love, it is my intention to bring history alive for my students."

"*Only* students?"

"What are you getting at, Mr. Toffit?"

The short fellow curled his fingers around his lapels, pulling himself up to full height—which barely brought the top of his head even with Bram's shoulders. "Earlier this year, the Royston Historical Society came into quite a windfall. One of our wealthiest benefactors recently passed, leaving his entire estate to us with the express wish that we create a museum. We have since found the perfect building to house our collection, which at the moment is woefully insufficient. To offset such a lack, the board members and I feel an educational approach would enhance what we have."

Bram set the brush back on the table, intrigued by such novel thinking. "What sort of educational approach?"

"Lectures, workshops, perhaps even small field trips for those of an interest."

Well, now. That was quite large thinking for such a small town . . . and therein lay the crux of the matter. The citizens of Royston had livelihoods to manage. Would they have time to involve themselves in such academic pursuits?

"Tell me, Mr. Toffit, do you really think the people of Royston would participate in this?"

"Oh yes." He bobbed his head vigorously. "I should say there's been a great deal of interest in the few town meetings we've held. And as you know, we're not all that far away from Cambridge. We could draw from that populace as well."

It could do. There were many deep pockets in Cambridge with a love of all things historical, and if this new museum was to partner with Trinity, why, the possibilities could be beneficial to them both. "It sounds as if you have thought this through."

"Indeed." The man sniffed again, then took a moment to retrieve a snowy handkerchief and honk a few notes into the cloth. "And what I am thinking now is that with your passion for education and flair for innovation, you are the perfect fit for our new curator. I have no doubt the other board members will agree."

He blinked. *Him?* Head of an entire museum? What a dream job. His gaze drifted out the flap to his students, who were enthusiastically pointing at their latest excavations. Young men like them made teaching worthwhile, and he'd miss them sorely.

But he wouldn't miss the politics of academia one whit.

He locked his gaze on Mr. Toffit. "I am honoured, sir. Most would seek out someone with years more experience, such as my uncle."

"There is a certain wisdom that comes with age, no argument there. But in order for this museum to be a success, it must have a fresh vision from a younger mind. A visionary, if you will. I see that in you."

His breath caught in his throat. As a lad, he'd longed for a father to recognize and encourage him just like this. But he'd had no father. He'd hardly had a mother to keep track of him.

"Thank you, Mr. Toffit." He barely pushed the words past the lump in his throat.

"Excellent!" He clapped his hands together. "Think on it, then, and we'll get back to you with a formal offer. Now, I am finally ready to see what your students have uncovered today." He strode toward the open flap.

Yet he barely made it there before Bram called after him, "Oh, Mr. Toffit, when were you hoping to fill the position by?"

"End of the year," he answered without missing a step.

Hefting a sigh, Bram plowed his fingers through his hair. So much for that grand career move. It didn't matter what sort of offer the historical society returned. There was no way he could take on a curatorship and keep his uncle out of trouble until the end of the school year at the same time.

Assuming he could keep his uncle out of trouble, period.

11

There was always a bite in the air on Bonfire Night, almost as if the world demanded an extra measure of warmth every November fifth. It was such a peculiar holiday, celebrating the failure of a group of men—most notably Guy Fawkes—who attempted to blow up Parliament several hundred years ago. The hoots and hollers of merrymaking carried all the way from the fairgrounds out to the field, where at least a hundred carriages were already parked. Eva fumbled with the top button on her coat as Bram tethered the wagon horses to one of the many metal spikes driven into the ground. She'd missed this festivity last year, and she'd expected to miss it again this time, yet here she was. And with a man, no less. But not just one man. A whole crew of men—Professor Pendleton and all three of Bram's students. Plus Penny and Dixon.

"Can I go?" Penny tugged at her sleeve, hardly taking a breath between words. "You must say yes. Professor Pendleton already gave me his permission. Oh, please, Eva!"

"Slow down, poppet." Eva straightened the girl's bonnet. "What are you talking about?"

"Everyone is going to the food tent, where there's treacle toffee and candy apples and cider and chestnuts and—"

"Enough. You will ruin your appetite for dinner."

Professor Pendleton appeared at her side. "That's what fair food is all about. It's only one night a year. Let the girl have some fun."

Eva bit her lip. He did have a point.

Dixon looped her arm through Penny's. "I'll join them, miss. We can catch up with you and Professor Webb later."

"Are you certain, Dixon?"

"It will be my pleasure. Truth be told, I fancy a bite of good treacle toffee." She leaned close, lowering her voice. "Mrs. Pottinger scorches hers, but you didn't hear that from me."

Eva laughed. "Very well. But mind your manners, sister."

"I will!"

"Come along, crew!" Professor Pendleton set off, waving for them to follow.

Bram held out his arm. "Ready for some fun?"

Caught up in his effervescent smile, she rested her fingers atop his sleeve. Even from this far away, music and laughter carried on the air. Bram whistled along, and it was surprising how endearing that simple habit of his had become. She peered up at him, the tip of his nose reddened by the brisk air, as was the scar at the top of his cheek. "Has it really only been three weeks since you have come to Royston? It seems so much longer. Almost like you are part of the manor now."

He gazed down at her. My, how accustomed she'd become to his face. To hearing his jolly laugh with his students. To meeting with him each evening when he showed her the treasures of the day. How empty the house would seem when he and his team returned to Cambridge.

"Is that a good thing or bad?" he asked.

An impish grin spread across her face. "I have not yet decided."

He nudged her with his elbow, sending her sideways, yet at

the same time, he anchored her grip on his arm so she wouldn't go sprawling. His tobacco smell wasn't as strong as when he'd first arrived. And yet there was that earthy scent, like a forest floor after an October rain. She breathed it in as they drew close to the fairgrounds before the aromas of all manner of foods and treats obliterated it.

Off to the far side of the grounds, a yellow-and-orange-striped hot air balloon slowly rose into the grey sky. Several riders hung over the edge of the basket, waving at friends below, a thick rope tethering them to the earth. Eva's step hitched.

Bram forced her face away from the horrid sight. "Still queasy about heights, are you?"

She sucked in a small gasp. "You remembered?"

A frown creased his brow. "What I remember is a very frightened little girl who was the butt of a vicious prank by Richard Trestwell. I daresay you would still be whimpering up in that apple tree had I not reset the ladder for you."

Her lips parted. That was right. The terror of the creaking branches and hard earth taunting her to fall and break her neck were still so vivid, she'd forgotten Bram had been the one to see her safely down. Had she inadvertently blocked other kindnesses by him—other soft feelings toward him—from her memory?

The question hit her sideways. She'd known the death of her mother and her sister's blindness, just six months after Bram's disappearance, had marked her deeply, but so deep that she'd wiped out all memories from that period? Maybe—just maybe—in an effort to never relive such a heartrending experience, she'd built walls around her heart, shutting out anything that was good . . . real or remembered.

Her throat tightened, so stunning was the revelation, and for a long while she said nothing.

Bram didn't seem to notice as he led her through the stalls lining the wide thoroughfares, selling everything from tin trinkets to elaborately feathered hats. The rich scent of roasted chestnuts mingled with the sticky-sweet aroma of apples dipped into hot toffee. Men, women, children, and sellers of all sorts of goods with trays strapped to their chests filled the walkway. Some pushed small carts. Even a goose and a few stray dogs snuffled about. The commotion was enough to pull Eva from her introspection. She truly had missed being amongst the jolly people of Royston.

"Here! I'll take one." Bram purchased a cone of sugared almonds, then handed them to her.

Spicy cinnamon wafted up to her nose, the fragrance raining water at the back of her mouth, but even so, she held them out to Bram. "Thank you, but I do not expect you to buy things for me."

"They are not for you. They are for *us*." He pinched a few, arced them in the air, and caught them on his tongue. "Besides, I always like to have something to crunch on when I watch fire eaters." He pointed.

Her gaze followed the length of his arm. With a flourish, two lithe men tossed flaming torches between them so quickly the fire blurred into an orange line. Simultaneously, they raised the blazing torches to the heavens. Tilting their heads back in unison, they plunged the burning length of their wands into their mouths, extinguishing the flames with a theatrical bow.

The crowd oohed, save for one white-haired woman who shrieked. All applauded.

"How do they manage to do that without blistering their mouths to cinders?" Eva wondered aloud.

"Easy enough." Bram grabbed a few more almonds, then guided her back into motion. "Before their performance, those men likely coated their mouths with a mixture of water and some sort of powdered chemical such as potassium or sodium salts."

"How do you know that? Do not tell me you eat fire in your spare time."

He shrugged. "You just never know when shoving a torch in your mouth could come in handy."

Bah. She didn't believe that for one second. "What is the real reason?"

"Dog with a bone, eh?" He chuckled. "All right. The sordid truth is, I am great friends with the chair of Trinity's science department. The man is full of all sorts of trivial information. Give him a pint too many, and there's no telling what sort of knowledge he will impart."

"There. Was that so hard?"

"What?"

"Being honest."

"I *am* honest. I merely do not always give all the details."

She snorted. "That is the truth. Remember that time we found those old bottles in the abandoned greenhouse? You told me not to go near them."

"It was for your own safety. I didn't know if they were poisonous liquids, and I didn't want you to get hurt."

"You could have simply said that instead of spinning some tale about magic potions and how I'd be turned into a toad if I went near them."

He grinned. "Where is the fun in that?"

"Fun, eh? Is that what you are after?" She upped her pace, holding the cone of nuts just out of his reach.

"Hey! Not fair." He made a swipe for them.

Giggling, she whirled away. "All is fair at the fair."

She strode off, steps lighter than they'd been for over a year. Why, she could almost kiss Lottie on the cheek for insisting she—and Bram—come to Bonfire Night. This was fun! Actual fun.

But then the malignant gaze of a passing matron wiped the grin from her face. Oh, sweet heaven. What was she doing? Laughing and prancing about like a schoolgirl. She had no business wasting time on such frivolities. She had a blind sister to care for. A house to manage. An overwhelming tax debt due in little over a month. One would think she hadn't a worry in the world.

She shoved the remaining nuts at Bram. "Here. You may have them, what's left, at any rate."

"You, milady, are fickle as the autumn breeze—which I suppose is a lady's prerogative." He finished off the treat, then tossed the paper into the nearest brazier barrel.

Eva glanced back the way they'd come. "Perhaps we should go home now."

"We have only just got here. Besides, I doubt you will be able to drag your sister away from all the merriment, and if you did manage to, we would all suffer some dreadful dirge of hers the whole ride home."

"I know but . . ." Worry upon worry crawled up her throat, and she swallowed. "It would be so easy for her to get lost in this mob. I can't expect Dixon to keep an eye on her every second. Penny will not even be able to see the bonfire tonight, so there is no point in staying any longer."

"Of course there is. I fancy seeing you by the light of the bonfire. It will be like old times when I used to set fire to the sawdust pile over by the mill."

She frowned. "That has nothing to do with Penny."

"Listen, Eva, your sister is a smart girl who will not wander off, for she is likely far too busy stuffing her mouth with spun sugar and sweetmeats. She has Dixon and my uncle and three students I would trust with my life. Penny is having a good time. Let her. And you should too."

"Roses fair and posies bright, get a daisy for the night!" A hump-backed old woman singsonged from her nearby perch on a dented milk can. She plucked a bloom from the bucket at her feet and aimed it toward Bram. "Lilies sing in moonlight's glow, whisper secrets lovers know."

It took everything in Eva not to roll her eyes at the poor prose, and yet she could heartily respect the woman's ingenuity to sell flowers.

"I'll take it." Bram swapped a coin for the pink rose.

"Bram." She huffed. Was this his way of distracting her from thinking about her sister? "I told you that you need not buy me anything."

"Actually, it is for me." Guiding her to a quieter space between stalls, he tipped her face up. "I happen to like the scent of roses, and this should be just about nose level." He poked the stem between her hat brim and ear.

Wheat-coloured stubble lined his jaw. Evidently he'd forgotten to shave again. He had unusually long lashes for a man, just as she remembered, for those lashes had dazzled her as a girl as well. She narrowed her eyes at the half-inch, faint-red pucker at the top of his cheek. "That scar on your cheek is new. How did you get it?"

"Hmm?" he rumbled while he moved the rose to her other ear. "Oh, merely a little something I received from a student, that's all."

"You are a history professor, not a boxing instructor."

"What do you suppose gladiators did in the Colosseum? Cutthroat games of whist?"

"You teach your students hand-to-hand combat?"

"No." He laughed as he wove the stem behind her ear. "I coach one of the sports teams. See? I am not as rough-and-tumble as you credit me, but you are every bit as lovely as I have told you."

He gave the flower a final tap and stepped away, appraising his work.

It was uncomfortable to be looked at as a piece of art. It wasn't true. Couldn't be true, no matter what Bram said. Nonetheless, the way his grey eyes brushed over her struck a chord deep inside. It was nice to be noticed.

She rejoined his side, and they moved on—but not far before a lad toting a Guy Fawkes effigy bumped into her as he dashed past. She barely caught her footing before another boy did the same.

Bram grabbed her arm and yelled at the retreating lads. "Watch it, you little scoundrels!"

Eva smirked up at him. "That would have been you fifteen years ago or so. But do let's go watch the Guy contest. I am sure that is where those boys are headed."

"Very well, but I am keeping a good hold of you. Come on." He laced his fingers through hers, then plowed through the crowd. They arrived at a stage made of old wooden boards just as ten boys holding up small Guy Fawkes mannequins stood in a line, front and center.

An announcer with a curled moustache planted himself in the far-right corner. "Step right up, ladies and gents! By a show of applause, I have a big blue ribbon here for the best Guy of the bunch." He waved a ruffly piece of shiny silk in the air, then motioned for the first lad to approach him. "What's your name, boy?"

"Olly Weaver, sir."

"Well, Master Weaver, show these fine people your Guy."

The man was barely finished speaking before the boy ran back and forth across the stage. Laughter rang from the audience.

And so it went from one lad to the next, until the last one advanced to the front. The effigy he carried was nearly as large as he was, and Eva recognized her friend's handiwork. She rose to her toes, whispering in Bram's ear, "That is Lottie's brother."

"Well then"—he arched a brow at her—"we shall see that he wins, eh?"

Bram started clapping before Freddie finished his parade across the stage. Eva joined in. Bram hooted and hollered. So did she. And when he stuck two fingers in his mouth and let out a shrill whistle, she did the same. Judging by his wide-eyed glance, she'd caught him off guard.

"And the winner is," the announcer shouted, "Master Frederick Channing! Step smart, lad."

As Freddie dashed over to the man, Eva tugged Bram's sleeve. "Let's go congratulate him."

Arm in arm, they wound around the stage toward the back side, where Lottie was already patting her brother on the back. "Good job, Freddie."

"Indeed," Eva chimed in. "Congratulations! And to you, too, Lottie. Your hard work paid off."

"More like Mother's nettling did. Off with you now, Freddie, but mind you don't get into any trouble." She made a grab for the effigy she'd worked so hard on. Too late. The boy dove into the throng with his effigy's head bobbing up and down.

Lottie puffed a sigh, then shifted her gaze to Eva and Bram. The longer she stared at them, the more a knowing gleam lit in her eyes. "Ah, the professor escorted you after all, did he? How lovely! I am so happy for you, Eva."

Instantly, Eva pulled her arm from Bram's, heat spreading like a rash up her neck. They were most certainly not a couple. She opened her mouth.

But before she could refute her friend's assumption, Lottie continued. "Congratulations, Professor Webb. I hear talk you're to be the new curator of the soon-to-be Royston Museum."

Eva arched a brow. Why had he not said anything?

"I do not know about that"—Bram grinned—"but I do think a museum will do this town good."

"A curator?" Eva stepped aside, allowing two giggling women access to the stage stairs. "I did not realize I was in such esteemed company."

"Really? I thought that was clear to everyone."

She bopped him on the arm.

He laughed. "But, yes, it is true the historical society is considering me, though I am in no position to take it on at the moment. That is all there is to it."

From the front of the stage, the announcer bellowed for one and all to hear. "Next contest is the Queen of the Bonfire. Who shall it be this year? Our reigning champion, Miss Charlotte Channing, will hand off the crown to some lucky lady, so gather in, folks! It's sure to be a tight competition."

"Ooh!" Lottie clapped her hands together, then looped her arm through Eva's. "Come on, my friend. We daren't be late."

"For what?"

"The queen contest, silly duck." She tugged Eva toward the stairs, pulling her away from Bram.

Eva dug in her heels. "I believe the professor and I can see just as well from the front of the stage."

"But you're not watching, darling." Lottie gave a great jerk, yanking her back into motion. "Besides, your new beau will wish to see you win."

Clutching the railing with a death grip, Eva jerked them both to a stop. "He is not my beau, and I cannot enter such a thing. You know I cannot!" She'd be laughed off the stage.

"What I know," Lottie drawled, "is you're sure to win. Besides, I've already signed you up, so off we go."

Bram watched Miss Channing tug Eva up the stairs to the stage, unsure if he ought to rescue her or dash around to the front for the best possible view. Either way she'd be mortified. He settled for a simple mouthing of *Good luck* and a reassuring smile as she cast a terrified glance his way. Poor girl. She'd have all her nails bitten off by the end of the contest.

He wound his way through the onlookers as the announcer bellowed, "I am pleased to proclaim, ladies and gents, that this afternoon's winner of the queen contest and her kingly counterpart—the winner of the men's archery competition—will be the lucky pair to ascend in the hot air balloon and begin tonight's bonfire at sunset."

Absently, Bram rubbed the scar on his cheek. Blast. As much as Eva would hate being up on that stage, she'd abhor it even more if she won. With her fear of heights, a balloon ride would kill her. Yet if he didn't cheer for her, what would that do to her already flagging self-esteem? And it would be easy enough to root for her, for she deserved to be the queen of the bonfire.

He anchored himself behind a group of perfumed ladies chattering together near the front of the stage. No sense wrestling them to the ground for their prime spot as he stood a good hand taller than them—even with their hats on.

"Let's welcome our first contestant, Miss Ivy Dewfeather of Cottington Cottage." The announcer gestured for a plump lady in a purple coat. "If you'd step up here, please, miss."

Covering her mouth with a gloved hand, the woman giggled her way to the front of the stage.

"Very good, Miss Dewfeather. Now then, speaking loud and clear, tell these good folks about a personal accomplishment or skill you believe sets you apart from the rest of the lovely ladies." He swept his hand toward the other nine in line. "What makes you a worthy candidate for queen of the bonfire?"

Though there was absolutely nothing to laugh about, she giggled again, then finally pulled her hand from her mouth. "Biscuits."

Egad. No wonder she kept her hand in front of her mouth. Her teeth stuck out every which way as if trying to decide which direction to run.

"Em . . . er . . ." The announcer fiddled with the curl on his moustache, evidently as baffled as Bram and the whispering crowd around him. "Care to elaborate on that, Miss Dewfeather?"

"Oh! Yes." Another giggle burst out as she bobbed her head. "Father says I make the best biscuits he's ever tasted."

"Ah, that explains it. How about you take a turn for everyone now, miss?"

She minced across the stage, which on a more graceful woman might have been attractive. But as it was, Bram had no time to think on her poor choice of gait. His gaze fixed on Eva, whose face had paled. How would she ever get a word out, let alone cross the stage without swooning? He gave an obligatory clap as Miss Dewfeather resumed her place in line.

"Next up is Miss Margaret Parkins, but we all know her as Meg the seamstress. Miss Parkins, what sets you apart from these other women?"

A petite woman in an ornately embroidered coat sashayed boldly to the front. "Everyone knows I make the tiniest stitches in all of Royston. None can compare. Why, just last week I—"

The woman continued talking for quite some time before she finally took her turn across the stage. Bram hadn't the faintest idea of what she'd blathered on about, nor what the next woman said or the next. There was no way he could concentrate while Eva nibbled on the nail of her pinky, curling in on herself more the closer it came to her turn. Now this was the timid girl he remembered, the one he hadn't seen since he'd arrived in Royston. He'd do anything to help her, but it wasn't as if he could leap up there and speak for her. She'd be a laughingstock. Blast! It was as if the calendar had been rolled back fourteen years, and he was as powerless now as he had been that time she'd stuttered her way through John 3:16 in front of the whole Sunday school.

God, please give Eva the confidence I cannot.

Men's voices carried over the top of the crowd, the mention of Eva's name quickly ending his prayer. "Say, is that Eva Inman next to Peggy Trestle? She's not been to any festivities for over a year."

"Kind of wide-mouthed for me, but those hips surely aren't."

Laughter followed.

Bram's hands curled into fists. Just like old times, the urge to protect Eva's good name pulsed through his veins. He craned his neck to confront the rude fellows, but a well-upholstered brute with jowls like mounds of mashed potatoes had stationed himself practically at his elbow, making it impossible to look past him.

And that's when the announcer called, "Our final contestant of the afternoon is Miss Eva Inman of Inman Manor."

Bram jerked his gaze back to the stage. Eva didn't move. Didn't blink. Didn't do anything but stare straight ahead. Miss Channing advanced from the back of the stage, whispering something into her ear, and still Eva stood as stiff as a Roman's javelin.

Bram's heart dropped in his chest just as Eva's head lowered and she swayed slightly. Stars and money! Would she swoon right here in front of all of Royston? He shoved his way through the tangle of women, prepared to leap up on the stage should Eva plummet to the planks.

But then her eyes snapped open. She squared her shoulders and marched up to the announcer as proud as you please.

Bram blinked at the transformation. Gone was the little girl, replaced by the tigress of a woman he admired more with each passing day.

"Now, Miss Inman," the announcer began, "what is a personal accomplishment or skill you believe sets you apart from the other women here today and makes you a worthy candidate for queen of the bonfire?"

"Nothing."

Everyone gasped.

Eva merely lifted her nose in the air. "The truth is, I am not remarkable, no more so than any other woman here. We are all created in God's image, each of us with our own unique giftings. Any one of these women would make a fine winner." She swept her hand toward the other nine, all in various states of dropped jaws, wide eyes, and even a bout of hysterical giggling from Miss Dewfeather. Whispers began to swirl around the crowd.

"I've never heard the like."

"Did she really just recommend the other ladies over herself?"

"What sort of trickery is this?"

Trickery? He frowned. Eva couldn't have been more sincere.

"Hear, hear!" he shouted, clapping his hands so hard his palms stung. "Cheers for a humble answer!"

"It were humble, weren't it?" the big man next to him mumbled, then slapped his meaty hands together in a clap that made Bram flinch. It did the trick, though. Applause broke out from the whole crowd. Instead of taking a victory lap, Eva gave a little dip to her head and retreated back to the line of women.

The announcer huddled with two other men. Judges, apparently. Eventually they signaled for Miss Channing to join them.

The crowd still murmured about Eva's unconventional answer, yet now the comments were favorable—save for one that traveled on a husky tone.

"Wonder if Eva Inman is as humble in the hayloft."

Another man joined in with the scoundrel's rude jesting.

Once again Bram craned his neck, this time spying two men with their heads bent together. Why, he ought to—

"It is with great pleasure, ladies and gents, that I announce this year's queen. Miss Channing, will you please place the crown on the lucky lady who will attend the king as he shoots a flaming arrow from the hot air balloon? And that lady is . . ." He paused for dramatic effect. "Miss Eva Inman!"

Bram whooped—then immediately clamped his mouth shut. As glad as he was that she'd won, she would hate going up in that balloon.

"Pardon me." He pushed his way through the throng, headed for the back stairs, when that same man's voice chuckled lewdly.

"Well, well. Inman Manor surely has its secrets. I bet that girl's got a hidden talent or two up those grand staircases."

That did it.

Bram wheeled about, rising to the balls of his feet and spying for those two men in the dark caps who'd had their heads together earlier. His gaze locked onto the shorter of the two.

He was a severe-looking gent with a bushel of wavy hair flowing from beneath his derby. His eyes were dark. His brows even darker, and so thick, they almost met in the middle. There was a cruel line to his jaw, with a patch of beard below his lip and on his chin. Beneath that finely sewn coat, muscles fought their way against the fabric. This man was the sort one didn't go against willfully unless broken teeth and pain were high on the priority list. Unbidden, Bram's tongue ran over the jagged molar at the back of his mouth, what was left of it anyway from a fistfight long ago.

Richard Trestwell.

He should have known.

Sucking in air, he shouldered through the dispersing crowd, closing in on Trestwell and his friend just as they turned their backs. "Hold it right there, Trestwell. I will thank you to voice no more randy comments pertaining to Miss Inman."

Slowly the man turned, his eyes narrowing. When recognition finally took root, his nostrils flared. "I was told you were in town."

"Who is it, Boss?" The younger fellow next to him looked from Bram to Trestwell.

"An old acquaintance. And you're just in time, Webb." A slow smile stretched his mouth. "Fitting that you should be here to watch me fly off with your pretty little pet."

"Over my dead body." The words barely made it past his clenched jaw.

"If you like." Trestwell shrugged.

"So we are to pick up where we left off, is that it? You haven't changed a bit, you boastful braggart."

"Ah, but that's where you're wrong. You're looking at the town's championship archer." He poked a finger into Bram's shoulder.

"Congratulations." He batted away Trestwell's touch. "But your reign ends now."

Without another word, Bram forged his way to the backstage stairs just as Eva and Miss Channing were descending. A glittery tiara sparkled brightly against Eva's hair, her flower and bonnet clutched in her fingers at her side, her face still a shade paler than normal.

"Well done, Eva. If you will pardon us, Miss Channing." He pulled Eva away from her friend.

"Where are you going in such a hurry?" Miss Channing called after them.

"Yes"—Eva peered up at him—"where are we going? Home, I hope. I cannot go up in a balloon!"

He shot off down the lane leading to the archery field. "We are going to settle an old score."

12

Bram's pen hovered over the archery roster. Should he really be doing this? The absurdity of engaging in a childhood rivalry gnawed at him. Ought he, a grown man, allow himself to be drawn into a contest fueled by petty animosities?

He rolled the pen between his fingers, debating. Even if he won—no, *when* he won—Trestwell would persist in his irreverent remarks about Eva and other women. Would a victory in this competition truly serve as a defense of female virtue?

And yet he'd be hanged if he'd watch Trestwell fly off with Eva in that balloon in the dark of night, especially knowing her great fear of heights. Now that she'd been named queen, she had no choice but to take that short ride or face the social stigma of refusing such an honor. Either way, he would make sure she felt safe.

He signed his name with a flourish and slammed down the pen.

"Here ye be, then"—the registrar squinted at his writing as he held out a bow, three arrows, and a number tag to pin to his coat—"Mr. Webb, is it?"

Bram collected the items. "Yes, sir."

"Very good. You're in the third heat. Best of luck."

He dipped his head at the man, then strode over to where Eva stood by a wooden railing marking the archery field from the main thoroughfare. She held her tiara, bonnet, and flower bunched in one hand. The other she held to her mouth, busily nibbling at the nail on her index finger. Perhaps they ought not have come to Bonfire Night at all.

But it was too late now.

"I am proud of you, you know." Gently, he pulled her finger from her mouth, then reset the tiara on her head. "I did not think I would be escorting a queen tonight."

"We both know I am no queen." Her lips twisted ruefully as her gaze drifted to the hot air balloon. "And I do not wish to go up in that awful balloon."

Footsteps approached, and a moment later Trestwell pulled alongside Eva. "What's this?" With a crook of his finger, he tipped her face up to his. "There's nothing awful about a balloon ride, for you shall have nothing to fear with me at your side, Miss Inman. It will be glorious indeed."

Eva pulled away from his touch.

Bram gritted his teeth. "That sure of your aim, are you?"

"I have won the last three years in a row, so yes." He eyed Bram with a malignant stare. "I am very sure."

Bram clicked his tongue. "I hope you won't weep overmuch when I take that title from you."

Eva stamped her foot. "It does not matter which of you wins. I cannot go up in that balloon."

"Oh, but I'm afraid I must insist." Trestwell's head swiveled back to her. "I look forward to collecting my kiss when I am proclaimed king of the bonfire yet again. Until then, Miss Inman."

He strolled off with a jaunty swagger.

Scoundrel! Bram stepped after him.

Eva tugged on his arm. "Let him go. You should know by now there is no sense arguing with that man."

"I was not planning on exchanging words." He flexed his free hand into a fist.

Eva huffed. "Neither of you have changed."

He white-knuckled the bow and arrows, her words hitting as kindly as a brick to the head. What was it about coming back to the place he grew up that made him revert to his old foolish ways?

"You are right." He breathed. "I suppose I am being childish. Would you rather I withdraw from the competition? We can go get a sausage roll instead."

"That will not divest me of this." She tapped at the tiara, her brow pinching. "Do you think you can best him? I cannot bear the thought of being a queen to Richard Trestwell's king."

"Remember when you asked me about this?" He ran his fingertip over the scar on his cheek.

"Yes. You said you got it from a student, from some sport you coach."

He nodded. "One of the underclassman's arrows shot wild. I dodged but not nearly quick enough."

"*You* are the Trinity College archery coach?"

He grinned, the wonder in her eyes oddly satisfying.

"What other secrets do you hide, Professor?"

Just then, the rest of the Inman Manor crew clustered about them, Jonathan Barker jamming his thumb against his own puffed-out chest. "Hah! That's the mark I left."

"It is not a prize to be heralded, Barker." Bram chuckled. "But if there are any prizes to be had at the moment, I should think Miss Penny would get a blue ribbon for the sheer amount of icing sugar on her coat."

"Oh!" Dixon whipped out a handkerchief and began scrubbing off the offense.

"Archers one through ten, to position!" a bass voice belted out. "All other contestants, queue up behind them."

"Guess this is it." Bram strode away to the jolly encouragements of his uncle and students.

Being in the third round, Bram found a spot at the back of two men. Apparently Trestwell was in the second heat, for he stood two rows over behind a burly man nocking his arrow. The announcer positioned himself between the archers and the onlookers.

"The rules are simple, gentlemen. On my mark, you will draw, aim, and release. The closer to the bullseye, the higher the score. There shall be one semifinalist chosen from each round, then those three men will face off to determine the winner. Understood?"

A rousing "Aye!" rumbled through the archers' ranks.

"Very good. Let the competition begin. Gentlemen . . . draw!"

Each man took a sharp stance, feet wide—some too wide—and pulled the bowstrings even with the corners of their mouths.

"Aim!"

Eyes narrowed. Some shut one completely. All focused on the haystacks twenty yards off with a paper bullseye secured to each mound.

"Release!"

Arrows flew. One by one the metal tips thunked into the targets. Only one hit close to center.

"Our first round goes to number eight, Mr. Thomas Golightly." Applause broke from the spectators, nearly drowning out the announcer. "Second round contenders—eleven through twenty—take your positions, if you please."

Trestwell cut him a smirk before stepping up to the line in the grass. He nocked his arrow, then planted his feet shoulder-width apart, perpendicular to the target. Bram frowned. There wasn't one thing wrong in the man's form, not even when he drew back the bowstring. The real test, though, would be on his follow-through.

"Release!"

Trestwell's arrow shot true—more than true, actually. Bram scrutinized the target. Trestwell's arrowhead appeared to be sunk in far deeper than the competition's. Granted, the man had tremendous upper body strength, but so much?

"The second round belongs to number seventeen, Mr. Richard Trestwell!"

Once again applause thundered. Trestwell arched a brow at Bram. Ignoring him, Bram glanced over at Eva. She stood ramrod stiff.

He smiled, praying such a nonchalant grin would ease her mind. Trestwell had hit dead center of the target, but so would he.

"Last group—twenty-one through thirty—to your mark, please."

Bram stepped up, taking care not to inch his toe too close to the chalk line. Too many of his students had been disqualified for such a careless stance.

"Draw!"

Bram pressed the tips of his three middle fingers to the string, pulling it even with the corner of his mouth.

"Release!"

He took a breath. Held it. Narrowed both eyes on the target, shutting out the world around him. Ever so slowly, the air whooshed from his lungs, his fingers moving slightly to release the arrow—

When something clattered behind him, shattering his focus. The arrow flew too soon. Too wide. The tip of it plummeted into the target's black dot, but not at dead center.

He wheeled about. Trestwell grinned hardly six paces behind him, stooping to pick up his dropped bow.

Immediately Bram's students yelled all manner of complaints—as did his uncle and even Dixon.

"Foul!" Bram agreed. "That man deliberately tried to distract me."

Trestwell held up his hands. "Untrue. All can see this divot here." He pointed at a dip in the ground as the judges neared him. "Lucky I didn't twist my ankle."

"Of all the—"

"Indeed, there appears to be a divot here, Mr. Gallen," one of the judges called to the announcer. "Nothing intentional."

"Even so," Bram objected, "he broke my concentration. That is not fair."

A round of ayes raised from the crowd, the loudest of which came from Eva and the crew.

Mr. Gallen held up a hand. "It is of no consequence, for you have won the third round, Mr. Webb. And so we have our three semifinalists. Gentlemen, take your positions as new targets are posted."

Trestwell sauntered to the far side of him, leaving Golightly between them. Just as well. Were Trestwell any closer, the temptation to knock him to the ground would be hard to resist.

"Release!"

Again Trestwell's sank deep into the center. Bram's hit spot-on as well. The other fellow's tip hit an inch too wide.

"This round goes to Mr. Webb and Mr. Trestwell. Sorry about that, Mr. Golightly. Good try and all."

The bald-headed man slumped away, the tip of his bow dragging on the ground.

Mr. Gallen approached Bram and Trestwell, speaking for them alone. "For the final round, gentlemen, you will be aiming for the same target. A flip of the coin will decide who goes first. Mr. Trestwell, being you were the better aim in the first round, you get the call."

"Heads."

A penny arced in the air, landing flat in Mr. Gallen's palm. "Heads it is. You're up, Mr. Trestwell."

Good. Bram stepped aside. He often told his students that being the last to shoot allowed one to time his shot strategically, ensuring proper focus and concentration without feeling rushed by the pace of competition.

"When you're ready, Mr. Trestwell," Mr. Gallen called.

A hush came over the onlookers. Bram didn't dare look at Eva. Better to keep an eye on Trestwell's form and prepare for his own shot.

Thwack.

Trestwell's arrow once again sank deep, hitting true.

Cheers raised. Bram absently rubbed the scar on his cheek. No wonder Trestwell had won the last three years. The power in his arms had to be magnificent to plant a tip into the target like that.

Trestwell wheeled about and took a formal bow.

Of all the arrogance.

"You have not won yet," Bram grumbled as he stepped to the mark.

"Now then, Mr. Webb." Mr. Gallen spoke above the crowd. "You will have to split that arrow in order to win, sinking your tip in deeper than Mr. Trestwell's, which has only been accomplished once to my recollection."

He tested the weight of his bow by lightly bouncing it in his hand. Mentally, he calculated the trajectory and force required to split the arrow. With unwavering focus, he drew the bowstring. Filled his lungs. Held the air. Aligned the tip of his arrow just to the right of Trestwell's.

And waited.

Sure enough, Trestwell sneezed loud and true.

Perfect.

Bram released.

The arrow flew, hitting dead center and becoming one with Trestwell's shot.

Silence reigned, eerie for such a festivity. The judges' shoes shooshed across the field as they strode to examine the target, Mr. Gallen being amongst them.

Time stopped as they conferred. Trestwell smirked. Bram blew out a long, slow breath. He'd done it. He'd split the arrow, even with Trestwell's ill-timed sneeze.

The judges strode back, and Mr. Gallen angled himself so he might face Bram, Trestwell, and the crowd at the same time. "It is with great pleasure that I announce the king of the bonfire for tonight's festivities."

Bram met Eva's gaze. Pride sparked in her eyes, a hopeful smile on her lips.

"And the winner is Mr. Richard Trestwell!"

Eva's jaw unhinged. How could this day possibly go from bad to worse in such a short amount of time? And not just for her. Bram stalked away, evidently as finished with this afternoon as she was.

"That can't be right!" one of the students grumbled.

"Professor Webb always wins," another one joined in. "Something smells of the highest stink."

"I don't understand." Bram's uncle shook his head.

"Behold, citizens of Royston, your king of the bonfire." Mr. Gallen placed a silver crown on Richard Trestwell's mass of dark hair, then he singled her out of the crowd with a wave of his fingertips. "Queen, if you would come and award His Majesty with a kiss, then we shall all disperse until the lighting of the bonfire at half past five."

"Oh dear," Dixon whispered at her side.

Eva gripped the railing with one hand, anchoring her feet. Nothing in the world could persuade her to kiss that man.

"We are waiting, Queen," Mr. Gallen called.

Slowly, then gaining momentum, a chant swirled like an unholy wind throughout the crowd. "Kiss, kiss, kiss, kiss!"

Penny bumped into her. "Eva, do you really have to kiss that man?"

"Do not be silly." Eva crushed her bonnet brim in her hand. Why had she ever let Lottie talk her into coming today?

"Your Highness." The man next to her nudged her sideways, as did another and another. Before she knew it, she'd been shoved all the way along the railing to where Trestwell waited with open arms.

"My Queen." A hungry smile spread across his lips.

Eva swallowed. Hard.

Just as footsteps pounded her way. "He cheated," Bram shouted. "Disqualify this man!"

Mr. Trestwell spun to face Bram. "Absurd! You always were a sore loser, Webb."

A low rumble thundered through the spectators, followed by a round of I-knew-its from Bram's students. Eva sucked in a breath. Could it be?

Bram held out an arrow. "This arrow is weighted. No doubt they all were. That is why they sank in so deeply. My arrow didn't stand a chance."

"You're just jealous." With a long reach of his arm, Richard Trestwell slammed her up against his body. The cloying stink of lime aftershave clung to his skin, and his breath was overly hot. "I shall take my rightful kiss now, Queen."

Eva wrenched from Mr. Trestwell's grip as Mr. Gallen gestured to the three men on the sidelines. "Hold please, Mr. Trestwell. Judges?"

"Give me that arrow." Richard Trestwell made a swipe for it. "You've probably tampered with it, and I should like to see."

Bram held it out of reach, handing the disputed item to one of the judges the moment they drew close. "As you will note here"—he ran his finger along the shaft toward the base of the arrow—"this twine wraps around thin lead weights."

"This is ludicrous." Mr. Trestwell lunged toward Bram, who

deftly stepped out of his way. "If my arrows are tampered with, it wasn't done by me."

A judge wearing spectacles gave him a stern look as he pulled out a pocketknife. Carefully, he slit the twine and, sure enough, long thin weights fell into his hand. He glanced at the other two judges, who nodded in unison, then faced Mr. Gallen. "Mr. Trestwell is disqualified."

Mr. Trestwell threw his arms wide. "I am most certainly not! You cannot prove I modified that arrow."

"Regardless, the arrow in question is the one you shot. You would have felt the difference. And so . . ." He plucked the crown off Mr. Trestwell's head. "Ladies and gentlemen, this is highly unprecedented, and yet I give you your new king of the bonfire, Mr. Bram Webb."

As he set the crown on Bram's head, Richard Trestwell stalked off, growling, "You'll get yours, Webb. I'll see to that."

A great cheer went up from the crowd. Mr. Gallen nudged her with a light touch to the small of her back so that she was face-to-face with Bram. "And now, Queen, you may kiss the rightfully reigning king."

Her gaze shot to Bram's, her heart racing out of control. The thought of kissing this man was entirely different from that of kissing Richard Trestwell. Part of her wanted to run into his arms and give in to his embrace, to know what it felt like to have his mouth pressed against hers, breath to breath.

Egad!

She stiffened. What sort of woman was she? She couldn't do this. There was no way she could do this! Especially not in front of Bram's uncle and students, and her cheeks fired even hotter when she thought of Dixon watching such a spectacle.

"Kiss! Kiss! Kiss!" the crowd chanted.

Bram leaned close and whispered for her alone. "Just put your cheek near mine. No one will know the difference. Trust me."

Trust him? The boy who'd played pranks on her as a lad,

teased her, and yet . . . while Bram had been a wild stallion no one could pin down, he'd never done anything with ill intent. She knew that now. Perhaps it was time to give him a second chance.

Swallowing hard, she rose to her toes and lifted her face so that her cheek was close to his. The heat of him radiated onto her skin.

Instantly he swept her up in the air, swinging her around and around so that his overlong hair flew about. Indeed, no one would be able to tell if her lips were truly on his cheek or not at this speed.

At last he set her down, her breathless, him grinning, the crowd roaring with delight.

"Ho ho! Very good!" Mr. Gallen laughed, then faced the onlookers. "One and all, gather near the brush pile at half past five when our queen and king shall rise above the fairgrounds and shoot the flaming arrow to start the bonfire."

Bram pulled her toward the dispersing crowd, stopping when they reached their friends and family.

"Well done, nephew. I see what you did there. Very gallant." Professor Pendleton clapped Bram on the back.

Instant relief loosened the knots in Eva's shoulders. At least Bram's uncle didn't think untoward thoughts about their display, though judging by the pinch of Dixon's lips, she hadn't caught on that the kiss had been faux.

Penny didn't care in the least. She bounced on her toes. "I want to go on a hot air balloon. Take me with you!"

Eva shook her head. "Not a chance."

"But you have to. You're the queen." Penny sulked. "At least allow Professor Webb's students and Dixon to take me for a ride."

Just the thought of Penny floating away into the sky made Eva's stomach flip. "No, absolutely not."

"You never let me have any fun!" Penny stamped her foot.

"That icing sugar still stuck to your collar says otherwise, sister."

Penny huffed, her lips flapping with the burst of air.

"What's this?" Bram stepped near after suffering countless congratulatory pounds on the back from his students. "Why such gloom when I just won a contest?"

Penny scrubbed her toe in the dirt. "I wanted to go on a balloon ride."

He fished some coins out of his pocket and pressed them into Penny's hand. "Here. This is your payment for the days you have helped on the dig. I am certain you and the fellows can find something else to do."

She fingered the money, her face lighting as she turned toward Dixon. "We can buy more fritters!"

"But . . ." Eva let the reprimand die on her tongue. Her sister deserved to have something to enjoy. "Do you mind, Dixon?"

"Not at all, miss." The housekeeper glanced at the students. "How about it, gentlemen? Another go-around at the food tent?"

"You don't have to ask us twice, eh, fellows?" Mr. Barker cuffed his friends on the back.

"I could go for a piece of taffy," Bram's uncle chimed in.

"Off with you, then, sister." Eva grinned. "At least we will know where to find you."

As the crew sped away, Bram nudged her with his elbow. "I am hungry as well. We could join them, but there is a sausage seller right over there. Shall we?"

She glanced across the lane, where a huge grate of smoked sausages sizzled over orange flames. The savory scent rumbled her stomach.

"Good idea."

He led her to the booth, but before she could pull a coin from her pocket, Bram was already handing her one of the pastry-wrapped treats.

"Bram, I have told you that you need not—"

"Tut-tut." He wagged a finger at her and chewed a huge bite before continuing. "I know you do not want me to buy you anything, but *I* wanted to."

Well. She couldn't refute that.

"Thank you." She sank her teeth into the flaky crust, which warmed her as the chill of evening settled over the grounds. It would be dark soon. Unbidden, her gaze drifted to the balloon glowing like a dragon with a fire in its belly at the far side of the grounds. No one was riding the thing now. No doubt the balloon master was preparing it for the king and queen's voyage—*her* voyage. Her stomach clenched, the sausage inside it rebelling.

She handed her roll over to Bram. "Here. I cannot take another bite."

"You are worried."

She lifted her chin. "Maybe I am just full."

"No, that crease in your chin always deepens when you're anxious about something."

Bother! He knew her far too well. "We should finish looking at the stalls."

She strode to the next booth, feigning interest in a pair of perfumed gloves. The dyed-green leather was soft and the embroidery lovely, but all she could think of was being stuck up in the air with no ladder to the ground.

Bram pulled out his pocket watch. "Fifteen minutes left. Perhaps we ought to start making our way to—"

"That watch." Choosing to deny the minutes ticking away until her doom, she pointed at the silver treasure in his hand. "I notice you always carry it on you. Even in the field. In fact, there is not a day I do not remember you pulling it out. Is it so very special to you?"

"Indeed." He rubbed his thumb over the engraved little swirls on the front. "This watch saved my life."

Setting down the gloves, she scrunched her nose. "How could such a small thing accomplish that?"

"Remember when I went away all those years ago?"

"You know I do."

A faraway glimmer lit his grey eyes. "I was fourteen when I arrived at my uncle's flat. My mother sent me off without the knowledge she was about to die, which would have been nice to know at the time." His jaw hardened.

Her heart squeezed. How hard that must have been for him.

"Still, looking back, she did the right thing. Uncle Pendleton was a bachelor. I was a delinquent—in most people's eyes. Certainly in his, though he never said as much. On that very first day he took me to the worst part of town. I had never seen such poverty or so much despair. It was there my uncle presented me with this watch and said, 'Mark the time, lad. Your life changes now. I will not ever see you living for one minute on these streets. Understood?' And, quite surprisingly, I did. I knew this would be the only second chance I would get, so I tucked this watch away, just as I am doing now." He dropped the silver disk into his waistcoat pocket. "And with God's help, I started a new life that day."

Eva's throat closed. "Your uncle is a very special man."

"That he is." Bram grinned, the effect warm as the golden glow spilling from the freshly lit lamps and torches.

"It is getting dark," she murmured, dread creeping over her shoulders.

"Eva, listen." Bram guided her from the stall, away from the crush of shoppers. "I want you to have a choice in this matter, but there will be nothing I can do to stop the gossip that will surely spread if you do not honour your position as queen. Believe me when I say there is nothing to fear. I will be with you the whole time."

She fiddled with the bonnet in her hand, feeling the weight of the tiara on her head. It was sweet of him to protect her like this, just as he safeguarded her from having to kiss him in front of all of Royston. If she was brave enough to set foot in that basket, surely he'd let no harm come to her in a tethered balloon. It was, after all, her social obligation.

Once again her gaze drifted to the orange glow of the big teardrop in the darkening sky. "It is not going to go so very high, is it?"

He turned his face toward the floating menace. "It will rise maybe twenty-five feet. Thirty at most. I will shoot a flaming arrow, and then we will descend right back to the ground." His eyes once again met hers. "But like I said, you do not have to do this. You have nothing to prove to me. You've already shown yourself to be a strong and capable woman."

And just like that, much of her fear melted from the sheer light of admiration burning in his gaze. He was right. Despite expectations, this was her choice. Yet if she never took the chance to change like Bram had, she'd never get over this fear of heights—and all because of Richard Trestwell trapping her up in an apple tree. Well, no more. She would not be controlled by the past. Bram had beaten the man at archery. Wasn't it about time she bested him as well?

Swallowing a lump in her throat, she lifted her chin. "I think I can manage a quick up-and-down ride that is controlled, as long as you are with me the whole time."

"I will be there every second." His brows gathered into a line. "Are you sure about this?"

"No," she admitted, "but let's do it anyway."

This time she grabbed his hand and led him on a merry chase along the lanes. Better to do this now while she still had the courage. Yet the closer she drew to that hellishly lit canvas, the more her bravery waned, especially when she pulled up breathless in front of the balloon master.

And Richard Trestwell.

Bram stepped in front of her. "What are you doing here, Trestwell?"

"As last year's king, it's my duty to hand you the bow and arrow to start the fire." Reaching behind him, he picked up a modified bow—shorter than the one they'd used earlier—and an arrow with a ball of wicking near the tip.

Bram immediately inspected both, and while he did so, Mr. Trestwell sidestepped him to face Eva. "I hope you have a memorable ride, Miss Inman. I daresay it would have been were I to accompany you."

The balloon master clapped his hands. "All my rides are memorable! Now, my dear, if you please. This way." He held the basket gate open, the glowing fire from the balloon painting his hair a devilish red.

"I—em." She pressed her lips flat. How could she ever do this? "I would prefer if Mr. Webb went in first, thank you."

"As you wish. Mr. Webb?"

Bram shouldered past Mr. Trestwell, and once inside the waist-high basket, he held out his hand for her. Encouragement sparked in his gaze, and his arm didn't waver in the least as she tentatively reached for his fingers. He guided her inside, the thick wicker beneath her feet feeling a bit lumpy against her shoes.

The overhead fire hissed like snakes as the balloon master shut the door behind her.

She whirled. "Is it very secure?"

"I've never once had anyone fall out of one of my balloons, so yes, my dear. There's not a thing to worry about. My stalwart assistant and I will be managing the rope the entire time." He pointed at a beefy man on the other side of the balloon, manning a thick tether that was mostly coiled on the ground.

"Now then, King, just place the tip of your arrow close to the overhead fire. You needn't put it all the way in for it to light. Once you shoot, my assistant and I will bring you down. Ready?"

Bram gazed at her. "Are you?"

Her breath stalled. How would she ever be ready for this? What a rash decision she'd made!

But there was no easy way to turn back now.

Biting her lip, she nodded.

"Right, then." The balloon master retreated several steps. "Ease her up, Mr. Hagethorn!"

The rope gave way. The basket tipped as it left the ground. Not much, but enough to cause her to clutch the side of the basket and face inward. There was no possible way she'd look over the edge.

Bram steadied her with an arm about her shoulder, and though it was rather immodest of her to do so, she leaned into him, soaking in his strength.

"How's the speed?" the balloon master called from below.

"Perfect," Bram shouted downward, then turned to her. "This is not so bad, is it?"

"As long as I do not look or move around, it is fine." And surprisingly, it was. God had blessed them with a calm night, and with the cloud cover, it was hard to tell how high they floated. If she set her mind to it, she could imagine being only a few feet off the ground, close enough to jump to safety, which was a calming thought indeed. "Actually, it is not as awful as I thought."

"That's my girl." He grinned as the balloon master's voice carried up to them.

"That'll do, Mr. Hagethorn. They're high enough. Have at it, O King!"

Bram gave her shoulder a little squeeze. "I am going to let you go now."

She gripped the top ridge of the basket a little tighter as he pulled away. The flooring beneath her canted to one side as he lit the arrow, and it took everything in her not to yelp. The flame caught, and with impossibly smooth moves, he drew the bowstring and released the fiery projectile down into the enormous woodpile at the center of the grounds. Cheers rose as red and orange began to lick over the smallest of branches, spreading into a bonfire that would light the night.

He turned back to her with a huge smile. "There we have it. Shall we return to earth, milady?"

"We absolutely sh—"

A curse belted out from below, overpowering the revelers near the bonfire. "It's loose! The rope has broken."

"But that's impossible!" the balloon master bellowed.

Eva froze. Surely she hadn't heard right. "What is he saying?"

Bram looked over the edge. "Hey! We are ready to come down."

"Ease the flame!" the balloon master shouted. "Lower the flame!"

Eva's legs shook, her knees threatening to give way. "Wh-what does that mean?"

But she didn't need Bram to answer. The clench of his jaw and the upward movement of the balloon told her all she needed to know.

And what she knew was that she was going to be sick.

13

He'd spent the first half of his life adrift, so free-floating in a runaway hot air balloon really ought not be so very unfamiliar. But this time was different. Bram's heart stalled in his chest as he stared, horrified, at Eva.

It wasn't only his life at stake.

She hunched over, arm to her stomach, hand to her mouth, her bonnet lying forgotten on the basket floor. Thank God there was no wind casting them to kingdom come, nor were they rising at a breath-stealing rate, but still Eva quivered with suppressed fear.

He slung his arm around her and eased her to sit with her back against the basket wall. The flickering flame overhead supplied enough light to witness the ashen colour of her skin. He tipped her face toward his. "Breathe, Eva. Come on. You can do this."

"I-I—oh!" Once again she slapped her hand to her mouth, her fingers muffling the rest of her words. "I am going to be sick."

"No, you are not." The words came out harsher than he

intended but did a fair job of sparking a bit of anger in her eyes. Good. A little fight was just what she needed.

"Now then, you are going to breathe with me. In and out. Like this." He sucked in then blew out an exaggerated lungful of air. "Ready?" Gently, he pulled her hand from her mouth. "In. Out."

She inhaled—albeit very choppily—and exhaled just as roughly. A start, at least.

"That's it. Keep it going."

Her pale blue eyes locked on to his. This time, while still shaky, she breathed somewhat easier. After several more tries—and a silent prayer on his part—her air flowed much more freely. Pink seeped back into her cheeks, and the sharp line of her shoulders relaxed.

"See? That was not so hard." Reaching for her hand, he smoothed his thumb along her palm. "There is nothing to fear. You are not alone. I am here. We will be fine."

"But how will we get down? There is no ladder. There is nothing and no one to save us." Her words ended on a shrill note.

The basket swayed. Her nostrils flared, and she flung out her arm as an anchor. Clearly she needed some sort of rousing speech to rally.

"Listen, Eva." Bah! What to say? He was much more fit to inspire a group of sweaty college lads than a frightened woman. "This . . . this is not the first time I have had to rely on God alone. And I daresay it is not yours either. So how about you pull yourself together and have a little faith, hmm?"

"Since when are you such a preacher?"

"Whenever I face death."

The whites of her eyes grew impossibly large. "*Are* we going to die?"

Blast. Poor choice, that. He forced a merry chuckle. "Not if I can help it. Sit tight. I shall have us down in no time."

Rising, he tipped his face to the burner above. The best way to make Eva feel better was to land this thing. How hard could it be?

The basket shifted, and he cut a glance her way. She stood, gripping the edge, her back to the drop below. No longer did she hunch over nor lift shaky fingers to her mouth. She still looked like a lost little girl with her tiara askew and pieces of hair straggling over her brow, but there was a definite change to the gleam in her eyes.

"If we are going to go down, I want to do so being a help, not a hindrance." She lifted her chin. "Tell me what to do."

Well. This was new. The Eva he remembered would have continued crying in the bottom of the basket. Evidently the strength he'd seen in her of late went deeper than he knew.

He scanned the basket, mind racing for a solution. Reducing the heat was the best way to land this thing, but what else? Nothing, really. But he had to give her something other to do than panic.

He faced Eva. "I will adjust the flame. You haul in the tether and hold tightly to it." He aimed his finger at the dangling rope. "See it?"

"Yes, but what will that accomplish?"

"There is no time to explain now. Just do it."

Thankfully, she did as he'd instructed because honestly, he had nothing else to keep her busy. Leastwise for now.

He studied the burner mechanism, searching for the— Ah, there it was. Ever so gradually, he turned the control valve counterclockwise, decreasing the flow of fuel. The more the fire shrank, the more its hiss gentled to a shush. He glanced out over the nighttime scenery, the black outlines of trees lifting toward the basket—or more like the basket lowered toward them.

"We're descending!" Eva gathered the length of rope to her chest, hugging it with a smile. "How brilliant!"

Indeed. He turned back to the control valve. If he lessened

it a bit more, they'd drop even faster, then he could search for a grassy knoll in which to land.

"Bram?"

"Hmm?" He eased the valve a bit more.

"We're going too fast."

He glanced away from the now-tiny flame. Blast! She was right. They plummeted toward the dark ground.

"Do something!" Eva cried.

He snapped his gaze back to the pilot light, a mere sputter of blue and yellow. Sweat popped on his brow. If that fire went out, there'd be no controlling their descent whatsoever. Desperate, he fiddled with the control valve.

And still the balloon picked up speed.

So this was it? Her body thrown to the ground like a discarded rag doll. Every bone shattered. And there'd be no saying good-bye to Penny. Eva dragged in a shuddering breath as she clutched the bundle of rope for dear life. Oh, sweet mercy. What would happen to Penny without her? Why did God not smile upon her?

A great sob stuck in her throat. No, things couldn't end like this. They wouldn't!

Trying hard to ignore the drop in her stomach as they plummeted earthward, she turned to Bram. "What should I do?"

He didn't so much as glance at her as he fiddled with the burner. "Crouch down and do not let go of that rope."

How in the world would that help? "Surely there is something more I can—"

"Do it!"

There was no ignoring that command. She hunkered low, making herself as small as possible, which was absurd, really. Sprawled spread-eagle or curled in the fetal position wouldn't make a whit of difference when the balloon collided with the ground.

God, please hear my prayer. I don't deserve Your help, and yet I plead for it.

A great hiss arose. She lifted her face toward Bram, his feet planted wide, his arms overhead—and an increasing orange glow casting a heavenly halo atop his loose hair. The freefalling sensation in her belly eased somewhat, creeping away in increments. Were they leveling off?

She rose an inch at a time and peeked over the basket's edge. Far back to one side, a red dot glowed—the Royston bonfire, she could only assume. Ahead, a dark bank of trees hovered just below them. Wait a minute. Trees didn't hover.

The balloon was hovering!

She rose to full height, smiling broadly at Bram. "We're not dropping anymore."

"True, but neither have we landed yet, and I need that help you wanted to give. I know it will be hard for you, but I dare not leave this flame. You must look over the edge and find us a clearing to land in."

"But I—"

"You can do this, Eva." He pulled his gaze away from the flame and looked directly into her eyes. "I know you can."

Encouragement radiated off him as tangibly as the reddish glow from the flame. He believed in her. She couldn't— *wouldn't*—disappoint him.

"All right." Summoning the remaining shreds of her courage, she set down the coil of rope and padded to the side of the basket. Sure enough, they slowly floated just above the bank of trees. At least she assumed they were trees. What else could such a black abyss be?

She clutched the rough edge of the basket, wicker splinters digging into the palms of her hands. Ahead, the inkiness gave way somewhat. "I think there is a field coming up."

"You *think*?"

He was right. She'd better be certain. She narrowed her eyes, and there, just beyond the dark tree line, was a large grey area with two dark blotches near the center. Four orange dots glowed on the smaller of the two shapes. A house, perhaps. Her gaze drifted to the larger outline next to it, the distinct black line of a cross atop the roof.

She'd clap her hands were she not clutching the edge of the basket in a death grip. "It is a glebe! And we may even get some help from the vicar for there are lights in the house."

"Very good. Let me know when you feel the slightest bump beneath your feet."

The flame hiss lessened. The balloon sank lower, but this time the descent was at a more controlled speed. Eventually something scraped beneath her feet. "I feel it."

"How many more trees to clear?"

La. She'd never been good at distance. "Twenty feet, maybe?"

"Tell me the instant we clear them."

The scraping grew louder. Sucking in a big breath, Eva looked directly down into grey instead of black. "Cleared!"

"And where is the church and vicarage?"

She went back to scanning the horizon. "Not far. To the left."

"Then here we go."

This time they descended gracefully, the burner's angry hiss softening to a steady whisper. The basket bumped the ground once, twice, then landed with a soft bounce hardly ten yards from the vicarage's front door, the balloon just inflated enough to keep aloft, but not enough to lift off again.

Bram let out a whoop, a grin as wide as a summer day flashing on his face.

They'd landed. Oh, how good it was to be on solid ground.

Without thinking, she wrapped her arms around his waist. "You did it!"

"No, *we* did it, and I could not be prouder of you." Ever so lightly, his lips brushed against her brow, his voice a soothing rumble. "You are amazing."

Warmth spread through her body from neck to knees. It was wonderful the way his arms pulled her close. Irresistible, really. She rested her cheek against his shoulder, breathing in his earthy scent, surprised at how right it felt to give in to this man's embrace.

"What is going on here?" The thunderclap of a booming voice cleaved the sweet moment in two.

Eva jolted away from Bram, whirling as she did so. Just past the basket stood Mr. Blackwood with another somber-coated man at his side. Each held lanterns. Both looked like monsters from the way the shadows elongated their features.

Mr. Blackwood lifted his light, the blue of his eyes as sharp as a kitchen knife as he studied her. "Miss Inman? Mr. Webb? Can it be?"

Behind her, Bram stepped closer. Just knowing he was at her back kept her from swooning. Of all the times and places for the reverend to show up.

"I—" She cleared her throat, willing words to flow. "I am as surprised to see you here, Mr. Blackwood."

"This is highly improper!" he spluttered.

"I could not agree with you more." Bram chuckled as he unlatched the basket door. He alighted the few inches to the ground, then offered her his hand. The grip of his warm fingers did much to right a world that was quickly falling apart.

The fellow next to Mr. Blackwood glanced amongst them all. "You are acquainted with each other? How very peculiar. But do tell, why have you chosen to land here in St. Andrew's Green, sir?"

"It was more a necessity than a choice." Bram doubled back to the balloon to retrieve the tether rope.

Mr. Blackwood shook his head. "And here I thought to escape all the madness of Bonfire Night." At length he lowered his lantern, which was a mercy and a fright, for now the features of his face once again stretched in macabre shadows. "I am afraid I shall have to cut short my visit, Mr. Tanbridge. Miss Inman here is a member of my parish, and I will not see her reputation tarnished any further than it already is. If you wouldn't mind having your boy harness my horse and give my thanks to your wife for such a hearty meal?"

"Straightaway, Mr. Blackwood. Until next time, Godspeed."

As the man retreated, Eva dared a step closer to the formidable reverend. "I assure you, Mr. Blackwood, nothing untoward happened between myself and Mr. Webb. The balloon broke loose, and we landed here. That is all there is to it."

His intense gaze drilled into her like the eyes of God, yet he said not a word.

"Pardon, Mr. Blackwood." Bram stepped between them. "Could you hold this rope for a moment? If I do not tie down this balloon, it could take off again."

Without waiting for a reply, Bram shoved the thick length of cording into one of the man's hands, then strode away.

The reverend frowned, then ever so slowly, he pointed to her head. "You are about to lose your crown."

"Oh." She yanked off the ridiculous tiara and patted her hair, tucking what wild strays she could. "I must look a fright."

"As you well know, Miss Inman, vanity is a sin . . . amongst others."

She gritted her teeth. He'd been suspicious of her and Bram ever since the dig had begun, for he'd warned her every Sunday to beware of what iniquity might be crouching at her door. That without a father or elder brother in the home to supply her with counsel, she might fall prey to the charms of Mr. Webb. Though she'd denied any impropriety, it seemed no matter what she said, there was no way to please the man. Must he be so harsh?

"I realize, Mr. Blackwood, that as a member of your parish, you are only doing your duty to look out for me. I appreciate that. I truly do. And yet a gentler approach would be better received by me, and no doubt would as well by other sheep of your flock. Was not Jesus a tender shepherd?"

"Not when He was flipping over money tables."

Thankfully it was dark enough that he'd not note the roll of her eyes. He always had an ominous rejoinder at the ready. Was that why her father had warned her against him? To protect her from verbal lashings? Could be, but deep in her belly, she suspected there was something more to it. What, exactly, she had yet to discover.

Moments later, grunts and heaves traveled on the air. Bram rolled an enormous rock their way, stopping just beyond the reverend.

"Thank you." He collected the rope, then tied the thing securely around the boulder. "With that tether—and barring any winds, of course—this ought to hold very nicely until the balloon master can get here. How far are we from Royston?"

"A little over two miles. I should have you back to town within the hour." The reverend turned on his heel toward a black carriage and an even blacker horse being led by a young lad.

"All's ready, Mr. Blackwood," the boy called.

The reverend merely gestured for Eva and Bram to follow.

"He is as dour as he is on Sundays," Bram whispered.

She hid a smile. It was true Mr. Blackwood rarely imparted lightness to his intense sermons, but in truth she'd hardly noticed the past month. She'd been too busy trying not to get caught snatching glances at Bram, who sat in the pew opposite her, for he cut a very fine figure in his Sunday suit.

The reverend pointed to the rear of the small coach. "You will have to stand on the backboard, Mr. Webb, though I always say brisk air is inducive to perfecting character. Teaches one to count his blessings."

Bram leapt up with a grin. "I am already grateful for your service, sir."

"As you should be," Mr. Blackwood muttered, then he offered her his hand. "Miss Inman."

His fingers were ice. The moment she hoisted herself up, she pulled from his touch. The ride in the balloon had been harrowing, yet it was preferable to an hour-long trek sitting next to a man who made her skin crawl. Would that she could be the one on the backboard instead of Bram, no matter how brisk the air.

The carriage canted to the side as Mr. Blackwood climbed in. Gathering the reins, he clicked his tongue twice. "Walk on."

Eva folded her hands in her lap, squeezing them tightly lest she chew on her fingernails and give the reverend something more to hold against her.

"It is not often, Miss Inman, that one finds oneself floating in the heavens, beholden to the whims of the wind . . . alone with a man." He cut her a sharp sideways glance.

She stifled a sigh. Evidently he wasn't going to let this infraction slip by so easily. "I did not fly away with Mr. Webb on purpose. I won the Queen of the Bonfire contest, and he was crowned king. As is tradition, it was our duty to go in the balloon—safely tethered to the earth and in full view of the entire town—in order to start the bonfire. Immediately after Bram released the flaming arrow, the rope somehow broke free, and we were set loose. There was nothing to do but try to land as quickly as possible, which we did. And so you have the full story. Believe me when I say none of this was of my choosing."

"I see." Simple enough words, but by the sour tone of his voice, what he saw was as appealing as a dishful of curdled milk. "I suppose God's providence does work in mysterious ways. Perhaps there is a lesson to be gained from the precariousness of your situation."

A smile tugged the corners of her mouth. "I prefer my lessons with solid ground beneath my feet."

"Solid ground is what we all seek, but life has a way of keeping us aloft, does it not? Much like that balloon of yours."

"I fail to see the spiritual metaphor here, Mr. Blackwood."

The carriage wheel hit a rut, juddering her bones. She flung out a hand to grip the side of the carriage. Hopefully Bram was still standing.

"We are all tethered to something, Miss Inman," the reverend continued after clearing another dip. "Responsibilities, relationships, even our own desires. When that tether snaps, as it is wont to do, this is when we realize the true extent of our faith." This time he turned his whole face toward her. "I pray you find that your faith is deeply anchored in Christ."

And there it was. The same doubt of his he managed to bring up every time he spoke a word to her. Must he always view her as a wayward lamb? Part of his responsibility as a clergyman, no doubt, but still such skepticism chafed.

She clutched the carriage wall all the tighter. "I appreciate your insight about being tethered to various aspects of life. It reminds me of the verse you preached on last Sunday, 'For I know the thoughts I think toward you, saith the Lord, thoughts of peace, and not of evil, to give you an expected end.' Perhaps even in the unexpected—such as my ill-timed balloon ride—there is an opportunity for God's plan to unfold. A testament to His wisdom, if you will, and our trust in His divine timing. All that to say, Mr. Blackwood, that, yes, though I do not know why God allowed such a dreadful nighttime ride, I assure you my faith is deeply anchored in Christ."

"Mmm." It was more of a growl than a word. "For your sake, I hope that is true, Miss Inman, for one never knows which tether will be broken free next."

14

After a night filled with dreams of a certain redheaded woman and how right it had felt to hold Eva in his arms, Bram swung into the manor's workroom with his uncle at his side. It wouldn't do any good to dwell on such pleasantries during the day. It wouldn't do any good to dwell on it at all. That embrace last night had been a spur-of-the-moment whim on Eva's part, nothing more. Any woman who feared heights would have been as equally grateful to land on solid earth.

So why did part of him yearn for something more?

Shoving aside the untamed thought, he pointed toward a leather messenger bag slung over the back of a chair. "There's that pouch you wanted, Uncle."

"Ah! So it is." Uncle Pendleton drummed his fingers against his ample belly. "How peculiar I don't remember leaving it in here. Could have sworn I stowed that bag in the cottage cupboard."

Bram strode past him, chest squeezing. The last several days his uncle had been more forgetful than ever.

Scanning the big table, Bram spied the calipers he'd need on-site today and was about to turn away when unease crept across his shoulders. Something was off. His gaze skimmed the tabletop from the amphora to the set of iron chisels, then beyond to . . .

He ran a finger over the empty piece of silk where a silver fibula brooch had been resting—leastwise it had been yesterday morning when he'd finished measuring it. He rummaged through the assorted tools and pieces that yet needed a good buffing, going so far as to peek beneath the table on the off chance the relic had fallen. "Did you move the silver fibula brooch? It's not here."

His uncle shouldered the messenger bag, then pulled off his perpetually dirty spectacles and huffed on the left lens. "No, I had nothing to do with a brooch."

"You are certain?" He waved the empty piece of silk. "That brooch was right here, sitting atop this fabric."

"Hmm." Uncle Pendleton slowly rubbed the dirty side of his spectacles along his sleeve. "No, no. I am positive I had nothing to do with it."

Setting down the cloth, Bram closed the distance between them. "Would you mind checking your coat pockets? It may have, em, fallen into one of them."

A great chuckle rumbled in his uncle's throat. "I hardly think so, but to make you happy . . ." He popped his glasses on the bridge of his nose and fumbled about in his pockets, eventually turning them inside out for good measure. Lint floated to the floor, as did a broken pencil lead and a balled-up horehound wrapper, but no jewelry clattered to the wooden planks. "As you can see, the brooch must be elsewhere."

"But it ought to be here. After I documented the depth of the engravings, I set it down and shut the workroom door just before we all left for the fair yesterday. You are the only other person allowed in here, so think, Uncle. Think hard!"

"Do not use that tone with me, young man." He aimed a finger at Bram's chest. "I am not one of your students."

Bram huffed a frustrated sigh. "You are right. My apologies. You have your bag, and I have my calipers." He waved the tool in the air. "We will simply stop by the cottage and give it a quick look over for that brooch. I am sure we will find it."

Brave words. Too bad they were false. He tucked the calipers into his pocket, feeling that if he didn't find that brooch, the blame would be pinned to his shirt. Dread sliced through him like a sharp knife. He knew exactly what it was like to be labeled as guilty for something he didn't do—and all because of his uncle, no less. This was uncomfortably familiar ground.

He turned toward the door, surprised to see a dark-haired girl buttoned up in a snug wool coat leaning against the door-frame. Once again he sighed. While he liked the girl—he truly did—he didn't have the patience today to answer Penny's incessant questions.

"Good morning, Professors. Are you looking for—"

"Sorry, Penny. This is not a good time."

"But I know—"

"You *are* a wealth of knowledge, a very bright girl, but I am in a hurry." He stalked past her—or tried to.

Her small hand snagged his sleeve. "Take me with you today. I can help on the field. I know I can."

"No, not today." He gently peeled her hand from his arm, still cross about the missing brooch.

"Oh, let the girl come," Uncle said merrily at his back. "I can keep an eye on her."

Bram coughed to keep from snorting. The man couldn't keep track of a simple brooch let alone a precocious twelve-year-old. "I am sorry, Uncle, but my answer stands."

"Please," Penny pled. "I spent all my coins on fritters yesterday. Allow me a chance to earn more."

"No. This is not a good day for me to have you underfoot."

It was eerie the way she tipped her face up to him, a storm brewing in her sightless eyes.

Blast. He plowed his fingers through his hair. "That came out wrong. What I meant to say was—"

"I revise my opinion of you, sir. You are *not* as jolly as I credited. You're not jolly at all, and I wish you'd never come to my house. You take up all my sister's time. She is forever closeted away with you either in this room or traipsing out to the site, and I am left alone with nothing but my songs to console me. You should leave." Her voice rose to a raging tempest. "You should all leave!"

"What is going on in here?" Eva strode through the door, her gaze bouncing between him and Penny.

Bram spread his hands. "I refused your sister's request to go out on the field today. That is all."

"Oh, Penny. Such theatrics." She closed in on the girl, curling her hands over her sister's shoulders and giving her a little squeeze. "A lady does not behave so passionately. If you are going to carry on like this, then you will have to do so in your bedroom and not come out until you are of a sounder mind."

"Fine. I don't want to be with you anyway." Penny shrugged away and advanced on him, one of her finger's poking him in the arm—barely. Any farther to the left and she'd have missed completely. "I don't want to be with you either. And I hope you never, ever find your stupid missing brooch!" In her haste to stomp from the room, the girl's hip smacked the table's corner, sending a few relics toppling and rolling several pencils to the floor.

"Penelope Rose!" Eva planted her fists on her hips. "You will come back here right this minute and apologize to Mr. Webb."

"Let her go." Bram collected the fallen pencils. "I do not require an apology."

Eva nibbled her lip. "Very well, but what was she going on about a missing brooch?"

"Nothing to worry about." Bram glanced at his uncle. "It's probably misplaced."

"Is it of value?"

"Like I said, do not worry—"

"Oh yes!" Uncle Pendleton cut in as he readjusted the bag strap on his shoulder. "I should say the piece is valuable. Quite rare in its design."

"Is that so?" Eva's brows gathered. "Then I pray you shall find it soon."

Bram couldn't agree more.

Eva stalked from the workroom, troubled by Penny's outburst and even more so by the missing brooch. She hated to question her few remaining staff members, but if that antiquity didn't turn up, she would have to ask around. Dixon would be hurt. Sinclair cross. Tom would snort like a horse and go right back to his work, totally ignoring her. And Mrs. Pottinger . . . well. There was no telling what that chary woman would do. Hopefully Bram would find the brooch, and it wouldn't come to such an unpleasant task.

But Penny could not be so easily put off.

Eva upped her pace, aggravated by her sister's ugly display of anger, and yet she ought to have seen it coming. Her sister adored learning on the dig site and was practically a sponge when it came to absorbing the students' answers to her questions. She would do well in school—but that had nothing to do with Penny's misbehaviour right now. Perhaps her sour mood was from lack of sleep. They had been out awfully late last evening at the bonfire.

As Eva neared the front hall, Dixon strode out of the sitting room, the lace of her mobcap flopping against her brow with each step. "There you are, miss, and just in time. You've got company."

"Who?"

"The Reverend Mr. Blackwood and his sister, Mrs. Mortimer."

Her shoulders tightened. She'd had plenty enough of Mr. Blackwood on the ride back to Royston last night. What more could he possibly have to say to her now? "Thank you, Dixon. Please bring in some tea."

She entered into a room smelling as if the very walls had been painted with violet toilette water. Mrs. Mortimer had really outdone herself today in the perfume department.

Mr. Blackwood rose at her approach, Mrs. Mortimer all a-smile as she perched on the edge of the highbacked chair.

Eva dipped her head at them both. "Mrs. Mortimer, Mr. Blackwood. Good day."

"Good day, Miss Inman." Mrs. Mortimer fluttered a lacy handkerchief near the top of her great bosom. "I heard about your disturbing brush with death last evening, and I told my brother I simply must come over to check on you."

"As you see, I am well, but he could have put your mind at ease about that." Eva glanced at the grey-suited man as she took a seat on the farthest end of the sofa from him.

"My sister is overly dramatic, a trait I have been trying to temper—unsuccessfully, I might add. Nor is the purpose of my visit to inquire about your well-being, though I am happy to see you whole and hale." His thin lips flattened to a straight line, belying his words.

Eva slid her hands beneath the fabric of her skirt, hiding her nails. "Then what is your purpose, sir?"

"If you will recall when I first learned of Mr. Webb residing on your property, there was something about the name that didn't sit right with me. I feel it was a nudging of the Spirit, if you will. That and a vague memory from years ago of a certain woman with the same surname. So I sent out discreet queries to a few of my associates in Cambridge."

Eva dug her fingers into the underside of her thighs. What business was it of his to needle about in Bram's private affairs? Or hers, for that matter. Still, it had already been done, so there was no point in calling out such a bold action. "That is very thorough of you, Mr. Blackwood."

"I take my position as shepherd quite seriously, Miss Inman." His eyes arced like a blue bolt of electricity she'd once seen at the fair. "At any rate, when the post arrived this morning, I opened a missive direct from Trinity College sent me by the head of the history department. Professor Grimwinkle informed me he is intimately aware of the details of Mr. Webb's past—a past that is riddled with infractions."

"I am well aware of Mr. Webb's history, sir. He grew up here in Royston. We were childhood friends."

Mrs. Mortimer tittered. "How romantic!"

Eva nearly choked. "It was nothing of the sort."

Though I'd like it to be now.

This time she did cough, and quite violently. Where had that unexpected thought come from?

"Here, dear." Mrs. Mortimer leaned to a dangerous angle on the chair, the legs of it straining as she held out her handkerchief.

Eva held up her hand. "Thank you for your kindness, but I have a handkerchief." She pulled out her own square of linen— nothing quite so fine as Mrs. Mortimer's—and pressed it to her lips.

Dixon entered, carrying a tray with the ivy-sprigged tea set, and placed it on the table between the sofa and the highbacks. "Will that be all, miss?"

"Yes, thank you, Dixon." She set to work, grateful for the distraction of pouring tea instead of having to face Mr. Blackwood.

But that didn't stop him from continuing. "Be that as it may, Miss Inman, I wonder if you know of a scandal involving Mr. Webb several years ago, long after he left the confines of Royston. The man was indicted for theft from a dig site."

The teapot shook in her hand, splashing tea onto the tray. Surely the missing brooch he'd spoken of couldn't have been taken by him.

Could it?

No. Of course not. Bram may have been a rascal in his younger years, but he'd changed. He'd said as much himself. Sucking in a deep breath, she continued pouring the steaming liquid into the teacups. "I was not aware of that information, sir."

"I assure you it is true. Such an esteemed academician as Professor Grimwinkle would not be given to exaggeration. Mr. Webb was eventually acquitted of the crime—for miraculously the relic in question showed up unscathed—but even so, the tarnish on his reputation remains."

She handed over a cup of Assam to Mrs. Mortimer, mulling on Mr. Blackwood's words. She'd like to believe it wasn't true, and yet why would a department chair take the time to pen a letter of falsities? But if Bram was so untrustworthy, why had Professor Grimwinkle not said anything when he'd been here that first day? Why had he allowed Bram to do the dig at all? She served the reverend his cup of tea, lost in thought as she poured one of her own.

". . . are you, Miss Inman?"

She snapped her gaze to Mrs. Mortimer. "I beg your pardon, what were you saying?"

"I wondered if you are well, dear. Your face has taken on quite a pallor."

"I am fine, thank you." She returned to her seat, swallowing a stout drink.

"I daresay this is all too much. You shoulder burdens that are not meant for a young lady such as yourself." Mrs. Mortimer rested her saucer on her ample lap and fanned her handkerchief at the side of her face. "Oh, my dear, I must insist you allow me to sponsor your sister for the Greenwell School for the Blind in London. It is for the best, you'll see. I shall write to them at once."

"Please do not, Mrs. Mortimer. I am grateful for your gener-osity, truly. And I have given this matter quite a bit of thought and prayer. The thing is, I feel Penny is not yet ready for such a big upheaval in her life. Her moods of late have been erratic." Eva set her cup on the table, the angry episode her sister had displayed with Bram fresh in her mind. "I cannot imagine what moving to completely different surroundings would do to my sister at the moment. Might it be possible to revisit this possibility in a year or two?"

Mrs. Mortimer tucked away her piece of lace. "The opportunity may not be available then. There are others I can help—others who will welcome my intervention. My offer to you cannot stand indefinitely. I am sure you understand."

Eva sank against the sofa cushion. She did understand. There were many others in Royston to whom Mrs. Mortimer could lend a philanthropic hand. The woman couldn't be expected to continue offering her aid when being told no at every turn.

And yet as frustrated as Eva was with Penny's recent behaviour, she couldn't stand the thought of sending her away. The idea of her little sister going off to school felt like a cruel twist of fate, leaving Eva feeling more alone than ever. Without Penny and her sweet singing, this house would be a tomb.

15

A week. Seven solid days and still that brooch hadn't turned up. Bram handed Eva the plan for today's work, a latent anger crawling under his skin. He ought to be riding out into the glorious November morn with his crew instead of wasting time presenting a schedule to a woman who looked at him with mistrust clouding her gaze. If only Uncle Pendleton could remember where he put that relic!

"So"—he planted his hands on the worktable to keep from slamming his fist—"does today's agenda meet with your approval?"

Eva pushed the paper across the table with one finger. "You make me sound like a harsh taskmaster."

"The harshest one I know."

Not to mention the most intriguing. For despite her wariness around him, he couldn't help but continue to admire her. This was no woman to be so easily taken advantage of, a trait he could respect.

A sad smile brushed across her lips. "Have I truly been an ogre this past week?"

"Not at all." He cracked his knuckles, working out his irritation. She had every right to be so vigilant. These were, after all, her antiquities. "Furthermore, I fully understand you wishing to tally our finds at the end of every day and going over the schedule each morn. Truth be told, I am growing rather fond of our time together."

"You, sir, are a rogue."

"I have been called worse." He shrugged. "And by you, no less."

She humphed, her gaze skimming along the line of relics they'd uncovered thus far. The room, with its grand chandelier now coated in dust, hung incongruously over the growing collection of Roman artifacts. The breakfast room had been transformed into a veritable nexus of history.

"We are compiling quite a lot of treasures in here." Eva ran her finger along the table. "And while I enjoy their beauty, I do have taxes to pay, and I am thirty pounds short. Now that you have catalogued and priced the bulk of these items, I think it is time I see about selling some of them to make up that deficit."

"Why not all of them?"

"Is it possible?" She rounded the table, eyes wide. "I do not mean to be greedy, but I really could use the funds."

No doubt she could, if one judged by the mean state of the cottage he and the men were staying in, the missing shingles on the manor, and the repetitious meals they'd been served.

"These relics"—he swept out his hand—"would be perfect specimens to use in the classroom, for it is quite a varied collection. How long do you have?"

"Taxes are due on December thirteenth."

"*Friday* the thirteenth?" He chuckled. He and Uncle were set to face the board on that ill-fated day too. "How fitting."

"Quite." Her eyes changed to a ghostly blue, the melancholy sort that songs were written about . . . and the sight drove a knife into his chest. Would that he could wave a magic wand and make things right for her. "Well then, how about I spend some time crating up these beauties, and we make a trip to Cambridge next Monday? I am certain I can persuade the powers that be at Trinity to purchase this lot for the college. The paperwork could take several weeks, which would be cutting it close to your deadline, but at least it is a possibility."

"*We* make a trip?"

"I hardly think you will let me take a load of valuables on the road by myself. Uncle Pendleton will join us, and we shall make a merry day of it."

"Oh, Bram." Sadly, she shook her head. "Please do not think I mistrust you so very much. It is just that I need to be cautious. I cannot afford to lose anything more that might bring in money."

"I understand, Eva. Truly, I do." But that didn't mean he liked it. He'd do anything to regain that gaze of confidence she'd given him the night of the bonfire. Absently, he laced his fingers and cracked his knuckles.

Eva frowned. "When are you going to stop doing that?"

He picked up her hand, hovering her fingertips in front of her face. "When you stop biting your nails."

The grin they shared did much to soothe the irritations of the past week.

"Of course, if we happen to unearth the Holy Grail, then I imagine you will be set for life monetarily. You shall never have to nibble your fingernails again."

Her lips parted with an intake of air. "Do you really think it could be here?"

"My uncle seems to think so. Personally, I highly doubt it . . . though I have learned to never say never."

"Hmm." Once again Eva wandered the length of the table before returning to his side. "Some say the grail has mystical powers. That it can heal. It would be lovely if that were true and Penny could regain her vision."

He shook his head. "God alone heals, though I suppose He could choose any means He likes through which to do so. Then again, I am no theological expert."

"Maybe not, but you are a man of faith." She glanced up at him, a glimmer of appreciation in her pale eyes.

Was she beginning to rethink her doubts of him? He chewed the inside of his cheek, wishing to God it were so. But even if it was, once she learned the truth of his parentage, she would no doubt put distance between herself and him.

And he wouldn't blame her.

Frustrated, he plowed his fingers through his hair. "Eva, I—"

Heels clicked into the room, the swish of the housekeeper's skirts rustling with each step. "A letter arrived for you, sir."

He took the sealed envelope. "Thank you, Dixon."

He studied it as she clipped away. The penmanship didn't look familiar, nor was there an official college seal. A simple paste glue wrinkled the edge of the back flap.

Eva handed him a pencil. "It is a far cry from a letter opener, but as you well know, I do not think my nails will be very effective at breaking the seal."

His lips twisted wryly as he slid the thing beneath the flap and shook out the folded paper that'd been tucked neatly inside. The more he read, the wider his eyes grew. Mr. Toffit hadn't been jesting about being impressed with his archaeological practices, initiative, and leadership. The curator position was his—with a hefty salary—all for the signing of his name on the bottom line . . . a signature that was due in two weeks. Blast! Why could this not have been offered next May when his uncle would be settled into his retirement?

"Must be important," Eva murmured. "You are quite engrossed."

He peered at her, the sense of her words slowly coming together. "Oh, yes, I suppose."

"May I ask what has you so pensive?"

"You may ask me anything." He smiled. "It seems the Royston Historical Society is making good on their offer of employment. This is a document for me to sign as their curator."

"I see." She brought her finger to her lips, then caught herself and dropped her hand. "What will you do?"

There was a tilt of genuine curiosity to her head. Interesting, that. "Would you like me to move back to Royston?"

The blush of a summer rose spread across her cheeks. "I would not think my opinion should make a difference."

"It matters to me."

"I-I would not presume to tell you where to live nor what career path to take."

No, of course she wouldn't, not unless pressed or possibly threatened. He would do neither. "And yet, Eva Inman, I suspect you have very definite thoughts on the matter, for I do believe you know your own mind."

Her chin lifted quite adorably. "You make that sound like a bad thing."

"Quite the contrary. I admire a woman with a little pluck."

A smile played on her lips. "Is it a good offer?"

"Yes, the salary is a bit more than I currently take in, and since I have been here this past month, I find that I rather like country living."

She studied his face. "So you are going to take it?"

Actually, he was surprised at how strongly he did wish to sign on that confirmation line, but with his uncle to mind, there was no possible way to do so.

"I, em, likely not. And now, if you will excuse me, I have some things to do and think about. I will see you later, Eva," he mumbled as he turned away, finished with the conversation and with the temptation to leave behind his teaching days.

He would pen a rejection letter later tonight.

It'd only been an hour since she'd last spoken with Bram in the workroom, and yet here she was, tethering her horse out at the worksite. She had been spending an inordinate amount of time with him, which was a mixed blessing. Bram was enjoyable to be around, and she found his insights into Roman antiquities to be educational and entertaining. Part of her wished he would accept that curatorship position. But it also meant time away from Penny, time that would have been spent reading or working on mathematics or history lessons.

Once again she felt that tug-of-war between caring for Penny herself and sending her off to school just like Bram, his uncle, and Mrs. Mortimer all urged her to do. Was she doing the right thing keeping Penny here, or was she being selfish? Was Penny ready to spread her wings and fly away, or would such a big move be traumatic for her at this age?

Sighing, Eva strode to the work tent—where a hundred more questions bombarded her.

Bram paced in front of the field desk, fists clenched at his sides. His jaw clamped so hard, iron cords stood out on his neck. The sight made her own stomach tighten. Whatever had him in such a high dudgeon couldn't be good.

She stopped just inside the door flap. "I got word from Sinclair you wished to speak with me. What has happened?"

He wheeled about so quickly his coat tails flew wide. "Come see for yourself."

She followed him—or tried to. His long legs ate up the uneven ground with bigger bites than she could manage. He led her to the farthest edge of the excavation site, where his students each hefted a shovel, digging out sand. Professor Pendleton stood nearby, supervising. Bram stopped abruptly, a low growl in his throat.

Eva peered up at him. "I do not understand. This is where you found the mosaic piece and had planned to see if any more might be discovered. Why did you fill it in with sand?"

"I had nothing to do with filling it in." His voice was a wire that might snap at any moment.

"Then who did?"

"If I knew, I would throttle the scoundrel!" He threw his hands in the air. "First the ripped tent, then the broken tools, the missing brooch, and now this. What is to be next? A sudden invasion of sandworms devouring everything in their path?"

"Sandworms?" She scrunched her brow. "Is that a thing?"

"No, but it is just as plausible as the catastrophes that have been striking here with regularity. Perhaps Sinclair is right, and these acres truly are cursed. Blast it all!" He paced once again.

She nibbled on a fingernail, concerned, yes, but also a fair amount of relief made breathing easier. Bram wasn't responsible for this, nor had he likely been for the other mishaps. Judging by the way his heels dug into the dirt and the fierce glower twisting his face, he was genuinely upset about the whole ordeal.

Or he was a consummate actor.

She discarded that thought and stepped toward him. "I shall report this to the constable at once."

"No." He faced her, crossing his arms against his chest. "That will mean interviews, paperwork, maybe even a site closure due to safety concerns. I would rather camp out here each night than risk such interruptions."

"But, Bram, you are already getting interrupted." She tipped her head at the crew diligently removing the sand.

"I know, and it is maddening!" He kicked a stray rock. "Every time we are on the brink of a breakthrough, something happens. It is like building a sandcastle at the edge of the tide, only to have the waves wash it away. This excavation is crucial. We cannot afford such setbacks!"

She stiffened at the raw fury in his voice. She'd hate to be the one to cross swords with this man.

His uncle approached, bold enough to pat Bram on the back. "Calm down. The fellows will set this to rights."

"They should not have to set anything to rights. They should be working on the dig. We do not have time for this!" He stomped away and grabbed a shovel. The students gave him a wide berth. Good call, for he pitched a furious storm of sand into the air.

Eva turned to Professor Pendleton. "I understand Bram is upset, and rightfully so. As am I. These ill happenings are vexing. But what I do not understand is why he feels so rushed. You and your crew are welcome to take as much time as you need. I hope you are not feeling pressured by me in any way."

"Oh, dear lady, you are ever so gracious." A wry smile quirked his lips. "Unfortunately, Professor Grimwinkle is not."

"What do you mean?"

His eyes glazed over for a moment as if Bram's uncle had vacated his body and nothing but a shell stood in front of her.

"Professor? Are you all right?"

"Hmm?" He squinted, studying her as if they'd just met, then gave a hearty chuckle. "Why, yes! This dig is quite important. I feel certain this is the site of Caelum Academia. We just need to prove it."

"To Professor Grimwinkle, I take it. But why the rush?"

"I'm in no hurry, but as I recall, there was something to do with someone's job being on the line." He massaged his temple with two fingers, late-morning sun glinting off the silvery hair he mussed. "I could be wrong about that, though. Sometimes things get a bit jumbled, you know. At any rate, it's nothing to worry about. We'll meet with the board at the end of the term, and all will be well."

Eva glanced at Bram, a pile of sand now behind him. He clearly didn't share the same calm as his uncle . . . perhaps because he knew exactly whose job was on the line.

16

A hint of frankincense wafted across the centuries. The tang of old leather and the mouldering dust of foreign lands floated on the air as well. Bram breathed deeply as he paced the length of the history department's large storage room. Artifacts of various sorts and regions lined the enormous shelves. If he listened hard enough, he'd hear the breath of a thousand whispers telling their stories. Of all Trinity College's prestigious halls and hallowed classrooms, this was his favorite place to be . . . usually.

Today he'd rather be basking in the sunshine of the unseasonably warm November morn, sitting next to Eva on the bench where he'd left her reading a book. There was no predicting what sort of mood Grimwinkle would be in—sour, antagonistic, or outright poison-tongued—and though it'd taken much convincing on his part, he'd talked Eva into allowing him to meet with the man on his own to spare her any upset.

For the man could upset a saint.

He cracked his knuckles. Hopefully no more mishaps would occur at the dig site during his absence. He didn't believe such poppycock about some ancient curse on a square of dirt and turf, but he did believe in the wickedness of men. Someone was up to no good. Then again, it could be pranking gone bad by his students, but to what end? They'd had to work all the harder yesterday, so that didn't make sense. Who else would wish to obstruct his work? Grimwinkle, perhaps, for the last thing that man would want was solid proof of Caelum Academia, but he was here in Cambridge. The motive was there but not the opportunity. A sigh barreled out of him. He could only hope whatever or whoever the cause was would soon be exposed.

Pausing in front of the three crates on the table, he pulled out his pocket watch. Eleven thirty. The man was a half hour late. Heaven help him if he were the one to arrive tardy to a meeting, a sickening double standard.

Wooden clogs *click-clacked* at a fast pace, growing louder. Bram tucked away his pocket watch as Professor Grimwinkle dashed in, the tails of his suit coat flapping against his backside. A fine sheen glistened on the man's upper lip and broad brow. Either he'd been participating in a marathon, or his morning classes had pushed him beyond his limits. Bram gave him a sharp nod. "Good morning, Professor Grimwinkle."

"What is left of it, you mean," he grumbled as he stopped across the table from Bram. "Since I have taken on your classes, my schedule has cinched tight. Where is Professor Pendleton?"

The same question Eva had asked him when he'd pulled the wagon up to the manor's front door. It had been a gamble she'd even accompany him unchaperoned to Cambridge—or allow him to go it alone. In the end, though, being that the artifacts had been packed neatly and were ready to sell, not to mention the glorious weather, she'd acquiesced.

"My uncle awoke with terrible back pain, sir. He must have wrenched it yesterday at the site, what with all the digging. I felt it best he stay behind and recuperate."

Disgust tightened Grimwinkle's already-thin lips to a thread-bare line. "It seems the man is unfit for anything. I should think the bulk of the excavation would've been finished by now. It wasn't that large of a site. Are you meeting with any setbacks I should know about?"

Blast. Had Uncle Pendleton told the man about their troubles? Bram gritted his teeth. "There are always challenges, as you well know."

"Yes, I do know." An unreadable gleam shone in Grimwinkle's eyes. "Now then, I haven't much time. What is it you wish to show me? Have you found the grail?"

"Not yet, but we have uncovered many valuable and varied artifacts." He pulled the already-loosened lid from one of the crates. "See for yourself."

Bending over the box, Grimwinkle poked about, removing relic after relic, and mumbling the whole while. "Of Roman origin, good, good. Second century, I'd say. Relatively well preserved. Interesting variety." At length, he set down a long-necked vase. "Of course, all this proves is that you have found an ancient site, not necessarily that it is from the supposed dwellings of Caelum Academia."

"I have every hope we shall yet find some evidence, but that is not why I requested this morning's meeting. As you have noted, this collection is diverse and in good condition, offering a comprehensive look at the historical evolution of the region. Such a variety could greatly benefit the education of our students, allowing them tactile learning instead of only what is printed in books." Squaring his shoulders, he sucked in a fortifying breath. "I propose the department purchase this lot."

"As you well know . . ." Grimwinkle plucked an errant wood shaving off his perfectly tailored sleeve, sneering at it as if he held a rat by the tail. "We only have so much money to go around, Professor Webb. Why should the college buy these items in particular?"

"The provenance of these artifacts is exceptional." Bram picked up a little lamp and rested it on his palm. "Take a look at this. It is not every day one finds such a wealth of treasures so close to home, which adds an extra layer of relevance to the collection. Think of it. With these pieces, Trinity College could become a hub for the study of regional history, and that is sure to please investors."

"Mmm." The sound rumbled in Grimwinkle's throat. "I am not certain. Investors are fickle creatures."

Bram set the lamp on the table. Money always talked, and he intended to give it the best voice he could. "Not if it comes down to increasing profits. Handled properly, once word gets out that our history department—and ours alone—houses such a unique cache, potential students will be drawn in like senators to the Forum."

"Possibly." Grimwinkle tugged at his sleeves, straightening imaginary wrinkles. "I shall have to give it some thought before I present it to the budget committee."

"But you will present it?"

"I make no promises."

A frustrated sigh leached out of him. He should have gone straight to the Fitzwilliam Museum. With a swipe of his hand, Bram set the wooden lid atop the crate. "If you are not interested, then simply say so. There are other buyers to be approached. I merely wished Trinity to have the first chance at these beauties."

"Leave it." Grimwinkle planted a well-manicured hand atop the box. "I will sort through these items later and get back to you."

Bram met the man's gaze with a steely resolve. "And when will that be?"

"I am a busy man, Professor. I cannot say for certain, but I will give you an answer."

Maybe so. Bram's jaw clenched. But would the man's answer be in time for Eva to pay her taxes?

∂X∂

She didn't deserve such a lovely day as this, having lounged about decadently in the uncommonly warm November sun, reading to her heart's content until Bram had returned. The history department head was considering the purchase of the relics, which wasn't exactly what she'd hoped for. She'd rather have the money in hand right now. But Bram had assured her in his usual convincing way that though it wasn't as quick of a turnover as she'd like, she would be paid for the antiquities sooner rather than later. A test of trust, she supposed, in more ways than one, and she wasn't sure she liked such uncertainty.

Still, the day thus far had been perfectly splendid, and now, leaving a cozy public room where she'd eaten her fill of a rich lamb pie with a flaky crust—and on the arm of a handsome man, no less—Eva couldn't be more content. Why, one might almost think she was a somebody. A lady of leisure. Her lips twisted into a smirk. How far from the truth that was. She couldn't even afford to buy new ribbons for her faded bonnet.

As she and Bram stepped out the door of the Pickerel Inn, that very bonnet took flight in a gust of wind. She shivered as she lunged for it. My, how chill it had turned. She just might use that old blanket they'd tucked between the crates on the drive here to wrap up in on the journey home.

As she retied the frayed ribbons beneath her chin, Bram flipped open the lid of his beloved pocket watch. After a glance at the time, he tucked it away and re-offered his arm. "How about a quick stop before we collect the horse and wagon?"

She tucked her fingers against his sleeve, grateful for the warmth against her thin gloves. While they strolled, she lifted her face to the sky. Thick clouds scudded overhead, gunmetal grey and looking quite cross. "Should we? Looks like we are in for some bad weather."

"And you are worried you shall melt?" He nudged her with his arm.

"Not at all." She elbowed him right back. "But you just might."

He chuckled. "I think we are both made of sterner stuff, but I also think you will be unable to refuse what I have in mind."

Against her will, she admired the strong cut of his jaw and the way his shaggy hair bounced against it. He needed a trim, but was he aware of what must surely be a triviality in his world of buried treasures?

"What makes you think, sir, that I would find one of your ideas irresistible?"

"Because, milady, though you may not wish to admit so, sometimes I do have brilliant ideas." He grinned as he stopped in front of a building with a long black awning, enormous windows, and a hanging placard that read *W. Heffer & Sons Ltd, Booksellers and Publishers*—her favorite Cambridge haunt. Well, well. He *was* entirely correct.

Threatening sky or not, there was no possible way she'd pass up an opportunity like this.

Bram paused in front of the door. "Shall we?"

She lifted her nose in the air. "Perhaps just for a minute."

Then she bolted through the door with a laugh, the chime of a brass bell matching her merriment. Strange how frequently she smiled with this man, but that didn't deserve a second thought as she gazed at the spines of stories galore. Ink and leather, paper and promises, she breathed it all in. So many books! How lovely it would be to pack up her traveling bag and simply move in here. To live, eat, and sleep surrounded by tales of all sorts. What a dream.

And what nonsense.

Come back to earth, girl.

For a while she wandered aimlessly, led by nothing other than fancying one book cover after another until she came across a lovely edition of *Little Women*. She ran her finger along the spine, appreciating the feel of the embossed golden letters, then slowly drifted her touch to the book next to it. Her lips parted on an intake of air as she pulled the beauty from the shelf. *Good Wives*. The sequel to *Little Women*. Oh, how Penny would love to hear this one. Actually, she wouldn't mind a bit herself.

Cradling the new book like a babe in arms, she sank onto a nearby chair and reverently opened the cover.

"A merry Christmas, girls!" someone called from the other side of the shop. "What are you going to do with yourselves today?"

Eva smiled softly. The cheerful words felt like a promise, even if her own Christmas seemed so uncertain. This book would be a grand surprise, wrapped up in paper with a sprig of holly tied to the front. She closed her eyes, imagining her sister's squeal of delight. The sound quickly faded, though. What sort of holiday could she possibly give Penny when she could barely afford to keep Mrs. Pottinger in flour?

Even so, she paged back to the front cover. Two shillings. Two! What an outrageous sum. She rose just as Bram cornered a long row of books.

"We should leave. We may need some extra traveling time."

"Very well. I am ready to go." She returned the book to the shelf with a last long look. Maybe someday—soon hopefully—she'd be able to buy her sister such a gift.

"What's that you have there?" Bram fished out the novel with one of his long fingers. "*Good Wives?* Planning to be an overachieving bride, are you?"

Heat burned up her neck, blossoming onto her cheeks. "Do not be absurd. Clearly you have not read Louisa May Alcott. She's an American novelist."

"Ah, Romanticism at its finest, then, hmm?" He waggled his eyebrows. "I did not take you for a daydreamer."

"Just because a girl reads novels does not mean she is a wool-gatherer. Literature can offer valuable insights into the human experience, allowing readers to explore different perspectives and emotions. A window, if you will, into worlds both real and imagined, fostering empathy and understanding. I should think that as a college professor you would recognize the intellectual stimulation such an exercise might render."

"Whoa, now." He held up a hand. "I did not mean to strike such a nerve."

Once again her face flamed, and she glanced away. What had gotten into her? "Pardon. I suppose I am a bit passionate when it comes to reading, especially since I hardly have time for it anymore. I was actually thinking of this book for Penny, that I might read it aloud to her."

"Yet if you sent your sister to school, she would learn to read for herself—and then you would have time to linger in whatever stories might strike your fancy. It would be a benefit to you both."

True. Penny likely would benefit from an education other than what she could give. The professor, Mrs. Mortimer, and Bram had all commented time and again on how smart Penny was. Eva really ought to consider it—and she would. But not yet.

She faced Bram. "School or not, there is still the issue of tax money."

"Which hopefully will soon be remedied." He tucked the book beneath his arm and strolled away.

She chased after him, but there was no chance of keeping up with his long legs. By the time she finally did catch up to him, he stood at the front desk, handing over two coins in exchange for a brown-paper-wrapped parcel.

"What are you doing?" she whispered.

"Thank you," he said to the clerk, then turned to her, pressing the package into her hands. "For you."

Her jaw dropped. "You bought *Good Wives*?"

He grinned. "I did. But if it makes you feel better, you may pay me back when your artifacts are sold."

"Oh, Bram . . ." She clutched the book to her chest, heart swelling. "Thank you."

"Think nothing of it." He yanked on the doorknob, the overhead bell chirruping—and a blast of icy pellets hit them smack in the face.

Eva grasped the collar of her coat tightly at her neck. If this sleet turned to snow, they'd never make it home by dark.

They might not make it home at all.

17

No mortal was framed for such weather as this. Sideways snow blurred the world into white blindness. Wind whipped so forcefully, it brought tears to the eyes and froze the lashes. Bram ducked his head against a particularly cruel blast. His sleeves were pulled down as far as the fabric would allow, covering as much skin as possible, but even so, his knuckles were cracked and raw from the blistering cold. Would that he'd have thought to bring his gloves along, for it was muscle memory alone that kept his grip on the reins.

He never should have suggested a stop at Heffer's.

The horses—God love them—plodded along. He could barely see their ice-encrusted rumps. They wouldn't last much longer. Eva wouldn't either. She huddled next to him, trembling uncontrollably.

And night would soon fall.

If his calculations were correct, they'd traveled a little over halfway to Royston. So close, yet so impossibly far in this dangerous weather. Though if he remembered right, the Robinson farm ought to be getting close. They could hunker down with them until morning—if he could find the turnoff.

He bent his face close to Eva's ear to be heard over the howling wind. "The Robinson farm—is it the next drive?"

Hard to tell if she shook her head yes or no, so violently did she shiver, but she did shift a bit, lifting her chin. "It is, but the Robinsons moved out years ago," she shouted. "The house is empty. We cannot stay there alone."

"It is that or die."

Without waiting for her consent, he squinted into the colourless world, scanning what he hoped was the right side of the road. If he turned too soon, they'd plow headfirst into a frozen hedgerow and be stuck. Too late and they'd miss the turnoff altogether.

An eternity later, an indistinguishable shape appeared. Maybe. Maybe not. Bram hunched forward on the bench seat, straining to see. Eventually, he focused on what could be a man in a charcoal coat, arms wrapped tight, standing immobile—the exact sight he was hoping for. The man-sized tree stump had guarded the Robinson farm lane for as long as he could remember. He slowed the horses with a slight tug—not too much lest they stop, but not too little or the back of the wagon would swing wide. With a layer of ice beneath the snow, it would be easy to lose control. Ever so carefully, he guided the horses in a gentle arc.

It was an excruciating dance, this delicate balance of trying to remain on a road he couldn't see. Thankfully the drive wasn't miles long. Just as the last of the day's light threatened to give up its ghost, the light grey mass of a structure grew darker in hue. He pulled on the reins with a "Whoa, now. Easy boys."

The crunch of wheels against snow ground to a halt. Bram climbed down from the driver's seat, stiff enough to shatter should he slip and fall, which he nearly did. He grasped the side of the wagon and worked his way around to the passenger side. "Come, Eva. I am here for you."

Gloved fingers shot out of the driving snow, flailing for his grip. He flung his hand toward her. Too late. A body hurtled at him, catching him off-balance. Bram flew backward, Eva sailing with him to the icy ground. He lay dazed, frozen, and completely out of breath . . . though it was nice to hold Eva so close.

"Sorry!" She pushed away and toppled sideways.

If he weren't so cold, he'd laugh.

With a few slips and slides, he made his way to his feet. Anchoring his step, he hauled her up. After a quick re-tucking of the blanket around her shoulders, he pulled her against his side. "Hold on to me and try not to lose your footing."

She gripped him without argument or mercy. As he trudged toward the old house, it took all his effort to breathe, so tightly did she cling. Ahead, the dark maw of a door hole opened in the whiteness. No actual door closed out the elements. Blast. Would this ramshackle old house be any protection against the storm?

He stumbled inside, pulling Eva along with him, and once his vision adjusted to the shadows, his spirits lifted. A door did still hang from its hinges. Likely the wind had blown it open.

He slid his arm from Eva's shoulders. "Stay here. I will see to the horses and return to make a fire in the hearth. Maybe look around for some wood, hmm?"

She nodded, teeth chattering.

He fought the door shut behind him—a brutal battle—and tromped back into a face full of snow. It was an even bigger fight to unhitch the horses, but eventually he prevailed and led them to a collection of wooden boards leaning together like a band of drunken sailors desperate to remain upright. Some barn. The roof was more of a suggestion than a covering. One of the horses snorted a puff of steam in protest.

"Easy now, Jasper." He patted the bay on the nose. "Let's see what we can find you and your mate."

Bram rambled around the big space, scowling when wind whipped snow through cracks in the walls. Two stalls toward the back seemed to be the best hope of protection. At least it was better than being out on the road.

It took him some time to remove the horses' tack, his fingers refusing to cooperate in the frigid air. Frequent breaks of huffing warm breath onto his hands helped somewhat. Eventually, he secured Quill and Jasper for the night, then shouldered his way back into the storm. Twilight settled like a dark counterpane pulled over the earth. He longed for a cheery fire, for light and warmth. Survival, actually. Thank God he'd purchased a new cigar and plenty of matches while in Cambridge.

After another tussle with the door, he staggered inside, numb with cold. Shadows gathered in the front room, but no woman did.

"Eva?" he called. "Have you found some kindling?"

Nothing but the howling wind answered.

It wasn't a big house. She ought to have heard him.

"Eva," he called again as he tread across warped floorboards to a side room. Blackness reigned, the only light from a single window. Snow stuck against what glass remained and a drift crawled across the floor. He pushed the door shut.

"Eva!" he shouted while striding into a back room. A kitchen, apparently. A broken range stood cockeyed on a few missing legs. An old sink against one wall. Part of a chair and what used to be a table heaped in the center.

But no Eva.

A gap-stepped stairway clung to another wall as if either may tip over at the slightest touch. Surely she'd not have gone upstairs . . . would she?

He dashed over to the steps. No. She absolutely would not have. The ceiling had collapsed on this part of the house, blocking anyone from traveling beyond the top stair.

He wheeled about, heart catching in his throat. He'd heard tales of those frozen to death, how delirium set in just before the poor soul wandered out into a perceived promise of warmth. Shedding clothing. Lying down to sleep. Forever.

"Eva!" He tore toward the rear door. "Where are you?"

She would die here, and not because of God's lack of smiling. This was all her fault. Stupid. Stupid. Stupid! Eva spun in a circle, clutching onto two small sticks for firewood. Snow pelted her face, blinding her. She couldn't even see her footprints to decipher which direction led back to the safety of the Robinson farmhouse.

"Eva!"

She tensed. Was this what it was like to die by freezing, hallucinating the wind called your name? Straining, she listened with every fiber of her body, hoping against hope what she'd heard was something more than wishful thinking.

"Where are you?"

She gasped, the air cold against her raw throat. That was no delusion. "Here!" she shouted. "I'm here!"

Moments later a shadowy figure appeared, and Bram's strong arm wrapped around her shoulders, gathering her close. "Try not to stumble. We are going to move fast."

Transferring her sticks to one hand, she flung an arm around his waist. He hadn't been jesting. He practically dragged her through the snow. They staggered through the door of the old house, and once inside, she pulled away and caught her breath.

"What were you thinking?" A great cloud of steam puffed out his mouth. "You could have died out there!"

"I—" She swallowed. Hearing him confirm her worst fear made it seem all the more real, yet he'd tasked her with finding firewood. "You told me to find kindling." She shook the paltry sticks in the frigid air, snow powdering off her upraised arm.

"Oh, Eva. I meant *inside* the house." Hefting a sigh, he once again wrapped his arm about her shoulder and guided her from the room. "Come. Let's get you settled, and I will make a fire."

"I doubt this will be enough wood." The two sticks weighed hardly anything against her gloved palm.

He laughed. "This whole house is made of wood—what is left of it, anyway." He stopped in front of a barren hearth in the main room. "Here, take a seat on the floor. It is hard and cold, but at least it is dry."

Exhausted, she sank without complaint. Bram lifted the blanket from her shoulders and shook it out, ridding the fabric of snow before he replaced it. But when he shrugged out of his own coat and began laying that over her as well, she pushed away his thoughtful offering. "Bram, no. You will catch your death. I am fine with just the blanket."

"A valiant refusal, yet I insist." He winked and strode into the shadows.

Eva tugged the blanket—and Bram's coat—closer to her neck, breathing in his mossy scent and the leftover sweetness of tobacco. He'd been nothing but kind, sheltering her as best he could all the way from Cambridge. She'd had the extra layer of a blanket. He'd had nothing but his coat. Surely he must be bone chilled. Though by the sounds of it, he was currently working up a sweat. The kicking in of a wall and cracking of slats being pulled free assaulted the cold air.

He reappeared with an armful of jagged-edged wood, dropped it in front of the hearth, then doubled back for another load. Eva shivered while he worked, torn between wanting to help yet unable to force her trembling body to move.

Methodically, Bram kicked away spent ash from the fireplace, then stacked the smaller sticks and scraps in the middle. When the pile grew to just below knee height, he disappeared once more and returned with a handful of splinters, which he carefully nested at the base. He then pulled out a small box of matches from his waistcoat pocket and struck one to life. Never had she been so glad to see a fire sputter into existence—nor so curious.

She cocked her head. "I am grateful, truly, but why do you just happen to have a box of matches? That seems very convenient."

"You will not like the reason." He blew on the tiny flames, coaxing them to life.

Reason, indeed. When had he found the time to purchase a cigar in Cambridge? Unless he'd stopped by his office at Trinity. Or possibly when she'd been looking at books inside Heffer's, he'd bowed out to the tobacco shop next door.

"Please do not smoke a cigar in here." She waved away a billowy grey cloud wafting from the hearth. It was hard enough to breathe with the smoke from the fire.

Bram fiddled with the flue handle. A jerk and a tug later, the thing creaked open, luring fumes and flames upward. After tossing a few of the bigger boards onto the fledgling fire, he sank to her side, stretching out his long legs toward the warmth. "If it were not for my bad habit, we would not have this fire now, would we?"

She humphed as she peeled off his coat and handed it over. Staying in a house alone with a fully dressed man was shameful enough. Better he should cover those shirtsleeves, where muscles bulged far too enticingly beneath the fabric. "The man I marry will not partake of such a filthy vice as cigar smoking."

"I did not realize you were looking for a husband."

Her cheeks heated as she pulled off her bonnet "I am not. It is just . . . Oh, what does it matter, anyway? When word gets out I have spent a night alone with a man, no one will have me."

"Any man would be a fool to listen to such blathering gossip. I would not." Resolution deepened his tone.

Of course he wouldn't give sway to what anyone said. He never had in the past. She set down her bedraggled bonnet on the dirty floor, then began working on shedding her sodden gloves. "You are not like other men."

He flashed a grin. "I shall take that as a compliment."

"You take everything as a compliment."

"Is that such a bad thing?"

She allowed the question to linger unanswered, weary of

banter. Weary of everything, really. She laid out her wet gloves to dry, then lifted her hands to the fire. As she slowly thawed, her thoughts turned toward her sister. How worried the girl must be. "I hope Penny is all right," she murmured. "I hope she did not venture out in this weather."

"She has more sense than you credit, I think." After tossing on a larger piece of wood, he returned to her side. "Still, your care for your sister is a noble endeavor."

"There is nothing noble about it. I made a vow to my father to look out for her and the house." A sigh deflated her, and she hunched farther into the blanket. "Though it seems I am failing miserably."

"None of it! Penny is well tended, and once those antiquities sell, you shall have your tax money and then some. Inman Manor will be restored to its former glory beneath your hand."

She peered over at him. "Do you really think so?"

"I know so." He bopped her on the nose with one finger.

She stared into the fire, doubting every word he'd spoken.

"You carry the weight of the world." His words were a soft rumble. "Why is that?"

Hah. As if she'd tell him all her deep, dark secrets. She fixed her gaze on the flames, ignoring the question.

"I know you may think otherwise, but you can trust me, Eva. I am a good listening ear. Besides"—he nudged her with his shoulder—"we have a history, you and me. We are friends, are we not?"

Slowly, she nodded. Despite his childhood pranks, he always had been there when she'd needed him most.

Until he wasn't.

Sorrow welled. As a girl she hadn't understood what she had done to make him abandon her without a single good-bye or even a note of explanation. "We were friends at one time."

"And we still are. I have not changed my mind on that matter—and I never will. So tell me what troubles you. I promise anything said here tonight will not be repeated. Now is your chance to unload your secret burdens and be free of them—at least for one evening."

Mesmerized by the flames, for the briefest of moments, she allowed herself to believe that could be true. "How lovely that would be."

"Then do so. It is a magical night. A storm like none other. Why, the winds that rattle these walls could blow your troubles all away."

Would that were true! Longing for just such a relief, she studied his face. The flames reflected sincerity in his grey eyes. Not a hint of jesting twitched his lips. All in all, he appeared to be deadly serious. "Do you vow you will not breathe a word of my secrets to anyone?"

Solemnly he nodded, one hand pressed flat against his heart. "I do."

She turned back to the fire. If she was going to do this—*was* she going to do this?—then she'd do so without making eye contact. Sucking in a breath for courage, she willed a confession she'd kept locked deep in her soul to rise to her tongue. "I . . ." She swallowed against the swelling in her throat. "I am to blame for my parents' deaths, my sister's blindness, and the dismal state of Inman Manor."

There. She'd said it. All of it. Aloud. Something she'd not dared to do since her father's accident. And just as she'd feared, hearing it come from her own lips opened up a fresh ache in her soul.

Bram was quiet for a while, then finally spoke. "I am at a loss to think how you could have possibly accomplished all of that."

Her chin dropped to her chest, shame a sickening weight. "My mother died about six months after you disappeared. I left open a window I had been told to close."

He turned her face to his. "A window?"

She tossed back her head, unwilling to give in to his tender touch. She didn't deserve such a kindness. "My mother was terribly ill during her confinement, though admittedly, she was never of prime health. Mother had weak lungs, you see, and during her pregnancy had suffered a terrible rash and fever. I simply wished to spare her any further torment. Dixon always forced me to take air whenever I felt ill, so I assumed such a measure could only be beneficial. My mother was too weak to leave her bed, so I opened her window. Father had bid me close it before I left her room, but I did not. I left the room with it open, and I forgot to go back and do as I was told." Eva scrunched her eyes closed, trapping hot tears. "Would that I had, for that one act of disobedience caused her to leave me forever."

"What happened?" Bram asked softly.

"Mother went into labour the next day. She died shortly after delivery. A month or so later, the wet nurse declared Penny to be blind. My father never recovered from such low blows, and I suspect it was his melancholy that affected his business sense. Though I did not realize it at the time, he simply could not manage anymore." She pressed her fists to her eyes. "Last year, I quarreled with him over a gown. A silly little gown! He had refused me, but I pushed and pushed until he stormed off for a ride—one that took him from me as well." Eva forced her eyes open and looked full in Bram's face. Better to bear his disgusted expression head-on than hear it in his voice. "So you see, it was all my fault, and now I am abandoned by them both."

"Rubbish. I hate that you believe such awful lies." Shooting to his feet, he threw a piece of wood at the fire, kicking up red sparks. "It is God alone who numbers our days, not a twelve-year-old girl doing what she thought best for her mother or a young woman who knew nothing about the state of her father's affairs. The strain of labour no doubt took its toll on your mother's lungs, and the horse hurt your father, not you. You had nothing to do with any of it."

"Maybe so, but had my mother not been so terribly ill, Penny wouldn't have been born blind. And if I had not been so insistent on my way, my father would not have gone out riding in such a frame of mind."

"Perhaps, and yet I repeat you are not God. He is sovereign. You are not. And the same goes for your father's melancholy. He made the choice to go riding when obviously he should not have been. You are not responsible for anyone's emotional state or choices made, save for your own."

Her heart squeezed, a fresh hope straining to be born. What if . . . this was truth? Dare she believe it? How freeing that would be, and yet also fearful, for to admit such a thing meant she wasn't in control . . . and she desperately needed to be in control. She didn't know any other way to live, for how else could she stop anyone else from abandoning her? "It seems you are determined to see the best in me."

"Oh, Eva." Face softening, Bram dropped to his knees in front of her and collected both her hands in his. "What I see is a woman who has blamed herself far too long for things she ought not."

She yanked from his touch. "But I left the window open on a drafty night! And the argument with my father—"

"Did you ask God for forgiveness?" With a swing of his legs, he settled back at her side.

"With every breath I still do."

"Then you may stop now. The very first time you asked to be pardoned, you were. That is what grace is all about. If we confess our sins, He is faithful and just to forgive us our sins, as far as the east is from the west. Even when we've done wrong, God does not abandon us."

Her lips twitched, wanting to smile, yet she wasn't quite ready for that much happiness. She wasn't completely convinced she deserved it. "I think you have muddled together several Scriptures, sir."

A slow grin stretched across his lips. "I told you I was no theologian."

True, but, oh, how his words resonated in her soul, lifting the weight that had pressed on her for so long. And buried beneath that weight was a fear she'd never faced, for she'd not been brave enough. But here, now, in Bram's safe and secure presence, she might even admit she'd been terrified that at some point, God might abandon her too.

She fidgeted with the hem of her sleeve. "Perhaps I have never moved beyond thinking of the past like a twelve-year-old. Why, I may just be as rash as my sister."

"We all have our moments of fear and doubt, Eva. It is part of being human. But I promise you, God's love and grace are constant whether we falter or not."

Tears stung her eyes as she drank in his words. "I have always felt like I needed to atone for my mistakes, to earn favor in God's eyes because of my wrongdoings. But hearing what you say is like—" Her throat closed, and it took her several breaths before she could even whisper. "It is like a burden being lifted."

"That is because it is," he said softly, reaching for her hand. "You do not have to carry that weight anymore. It was never meant for you to begin with."

She squeezed his fingers, wanting—needing—to hold on to all the truth he'd imparted. For the first time in years, she felt a glimmer of hope. Of lightness. She could let go of her past and embrace the grace she'd always believed in yet never truly accepted. "Thank you, Bram. Your words mean more than you could ever know."

"You are stronger than you think, Eva. And you are never alone. Not with God, and not with me."

"You speak as if you have already dealt with the same demons I have been wrestling all these years." She peered up at him. "How do you know so much about God's mercy?"

"Hard-earned experience." He chuckled.

"Is that so?" She lifted her chin. "Then I should like to hear of it."

"Of what?"

"Your experience. It is, after all, only fair. I have shared with you my deep, dark secret." She leaned close. "So tell me, Bram Webb, what is yours?"

18

Wind rattled the shutters against the house, howling through cracks in the walls, a violent echo of Eva's demand to know his secrets. Bram pushed to his feet, plowing his fingers through his damp hair. He couldn't sit anymore. He was too antsy. Too . . . off-center. For years, he'd kept sentry over the ghosts of past wrongs that lurked in his heart's shadows, for those specters refused to be laid to rest. And if he let them loose now, then what?

He crouched in front of the fire, rubbing his hands together, more of a stalling tactic than a true need. He certainly wasn't cold anymore, not with the burn of shame firing in his gut. Ah, but it was a sticky residue, this fear and uncertainty. The prospect of exposing what he'd hidden for so long waged a silent war with a hunger for connection with Eva. After all, she'd bared her soul to him. Ought he not do the same?

Yet this was entirely different. He dropped his hands, allowing them to hang between his thighs like dead weights. Eva's confession had been naught but the misguided thoughts of a girl who'd deeply mourned the loss of her parents. His mother's situation was nothing so innocent. It was an all-too-real, undeniably ugly truth. His jaw clenched. No, it would be better not to voice such atrocities.

He flashed a smile over his shoulder, pretending for all the world that nothing ate at him from the inside out. "You have known me all my life. If I had any secrets, you would be well aware of them."

"That is not completely true."

Firelight flickered over Eva's pale skin, an eerie illumination—or maybe a reflection of the dark mood that suddenly choked him.

She pursed her lips. "It was always a mystery to me why you moved away."

"I told you." He turned his face back to the hearth lest she read more on his face than he intended. "My mother was about to die. She did not wish for me to witness her decline. That is no secret."

"No, not anymore." Fabric rustled at his back. Floorboards creaked. A light touch rested on his shoulder. "Yet I cannot help but wonder what else you may have omitted in that story. It doesn't quite make sense. No one likes to die alone."

A bitter laugh strangled in his throat. "My mother was unlike other women. Most other women, at any rate."

"Which could account for your distinctiveness."

He shot to his feet. "I hope I am nothing like my mother." The words squeezed out like blood through a clenched fist, so tight was his jaw.

Eva blinked, gasping softly—a direct contrast to the storm raging outside and the one within him. "You sound as if you did not love her."

Hah! How did one love someone he did not know? And yet love really had nothing to do with the strained relationship between him and his mother. "It is not that."

"Then what is it?" Eva angled her head, the picture of a curious tot.

Suddenly far too warm, he stepped away from the question and the fire, pacing into the shadows of the empty room. How could he tell her, a woman of innocence and virtue? It seemed ungodly, somehow, to share such a naked wickedness with her.

"Bram? You need not be afraid of what I might think. As you have said, we are friends."

Her words were a soothing balm. She was trustworthy—always had been, even as a girl. Were he to finally give voice to the dark side of his mother's past, Eva was the only possible choice to whom he would speak of such things. He doubled back to her, hardly daring to believe he was even considering this. "I am afraid I shall need the same vow of secrecy you required of me."

"Of course." Her fine brows cinched tight. "I would not dream of sharing anything you tell me with anyone else. You have my word on it."

"All right." He sucked in a breath, retreating a step. Better to allow Eva some space to recoil or turn away altogether once she heard the full truth of his parentage. "Being a girl at the time, you may have been too young to notice such a thing, but my mother did not socialize with the other women in town. She did not join their clubs or go to teas. She could not, for they would have nothing to do with her despite her carefully crafted story. I am not sure why they did not believe her, for there was no proof otherwise, and yet I suppose a harlot's ways can never fully be erased."

Eva shed her blanket, folding it up as her nose scrunched. "What are you talking about?"

And here it was. The moment of truth. Once he crossed this threshold, there'd be no going back.

He stiffened like a condemned man awaiting a firing squad. "My youngest years were spent in a London brothel. The truth is, I was born out of wedlock, the whelp of any one of several men who had visited my mother. I have no memories of it—

thank God. I only know so because my Uncle Pendleton told me as much."

Her lips parted. Closed. Parted again. A fish out of water. "I . . ." It was more a breath than a word. "I had no idea."

"Of course not. Such a disgrace is better left in the shadows." He rubbed the back of his neck, his fingers digging hard into the damp fabric of his collar.

"How did you come to be in Royston?"

"My mother struck it lucky—as she said, though I prefer to think of it as God's providence—when a well-to-do toff took a fancy to her. He kept her as his mistress, giving her a steady income and the means to advance us to a flat of our own. I could not have been more than three years of age at the time." Disgust twisted his gut into a knot. "When the man died, he left her a substantial amount of money, enough to allow her to move to Royston to live out the rest of her life. She concocted a story of having been married to a navy man who was lost at sea."

Recollection dawned on her face as she set the blanket on the floor. "I do remember that. You always said your father sailed the seas and would one day return with a walrus tusk for you."

"So I was told. So I believed."

"Well, at least that wealthy gent did some sort of right by your mother in giving her money when he passed on."

"That was not all he gave her." Bram snorted. It couldn't be helped. And now that he was this deep into dredging through the truth, he might as well scrape out the rest of it. "He gave her the pox as well—the slow kind that rots you from the inside. Much to my shame, and hers, my mother died of the French disease."

Rage welled, hot and thick. What sort of man did such a thing? What sort of woman allowed him to? And what sort of misbegotten aberration must Eva think him? He hung his head. "So there you have it. Now that you know, perhaps you would prefer if I sleep out in the barn with the horses. Is that what you want?"

He dared a peek at her. Her brow crinkled, not in judgment or contempt, leastwise not what he could detect as she stood with her back to the fire and her face in the shadows.

"It seems to me your situation is no different than mine," she murmured.

"How can you possibly say that?"

"Like me, you have blamed yourself far too long for things you ought not."

He flung his arms wide. "My mother was a strumpet, Eva. There is no getting around that."

"Exactly. Your mother, not you. You did not have any more control over her behaviour than I did over my father's melancholy. It was not you who caused her to take up such a lifestyle any more than I caused my mother to die or inflicted my sister's blindness . . . if, that is, I am to trust your earlier words of God's sovereignty. Do you still stand behind that sentiment or not?"

He shook his head, hardly able to grasp that she extended such grace to him—the illegitimate child of an unknown father. "Unbelievable," he breathed.

"What?"

"Any other woman would be aghast at what I just shared, and yet you—" His voice cracked, far too many emotions welling, and he cleared his throat. "You challenge me with the very hope I gave you."

A lovely smile radiated on her face. "We are a pair, are we not?"

Somewhere deep, humor bubbled up and broke free. A great belly laugh roared out of him. Eva joined in until they both collapsed onto the folded blanket, clutching their stomachs. It was hard to remember that barely an hour ago they'd been frozen to the bone.

Bram glanced over at her. "No wonder they say confession is good for the soul."

"Indeed." Her smile faded. For a long while she said nothing, her pale blue eyes almost ethereal in the firelight. "I suspect, though, you are not quite finished confessing. There is more, is there not?"

"I have told you everything about my mother. There is no more that I know." He narrowed his eyes. "What is it you suspect?"

She toyed with the frayed hem of the blanket, picking at strings for a while before turning back to him. "If we are being fully honest with each other here tonight—and I think that we are—then you should know I have heard you were indicted for theft from a dig site. Is it true? Did you do such a thing?"

His gut sank.

How was he to answer that?

Eva watched Bram as he rose and silently paced, clearly lost deep in thought. Was he truly a thief? And if so, how could she keep him on at the manor? She needed those relics—all the relics—to bring in money, yet it would cut deep to send Bram away. Though she hated to admit it, she'd become attached to this man over the past month and a half. Too attached for her own good, apparently.

The fire snapped, and she jumped. If—and that was a big if—Bram was behind the missing brooch, what about the other suspicious mishaps? He couldn't be the cause of all the unfortunate incidents if his job was on the line with this dig. It just didn't make sense.

Bram returned with an armful of broken wall slats and table legs. After dumping the pile on the floor near the mouth of the hearth, he leaned against the mantel, his face inscrutable in the shadows. "Where did you hear a tale like that?"

Her shoulders sagged. The reverend's words must be true, or Bram would have denied the accusation.

Oh, Bram.

A chill shivered down her spine, and she scooted closer to the fire. "The Reverend Mr. Blackwood has connections at Trinity. For my sake, he inquired about you."

She couldn't be sure, but it sounded like Bram whispered something beneath his breath. He scrubbed a hand over his face, and when he lowered it, his head dipped as well. "Whatever he told you is likely true. I was indicted for the theft of a first-century signet ring at Verulamium—St. Albans, as you know it." His shoulders straightened as he stepped away from the hearth. "But I was also fully acquitted as the item was never proven to be in my possession because the ring was returned. So there you have it."

Once again he sat next to her, legs stretched out, staring into the flames as if he'd put an end to the conversation.

Which was absurd. More questions than ever sprang to her tongue. She shifted on the blanket, facing him instead of the hearth, the side of her body away from the heat feeling the chill of the old house. "Surely whoever returned the ring must have been the one to have stolen it."

"Possibly, but no one knows who replaced it."

She pressed her fingers to her temple, the slight throb of a headache beginning. "Why were you under suspicion? And why do I feel as if you are only giving enough information to appease me so I stop asking questions?" She searched his profile, for he had yet to face her. "I would have the truth, Bram, and I would have it now."

A muscle jumped on his jawline, several times, as if he chewed on a bite of gristle he'd rather spit out. For a long while only the fire spoke in pops and crackles. The wind yet howled, not as forcefully, but strong enough to make her lean toward Bram when he finally opened his mouth.

"It was not me who took the ring. It was my uncle."

"Professor Pendleton!" She leaned back on the blanket, planting her hands on the icy floorboards behind her. "I find it hard to believe that dear old man is a thief."

"He is not." Bram sighed and finally faced her, though she doubted he saw her. He was somewhere in the past, out of this storm, away from this house, reliving an event that clearly distressed him, such were the lines on his brow.

"It was a busy afternoon, that day," he began. "My uncle was the site director, and anything that could go wrong did. He had been working on cleaning the signet ring when he was called away for an emergency. I found out later that one of the support structures had collapsed, trapping two students. One of them broke his leg, not that it matters now. At any rate, my uncle shoved the ring into his pocket and tended to the emergency, then promptly forgot he had done so. The ring had already been documented, so it was reported as missing."

"That was a simple oversight, not a theft."

His gaze sharpened on her. "Any missing antiquity on a proper dig site is considered stolen unless proven otherwise."

"Your uncle could have proven it. All he had to do was take the ring out of his pocket and explain the situation."

"He did not remember it was there." Bram flailed his hand in the air. "And being I was the last one left in the work tent, the blame fell on me. The college has a strict policy that the person nearest an artifact at the time of its disappearance is the responsible party. I became the scapegoat, with charges brought against me."

"How unfair!" Eva sat upright, incensed at such an injustice. "So what happened? You said you were acquitted."

"My uncle and I were scheduled to go before the disciplinary board, and wishing us both to be in fine form, I retrieved my uncle's suit coat in order to brush it clean, make sure no buttons were missing, and the like. That is when I discovered the ring in his pocket. Before the board met, I simply snuck in and restored the relic to the collection." His lips twisted wryly. "The board had no choice but to drop the charges once my uncle discovered the lost had been found."

"And you never told him it was his oversight for which you took the blame?"

"No. He sacrificed so much by taking me in and making a respectable man of me that I couldn't expose his mistake. Some burdens are worth bearing."

"At the cost of your reputation?"

"Yes." Bram rose, offering his hand to pull her to her feet as well.

She wrapped her fingers around his, all the while mulling on what sort of man would take the blame—still took it, in fact—for the sake of another. "Have you always been so noble, and I just did not recognize it?"

"Of course." He shook out the blanket, then folded it into a bedroll. "Hopefully we can get an early start in the morn. It sounds like the wind is taming down a bit, leastwise there is less snow drifting through that crack in the door. How about you bed down?" He swept his hand toward the blanket. "I will manage the fire."

"When will you sleep?"

"I am a college professor. I go without sleep during final exams every semester."

She lowered to the scratchy wool, a thin barrier to the cold floor, but at least the fabric was mostly dry now. Closing her eyes, she willed sleep to come, but all she could think about was an innocent man bearing the censure for a crime he didn't commit, and the old dear who didn't have a clue such a mercy had been extended to him. And now that she thought on it, there were other things Bram's uncle didn't seem to be aware of either, like the constant misplacing of his satchel, his many lost tools, or the time he'd come in for breakfast and was surprised to see eggs in a dish instead of dinner.

Eva pushed up on one elbow. "Bram?"

"Hmm?" He glanced over his shoulder from where he sat by the fire.

"About your uncle . . . that pocketing of the signet ring was not the only time he has overlooked something, is it? I have noticed he is quite absent-minded."

"Have you?"

"Is there something more serious going on with him?"

He gazed at her a moment longer, firelight playing over the far side of his face, the other half-hidden in shadows. Without a word, he picked up another piece of wood and swiveled back to the hearth.

Her heart squeezed. She'd had a great-aunt who slowly yet steadily lost her faculties, declining so much that one day she'd ended up lost in the woods . . . only to be found after she'd breathed her last. Eva laid her head in the crook of her arm, deeply troubled.

Would to God such a thing might never happen to Bram's uncle.

19

Sunlight sparkled like handfuls of diamonds cast across the snowy lawn. As Bram pulled the wagon to the front door of Inman Manor, Eva could hardly believe yesterday's landscape had been so brutally harsh in the serenity of this fine morn. Though it was just as chilly. She held tightly to the blanket around her shoulders as Bram helped her down to the drive.

He didn't pull away when her shoes crunched into the snow. Rather, he straightened her bedraggled bonnet atop her head. "I wager you have never been so glad to return home."

"We did have quite an adventure, did we not?" She angled her head. "Then again, it seems I always do when I am with you."

His easy laugh was as brilliant as the sunshine. "And after such a harrowing journey, I suggest you take it easy today." His smile faded. "I would not have you suffering any illness from being so chilled."

"Oh, I intend to—take a care, that is. Listen." Cupping her hand to one ear, she leaned toward the house. "I believe I hear the call of a hot bath."

He mimicked her gesture. "And I hear a steaming pot of tea saying, 'Bram, drink me. Drink me now.'"

She couldn't help but grin at his falsetto voice. "It would be a crime not to heed such calls. Until later, sir."

He swung back up to the driver's seat. "I will meet you in the workroom after dinner as usual."

Thankfully the front stairs had been swept clean, but even so, Eva gripped the railing until she reached the door. Once inside, she pulled off the blanket and hung it on the coat tree while calling, "Poppet! I am home."

As she fumbled with the ragged ribbons knotted beneath her chin, footsteps clacked down the corridor toward the hall. She pulled off her bonnet just as Dixon sailed around the corner.

"Oh, miss! I was so worried! Why, Sinclair was just about to organize a search party for you and Professor Webb." The housekeeper frowned at the dirty blanket hanging like a collared cat. "I'll have Mary see to your wraps straightaway. I am so thankful to see you remained in Cambridge overnight. How were the roads this morning?"

"Em . . ." Stalling, Eva hung up her bonnet. How deceitful would it be to allow everyone to think she and Bram had stayed at an inn in the city?

Probably very deceitful, judging by the hitch in her spirit.

She unbuttoned her coat, loathing to disappoint the woman yet hating even more to lie. "Now that the sun is up, the roads are passable. I think you should know, though, that the professor and I did try to make it home yesterday, but the storm turned so fierce, we ended up staying at the Robinsons' farmhouse."

"The Robinsons'?" The tail end of the name hissed like the whisper of Satan himself. Dixon's lips pinched tightly. Clearly she was mortified—as she had every right to be. "Well, I won't speak any more on the matter. Suffice it to say you made it home in one piece, and for that I am grateful."

Eva reached for the old housekeeper's hands and gave them a little squeeze. "You are a dear."

"I trust you, miss. It's that young professor I have my doubts about." Dixon sniffed as if she smelled something rotten.

"I assure you Professor Webb was a perfect gentleman the entire evening. He kept me safe and warm by staying up all night to tend the fire. Now then, after such an ordeal I crave a hot bath. Would you have one drawn as soon as possible, please?"

"Yes, miss, but a few things first. If you intend to see Miss Penny, you'll have to go out back, for she is currently engaged in building some sort of snow fort with the college gents. Professor Pendleton is yet abed with a sore back and didn't think it prudent to send the students to the dig unattended. I have every hope, though, that Mrs. Pottinger's mustard poultice will have him back on his feet by tomorrow."

"Indeed, I shall pray to that end." Poor fellow. Eva smoothed her palms along the wrinkled fabric of her skirt, not that it did any good. This gown needed a good washing as much as she did. "I guess it is straight to the bath for me, then."

"Not quite." The short housekeeper held up a rigid finger. "Mrs. Mortimer and Mrs. Quibble are waiting for you in the sitting room. I told them you weren't at home and didn't know when you'd return, but they were quite adamant about waiting around on the off chance you arrived soon."

"Oh dear. I look a wreck. Would you please distract them so I can at least change out of this rumpled gown and do something about my hair? Maybe you could—"

"I thought I heard voices." A voice chirpier than a wood warbler drew both their gazes. Mrs. Quibble peeked out the sitting room door, an absurdly feathered pelerine half cape draped about her shoulders. "Ahh, Miss Inman. Just the woman we were hoping to see." And yet as her gaze swept over Eva, the widening of the woman's birdlike eyes expressed she wasn't hoping to see Eva in such a state of dishevelment.

Eva's fingers frantically tucked and poked at her hair to somehow contain the wild nest. "Good morning, Mrs. Quibble.

Please pardon my appearance. I had quite a ride from Cambridge."

"You drove all the way from Cambridge this morning?" The question pipped out of her.

"Not quite, but I am sure you are not here to discuss such trivialities. Shall we make ourselves more comfortable?" After a nod of dismissal to Dixon, Eva crossed to the sitting room.

"Oh, there you are and—my!" Seated on the sofa, Mrs. Mortimer pressed her sausage fingers to the pearls at her neck. "Pardon my saying so, Miss Inman, but you look atrocious. Tsk, tsk. You have overtaxed yourself once again. I daresay you take on far too much."

"I, em, yes. I suppose so." Desperate for a different line of conversation, she spied the tea set on the table. Perfect. "Let us have some tea, shall we?" Yet she was sorely disappointed when naught but a few drops dribbled from the teapot. She set it back down and strode to the service bell. "I will ring for more."

"Please don't do so on my account." Mrs. Quibble sat on a wingback, the feathers on her capelet taking flight with the movement.

Mrs. Mortimer held up a finger. "If you're going to the trouble, dear, I wouldn't mind a few more of those tasty jam toasts."

Of course you wouldn't.

Eva bit back the retort as she took the opposite end of the sofa. "I am sorry to have kept you both waiting. What is so urgent you felt you must await my return?"

Mrs. Quibble opened her mouth, but Mrs. Mortimer beat her to the punch. "Miss Ellsworth's aunt died last Friday, God rest her. Apparently the woman had a London town house that must be disposed of. Being that her next of kin is Miss Ellsworth's mother, Miss Ellsworth now finds herself in the position of having to accompany the woman—for her mother is, as you'll remember, confined to an invalid chair. They departed yesterday."

Just then, Dixon entered. Eva ordered more tea *and* toast before turning back to the ladies. "That is dreadful news. Please convey my condolences to Miss Ellsworth when you next speak with her."

"We shall," Mrs. Quibble said before Mrs. Mortimer could steal the entire conversation. "And yet we did not come all this way simply to elicit sympathy. The thing is—"

"Miss Ellsworth was overseeing the annual Christmas fund-raising gala," Mrs. Mortimer cut in. "And we should dearly love for you to take it on. You have such an aptitude as a hostess."

Eva leaned back in the chair, one finger tapping on the arm of it. She had missed serving with the relief society. The cama-raderie of banding with other women for the good of others made her heart happy. She was beyond weary of always thinking about money and Penny. How delightful it would be to set her mind on something else—and a worthy cause at that—so the prospect was tempting indeed.

Her finger tapped faster. The society was in a conundrum. They needed her, and it would pain her to refuse them.

Yet life was often pain, was it not?

She stopped tapping. "As much as I would like to accept, I am afraid I shall have to decline. As Mrs. Mortimer has pointed out, my hands are quite full here at home. Not only have I my sister to look after, I am also hosting a team of archaeologists from Trinity College."

"I had heard the rumour." Mrs. Quibble's beakish nose lifted as she stared down the length of it. "Yet as Mrs. Mortimer also pointed out when we were discussing replacements, you could organize the gala with your eyes closed and hands tied, so well suited are you for such a task."

"I am surprised to hear it, for she knows how overtaxed I am."

"Look! Here is the tea now. How lovely." Mrs. Mortimer shifted on the sofa cushions, beaming at Dixon as she set down a new tray.

It was nearly impossible for Eva not to roll her eyes as she poured the woman a fresh cup and handed it over.

"Thank you, dear. Now, as Mrs. Quibble was saying, in the past you have elevated the fundraiser to one of the most well-attended social events of the season. I am loath to admit Miss Ellsworth hasn't had quite the same success. Don't get me wrong, she is a fine young woman, yet she does not own the same attention to detail you possess, so please say you will take the reins on this."

Eva shook her head. "As I said, I have a lot to manage as is."

"Oh, do say yes. The entire fate of the relief society hinges on this one evening." Mrs. Mortimer's lower lip quivered. With a great flourish, she produced a flowery handkerchief and clutched it to her chest.

Such dramatics. Overly so, actually, for despite Mrs. Mortimer's distress, Eva would swear before a magistrate that she caught something calculating shining in the woman's eyes, almost as if Mrs. Mortimer wanted to push her to the brink of overexertion. But that made no sense, not with the way she was always harping on her about being far too busy.

"At least consider it, Miss Inman," said Mrs. Quibble.

Eva poured her own cup of tea. Planning a gala would be a welcome distraction to brooding over the unpaid tax bill and the endless waiting to hear about the relics sale. Honestly, though, it would be more than that. She had always found her charity work to be profoundly fulfilling. When she was helping others, she felt a sense of purpose and belonging that nothing else quite matched, as if she was making a real difference in the world—for she had been, leastwise to those in need.

She fortified herself with a stout swallow of black tea. "Can you tell me what Miss Ellsworth has accomplished thus far?"

"The Rosewood Assembly Hall has been reserved," Mrs. Quibble answered. Mrs. Mortimer's mouth was too full of toast now.

"And?" Eva asked.

"And what?"

An uneasy feeling settled like a layer of oil over the swallow of tea in her belly. "Have invitations been sent? Musicians held on retainer? A menu planned with a cook and serving staff hired? How about table linens and dishes, someone in charge of giving a speech, and take-home pamphlets ordered from the printer to remind the guests of what the whole occasion is about?"

"She didn't say, exactly, but I do believe she left behind a list."

"That is good. It would be impossible to know where to begin without that."

Mrs. Mortimer clapped her hands together, twittering a squeal of delight. Crumbs flew past her lips. "I knew you were the right woman for the job, and I don't mind telling you how much we have missed your attendance at the society meetings. It is so lovely to have you back." She rose, beckoning for Mrs. Quibble. "Come along, Marian."

"Wait a moment." Eva stood as well. "I have not said yes yet. How many days remain until the gala?"

Worry marks traveled across Mrs. Quibble's brow like tiny bird feet. "The event is slated for December seventh, so—"

"Eighteen days," Mrs. Mortimer answered. "And I'm sure I needn't remind you it is this occasion during which the relief society garners most of its funding for the entire year. If we do not hold the gala—or the affair is such that it leaves a bad taste in the mouths of donors—then I daresay the poor of Royston will suffer the most. None of us would want that on our conscience."

Sweet heaven. The woman certainly knew how to go right to the jugular. But la! In the past Eva had started planning for the gala by the end of August, and here it was with November more than half spent. If she agreed, how in the world would she pull off a successful fundraiser in a little over two weeks? That would be more than a challenge. It would be impossible.

Mrs. Quibble reached for Eva's hand. "Please, Miss Inman. You are the relief society's one and only hope."

Bram ducked—barely in time. An icy ball of snow whizzed past his ear and splatted against the cottage doorframe. Frozen flecks hit his cheek. Hoots and hollers rang out at his back.

"Did you get him?" Penny shouted.

"Not yet," yelled Jonathan Barker.

Bram yanked open the door and slid inside, the distinct thwack of another snowball hitting the instant he shut it. Boys . . . and a tomboy girl. Playful pups all.

He doffed his hat and shook off the ice crystals from the shot that had skimmed the top of his head.

"Well, well," Uncle Pendleton called from across the room. "I see the lost sheep has returned to the fold at last."

"I could not leave you and the fellows unattended for too long. Heaven knows what sort of tomfooleries the lot of you would get into—or are getting into, as is the case." Bram dragged a chair over to his uncle's bedside, the strong scent of a mustard-glazed ham hanging like a cloud above the man. "How are you?"

With only a slight wince, his uncle pushed up from the mattress, stationing himself higher on the mound of pillows behind him. "I find I am unable to shake the craving for Scotch eggs with mustard sauce, but other than that, thanks to Mrs. Pottinger's poultice, my back is feeling much better."

"Excellent. That is exactly what I wanted to hear, though I insist you continue to lay low until tomorrow. We won't get much accomplished today, what with the snow, though with the sun shining so brightly, I expect it should mostly be gone by tomorrow." Hopefully, at any rate. They could not afford any more delays.

"And how did things go with Grimwinkle?"

Bram smirked. "As well as can be expected. He gave no answer about purchasing the goods, yet bid that I leave them in his care instead of shopping them around anywhere else."

His uncle scowled. "Odious man."

"Here. This ought to make you forget about him." Bram pulled the cigar he'd bought from an inside pocket and handed over what was left of the matches in the box.

Uncle Pendleton's thick brows lifted. "A cigar? I can hardly believe you didn't smoke this on your way back to Royston."

"Miss Inman would not have appreciated that nor, I suspect, would she welcome me smelling of tobacco when I meet with her to go over the day's findings. Speaking of which"—he rose— "I should see about pulling the students away from their snow frenzy, though I suspect the bigger fight will be convincing Penny it is time to head back to the house."

Uncle Pendleton reached for Bram's sleeve, giving it a slight tug. "Tarry a moment, will you?"

Alarm crept down his spine. Slowly, he straddled the wooden chair. "What is on your mind, Uncle?"

"You . . . and Miss Inman."

Oh. Of course. He might have known being gone all night alone with the woman would raise a few eyebrows, though he hadn't expected his uncle to play the part of a suspicious old aunt. "I swear nothing happened between us." He held up both hands. "We stayed the night in a farmhouse where I kept a fire going and Miss Inman slept. That is all there was to it."

A grumble rumbled in his uncle's throat. "I don't think so. I know my mind has been slipping of late, but on the matter of you and Miss Inman, I have complete clarity."

Sadness twisted Bram's empty gut. Since when had Uncle Pendleton noticed his faculties were dimming? This was the first he'd spoken of it. Had the old fellow been silently harbouring angst and fears about the situation?

Unwilling to see the pain or confusion that would surely be

in the man's eyes, he snagged a blanket off the floor and draped it over his uncle's feet. "We all grow absent-minded as we age. There is no shame in it."

"No, no. That's not at all what I'm talking about. This discussion focuses solely on you and Miss Inman." With a small groan, he stayed Bram's hand from fussing with the blanket. "What are your intentions toward the woman?"

Bram pulled away, regretting that he'd caused his uncle pain and bemoaning even more the turn of this conversation. "I intend to perform the most professionally successful dig for Miss Inman that I can."

"I meant personally." Uncle's dark eyes drilled into him, seeking depths Bram wasn't about to allow him to descend.

"We have been friends since childhood, and I see no reason why we should not always be."

"And yet you wish it was more than that, don't you?"

Bah! How could the man possibly know that? Then again, Uncle Pendleton had always seen past any façade he constructed. Bram folded his arms over the back of the chair, a weak shield but the only one he had at the moment. "Is it so obvious?"

"Perhaps not to everyone, but I've become adept at deciphering you like an ancient codex." A merry twinkle gleamed in his uncle's eyes. "Do you love her?"

Did he love her? What a question. His uncle may as well have asked the moon if it adored the night sky, or the wind if it fancied caressing tree branches. Those things just went together—and always would. Bram rubbed the toe of his boot over the rag rug. Honestly, he wasn't sure what love was, but he did know he had a driving need to be in Eva's presence.

Though he'd never speak a word of that aloud.

He grabbed the chair to drag it back to the door. "My feelings for Miss Inman are irrelevant. Now, I should get those students off to work."

Uncle Pendleton grabbed his hand, the man's fingers hot

against Bram's. "Matters of the heart are never irrelevant, my boy, a lesson I learned the hard way. Believe it or not, I was young once, determined to make a name for myself. There was a woman—brilliant of mind, gentle of spirit—whom I loved with all my heart. But I was too slow to let her know my feelings, too entangled with my career, and she found someone else. I never got over Catherine, and I never will. Do *not* make the same mistake."

Bram's jaw dropped. "I had no idea. Why did you never tell me this?"

"It was long ago, years before you came to live with me. The only reason I'm telling you now is so you don't go to the grave with the same regrets as I. Love is a gift, worth risking everything for, and if Eva is the one you love, then go after her—and let nothing stand in your way."

A hammer to the skull would have been a kinder blow. His love for Eva did run deep, but he was trapped in a tangled web of duty and practicality. As much as he longed for a future with her at his side, that reality was as distant and improbable as the curator position he'd turned down at the new museum. His immediate priority was keeping a sharp eye on Uncle Pendleton until the end of next spring. Without securing his pension, the older man would die with more than regrets. He'd die a pauper.

Bram gave his uncle's fingers a squeeze, then pulled away with a dip of his head. Even if Uncle Pendleton's welfare were not a concern, Bram couldn't ignore the harsh realities facing Eva. She bore the heavy burden of caring for her blind sister and maintaining a dilapidated home that threatened to collapse under the weight of neglect and mounting taxes. Love alone wouldn't meet those needs, nor would a lowly professor's salary . . . though the sale of the relics would surely turn around Inman Manor to a respectable state and provide a suitable yearly income for Eva and Penny.

But he couldn't very well live off her earnings, not with any self-respect intact.

He lugged the chair across the floor. As much as he'd like to take his uncle's advice and pursue Eva, how could he possibly overcome the very real obstacles standing in his way?

20

The Old Bull Inn was quite a different place on a Saturday morning than on a Saturday night. Thankfully. Eva was harried enough without having to elbow past patrons, and this early in the day it smelled of freshly washed tables instead of spilled ale. She shifted on the chair, a yawn stretching her jaw, her backside cramped from sitting there the past fifteen minutes. After ten full days of scrambling to pull together a fundraiser worthy of inspiring generous donations, she was weary to the bone.

And dwelling on her money matters didn't help. Though she pestered Bram daily, there was still no answer on the sale of the relics they'd brought to Cambridge. She'd even suggested they bring another load, this time to the Fitzwilliam Museum instead of the college. He'd been too preoccupied with the dig, though, almost in a frenzy to uncover some proof of Caelum Academia—and she didn't blame him, especially since his job might depend upon it.

The kitchen door swung open and out stepped Miss Thompson, the Old Bull Inn's head cook and begrudging miracle worker. Her flour-dusted apron left a sprinkling of white on the floorboards as she strode like a burly stevedore ready to heft a mountain of crates. Truly, with the size of the woman's biceps and meaty jowls, she looked more suited to a dockyard than a kitchen. Eva would have much preferred to have hired the tried-and-tested Mrs. Havery over at the Coach and Horses Inn, but she had already booked a private dinner for the same night as the gala.

Eva rose. "Thank you for meeting with me, Miss Thompson. Being that it is only a week away from the relief society's gala, I wished to see how the menu is coming along and that everything on your end is running smoothly."

"Humph." The woman planted fists on her hips, her jaw moving as if she chewed on a tough old biscuit. "I'm not sure why ye think I have time for a silly meeting such as this, Miss Inman. I've a kitchen to run, ye know, one that'll soon open for the lunch hour, so I'll thank ye to be quick about it."

"This should not take long. The gala is crucial for the society's fundraising efforts, so I merely need to ensure everything is perfect."

"Perfect? Ha!" She spit the word like a bitter almond, derision sharpening her tone. "Easy for ye to say, sittin' in yer cozy parlour up in yer fancy house. Ye have no idea what it's like tryin' to make magic happen in a cramped kitchen with a staff who wouldn't know a mushroom from a potato."

Eva bit her lip to keep from smirking. If only the woman could see the buckets in the back half of the house catching water whenever it rained. "I am sure you suffer many trials, Miss Thompson, but if you would not mind keeping this to the menu? You are, after all, in a hurry."

"Aye." She finally dropped her fists. "About that menu of yers, I've made a bit of a change. A hearty tongue and ale soup should be just the thing for yer little"—she swirled a podgy finger in the air—"soiree."

Eva pressed her hand against her belly. Just thinking about

serving such a common meal made her ill. "But that is not what we discussed. I ordered chicken with a garlic-cream sauce."

"And I landed a great bargain on tongue." She folded her arms, her ample bosom nearly spilling out the top of her apron. "I should think ye'd be glad fer a savings. This is Royston, not Buckingham Palace."

"Even so, Miss Thompson, I insist you remain with the chicken. I intend to impress the guests with an elegant experience, not a night out at the pub. No offense."

A magnificent scowl etched deep lines into the fleshy part of Miss Thompson's forehead, casting a shadow over her narrowed eyes. "Then I suppose ye'll not want the croquembouche swapped out for spotted dick either."

Eva choked, immediately turning the horrified sound into a polite cough. "No. As I said, please stick to the dishes we agreed upon. Nothing more. Nothing less."

"Fine, Miss Inman. Have it yer way. But mark my words, ye'll be singing a different tune when the guests are clamoring for a taste o' my tongue and ale. Now, if ye'll excuse me, I don't have the luxury of standing around discussing lavish menus." She turned on her heel, a huff puffing from her nostrils.

"I shall expect the food delivered by six o'clock next Saturday. Thank you, Miss Thompson."

The woman waved her thick fingers in the air.

Eva frowned. Oh, that Mrs. Havery had not been booked!

But there was nothing to be done for it now. Gripping her reticule, Eva strolled down Market Hill toward Campbell and Sons Press. Halfway there, she paused in front of a window with a dazzling jade green evening gown for sale. Longing welled from her toes to her head. How lovely it would be to wear such a dream to the gala instead of the brown gown she'd worn two years previously.

Refusing to sigh, she marched the rest of the way to

Campbell's. She pushed open the door to a small office, the scent of ink and paper thick on the air.

"Good morning, Mr. Campbell." She smiled as she approached the counter. "I am here to pick up the pamphlets for the fundraiser."

A fellow as slender as the metal ruler sticking out of his apron pocket faced her, a smudge of ink near his upper lip vying for attention alongside a dark moustache. "Ah, good day to you, Miss Inman. I've got your order all ready. If you'll wait here, I'll be back in a moment."

He opened a side door that let out the clack and hammer sounds of printing presses, then disappeared just as the front door opened and in bustled Mrs. Mortimer.

"Miss Inman!" The woman beamed as she approached, the cloying scent of violets a sickening cloud around her. "You have saved me a trip to your house."

"Oh?" Eva retreated a step. A noble effort, but one that didn't do much to lessen the flowery reek. "Did you wish to speak with me?"

"I do." The reverend's sister pulled out a lacy handkerchief and dabbed her brow. "I have found a suitable position for you."

"I do not recall mentioning I was looking for one." Indeed, she'd not even told Lottie she must find some sort of employment if she couldn't pay the tax bill.

"No matter." With a flourish, Mrs. Mortimer tucked the handkerchief into her pocket. "Mrs. Eleanor Pempernill of Pempernill Hall is looking for a traveling companion. The old dear wishes to go abroad, you see. Tuscany, I believe. I spoke to her of your many admirable qualities, so all you need do is apply to her by post."

"Travel abroad?" Eva grabbed hold of the counter, shocked at the thought. "I could not possibly leave my sister. Surely you must know that."

"But do you not see, my dear? This would be a prime opportunity for you to send Miss Penny to school while you gain some worldly exposure that I daresay will be good for you." With far too much familiarity, Mrs. Mortimer reached out and straightened Eva's hat, her lips pursing. "Why, a young lady such as yourself ought not be cooped up way out in the country all alone. Who knows? You may meet some dashing count or baron, or mayhap even a prince, who will sweep you off your feet."

Bah. The thought of meeting any man other than Bram didn't interest her in the least, and she didn't care two figs for traveling the world. The only thing of value in Mrs. Mortimer's speech was the point she made about Penny, for more and more often she did think it would be good for her sister to go to school.

She traced her finger along the edge of the counter. "How long does Mrs. Pempernill expect to be in Tuscany?"

"I cannot say for certain, but I should think at least the better part of a year. Tut-tut!" Mrs. Mortimer wagged her finger in the air. "I see the objection in the downturn of your mouth. Naturally, you and your sister shall correspond, so there is no need to plague yourself about Miss Penny being heartsick over your absence. I should think it will be a growing experience for both of you. Please, my dear, at least consider this opportunity, for I don't know of any others. Many a young woman would jump at the chance."

Eva gnawed on her fingernail, chewing on the information. It might not hurt to at least inquire about the details of Mrs. Pempernill's employment offer in case Trinity College didn't agree to purchase those relics and she couldn't afford to pay the property taxes. Eva had never traveled any farther than Cambridge, and Tuscany did have its charms, or so she'd heard. She could put Penny in the boarding school that was so enthusiastically encouraged by Mrs. Mortimer. After all, her sister had hungrily been learning so much from Bram and the students that she truly would relish the hope of getting a proper education.

And as Mrs. Mortimer had pointed out, there weren't any other opportunities out there.

Bram leaned over his uncle's shoulder, eyes narrowing on the bone needle sitting atop the man's upturned palm. A cool morning breeze wafted through the canvas flap of the work tent. Winter would soon call in earnest, but thankfully they'd had a somewhat balmy reprieve from the recent storm, and the snow had completely melted.

Uncle Pendleton glanced up at him. "What do you think, Professor?"

"I think your assessment is one hundred percent correct. That does appear to be a second-century—"

A harsh grunt of pain came from outside, followed by an anguished cry for help.

Bram took off running, heart in his throat. He should have been out with the students instead of tarrying over his uncle's latest find. His boots sank into the damp earth with each pounding step, the cries of pain growing louder as he closed in on the huddle of young men at the far side of the field.

Barker was on the ground. Mostly. One of his legs was buried knee deep, the other bent beneath him. Hammet and Wimble each had hold of one of his arms, yanking him upward—and with each pull Barker let out an unearthly yowl.

"Stop tugging on him, lads!" Bram pulled alongside them. "Just support him."

Sidestepping Hammet, he crouched beside Barker just as Uncle Pendleton wheezed behind him. "Easy now, Barker. We will get you out of here, I promise. Where is the worst pain? Foot, ankle, shin?"

Barker winced. "It's my ankle. Feels like it's caught on something."

Uncle Pendleton laid a hand on Bram's shoulder, speaking

for his ears alone. "We don't want to exacerbate his injury, yet at the same time we cannot afford to damage any relics that may be down there."

Bram rubbed the back of his neck as he formulated a plan. Uncle was right. If there were antiquities in that hole, tearing into it would damage the goods. But neither would he subject Barker to further suffering. He glanced at the sky, as if some miraculous answer might be found amongst the gathering clouds. Fabulous. Rain would only compound the problem. He had to do something. Now.

He turned to the other two students. "Let him go, boys. Wimble, grab the long shovel from the work tent. Hammet, get the rope off the wagon."

As they scrambled to do his bidding, Bram once again squatted next to Barker. "Tell me what happened."

"I was just digging with my hand trowel, Professor, nothing out of the ordinary, when I decided to explore this pile of rock and scrub." His curly hair ruffled wild in the breeze, the tips of his ears as red as his cheeks.

Bram topped the man's head with his own hat for some warmth. "Then what?"

Barker leaned back on his elbows. "To be honest, I'm not quite sure what happened. It was like the earth just opened its maw and took a bite of me. I couldn't pull out my leg, so I called the lads to help . . . and so you found me."

"Hmm." Bram's mind raced as he reached for Barker's forgotten trowel lying on the rocky soil. Perhaps if he poked around a bit, he'd find the source of the strange sinkhole. He could only pray it *was* a natural formation and not another act of the cursed acres or, worse, a saboteur.

Uncle Pendleton pawed away some rubble on the other side of Barker's leg. Shortly thereafter, the other two students returned.

Bram peered up at them. "Hammet, tie that rope around

Barker's waist in case we need to pull him out quickly. Wimble, help me loosen this top layer of soil. Take over where Professor Pendleton has been working. And Professor Pendleton—"

"No need to tell me what to do." His uncle straightened, pressing his hand to the small of his back with a slight groan. "I shall keep a sharp eye for structural instability lest we all end up in the depths of hades."

They set to work, carefully, methodically, and after an eternity, Bram finally reached the source of Barker's predicament—two large rocks pinning his calf in place.

"Egad!" Hammet gawked at the exposed rocks. "How are you going to get his leg out of there?"

"Amputation?" Wimble chuckled.

"Now see here!" Barker bellowed. "I will not allow anyone to—"

"Calm down. Wimble is merely jesting." Bram shot Wimble a noxious look before dragging his gaze back to the rocks. What were they to do? He'd never had a student caught in such a predicament before . . . hold on. Not a student, maybe, but . . . He turned to his uncle. "I realize this situation is a bit different than the wedged urn at Verulamium, but what do you think?"

Uncle Pendleton nodded. "Indeed. A pickax will be just the thing."

"Wimble, fetch the pickax and a pry bar."

Hammet's brows shot to the now-sullen sky.

Barker pushed up as far as his jammed leg allowed, bits of gravel beneath him flying from the sudden movement. "What the blazes are you intending? How is mutilating my leg any better than amputation?"

"Be still." Bram rested a light touch on the young man's arm. "We shall have you out in no time with legs and feet attached."

"Caw!" Hammet laughed. "If only the other lads were here to see you caught like a fat rat in a trap."

"That's enough ribbing." Uncle Pendleton frowned. "Or I

shall have you write a ten-page essay on the proper manner of behaviour at a dig site—in Latin."

Hammet's Adam's apple bobbed.

Despite his pain, Barker flashed a smile.

Wimble returned with the tools.

"Very good. I'll take that pickax. Now, Wimble, stand opposite me with the pry bar. Hammet, hold my coat in front of Barker's face and see that you do not watch what I am doing either. I will not have either of you taking a flying piece of granite to the eye." He handed over his coat. "Ready?"

Everyone nodded.

With carefully aimed swings, Bram chipped at the compacted earth by the side of the rock, working his way down to find an edge. When he did, he straightened, breathing hard. "Try that pry bar, Wimble."

Crouching, the young man planted the tip of the iron and gave a great heave. Nothing happened.

So Bram went at it again.

And again.

Increment by increment.

Until finally, the rock budged. Not much, but enough to notice. Bram gave it a few more swings. "All right, Hammet, I think I am finished chipping rock. Try gently easing out Barker's leg on the next pry." He nodded at Wimble. "Give it your all, lad."

Wimble strained.

Hammet pulled steadily, Barker groaning as his leg slid out inch by inch until at last his foot cleared the hole.

"Oof." Barker rubbed his ankle, colour draining from his normally ruddy cheeks.

Bram dropped to his side, as did the other students. Uncle Pendleton bent as far as he could with his sore back. All of them peppered Barker with questions.

"Have you any feeling in your foot?"

"Is anything broken?"

"Can you move?"

Slowly, Barker extended his leg and circled his foot. A little stiff, but it rotated, thank God! Bram hefted a huge sigh of relief.

Uncle Pendleton patted the young man on the shoulder.

The other two lads threw their hats in the air with a loud whoop.

"What sort of unorthodox site protocol is this?"

Everyone froze at the indictment.

Bram pivoted to face Professor Grimwinkle, the man's lips pressed so tightly they looked like two thin earthworms. Blast. Of all the times for the department head to show up. "Barker here was merely testing for soil composition."

"With his foot?" Grimwinkle tucked his orange-herringbone scarf tighter at his neck. What was he doing here? Clearly he hadn't dressed for a dig site in those ridiculous clogs of his.

"That's right, sir." Barker pushed up to his feet, though leaned most of his weight on only one boot. "However, I have since learned from Professors Webb and Pendleton that I shouldn't have gone about it in such a way."

Bram glanced at the students. "Put away the tools, lads, then take an early lunch break while Professor Pendleton and I meet with Professor Grimwinkle." He swept his hand toward the work tent. "Shall we?"

His uncle fell into step on the other side of Grimwinkle. "What brings you all this way, Professor?"

Bram cast the man a sideways glance. Hopefully he was here about Eva's relics.

"A few reasons." Grimwinkle lifted his trouser hems to step over a ridge of dirt. "First and foremost, I came to check on the welfare of the students. I wouldn't wish any mishaps to harm them."

Bram clenched his jaw. No doubt he and his uncle would be written up for endangering the life of Jonathan Barker or some other such nonsense.

Uncle Pendleton let out a merry laugh. "As you saw, they are a hardy set of lads having the time of their lives."

"Mmm." Grimwinkle grumbled ominously. "I wonder if Mr. Barker will say the same when he wakes with a bruised ankle tomorrow morning. You're going to have to shore up that area of soil before any further exploration. I will not have Trinity students at risk of harm."

Bram turned away his face lest Grimwinkle witness the roll of his eyes. Did the man truly think Bram would endanger one of the young men on purpose? "I will personally see to it, Professor Grimwinkle." He opened the flap to the tent and dusted off the nearest folding chair. "Have a seat, Professor."

"No, I prefer to see what you are working on." He strode straight to the relic table and gave it a cursory glance before turning to Uncle Pendleton. "No grail?"

Uncle lifted his chin. "Not yet."

"Nor any proof of your Caelum Academia?"

So that's what the man was truly here for, making sure his plan was on track to oust Uncle Pendleton at the upcoming board meeting. Bram cracked his knuckles. They had to find some proof—and soon—not only to persuade Grimwinkle they had found Caelum Academia but to sway the board as well. "We have not uncovered anything conclusive, but as you can see, we are making fine progress."

Grimwinkle squinted at the bone needles. "For a regular dig, I suppose I could grant you as much, but this is no ordinary dig, which brings me to my other reason for coming here today." He turned his back to the antiquities, facing Bram and his uncle with a dip to his manicured eyebrows. "The review board will meet on December thirteenth at ten in the morning. However, I shall expect you to have the students returned by the twelfth so they may get their affairs in order before leaving on holiday break. Until then, try to keep the students in one piece. Good day."

He stalked toward the door flap, leaving Bram and his uncle to gape at each other. They'd both known the time was drawing near, but this just seemed so final.

Bram dashed after the man. "Professor Grimwinkle, one more thing if you don't mind."

He glanced over his shoulder, not loosening his grip on the saddle. "Yes?"

"About Miss Inman's antiquities. Have you met with the budget committee to set a purchase price for the items?"

"I have."

"And?"

Grimwinkle launched up to seat himself, his horse bobbing its head at the sudden movement. With a great sniff, the professor looked down his nose at Bram. "We are in negotiations. I suspect you'll have an answer when you return to Cambridge. Good day, Professor."

Grimwinkle wheeled the horse in a tight circle.

Bram's gut turned as well. Eva couldn't wait that long for tax money. Either he must bring up the prospect of taking another load to Cambridge—and this time bringing it to the Fitzwilliam Museum—or he had to figure out another way for her to pay her debt.

He watched Grimwinkle ride off, a scowl tightening his brow. For good or for ill, December thirteenth would be a providential day indeed.

21

So many things could go wrong. An ill musician. Cold food. A quarrel between Mrs. Grample and Mrs. Lingerton that would leave a bad taste in everyone's mouth. Eva inhaled deeply of the cool night air as she, Bram, and Penny entered the Rosewood Assembly Hall, trying desperately to ball up her fears about tonight's gala and shove them into a dark corner of her mind.

They paused in the foyer, where a coat-check girl collected their coats.

Bram leaned close, his breath warm against her ear. "Are you ready for this?"

"I hope so." She peered up at him, and yet again her breath caught in her chest. For once, he was completely clean-shaven with his hair slicked back and smelling of sandalwood tonic. His usual devil-may-care appearance was undeniably attractive but this transformation? The stunning man smiling down at her was actually a little intimidating. She'd be completely tongue-tied if she didn't know the same old Bram lived and breathed beneath the fancy suit he'd rented for the occasion.

"Do not worry. All will be well. The Inman sisters will be

the loveliest ladies in the room tonight, and I am honoured to be their escort." He planted their hands in the crook of each of his arms and led them from the foyer into the receiving hall.

Eva scanned from wall to wall. The drink table appeared to be well stocked. Hors d'oeuvres graced several plate towers on another table, exactly as she'd instructed. Ivy swags crisscrossing from the ceiling added a festive touch, and all in all, everyone seemed to be enjoying themselves—if one were to judge by the drone of conversation. Truly, it was a lovely sight to see everything so pulled together.

But was the dining room as impeccable? Craning her neck, she slipped a glance toward that doorway, but only succeeded in attracting a wave from Lottie across the room. "Would you mind if I—"

"Well, well, if it isn't the belle of the ball and her lovely sister." Richard Trestwell swooped over, pulling her and Penny's hands free from Bram's arms, and gave them each a kiss on their fingers. Straightening, he raked a cool gaze over Bram. "Webb, I'm surprised you were allowed in the door. Won't you be a bit out of your depth amongst Royston's high society?"

Bram's jaw tightened. "Good evening, Trestwell. There is no need to bedevil yourself on my account. I'm quite capable of navigating social gatherings regardless of their refinement."

One side of Mr. Trestwell's moustache twitched upward in a smirk. "Navigation is one thing, but doing so with grace and decorum is another matter entirely. Try not to trip over your own feet, will you? Miss Inman wouldn't want any unfortunate accidents spoiling the evening."

Tension ran thick between the two. Eva forced a soothing tone to her voice. "I have every expectation tonight will run smoothly, Mr. Trestwell."

"I am sure you do, Miss Inman, but one can never predict when the unexpected might happen. Disasters often strike at the most inopportune times, do they not? Even the most well-laid plans can unravel in the blink of an eye. But don't worry, I'll be sure to keep a close watch on Webb here." He cuffed Bram on the back too forcefully, jerking him forward. "Wouldn't want him causing any undue disturbance to ruin the evening, now, would we? Please let me know if you require any assistance, for, as always, I am your servant."

Eva held her breath until Mr. Trestwell eased back into the mingling crowd. Irritation radiated off Bram in waves. His hands were fisted at his sides, yet to his credit, he let the bully go.

"Do not mind him," Eva whispered. "He is only trying to spoil your night."

Bram turned his gaze on her, a charismatic smile curving his lips. "It will not work. With you at my side, there is nothing that could ruin it."

"Ah, the Miss Inmans." Mrs. Mortimer closed in on them, turning her large girth sideways to edge between a servant carrying a silver tray and two gentlemen deep in discussion. "Exactly who I was hoping to see. And of course, you as well, Professor Webb." She stopped in front of them, violet toilette water wafting around her. So many ruffles adorned her ample figure that she looked more like a decorated cake than a woman.

"I am happy you could make it tonight, Mrs. Mortimer." Eva bobbed a small curtsey. "I did not realize the reverend would attend such an event."

"Oh, my brother isn't here. I came on my own—scandalous, is it not?" A laugh trilled past her painted lips as she looped her arm through Penny's. "You, my darling dear, have been indisposed the last few times I've been to your house, and I was hoping to have a chat with you." Mrs. Mortimer lifted her face to Eva. "May I steal away your sister for a few moments?"

Penny pulled from the woman's grasp. "Thank you, Mrs. Mortimer, but I would prefer to stay with my sister. She's promised to let me sample the croquembouche before dinner."

"My sister is correct. Another time, perhaps. Do enjoy the

refreshment table, Mrs. Mortimer." Collecting Penny's hand, Eva led her sister toward the dining room.

"Mind if I tag along?" Bram joined them. "You may not know this, but I happen to be a croquembouche expert."

"I did not know." She arched a brow. "Another one of your secrets, eh?"

Bypassing the tables with a glance to make sure the centerpiece candles were lit, Eva led her sister and Bram to an adjoining large room that bustled with serving staff and smelled divine. Miss Thompson reigned supreme, barking orders and waving a wooden spoon in the air.

Eva approached the woman. "Excuse me, Miss Thompson. I wondered if we might taste the dessert?"

"It's not properly plated yet, but there are a few broken pieces in that box over there." She tipped her head toward a corner table. "And mind yer not underfoot."

"You will not even know we are here. Thank you." Guiding Penny behind her, and with Bram at the rear, they made their way single file through the melee. Sure enough, a box of subpar profiteroles sat on one corner, the balls of caramel-glazed choux too irregular in size or misshapen to be added to the final towers. The sweet scent made her mouth water.

Penny leaned over the box. "It smells magnificent."

Bram popped a piece into his mouth. "It is magnificent."

"Beast." Eva gathered a few small plates from nearby and, using a pair of tongs, served them each some imperfect croquembouche.

Penny closed her eyes as she chewed. "I could eat this every day."

Eva smiled. So could she. Miss Thompson had her rough edges, but the woman surely could cook—and bake.

"As long as yer takin' up space, ye might as well try some of the meal as well." The ruddy-cheeked cook set down a platter with odds and ends of chicken pieces, buttered potatoes, and a thick gravy.

"What a surprise." Eva grinned. "Thank you, Miss Thompson."

"This is the best!" Penny felt for the serving spoon and plopped a large portion onto her plate.

Eva's chest swelled at the delight on Penny's face. It was lovely to see her sister so happy . . . though she didn't really know how to break it to her that they didn't have time for sampling everything. She had to make sure the speaker had arrived.

"Penny," she began, then thought better of it. *She* had to check on the speaker, not her sister. "I have something to attend to. Do you mind if I leave you here with the professor?"

"Not as long as I get to keep eating." She shoveled in another bite.

"Actually," Bram cut in, "I have something to attend to as well. Think you can manage that plate and still have room for dinner later on?"

Penny laughed. "Mrs. Pottinger says I must have hollow legs and that she's never seen a girl tuck away so much food."

Eva bit her lip. Was it safe for Penny to remain in this area by herself? Then again, as long as she stayed in place, she would be just fine. "All right, Penny. I shall only be a minute. Enjoy."

"Well done," Bram whispered as he led her through a side door adjoining the reception hall, then abruptly stopped her behind a framed screen strategically placed to separate the gala goers from witnessing the comings and goings of the waitstaff.

Eva's brow tightened. "I thought you had something to attend to?"

"I do, and it involves you."

"Will we not be in the way of the servers here?"

"Not if we huddle close together." Gently, he pushed her against the wall and stepped near enough that the bottom of his trousers kissed the hem of her gown. "Hold out your hand."

"I do not have time for games, Bram. I should be checking on the speaker."

"And you shall. This will only take a moment."

Conflicted—yet curious—she slowly maneuvered her open palm upward in the thin space between them. Only God knew what he'd put into her hand. A Roman coin? A ginger drop? A new ribbon for her bonnet since he'd overheard her grumping about it?

Yet nothing could have prepared her for the small rock he planted on her palm.

A rock?

Indeed, it was a smallish pebble. Shiny, smooth, oval. One end had a notch on it, and the whole thing had a reddish sort of grain to it. Her nose wrinkled.

A jolly chuckle rumbled in his throat. "I know how important this evening is to you and how anxious you have been about it. I remember as a young girl you fancied a smooth river rock to keep in your pocket when the world treated you ill. I happened upon this one on the dig today, unusual for its glossy finish, and, well, I know it is not a river rock per se, but I thought you might like to keep it in your pocket tonight as a token that I am here cheering for you."

"Oh, Bram." His name was a breath, for how to speak when her throat practically closed from such a thoughtful gesture? "I cannot believe you remembered such an insignificant detail."

He curled her fingers over the offering, his hand warm against her skin, sending a thrill up her arm. "I remember everything about you."

She swallowed past the lump of remorse in her throat. The last two months had revealed a Bram she hadn't known before, a man of depth and kindness that shattered her childish preconceived notions that he was often selfish and secretive. Slowly, she shook her head. "I am afraid some of the things I recall about you are dreadfully wrong, for you are not anything like I remember. You are compassionate, generous to a fault, willing to listen and offer an insightful word. Plus, you make me laugh, and I think . . ."

Words failed her, so enamored was she with the gleam in his grey eyes. She could live in that look of affection. Be healed of old doubts and fears. Maybe even believe that he cared for her—a plain spinster with nothing to offer but debt and a blind sister.

"What is it you think?" A husky undertone ran beneath the surface of his question.

Tentatively, she brushed her fingers over the small ridge near his eye. "I think that even with this scar, you are the most handsome man I have ever seen. And please do not try to tell me I am beautiful, for I know—"

He stayed her words with a touch to her lips. "Maybe you are just as wrong about yourself as you were about me, for what I see is a striking woman any man would be proud to call his own. And yet what I desire even more than beauty is a woman with a brilliant mind and a selfless heart. One who will not turn away from me despite my misbegotten birth or flaws and weaknesses."

"Well"—she grinned—"you do smoke cigars and crack your knuckles."

"And you bite your fingernails." He grabbed her hand and kissed her fingers. "But none of that matters. You, Eva Inman, you are the one who matters most to me." His gaze lowered to her lips. "And with your permission, I should dearly love to kiss—"

"Why are you two whispering in here? I thought you had things to attend to. What are you doing?"

Eva stiffened at Penny's voice, then immediately ducked around Bram to face the girl. "Professor Webb and I were just talking, poppet, that is all." Her words came out in a rush as she squeezed her sister's shoulders, hoping to steer the conversation and Penny away from the awkwardness.

Penny planted her feet. "People don't whisper their conversations. I think you were kissing."

The accusation swung in the air like a noose looking for a neck, and though she'd not actually kissed Bram, guilt burned hot in Eva's chest. "Hush, Penny. Do not be absurd. Of course we were not—"

"You were! That's why you snuck off together. Something to attend to, indeed." She flashed a huge grin. "You two were kissing!"

A unified gasp whooshed behind her sister. Eva lifted her gaze toward the opening of the room divider—and instantly died a thousand deaths.

There stood Mrs. Mortimer, Mrs. Quibble, and Mr. Toffit, all three of their mouths hanging open.

Facing a firing squad would be less deadly, leastwise for Eva's reputation. Bram flexed his fingers at his side, unsure how to salvage the situation. Blast! What had he been thinking to have put her in such a compromising position?

Stepping beside her, he cleared his throat, drawing the gawkers' attention. Even Penny cocked her head toward the sound. He'd have to talk fast to defend Eva's character, but what to say? He *had* been about to kiss her, but he couldn't very well confess such a truth.

Wait a minute.

Truth?

Now there was a thought. It would be a long shot, but he'd never been one to shy away from a hard-to-hit target.

"As much as I would love to admit to a romantic interlude with Miss Inman, we did not steal away for such a clandestine motive as that. The reality is, I gave her a rock, and I thought it only decent to do so in private as I didn't have enough for everyone."

Mrs. Mortimer clutched her pearls. "Pardon, but did I hear correctly? You gave Miss Inman a rock, sir?"

"He did." Eva held up the shiny pebble for the three adults to view, then bent and folded her sister's fingers around it.

Penny rolled the rock between her palms, then, evidently satisfied, she lifted her face toward his general direction. "But why give my sister such a silly thing?"

"It is a bit of a long story, but the gist of it is I thought it might bring your sister some encouragement on such an important night. She has put a lot of work into this event, and I think I speak for us all to say how much we appreciate it."

"A thoughtful gesture, Professor Webb." Mrs. Quibble angled her head at him, lips pursing into a sharp beak. "If not a little eccentric."

Beside her, Mr. Toffit ran his fingers along his thin moustache. "A trait of the best history professors, I daresay."

Penny cast the little rock back and forth between her hands, lips twisting. "I suppose I could have been wrong. It is quite loud in here." She lifted her face in Eva's general direction, a sheepish dip to her brows. "I am sorry, sister."

"I forgive you. Now, I still have that speaker to check on. Would you like to come with me?"

"I suppose. I have finished all the sampling, and everything was delicious."

Eva plucked the pebble from Penny's hand and faced the three onlookers. "If you will excuse us, please." She guided her sister around the divider, mouthing *Thank you* to Bram over her shoulder.

Well. Crisis averted, apparently. For a moment, he leaned against the wall where Eva had been only moments before, the sweet scent of the rosewater perfume she must've dabbed on before the gala lingering on the air. What would she have said to his request had Penny not interrupted? Would she have allowed him to kiss her? Heat flashed through him, and he tugged at his collar, suddenly unable to breathe.

Stars and thunder! What was he thinking? He'd be leaving for Cambridge in five days. He had no business starting something with Eva he couldn't finish.

He strode into the fray of powdered ladies and gents smelling of too much aftershave, working his way to the drink table on the opposite side. Bypassing the flutes of champagne, he grabbed a glass of punch—then nearly spilled it when a tipsy fellow shouldered into him.

"Easy there." Bram caught the man's arm and squared him up.

"Say," the fellow slurred as he tried to focus on his face. "Do I know you?"

"Likely not. I am Professor Bram Webb. And you are?"

"Mr. Finebridge." He hiccupped, then pounded his chest with his fist. "Robert Finebridge."

The name traveled on the stench of spirits, and Bram fought a strong gag reflex. "Well, Mr. Finebridge, take a care tonight. There are ladies present."

"Don't I know it." Finebridge waggled thick eyebrows as he poked Bram's chest—or tried to. His finger slid off his ribs. "Now I remember, you're the fellow Trestwell badgered at the door. Ho ho! If you knew what I know about that man, you'd have not been so civil."

Bram tossed back his punch, debating if he ought to engage in a conversation with a fellow merrier than he should be for so early in the evening.

Curiosity won out. "What do you mean?"

"Why—" Once again Finebridge pounded his chest, staving off another round of hiccups. "Trestwell's the fellow who cut that rope at Bonfire Night."

Bram tensed, unsure how much truth could possibly be in a drunkard's words. "How do you know?"

"Watched him do it. Watched you sail away with that pretty filly as well." He twirled his finger upward in the air with a whistle.

A spark lit in Bram's belly. Trestwell *had* been skulking about that balloon just before he and Eva had entered the basket. And the balloon master had said it was impossible the rope could have broken on its own, though after he'd examined it, he had admitted it was one of his older ropes. Still, the prospect ought to at least be entertained, and the more he thought on it, the more he believed it could be true. "Thank you for the information, sir."

Bram stalked into the crowd, craning his neck to spy a certain pompous man in a dark blue frock coat with a cruel line to his jaw.

There. Standing near the hors d'oeuvres table with a puff pastry in hand, Trestwell conversed with a shorter fellow who looked as if he'd welcome a reprieve.

Bram closed in on him. "I would have a word with you, sir."

Trestwell's dark eyes raked over him, one of his brows rising like a black cloud. "Ah, Webb. I see you've lost Miss Inman so early in the evening. Do you need me to give you some guidance in matters concerning women?"

Bram flattened his hands against his thighs to keep from throttling the man. "What I need is to know if you cut the rope to the balloon on Guy Fawkes Night."

His left eye twitched as if a nerve had been struck. "Why would I involve myself in such an affair?" The words were barely past his lips before he turned to continue talking with the other fellow.

Though Trestwell hadn't admitted anything, it appeared Finebridge had been right.

Bram spun the scoundrel around. "I'll tell you why. Because you are a sore loser, a low-lying serpent who strikes only in the shadows. Miss Inman and I could have been gravely injured."

Trestwell wrenched from his grip. "Then she never should have accompanied you."

"So you admit to such skullduggery!"

"I admit to nothing."

"Of course not. It takes a man of honour to own up to his deeds, which we both know you are not."

Trestwell shoved his face into Bram's, the pastry in his hand crushed to crumbs and raining onto the carpet. "I take offense at your words, sir."

"And I take offense at you."

Trestwell's nostrils flared, the jut of his jaw diamond hard. "Then perhaps we should settle this outside like men."

Good. With the rush of fury running through his veins, the thought of a fight suited him very nicely. "I would not decline the invitation."

A snort huffed out of Trestwell. "Excellent. Then Miss Inman will finally see you for the fool you truly are. She needs a man of substance, not a scholar seeking treasures where none exist."

"Miss Inman deserves respect, which you clearly lack."

"Respect?" A feral smile sliced across Trestwell's dark countenance. "You're one to talk respect, considering your history—or shall I say your mother's?"

Bram's hands curled into fists, clenching so tightly his fingernails cut into his palm. Where the deuce had Trestwell dug up such information? Then again, rats always snuffled about in dark corners. There could still be an older woman or two yet alive who held their suspicions about his mother. "Neither my history nor Miss Inman has any bearing on the treachery you committed. You sabotaged that balloon because you lost at the archery tournament. We could have been killed."

"Too bad you weren't. It would have saved me a heap of trouble, but I am more than willing to rectify that now. You should have packed up and left when your dig site was sabotaged as well, but you always were a dullard."

The dig site?

Bram sucked in a lungful of air, the realization so stunning, he could hardly breathe even with the action. "That was all you?" He threw back his head, laughter shaking him to the core.

"You're mad," Trestwell sneered.

"You shot yourself in the foot this time." After a few more chuckles, all his mirth faded, and he poked a finger into Trestwell's chest. "I shall have you arrested for the theft of that brooch."

Trestwell slapped away his hand. "I may be handy with a shovel and knife, but I am no light finger. Go ahead, call the law down on my head. They'll not find a thing."

"I ought to—"

"You can try." He flicked his index finger beneath Bram's chin. "I will see you on the front lawn, sir, if you dare."

22

It was hard to contain such white-hot anger—yet it must be done, at least for the moment. He couldn't very well pummel Trestwell in the pressing crowd. He really shouldn't do so outdoors either for Eva's sake, and yet Bram shouldered his way through the mingling gala attenders, schooling his face to some semblance of pleasantry when all along fury shook every muscle. Hopefully Eva would be detained in the dining room until he served Trestwell the comeuppance the scoundrel deserved.

He gripped the front doorknob and forced a calmness to his movements he certainly didn't feel. Cold night air slapped him in the face as he stepped onto the drive, which he welcomed. He could do with some cooling down.

The driveway curved in a large circle, a grassy expanse at the center. In summer, the ornate fountain in the middle of the lawn would be flowing with sparkling water. Tonight the barren plaster held nothing but the drape of Trestwell's coat on the bottommost tier. Trestwell scoffed at his approach while busily engaging in rolling up his sleeves.

Leaving behind the pea gravel for sturdier turf, Bram plowed his fingers through his hair. He sucked in a deep breath as he approached the man, the sharp bite of air momentarily clearing his mind. Yes, such a tormentor ought to take a fist to the jaw, but was he really the one to mete out such justice? Perhaps he should get the law involved. And what would Eva think?

He glanced at the event hall, golden light spilling out the windows. She'd worked hard to make this fundraiser a success. A walloping on the front lawn wouldn't sit well with her or the donors she'd hoped to impress. While he'd love nothing more than to see Trestwell writhing on the ground, taking him down here and now could ruin the entire evening.

Though it killed him to do so, Bram held up his hand in peace. "Listen, Trestwell. This is not the time or place. Put your coat back on."

Trestwell crouched, fists raised. "I knew you'd turn yellow. But it's too late now. Defend yourself or take a beating. It's all the same to me."

"We are no longer lads given to fisticuffs. Just be a man and apologize to Miss Inman for putting her in danger. That is all I ask. And if one more thing happens to my dig, I will hunt you down." He turned away, the ebb of wrath making him weary to the bone.

Fingers dug into his shoulder, spinning him around. Trestwell's thick brows gathered like a squall line on his brow. "You have no idea how much I'm going to enjoy this."

"Did you not hear a word I said? This is highly inappropriate. I will not fight—"

"What is going on out here?" Light footsteps rushed across the pea gravel.

Bram swiveled his head to see Eva running pell-mell toward them, her skirt bunched in one hand, part of her carefully crafted hairstyle now loose and flopping against her cheek. At least this provided the opportunity for Trestwell to apologize and put the ugly balloon incident behind them.

"Good timing, Miss Inman. Mr. Trestwell here has—"

Something hard rammed into his gut, stealing his breath. Instant nausea rose. So did his fist. Ignoring the pain, Bram cranked back his arm and swung a right hook. His knuckles connected with Trestwell's nose, the cartilage giving beneath the blow.

With a grunt, Trestwell stumbled aside, one hand reaching for the fountain to shore him up.

Eva swooped in between them, arms held out like a constable. "Stop it!"

Protecting his gut with a crooked arm, Bram shook out his hand as he sidestepped Eva, every nerve on high alert. Who knew what the enraged man would do next.

"This isn't finished, Webb." Blood oozed through Trestwell's fingers as he probed his broken nose. "This isn't finished at all."

"Yes, it is. I will have nothing more to say or do with you, and if you come after me, Miss Inman, or the dig in any way in the future, I shall press legal charges. Is that understood?"

. Trestwell's upper lip curled as he wheeled about. Slinging his coat over his shoulder, he stalked toward the carriage yard.

Finally able to let down his guard, Bram doubled over, catching his breath while nursing his sore gut.

A light hand rested on his shoulder. "You are hurt."

"I am fine." But a groan slipped out, belying his words.

"You are most certainly not! Let's get you inside. You need to sit down."

He straightened like a rheumy old man, putting on a brave front to calm the concern in Eva's voice. "I merely needed to catch my breath. Do not fret."

"Do *not* fret?" She flailed her arms. "What am I supposed to think when I am told by a guest that two men are on the front lawn bent on brawling? This is a fundraiser, Bram, not a ringside match. If those people in the hall were to witness flying fists, it would have spoiled the whole evening."

"I know, which is why I never even took off my coat. It was

foolish of me to give in to Trestwell's baiting. I allowed anger to rule over common sense, and for that I am truly sorry." He drew in a deep breath, shoving down the remaining pain. "Will you forgive me?"

A great sigh deflated her, an incongruous sound with the merrymaking filtering out of the event hall. "Yes, I suppose I must. You were only defending yourself, after all."

"Thank you." He dipped his head.

"I am curious, though." She stepped closer, her pale blue eyes searching his face. "What sort of legal charges could you bring against Mr. Trestwell for a mere blow to the belly? What else has Mr. Trestwell done?"

He tucked away the stray curl hanging against her cheek, the silkiness of it doing much to soothe the frayed ends Trestwell had unraveled. "Besides trespassing—for it was not the curse on the land that has been causing all the setbacks on the dig—it seems our balloon ride the night of the bonfire was compliments of the man."

Eva angled her head. "What do you mean?"

"He cut the rope. I was told as much by one of the guests inside who witnessed the event."

"But . . ." The curious scrunch of her nose vanished, replaced with a fire in her eyes and flames on her cheeks. "We could have been killed!"

"Thank God we were not." Ever so gently, he rubbed her upper arms, hoping to calm the same rage that had shook through him and now made her tremble.

"How dare he? How dare that man risk our lives!" She whirled toward the carriage yard.

"Eva, what are you about?"

"To finish the job you started." One of her hands flew in the air. "That man deserves a good pop on the nose and then some."

Eva had seen a wide leather belt snap once, flying off a steam-powered thresher and nearly taking off the head of a nearby farmhand.

She was that belt.

Until Bram pulled her back around, his fingers a vise on her arms. "Enough, Eva. We are finished with Trestwell. His absurd vendetta is his own burden to bear, not ours."

"But I am not finished!" She wrenched from his grasp. "He needs to know what he did was wrong."

"Deep down, I believe he does. God puts a moral code in us all, does He not?"

She snorted, wholly unladylike yet completely unstoppable. "Richard Trestwell's conscience was seared long ago. He is a manipulative schemer who expects to get his way in everything."

"Yes, he is, but . . ." Bram huffed a sigh. "Perhaps his conscience is buried beneath layers of deceit and bitterness, yet it is not beyond redemption. Harsh words and flying fists will not change his heart. Only God can do that. Besides, giving in to Trestwell's provocations only grants him power over us, allowing him to dictate our actions and emotions. I will give him that power no longer. What about you?"

She rubbed her arms, suddenly chilled by the truth in his words, and not just a little bit missing his touch. He was right, of course. It was childish of her to think anything she said would instantly change Mr. Trestwell's villainous ways.

"Fine." It was more of a groan than a word. "But that does not mean I am not still angry."

"You have every right to be, and yet, perhaps, Trestwell does not deserve all our wrath."

"What do you mean? Of course he does!"

"Maybe, but we must consider his motivations. Yes, there may be some minor jealousy or downright pettiness, but that is not enough to make the man go out of his way to break the law. There is something bigger going on here. I suspect he was paid off to commit such skullduggery. He has always been insatiably greedy for a coin or two."

"By whom?" she demanded.

"I do not know—yet." Bram flashed a grin, his teeth white in the flickering light from the driveway torches. "You know, your nose crinkles in the most charming way when you are fiery like this." He ran a light touch down the length of her nose. "And there is the slightest quiver at the bottom of your chin, which I find quite attractive." His finger brushed over her lips—inducing a shiver—and made a home on her chin. It was all quite delicious.

But she turned away her face. "You are just trying to make me feel better."

"Mm-hmm." The sound rumbled in his throat as he crooked his knuckle and directed her face back to his. "Is it working?"

My, my. Was it hot out here? Despite the chilly evening, heat radiated off her in waves—or was it from him? Either way, she was completely helpless to look at anything but his enigmatic grey eyes. "You are quite the dichotomy, sir."

"How so?"

"On one hand, you are a fearless defender of justice, ready to take on any challenge that comes your way, even if that justice requires you to allow a man to walk off and let God deal with him. And on the other hand"—she leaned closer, fully drawn in by the spark of pleasure in his gaze—"you have an uncanny ability to make me forget all my worries with just a few words and a curve of your lips."

Lips she had no business fixating on, yet here she was.

"Flattery will get you everywhere, Miss Inman."

"It is not flattery if it is the truth."

"In that case, then, you are doing an excellent job of it." He pulled her to him, his breath mingling with hers.

"There you are! I've been looking all over for you, Eva."

Eva gritted her teeth. Again with an interruption at the most inconvenient time? She turned to face Lottie marching across the lawn.

"What are you two doing out here? The gala is inside." Lottie's gaze bounced between her and Bram, questions galore in the tilt of her head.

And Eva couldn't blame her. It surely must look as if she and Bram were engaged in a tryst. "I was informed by a guest that Mr. Trestwell had challenged the professor to a bout of fisticuffs. I came out to break it up."

"He didn't! Though I cannot say I am surprised. Obnoxious man." She stamped her foot against the turf. "But we will have to speak of it later. You must return to the gala, Eva. Dinner is ready to be served."

"Then you should run along, Miss Inman." Bram smoothed back his hair with a swipe of his palm. "I will slip in after a few moments. I think you and I have provided enough tongue-wagging fodder for one evening." He winked.

Lottie giggled. "I'll say."

Oh bother. Eva joined her friend's side, more anxious than ever about making the gala a success. Thus far, she'd been sorely neglecting the guests.

As they crossed the drive, Lottie singsonged beside her, "I wonder if I shall hear wedding bells come spring."

"Pish. How absurd."

"The way you two have been looking at each other?" Lottie looped her arm through Eva's. "I'll be surprised if you make it till spring."

Rolling her eyes, Eva opened the front door. Better to leave that prediction outside, where she may or may not pick it up to consider on her way home later that night. She crossed the foyer, and inside the receiving hall, she retrieved a handbell from a side table.

"Attention, ladies and gentlemen." She gave the bell a hearty ring. "Attention!"

The buzz of conversation lulled to a low drone as faces turned her way. "I am pleased to announce that dinner is ready to begin. You may all make your way into the dining room now, and after we eat, please remain seated for a few short words from Mrs. Quibble and Mr. Heathridge, our guest speaker for the evening."

A herd of skirts and suits moved toward the dining room door. Eva turned to Lottie before her friend joined the throng. "Where is Penny?"

"She's in the ladies' retiring room with Mrs. Mortimer."

Oh dear. The woman was no doubt filling the girl's head with the prospect of enrolling in school immediately.

"Thank you, Lottie." Eva doubled back to the foyer, then padded down the passageway. Perhaps she ought not have brought Penny along tonight. The girl had been out of sorts ever since Eva hadn't allowed her to wear their mother's old mink stole, for it was dreadfully out of date. What an evening this was turning out to be.

With a sigh, she entered the first door on the left, and a waft of violet toilette water nearly knocked her backward. The room was a lavish space with its flocked rosebud wallpaper and scrolled trim along the ceiling and baseboards. Gas lamps burned merrily, bouncing light off gilt-framed mirrors. Mrs. Mortimer sat on a padded bench next to Penny.

"Ah, the lost is found, or so my brother would say." Mrs. Mortimer laughed as she pushed up from the velvet seat. "Your sister is here now, Miss Penny, and so I shall leave you, though it has been a delight to visit with you so intimately." Stooping, she pinched Penny's cheek, and—miracle of miracles—Penny didn't flinch away.

Instead, her sister patted Mrs. Mortimer's hand. "You don't have to leave on my sister's account, Mrs. Mortimer. I am sure she would be more than happy to leave me in your care for the rest of the evening."

"Penny!" Eva gasped.

"Oh, the capricious words of youth. Does the body good to partake of such stimulating dialogue. Keeps you on your toes, eh, Miss Inman?" She fluttered her fingers at Eva, then patted Penny on the head. "Do not be too hard on your sister, dear. She has a gala to run."

"Yes, she is often quite busy of late," Penny grumbled.

Eva ground her teeth. Of all the impertinence.

"I shall see you at dinner, Miss Penny." Gathering her hem, Mrs. Mortimer strolled over to Eva and lowered her voice to a whisper. "I spoke to her about the school for the blind. Please rethink your stance, for I believe she is willing to give it a try." Then louder, "Until later, ladies."

The woman swept from the room, leaving Eva with every muscle clenched. Truly, she shouldn't be so annoyed at Mrs. Mortimer's offer, and yet for whatever reason, it just did not sit well.

She crossed over to Penny and sank onto the bench's velvet cushion. Though the evening had barely begun, she was weary of it. Regardless, she reached for her sister's hand and forced a pleasant tone. "I understand you are cross with me, sister."

"I am." Penny pulled away her hand. "It seems every time I turn around, you're off somewhere with the professor."

That stung. It wasn't as if she'd chosen to break up a fight between two brawling men. She shoved her fingers into her pocket and ran her thumb over the smoothness of Bram's rock. "Your words are patently untrue, and I think you know it. I am not trying to get rid of you in order to spend time with Professor Webb."

"I know, but it sure feels like it sometimes." Penny scuffed her toe along the carpet. "You've been so occupied these past few months, I hardly think I matter anymore."

"That is not true either. You mean the world to me." She pulled her sister into a sideways hug. "I have you here with me now, do I not? We are sisters. Nothing will ever change that."

"No, but as Mrs. Mortimer says, things do change, and she thinks I'm ready to go off to school. Even the professors have told me what a quick mind I own and that I ought to think about school as well. You know, spread my wings and all that. Maybe it *is* time for something different for me, something more than just being your sister."

Eva scrunched her brow. "What are you saying?"

"I shall be thirteen in a couple of months. Perhaps it is time I grew up."

"Not too quickly, I hope. Though it may seem otherwise to you, I am not ready to let you go into the world." She pressed a kiss to the crown of Penny's head.

For a moment, Penny leaned against her just like old times, then pulled away and rose to her feet. "Well, I know what I am ready for. The samples I tasted were good, but I am hungry for more. Shall we go to dinner now?"

"Brilliant idea." Though she used a pleasant tone as she looped her arm through Penny's, Eva's heart weighed heavy. No harsh words had been exchanged, and yet something had shifted in their relationship—or more like had been shifting ever since Bram and the team had arrived. But did the blame for that really land at his feet? Penny was no young girl anymore. These growing pains were only natural, and Eva had no idea how to navigate them. There was one thing she did know, however. Change was on the horizon.

A change she wasn't sure she'd like.

23

After two cups of *very* stout black tea, Eva still couldn't contain a yawn the size of all Cambridgeshire. She should be glad for being the sole occupant of the dining room this quiet Sunday morn, but Penny really ought to be down here by now.

Oh, Penny.

She poured a third cup, inhaling the fragrant steam as it flowed from the spout. No doubt her sister was a bit sluggish after being out so late last evening. The gala had gone surprisingly well after the rough start. Leastwise Mrs. Quibble seemed to be pleased when Eva had wished her good night. Hopefully the relief society's funds would be replenished to cover the whole of next year.

Setting down the teapot with a gentle clink, Eva pressed her fingertips against her tired eyes. She wouldn't be quite so tired if she'd actually slept the few hours between arriving home and sunrise. Instead, she'd wrestled with the bedsheets, reliving the two times Bram had nearly kissed her last night. She'd wanted him to—which frightened her to no end. She'd never entertained feelings so powerful for a man before. What was she to do with all these unexpected pangs and desires? And there was no one to ask. Lottie was as inexperienced as she. Dixon—having never been married—would blush herself into oblivion. It wasn't something she could—or would—discuss with the reverend, and Mrs. Mortimer was far too flamboyant to have a serious discussion . . . though apparently the woman had held a thoughtful conversation with Penny.

Dropping her hand, Eva blew on her hot tea. Was she being stubborn in refusing Mrs. Mortimer's offer to sponsor her sister for that school in London? Penny hadn't said anything about it on the drive home, though to be fair, the girl had not said much of anything, for she'd been far too exhausted.

Eva sipped her scalding drink. *She'd* promised to care for her little sister, not some hired instructors at an academic establishment in a big city so far from home. But Penny wasn't so little anymore. Was the girl really turning thirteen in February? Perhaps letting her get the schooling she so desired was the best way to care for her.

Eva rattled her teacup against the saucer. How had the past half hour gone by so quickly? They ought to be leaving for church soon, and her sister had yet to eat.

Striding from the room, she wound her way upstairs to her sister's bedroom and rapped on the door. "Penny?"

No answer.

"Poppet, are you in there?" Eva tried the knob, which gave. She swung open the door to morning sunshine streaming into the room through open draperies, casting light on a very rumpled—and empty—bed. The counterpane was completely missing.

And so was Penny.

"Oh, sister, where have you gone?"

She whirled, then paused, something shiny catching at the corner of her eye. Turning back around, she crossed the few steps to the washstand and fished out a pendant caught between the stand and the baseboard. She held it up to the sunlight, then gasped. A brooch. *The* brooch. The one that had gone missing from the Roman collection. What in the world was it doing here?

She shoved the relic into her pocket and strode out the door, not even bothering to shut it. She was on a double mission now—to find Penny *and* ask what the girl knew about the valuable antiquity.

She ran into Dixon the moment she descended the stairs. "Do you know where my sister is?"

The housekeeper angled her head. "I assumed she was with you now, miss."

"So you did see her? Did she tell you where she was going to look for me?"

Dixon cradled her feather duster like a babe in arms. "I never spoke with her, miss. When Mary went in to draw the drapes, she said your sister's bed was empty. I merely thought the girl had woken early—maybe suffered a bad dream or the like—and crawled into bed with you as she used to when she was little."

"No, she did not." Eva's finger flew to her mouth, but at Dixon's frown, she clasped her hands in front of her. "I hate to ask you this again, but would you mind searching the house, please? I will check with Professor Webb, since she visited him the last time I could not find her."

The housekeeper bobbed her head. "I'll get on that straight-away, miss."

After retrieving her hat and coat, Eva crunched across the backyard's gravel all the way to the cottage Bram shared with his uncle and crew. She rapped on the door, and it swung open.

"Good morning." Bram grinned as he knotted his bow tie. "I am afraid we're running a little late for church. Go ahead and leave without us. I shall make sure the fellows sneak in the rear entry on mice feet to avoid Mr. Blackwood's evil eye."

"Very good, but my sister should come with me. Is she here?"

Bram's fingers stilled at his neck. "No."

Alarm tightened Eva's throat. "Has she been here?"

Bram shook his head.

Eva froze as Penny's words of the night before barreled back to slap her in the face. *"Maybe it is time for something different for me. . . . Perhaps it is time I grew up."*

Her throat didn't just tighten, it closed. Those were the sentiments of a desperate girl, one who wouldn't think twice about running away.

"Eva, are you all right?" Bram clutched her arm, shoring her up. "You have gone pale."

She stared up at him, horror wrapping around her like a cold mist. "I need your help."

Bram would rip out his heart and offer it on a platter if doing so would remove such a frantic look from Eva's face. Whatever help she needed would be hers, no matter the cost.

"You always have my help, Eva. What do you need?"

"It is Penny. She is gone, and this time she is not with you." Eva wrung her hands. "It is all my fault! She is probably still cross with me. I should have checked on her earlier this morning. Oh, why did I not check on her?"

"Blaming yourself will not help the situation. Give me a moment while I fetch my hat and coat." He gently pulled her inside the cottage.

"Good morning, Miss Inman," Uncle Pendleton called from across the room. The students dipped their heads in greeting as well. Thank heaven they were all in the last stages of getting ready for Sunday service instead of lounging about in shirt-sleeves as was the usual.

"There is no time for pleasantries, men." Bram shrugged into his coat. "Young Miss Penny has gone missing. Lads, I need you to split up. One of you take the barn, the other two walk the route to the dig on the off chance she wandered out there."

Uncle Pendleton grabbed his hat, wincing from the reach. His back, while better, yet pained him. "I'll stroll along the front drive and see if Miss Penny has gone that way."

"Thank you." Tears strained Eva's voice.

And broke his heart.

He grabbed her hand and led her out across the drive.

"Where are we going?" The morning sun illuminated the tears shimmering in her eyes. Would that he could pull her to his chest and cradle her until every last one dried up.

But there was no time for that now . . . and who knew if there ever would be?

He guided her down an overgrown path that followed a creek. "Remember that old greenhouse? As I recall, there was a time or two you hid in there when you did not wish to be found."

"An old . . . ?" Slowly, recognition dawned on her face. "Of course! You always found me there—or anywhere else I happened to scurry off to."

"Apparently I was drawn to you even then." He grinned. It was true he'd always cared for Eva, even at a young age, though he'd been too naïve to admit it.

"Wait here." He picked his way down the decline of a rocky path. It ended at a glass building so overgrown with ivy that if one didn't know the greenhouse to be here, one would never find it. He pulled away some of the thick greenery, then scrubbed at the glass wall with the heel of his hand. Through the shadows, beyond a stack of old pots and a pile of rusted tools, he spied a girl-sized lump curled on a weathered bench, a counterpane wrapped tightly about her.

Thank You, God.

He climbed back to Eva and entwined his fingers with hers. "She is there. Come on."

A small cry rushed past Eva's lips. "You, sir, are a genius."

"I just happen to have inside information on the Inman girls, that is all."

He led her down the frosty trail to the front door, holding tightly to her hand to keep her upright. At the entrance to the greenhouse, just as he'd suspected, the ropey vines had been cleared, enough for a girl to crawl through. Bram yanked away a bit more, then pushed open the door. "I think it is best if you go in alone, for you two may have much to say. I'll let the others know we found her, and I shall see you at church. Make sure you sneak in the rear door so you do not get the evil eye from Mr. Blackwood." He winked.

Eva kissed him on the cheek. "Thank you."

He turned away, lifting a heartfelt prayer that Eva would be able to manage whatever was troubling young Miss Penny.

Eva ducked inside the greenhouse, the air surprisingly warmer than outside, enough to notice her cheeks weren't so prickly with cold. Nor did her breath steam out of her nose. She gingerly stepped over some broken pots to the wooden bench at the center, where her sister lay wrapped like a mummy in her counterpane. How many times as a young girl had Eva cried herself to sleep on this same lichen-covered slab of wood when she'd felt the world hadn't treated her properly?

With careful steps, she approached the bench, mindful of the fragile shards beneath her feet. She settled beside Penny, heart heavy with a mix of frustration and affection. She wanted to throttle the girl for giving her such a scare—and yet, what had driven her little sister to brave the cold of a December morn to come out here in the first place?

"Poppet?" Gently, she nudged her sister's shoulder. "It is time to wake."

"Hmm?" The sound was a feather, nothing more.

Her gaze lingered on her sister's rosy-cheeked face. How young—yet how grown—Penny looked. She was so childlike as she slept, but those thick lashes and full lips belonged to a young woman. A tender smile graced Eva's lips as she brushed a stray lock of hair from Penny's forehead. She would—she must—cherish every precious moment she shared with this girl, no matter how often the little mischief-maker irked her.

She nudged her again. "Sister, you must wake now."

"Eva?" Penny's head swiveled, but her eyes remained closed.

"Yes, I am here." Working her arm beneath her sister's shoulder, she eased her up. "But the real question is, What are *you* doing here?"

Penny yawned. "I guess I fell asleep."

"That is what your bed is for, not this old bench." Absently, she ran her fingers along the cold surface, the seafoam-coloured lichen rough beneath her touch. "Why did you leave the house?"

"I needed to think."

"Well, next time could you please let someone know where you can be found? I was terribly worried."

"I didn't know you'd notice. I mean, you wouldn't have if I'd not fallen asleep. It wasn't my plan to be away for so long." Another yawn stretched her sister's jaw, and she covered it with the back of her hand while mumbling, "Have we missed Sunday service?"

"Not yet, but we may unless you tell me right now what was so important that you needed to steal away to think about it."

"I had a decision to make—one I was going to tell you about after church . . . after I had a word with Mrs. Mortimer."

Mrs. Mortimer? Ah. "This is about that school in London." Drat that woman for ever having mentioned anything to Penny in the first place. "And have you formulated some sort of conclusion about the matter?"

Penny swung one of her legs, the edge of the counterpane swiping a clean line in the dirt on the floor. "I should like to go. Mrs. Mortimer says there's even a chorus I might join."

"Are you so very unhappy here with me? You know the professors and their team will be leaving this week. Things will go back to normal then." Hah! Not likely, not if she didn't come up with the tax money by Friday—and she was still thirty pounds short. A shiver ran along the top of her shoulders—and not from the chill of the greenhouse. If she couldn't pay that debt, the school Penny wanted to go to would be the best place for the girl, for she was out of options.

"I am not unhappy with you, Eva . . . not anymore, at least." The swoosh of Penny's foot stopped. "I admit I have been jealous of how much time you've spent with Professor Webb."

"Is that why you took this?" Eva pulled out the brooch she'd rescued from her sister's room and pressed the relic against Penny's fingers.

Penny jerked her head up to face her—though not quite. "You found it!"

"Yes, it had fallen behind your washstand." Though she wanted to say more, to indict, to convict, instead she kept her tongue still. Accusing the girl wouldn't be nearly as valuable a lesson as Penny admitting to the theft herself.

Penny's arm snaked out of the thick blanket, offering back the brooch. "I only meant to examine it for a bit. No one was around for me to ask permission, and I figured since I was part of the crew—or so Professor Webb had said—that it wouldn't be an offense. When I went to return it, I tried to say as much to the professor, but he was very short with me that day. I wanted him to take me to the field, you see, but he wouldn't, so I . . . I brought the brooch back to my room, thinking to spite him—and you. I know it was very wicked of me, and I was going to put it back the next day, but then I couldn't find it. I am sorry." Penny's head dipped with remorse.

Eva sighed and pulled her sister in for a sideways hug. "I accept your apology, but you will have to make amends with Professor Webb yourself."

"I will. I promise I'll make things right." Penny nuzzled

against her for a beat, then lifted her face. "But there's something I want you to promise as well."

"And what is it?"

"That you'll not miss me overmuch when I'm gone to that school in London."

Despite the gravity of the girl's tone and furrowed brow, Eva chuckled lightly. "Just because you have decided to go does not mean I give you permission to do so."

"But that's exactly why you must. Don't you see?" Penny rose, facing her, the counterpane rustling a scattering of old leaves over the ground. "You cannot always be in charge of me. I want to be my own person. I want to learn to live in this world, even though I'm blind. They can teach me such things at that school. Mrs. Mortimer said so."

"I admit I have been a bit overprotective at times, but it is only because I love you so much." Tears welled, tightening her throat. All the work, doubt, and fears of the past year closed in on her. "I have tried to do my best for you since Papa died, it is just . . ." She choked. "I would prefer if we could wait another year or two."

"And where will the money come from then?"

"How did you know—"

Penny must've heard the crackle of emotion in her voice, for the girl's face immediately softened. She reached out her slim hand, searching for Eva's cheek, and once found, she pressed her palm against it. "I may be blind, but I can see what's been happening. I notice the same old soup and bread for dinner and that you've not gotten a new gown for over a year. Mother's desk is gone, as is a lot of the furniture that once filled the house. We are barely getting by, are we not?"

Eva sighed. She should've known Penny would note such things. "The budget is not your concern. I promised Father I would look after you, and I shall, so there's no need to fuss."

"I'm not fussing. I'm just saying that if I went away to school, there would be one less mouth to feed. Please, just think on all I've said."

Eva pressed her own hand over her sister's, cherishing the connection. It would kill her to send Penny off to London . . . but as Bram and his uncle had said, the girl *did* have a quick mind, one that deserved to be educated beyond what she could give her. "All right, Penny. I will think on it. But if I decide the answer is no, I will not suffer any dramatics, is that clear?"

"I suppose." A playful smile danced on Penny's lips. "Though I shall be disappointed."

"We must all learn to cope with disappointment, for there is nothing on this side of heaven that is perfect." Eva pushed up from the bench and snugged the counterpane tighter around Penny's shoulders. "Come, let's get you in something more suitable for morning service."

She led the girl through the ivy-strangled door, then up the rocky incline. By the time they rounded the corner of the barn, Bram was already driving his uncle and the college boys in the wagon across the yard. As she watched his fine form, a bittersweet ache settled deep in her chest. The sight of him, strong and steadfast at the reins, stirred emotions she'd been trying to suppress. There was no more denying the pull he had on her, a force that defied reason and propriety—for, yes, indeed, she would have allowed him to kiss her last night—and she would have kissed him right back.

And the truth of her own words of only moments before slapped her hard in the face.

"We must all learn to cope with disappointment."

He'd be leaving in four days. How was she to cope with that?

24

Good-bye was too harsh of a word. Too jarring, like the slamming of a door in an empty house, the echo of it sharp on the ear. Bram had stayed up half the night trying to figure out a way to soften the blow of parting from Eva, and yet here he was in her sitting room, his tongue lying impotent in his mouth. He'd arrived early to have a moment alone with her before departing for Cambridge, to speak heartfelt words that would leave behind a sweet memory for them both.

But all he could do was stand there, twisting his hat round and round in his hands.

Eva wasn't much better. Her fingers toyed with the delicate lace edging of a handkerchief, folding and unfolding it in restless motions. The ticking of the wall clock filled the silence, each second amplifying the silent scream of their impending farewell.

"I suppose I should be thankful you are not cracking your knuckles." Eva directed a pointed look at his hat.

"And I am glad you are not biting your nails."

A small smile traveled across her lips. "So you are all ready to go, then?"

Ready to leave her? Never. But the lads were likely even now parking the wagon at the front door, preparing to enter for their own good-byes.

"As ready as I can be," he murmured.

"Bram." Worry creased her brow. "I do not mean my words to be a harbinger of ill will, but I am wondering . . . what if your meeting tomorrow does not go well? What if Professor Grimwinkle does not believe you have enough proof of Caelum Academia? I mean, you did not find anything with the name engraved onto it."

Ah, leave it to her to cut right to the heart of the matter. He flashed a smile and, striving for a bit more levity, bopped her lightly on the nose. "It's nothing to worry about. Grimwinkle needs us until at least the end of the school year, and after that? Well"—he winked—"my uncle and I can always take on something more lucrative, like rat catching or sweeping chimneys."

Her jaw dropped. "That is horrible!"

He laughed. "You know, your chin quivers quite adorably when you have swallowed a tall tale."

"Then I take back what I said." She poked him in the chest. "*You* are horrible."

"Yes, but you already knew that. And speaking of horrible, I forgot to tell you we spent every last minute on the dig, so I am afraid there was no time to fill in that sinkhole. I did, however, have one of the students rope it off. At least you will not have to worry about any more damage to the land, what with Trestwell behind bars for trespassing."

"He has been arrested? When? Why?"

"Last night. As a parting gift to Trestwell, I visited the constable and told him all about the man's trespassing and attempted harm when he cut the balloon tether. The constable agreed there likely was not enough evidence to convict him but thought a night in jail ought to put the fear of God into him. Besides, with me out of the picture, he will not try anything more, though I would dearly like to know who put him up to such skullduggery to begin with. At any rate"—he fiddled with his hat—"perhaps your farmhand could see to filling that hole, for I would hate to think of anyone getting hurt. Barker still complains of his ankle now and then."

Blast! What was he doing talking about Trestwell and sink-holes and sore ankles? What happened to heartfelt words? He crushed the brim of his hat, forcing his hands to still.

Eva nodded. "I shall let Sinclair know, and I promise I will not go wandering around out there."

"Your sister should not either."

"I do not think that will be a concern." She wrung her hand-kerchief so forcefully that were it a chicken, the poor creature would be lifeless on the floor by now.

And yet had he not been as merciless with his hat? He set the beat-up felt on the nearest chair. "Found a way to wrangle the girl into submission, have you?"

"Of a sort."

"How cryptic."

"Not so much." Wadding up the fabric, Eva shoved the handkerchief into her pocket, apparently finished with her fiddling as well. "The truth is, if I do not pay those property taxes tomorrow, there will be no one here to fall into any sort of hole."

"Do not give up hope yet. Finding out about the sale of your relics shall be my first order of business when I am back on campus. I shall wire word to you at once, so check with the telegraph office in the morning. And if the antiquities did sell, I will have the money sent straightaway, so you will have it in your hands before the revenue office closes."

"Thank you." She averted her gaze, eyes now shimmering. "That is very kind."

His chest squeezed. Would that he could do more for her. Pay the revenue man. Fix the roof, the barn, the sadness creasing her brow. He took a step toward her. "Furthermore, I will do my best to sell the rest of the relics we have loaded in the wagon, and I shall personally deliver those funds into your hands."

She shook her head slightly, morning sunlight setting her hair aflame so beautifully his throat ached.

"You could simply send a courier, Professor. I am sure you will be busy with college business. You need not travel all this way on my account."

"You credit yourself too much, milady. It is for selfish reasons alone I would do so."

"Such as?"

"To see you again, of course." He inhaled deeply as he crossed the rug, closing the distance between them. "I have enjoyed my stay very much, and I am loath to leave. You are good for me, I think."

"It has been nice having you here." She straightened one of his lapels that'd apparently gone rogue after such a violent maneuvering of his hat. "Inman Manor will be empty without all the comings and goings of your crew."

"So it is the crew you shall pine for, hmm?"

A playful grin spread on her face. "You did not seriously think I would miss you, did you?"

"I had hoped." He gathered one of her hands and pressed his lips to her finger. "For I shall dearly miss these bitten nails of yours."

"Is that all you shall miss?" There were far deeper questions than that swimming in the blue pools of her eyes.

"No." Slowly, he pressed a kiss to each of her fingers. "I will long for far more than these hands of yours."

Men's bantering, Penny's laughter, and a great chuckle from his uncle entered the sitting room. Bram stepped away from Eva as Uncle Pendleton approached and folded into a formal bow.

"Well now, my dear, it is never easy to part, but we are not really, for I shall take a piece of you along in my heart back to Cambridge."

Eva smiled. "You are quite the charmer, Professor."

"Where do you think my nephew comes by it?" His dark eyes twinkled behind his spectacles.

A tug on Bram's sleeve pulled his attention down to a brown-haired twelve-year-old with a pixie face.

"Good-bye, Professor Webb. Thank you for allowing me to be part of your crew."

"Good-bye, Miss Penny. You are very welcome, and try not to give your sister too much trouble after I leave, hmm?"

The girl's face clouded. "I wish you weren't going."

He squeezed her shoulder. "Here, I have a little something for you." He handed over a canvas-wrapped tool kit from inside his coat.

Penny's fingers examined the thing. Nimbly, she untied the cord and spread it open, touching the small picks and brushes. "My own field kit!"

"Indeed." He grinned. They were old tools, not particularly effective for fieldwork but good enough to suit her. "But no wandering out to that dig site alone, you hear?"

"Of course." Clutching the pouch in one hand, she flung her other arm around him, hugging him tightly. "Thank you. I shall treasure it always."

He kissed the crown of her head, more moved by her reaction than he cared to admit—for it just might be his undoing.

Picking up his hat, he punched the felt back into shape. "Time to leave, lads."

One by one, the students bid their thanks and good-byes to Eva.

"Safe travels, everyone." Though she spoke to the room, Eva's gaze lingered on him.

He dipped his head and turned away, saying nothing more—for there was nothing more he could say. He'd failed at proving the relics on Eva's property belonged to Caelum Academia, so there was no way Grimwinkle would pay for him to return to the site. He'd be lucky to keep his job as is. Perhaps another team would poke about the remains of all their hard work, if Eva allowed it, but by all that was holy, how he wished it would be him to return. His shoulders sagged, defeat bitter on his tongue.

Good-bye was too harsh of a word indeed.

Eva grabbed the back of the overstuffed chair, grateful for something solid to hold on to. She'd known seeing Bram leave would be hard, but this? It felt as if someone had carved a great hole in her chest, leaving nothing but an empty space for cold wind to whistle through.

She lifted her fingertips to her mouth, remembering the feel of Bram's lips against them. There'd been several times over the past few days when she was sure he'd kiss her—had longed for him to do so—and yet it was probably a good thing he hadn't, for the pain of his leaving would be even greater.

And it was bad enough as is.

Penny leaned her head against Eva's arm. "It will be very empty around here without them, won't it?"

"It will." Eva glanced down at her, inhaling deeply. She'd reached a decision about the school, and now was as good as any time to say as much. "But it will be even emptier without you."

Penny jerked up her head. "What?"

"You heard me, for those ears of yours are very keen." She ran her hand over her sister's plaited hair. "Though I regret there is no extra money to order you some new gowns."

"Do you . . ." Penny's lips parted and closed several times. "Do you really mean I can go to school?"

"I really do."

"Oh, Eva!" Penny flung both arms around her, hugging her so tightly it hurt to breathe.

Eva peeled her off, laughing. "Now there is the happy poppet I remember. I love you, you know."

"I love you too, sister! And I shall miss you very much."

"Let us save such talk for tomorrow when I bring you to Mrs. Mortimer's. I have had enough good-byes for one day." She straightened her sister's collar, all askew from such exuberance. "How about you enlist Dixon or Mary to haul down a trunk for you? I will be up shortly to help pack your belongings, after I have had a word with Sinclair."

"You are the best sister ever!" Penny raced from the room, a rousing rendition of "Rule, Britannia!" on her lips.

Eva nibbled on her nail. She'd still rather hold off on sending Penny to school, but she was out of options. Unless Bram's money came through, the estate would be gone. So would she—to Tuscany with Mrs. Pempernill if the woman took her on as Mrs. Mortimer had suggested she might.

She strolled from the sitting room, intent on finding Sinclair, when a knock rapped at the front door. Eva opened it to a lad wearing a brilliant scarlet cap, his nose just as red and no wonder. A December wind barged in uninvited, nipping Eva's cheeks.

"May I help you, young man?"

"Aye, miss. I were to deliver this letter to Inman Manor." He held out a creamy white envelope.

Her heart raced as she retrieved it. She wouldn't be surprised at all if it was yet another revenue addendum adding on even more to the property taxes. Yet this paper was far too fine, and with a bloodred wax seal securing the back of it, it was clearly a missive from someone of stature.

She glanced past the young man. No pony cart. No horse. Odd, that. Her gaze drifted back to the young fellow. "Did you walk all the way from town?"

"I did, miss." He tipped his hat.

"Well then, I should think you will need a cup of warmed milk before braving a return journey. Go to the kitchen entrance and tell the cook that Miss Inman sent you."

"Caw! Thanks, miss." He tore around the corner of the house before she could even say *good day.*

Eva pushed the door shut against the cold air, then set off down the corridor, still intent on her mission to find Sinclair. As she walked, she ran her nail beneath the seal, then immediately popped her finger into her mouth, the sting of a paper cut sharp on the skin . . . which probably wouldn't have happened if she'd had an actual nail to slit the thing in the first place.

Or a letter opener.

Sighing, she unfolded the letter.

Dear Miss Inman,

Your inquiry into the position of lady's companion at Pempernill Hall has been accepted. Your qualifications and references meet the criteria, and we are delighted to inform you that your duties of lady's companion to Mrs. Eleanor Pempernill may begin at once. Please send your acceptance correspondence as soon as possible, and we will work out the details of your compensation.

Sincerely,

Miss Fanny Goshorn
Assistant to Mrs. Pempernill

Eva stopped right there in the corridor, shock a cold shower tingling over her body. While it was good to know she had some employment lined up, she didn't really want to be a lady's companion. Always at the beck and call of a demanding older woman. Making travel arrangements to places she'd never been. Worst of all, she'd miss her home. Inman Manor was all she'd ever known. And yet, still shy of the full tax amount, she'd miss her home anyway—for tomorrow she would lose it unless Bram came through with the relic money.

She stuffed the note back into the envelope, chafing at the

unfairness of it all, for her, for Penny. And then there was Bram. He'd worked so hard on the dig. If that curmudgeon Mr. Grim-winkle let him and his uncle go at the end of the year, what would they do?

The more she thought on it, though, the more a beautiful thought took root. Growing deeper. Practically bursting out of the soil in her heart. She might lose her house, but that didn't mean Bram and his dear uncle had to lose everything as well. As soon as she dropped Penny off at Mrs. Mortimer's tomorrow morning, she would pay Mr. Toffit a visit and persuade the man to keep that curator position open until the end of the school year. After all, the society didn't even have the building ready for a museum yet, so it shouldn't be a problem.

Hopefully, at least.

25

Bram tagged his uncle's heels as he strode the long college corridor toward the board room, his irritation palpable. Grimwinkle's refusal to see him yesterday had left him seething, his frustration compounded at the lack of information regarding the sale of Eva's relics. Nor could he shake the annoyance over the fact he and Uncle Pendleton had not found definitive proof of Caelum Academia—though they had more than enough evidence of a second-century Roman settlement. And to top it all off, an unwelcome eight-legged visitor had taken up residence in his quarters during his absence. The sight of the hairy intruder scurrying across his desk upon his return had nearly sent him into a fit of arachnophobic rage as he'd hunted the thing with his shoe all night. But to no avail. He had yet to slay that monster.

"Step lively, nephew." His uncle beckoned him with a swing of his arm. "We don't want to be late."

"Why not?" He smirked. "I guarantee Grimwinkle will not be on time."

"That doesn't mean we ought not be."

Begrudgingly, he upped his pace, and they entered the board room. The first thing that caught him off guard was the two piles of muscle stationed at each side of the door, as if he and his uncle were on the dock for murder at a Bow Street court. The second—and at this he blinked in surprise—was that not only were the six committee members already spaced out along the extended table, but Grimwinkle sat at the center, wearing a herringbone suit, a tobacco-brown bow tie, and a curl to his lip that could stop a cohort of Roman soldiers.

He knew. Impossibly, somehow the man knew they didn't have the proof of Caelum Academia or Grimwinkle would never be here on time with that smug look on his face.

Uncle Pendleton strolled to the small desk in front of the review board and set down his leather satchel. Bram stood at his side, and once the echo of his own footsteps faded, silence reigned.

Grimwinkle looked down the table to where the secretary, Mr. Clem, perched on his chair like a fat slug. Clem gave him a sharp nod, then Grimwinkle banged his gavel even sharper. "This disciplinary meeting is called to order. We are convened today—as previously scheduled—to decide the matter of academic fitness on behalf of Regius Professor Sebastian Pendleton. Mr. Clem, can you please confirm?"

Mr. Clem shuffled a few papers. "As recorded on Monday, October seventh, in my own hand—" He cleared his throat. "'This board shall reconvene on December thirteenth, at which point irrefutable confirmation will be presented by Professors Webb and Pendleton authenticating the existence of Caelum Academia, the supposed refuge of Roman Christians and artisans. If no such evidence is provided, Professor Pendleton will be deemed unfit as an instructor of excellence in the classroom and immediately dismissed.'"

"Thank you, Mr. Clem." Grimwinkle swiveled his head toward Uncle Pendleton. "And so, Professor, the board members and I are now prepared to evaluate your evidence. Please present your findings."

After an excessive amount of rummaging in his bag, Uncle Pendleton pulled out an old wooden horse—a child's toy that had absolutely nothing to do with the dig. Bram quickly stayed his hand.

"Uncle, not that," he whispered urgently. "The report you wrote. Please tell me you have it."

"Hmm?" His uncle peered over the rims of his spectacles, confusion rife in his eyes.

"The report." Bram enunciated each word in a desperate undertone.

"The . . . ah!" He dove back into his bag. Thankfully, this time he retrieved a small sheaf of bound papers, then reverently set it in front of Grimwinkle.

Grimwinkle merely sneered as he stabbed the document with his finger. "This is not the Holy Grail as you promised."

Bram tugged his collar, gut churning. He knew this would get ugly but so soon?

His uncle brushed away Grimwinkle's finger as if it were a gnat to be swatted, "Nevertheless, this is a complete log of what Professor Webb and I preserved. Most items date back to the second century and are indisputably of Roman Christian origins. You already have a wagon load of many of the relics listed here, so you have had time to assess authenticity for yourself. There is no denying we unearthed a historic and valuable settlement, as I knew we would."

"I do not deny it, though I am surprised in light of all the . . . shall we call them *setbacks* that you suffered. But even so, Professor Pendleton, that is not what this review board charged you to accomplish. You have no proof of Caelum Academia whatsoever, and so as stated—" Once again he peered down the table at Mr. Clem.

The secretary reshuffled his papers. "As it is written, and I quote, 'If no such evidence is provided, Professor Pendleton will be deemed unfit as an instructor of excellence in the classroom and immediately dismissed.' End quote."

"Thank you, Mr. Clem." Grimwinkle cast a cankerous gaze at Bram's uncle. "In light of such, it is my duty to dismiss—"

"Now see here!" Bram stepped to the front of the desk. This was going too fast and too far. "You have seen for yourself the antiquities we brought in, Professor Grimwinkle. That proves—"

Grimwinkle held up his hand. "That's enough, Professor Webb."

No, it wasn't. Not nearly enough. He jutted his jaw. "You have had nearly three weeks to inspect the validity of those antiquities and—"

"I said that's enough."

"—we uncovered a legitimate second-century Roman settlement of Christian origin, not to mention—"

The gavel banged like the slamming of a guillotine. "Silence! Or I shall have you bodily removed from this room."

Bram gritted his teeth. So that's what the muscles were for. The man had planned all along to terminate his uncle!

"Now then, Regius Professor Pendleton, it is my duty to inform you of your dismissal from Trinity College. Kindly vacate your office by Monday morning, lest your belongings be removed by the cleaning staff during the Christmas recess."

"Vacate?" His uncle stood like a lost little boy wondering where his mam had gone.

Completely breaking Bram's heart.

Then birthing a rage so molten, he stiffened to a ramrod.

"You cannot do such a thing! That man has served this institution with high honours for the past forty years." Bram stormed up to Grimwinkle and slammed his fist onto the report Uncle Pendleton had so painstakingly written. "You, sir, have your proof right here of my uncle's service and dedication. You cannot simply discard him like yesterday's newspaper. It is unjust.

You are tarnishing his legacy, his entire career, based on some arbitrary technicality and your own personal vendetta. He always was the better scholar, and you know it. It was you who stole his notes on the Ostia Antica dig, writing the award-winning article that belonged to him!"

A rumble traveled around the faculty members.

And was immediately quashed by another thunderous strike of the gavel. "That was hearsay of years ago, and your belief in the matter calls into question your own judgment." Little flecks of spittle flew from Grimwinkle's mouth. "Furthermore, Professor Webb, in light of your complicity in the matter of Caelum Academia and your unwavering support of former Professor Pendleton's unfounded endeavors, I must also terminate your position at Trinity College as well."

"This is preposterous!" Bram threw his hands in the air. "You cannot punish me for supporting a fellow scholar in his pursuit of knowledge."

Uncle Pendleton stepped between him and Grimwinkle, head dipped like a bull on the charge. "Do not commit such a vindictive act, Grimwinkle. It's me you hate, not my nephew. Catherine never loved you. She loved me—though I was too preoccupied to act on my feelings at the time."

The gavel banged so hard, the head flew off and ricocheted from the table, bounding its way along the floor until all that could be heard were the great snorts of air huffing from Grimwinkle's nose. He snapped his gaze to the men on his left, then his right. "Has any man here an objection to my decision?"

Bram scanned from face to face. Only one man opened his mouth, then just as quickly closed it. If anyone naysaid Grimwinkle, their own head would be on the chopping block. And while Bram understood such a truth, nothing but contempt for each man roiled in his gut.

"Mr. Clem," Grimwinkle thundered down the table. "Be it therefore written the dismissal of Professors Pendleton and

Webb was unanimously voted upon and deemed the proper conclusion to this meeting."

Then he skewered Bram with a razor-sharp stare. "Like your uncle, vacate your office by Monday morning. Furthermore, the two of you are banned from completing the dig at Inman Manor, which I will personally see to finishing."

Bram's jaw dropped. This was not to be borne! He side-stepped his uncle, facing the bully man-to-man. "Because *you* wish the glory of publishing what *we* found. That was your plan all along, was it not? You were the one who hired Trestwell to foul up our work, hampering our progress just enough to get us out of the picture so you could swoop in and claim victory for yourself!"

A collective gasp hissed throughout the room.

"Nonsense. Guards, take this man outside." A demon couldn't have sounded any more ominous than the rasp in Grimwinkle's tone. "This meeting is adjourned."

"You cannot do this!" Bram lunged.

And was immediately yanked back by a steel grip to each of his arms. His feet slid across the floor, his voice the only weapon in reach. "The Lord judge you, Grimwinkle!"

What a horrid day.

Cold air nipped Eva's cheeks as she halted the pony cart in the vicarage's drive. The entire ride here Penny had either been chattering like a magpie or singing at the top of her voice. Not anymore. She went strangely silent when the wheels stopped their grind. Hardly ten feet in front of them, an enameled carriage stood at the ready, horses snorting. Mr. Blackwood strode their way, completely absent of colour in his grey garb, save for those electric blue eyes of his.

Eva looped the reins as the reverend reached for Penny's hand. "Allow me to help you down, Miss Inman. Mrs. Mortimer awaits you in her carriage." He lifted his face to Eva. "No need to alight, Miss Inman. My man Henry will see to your sister's trunk."

Sure enough, the driver from the other carriage loped over to the back of the pony cart, where Sinclair had secured Penny's belongings.

Eva gave Mr. Blackwood a tight smile. "I should like to say a proper good-bye to my sister, Mr. Blackwood."

"For her sake and yours, I think it best if we keep emotions to a minimum. Excess is akin to gluttony. Come along now, Miss Inman." He guided Penny away.

"Good-bye, Eva." Penny flailed her free hand.

No. This was not how it should be. Not how it *would* be!

Eva flew from the cart, shoes landing with a crunch in the pea gravel, and dashed over to her sister before Mr. Blackwood could stuff Penny into the carriage like an order of feed to be delivered. In one quick movement, she pulled her sister from the reverend's grasp and wrapped her arms around the girl. "Good-bye, love. I shall write to you often and expect you to as well, as long as it does not deter you from your studies. I am sure one of the school attendants will not mind taking dictation from you. Make sure you mind your manners and remember that I—oh, poppet."

Fighting tears, she pressed her cheek against the top of Penny's head. How could she possibly do this? This would be the last chance she had to breathe in her sister's rosemary scent. "I love you so much that I have not words big enough to express it. But here, I have something special to give you. Keep it in your pocket, and if you should find yourself missing home, just rub your thumb over the face of it." She handed Penny the same small rock that Bram had given her.

Penny sniffled as she wrapped her fingers around it, then buried her face against Eva's coat. "Maybe I shouldn't go." Her words muffled out on a cry. "Maybe I ought to just stay here with you."

"Tut-tut, Miss Penny!" Mrs. Mortimer shrilled from the carriage door, one of her plump hands waving toward them. "We've a long drive ahead of us. You'll feel much better once we begin your adventure. Brother, help the girl into the carriage."

"My sister is right, Miss Inman. You've made your decision to send the girl to school, so let your yes be yes." Harsh words, yet a surprisingly soft current ran beneath them, almost as if Mr. Blackwood had a heart after all.

One last time, Eva hugged her sister fiercely, then set Penny from her and produced her handkerchief, dabbing the girl's eyes. An education was the best thing for Penny. She pressed the cloth into her sister's hand and stepped away. "The reverend is right. We have made our decision, have we not?"

"I . . . I guess so." Penny drew in a shaky breath. "But you will come to visit me soon and often, will you not?"

Eva bit her lip, her hand absently traveling to the outline of an envelope in her pocket. If Bram's telegram didn't say money would soon arrive, she'd have no choice but to accept Mrs. Pempernill's employment. Not that she could tell Penny that, of course. She straightened her sister's bonnet. "I would never turn down an opportunity to see you."

"Off we go, Miss Inman." Mr. Blackwood gathered Penny and lifted her into the carriage.

In light of her father's warning about Mr. Blackwood, it chafed to see her sister in the man's hands—but at least he would not be accompanying them to London. Mrs. Mortimer's maid, sitting pinch-faced opposite her employer, was an improvement over Mr. Blackwood.

Mrs. Mortimer immediately reached for the door handle, then paused and smiled at Eva. "Oh dear, Miss Inman, I ne-glected to tell you the school allows no visitors for the first year. It is better for the students to acclimate without inter-ruption. Good-bye." She pulled the door shut with a clack and the carriage rolled off, leaving Eva standing with her mouth agape. A whole year? She was to be parted from her sister for so long?

A sob strangled in her throat.

"Now, now, Miss Inman. Your sister is merely making a natural progression from girl to young lady. I understand these things are hard on the heart, but ultimately they're good for the soul in that she—and you—will have to trust God with each other all the more." Mr. Blackwood reached a hand toward her but, inches from contact, withdrew it. "After all, you and your sister are in God's hands, and there is no better place to be. Now, if you'll excuse me, I have an excessive amount of paperwork to finish. It's revenue day, you know. Good-bye."

He wheeled about, the grey tails of his coat flapping in his haste.

Callous, harsh man. Leaving her to mourn the loss of her only family member alone on this grey December morn. Could he not have tarried just a moment more?

Then again, did she really want him to?

Eva stomped back to the pony cart and, with a sharp click of her tongue, ordered Dusty to walk on. A snarling mess of sorrow and anger chased circles in her belly all the way to High Street, and she fought tears the entire drive. Letting loose a torrent now would be a disaster. Penny had her handkerchief.

She stopped the cart in front of the Royston Postal Office, then secured Dusty's reins. If God would but smile upon her—*Oh, God, please!*—then a telegram from Bram awaited her just inside. Tossing back her shoulders, she marched through the door, the jingle of the bell more grating than merry. Even so, she approached the telegraph window, determined to think only the best of what might be.

A silver-haired fellow with pockmarked cheeks peered at her from his stool. "May I help you?"

"Yes, have you a telegram for Miss Eva Inman?"

He reached for a spindle of papers and riffled through them

one by one. There weren't many, yet it seemed like an eternity before he glanced back up at her. "Sorry, miss. There's not one here."

"Are you certain?" She clutched her reticule, acutely aware of how light it felt. "Perhaps the message is addressed to Inman Manor?"

Once again the clerk fingered through the yellow squares of paper, a slight shake to his head. "Nothing, Miss Inman. Sorry."

Her heart dropped to her shoes. No telegram meant no money would be arriving today.

So she had no choice.

"Thank you." The words barely pushed past her teeth.

Her steps dragged over to the postal counter on the other side of the shop. She pulled the acceptance letter to Mrs. Pempernill from her pocket and a coin from her purse. "I should like this delivered right away, please."

"You're in luck, missy. The morning delivery is just out back." He shoved the coin in the register drawer, then waved the envelope in the air. "I'll see this gets in today's load."

He disappeared out a side door before she could thank him, which was just as well. She wasn't feeling very grateful at the moment, not with what she must do next.

Heart heavy, she trudged from the postal service to the revenue office. Bram was gone. As was her sister. And if she didn't do some elaborate talking, her house would be too.

She reached for the office door just as a man with a red face and monstrous scowl thundered out. "Thieves!" He shook his fist in the air. "The lot of them! Blasted bloodsuckers."

Eva jumped out of his way, doubtful he even saw her, so noxious was his wrath.

That didn't bode well.

Sucking in a breath of courage, she entered into a barebones office. She approached Mr. Buckle's desk. "Good day, Mr. Buckle."

"Good day, Miss . . ." He narrowed his eyes, his moustache crawling ever farther down the sides of his mouth. "Inman, is it not?"

She dipped her head.

He pulled a wooden box across his desk and fingered through some cards, eventually retrieving one. "I've got your statement right here. Once you pay the total amount, you may sign on this line." He set the paper down and tapped his finger on the mark.

She retrieved the few banknotes in her reticule, reluctant to part with them, then handed them over. "I, em, it is not all quite there, but mostly is."

His lips moved as he silently counted, then recounted. His gaze sought hers. "You are thirty pounds short."

"I am." She forced a brilliant smile. "But you will be happy to know I have taken a job and will make payments to account for the difference."

He shook his head. "Today is the deadline."

"I realize that, but as I said, I shall have all my wages sent here, and the shortfall will be eliminated in no time." She reached for the pen on his desk. "Shall I sign that card now?"

"That's just it, Miss Inman. Your time has run out." He snatched the pen from her fingers. "I shall have a possession order drawn up and served on Monday, which will state your eviction date. As it is closing in on the end of the year, I would expect that to be very soon. Property auctions of homes acquired this quarter are to happen in the new year when transfer of ownership will be complete. All that to say, will your wages cover the thirty pounds within the next fortnight?"

Eva gripped her empty reticule so tightly, her fingers ached. She had no idea what Mrs. Pempernill would pay her nor when she'd be paid.

"I-I do not know."

"Then I suggest you remove whatever personal belongings

you have as soon as possible, for whatever remains will be sold with the home. Good day, Miss Inman."

"But . . ."

Deep furrows dug into his broad brow. "Was I not clear in my explanation?"

"No, it is not . . . I mean . . ." She sighed. "You were very thorough, Mr. Buckle. Good day."

She tramped outside to a day devoid of any sort of cheer, the bitter sting of failure prickling down her back, dragging her shoulders to the ground. She'd failed her father in the worst possible way, losing the house, losing her sister. Losing the small remnants of whatever self-respect she owned.

Indeed.

What a horrid day.

26

It was quiet—*too* quiet. To be expected for a Saturday morning on campus, though, especially since it was the first day of Michaelmas recess. Students always bolted at the end of a semester. Bram had done so himself as a younger fellow. But now? Normally, he'd embrace such peace with no one to barge into his office or interrupt his study, but not today. He longed for noise. Laughter. Shouting. The thunderous roar of running feet that ought not be tearing about in these hallowed halls. Anything to drown out the hollow sound of packing the last of his belongings into the wooden box on his desk.

Reverently, he laid his worn copy of *The Twelve Caesars* on top of the pile. The text had been invaluable when teaching Roman history. He ran his finger over the cracked leather, a sudden wave of loss breaking so strongly over his head that he sank onto the chair he'd warmed these past six years. Everything he'd worked for, everything he'd gained—rapport with the students, an award-winning archery club, a salary on the rise—Grimwinkle had yanked from his hands, leaving him with nothing. Nothing! And now what? With a scarred record, no other institution would hire him. Extensive knowledge of the Roman Empire wasn't exactly a marketable skill.

He folded over, forearms on his thighs, a curtain of unkempt hair falling over his eyes. There was no way out of this mess. Grimwinkle had spoken, and that was the end of it.

"Oh, God." A moan more than a prayer. "I cannot fix this. I cannot even pretend to. All my life I have kept one step ahead of trouble, but this time . . ." Bitter laughter gurgled in his throat. "This time, Lord, it has caught up. You must make a way for me and my uncle, for I cannot, nor can he. We are in Your hands, as is Eva. Grant us all mercy."

He exhaled long and low, heart heavy at the thought of Eva. Leaving her had been hard. Leaving her to deal with a financial crisis had been reprehensible. Yet what choice did he have? It wasn't as if his bank account could solve her money problems.

Feeling a million years old, he slowly straightened. He ought to have sent her a telegram yesterday, explained that he'd withdrawn her relics from the college and delivered them along with the second load to the Fitzwilliam Museum—where he should have brought them in the first place. But by the time he'd finished the task, the telegraph office had been closed, and it'd not been open when he'd stopped by there on his way to Trinity this morn. Perhaps now would be a more suitable time.

He pulled out his trusty pocket watch. Half past nine. Funny how loading up years of his life had taken only the better part of an hour. Flipping the lid shut, he ran his finger over the embellishments, a new idea slowly taking root. He'd not been able to get Eva the money to fix up Inman Manor, but he could still provide her with something for her taxes. Hopefully it wasn't too late. The revenue man couldn't have processed the foreclosure paperwork yet, could he?

Bram shoved the watch into his pocket, then reached for his crate. Moments before his arms wrapped around the wood, he thought better of it and instead retrieved *The Twelve Caesars*.

He set the beloved book on the shelf behind the desk as a makeshift blessing. Perhaps the next professor would take as much joy from it as he had.

Then he grabbed his box and, without a backward glance, strode from the room.

Uncle Pendleton's office was farther down the corridor, where windows banked the entire south side. His door stood open, and Bram paused on the threshold. His uncle's workspace spanned twice the size of his, with great oak bookcases flanking one wall and a cheery hearth on the other, leather chairs sitting cozily in front of it. Uncle Pendleton stood at his desk, his back to the door, shoulders stooped over a box.

Bram's heart squeezed at how frail the old man looked. Uncle had been in surprisingly good spirits about the whole affair yesterday, but now the sledgehammer had clearly landed square on his head. And Bram could hardly blame his uncle for lacking the gumption to store away pieces of his life like some sort of squirrel burying nuts.

"Uncle?" Bram set down his box just inside the door. "Can I help you?"

"Hmm?" Uncle Pendleton faced him. "Oh, it's you. No, no. I, em, I should like to do this by myself, if you don't mind."

"I understand."

His uncle held up a dip-and-scratch ink pen, the ornate metal nib between his fingers. "Remember this?"

Bram smiled. "From Vindolanda."

"That was a proper dig, was it not?"

"Indeed." He took the pen from his uncle's hand, admiring the craftsmanship himself before setting the relic back on the stand . . . and that's when he noticed that hardly a thing had been packed up. A mere few items sat inside the box.

Bram laid a light touch on Uncle Pendleton's shoulder. "Look, Uncle, I know you are going to miss this. It is your life. But we will get on, you and me. I promise."

His uncle chuckled. "You think I'm mourning the loss of my tenure?"

"Are you not?"

His uncle paced the length of the desk. "After staying at Inman Manor these past few months, I realize just how ready I am to be finished here at Trinity. I rather enjoyed being in the country. The fresh air. The quiet mornings. No, my boy, I shall not miss the rigors of teaching, for I am ready to be done with that taxing business. But"—he held up a finger—"what I will pine for is the profound sense of fulfillment and connection I had in the classroom on a personal level. Igniting curiosity, instilling a love of the past, these are the things I shall always hold dear."

Of course he would, for Bram would miss the same. Blast that Grimwinkle! Blast him to Mount Vesuvius and back for inflicting such a wound upon them both.

Bram heaved a sigh, yet it did nothing to remove the ache in his heart. "I am deeply sorry, Uncle."

"No more than I am for you." Uncle Pendleton removed his spectacles and rubbed one of the glasses with his handkerchief, his eyes watery. "And I daresay I hold the greater sorrow on your behalf, for you had your whole teaching life ahead of you."

Bram forced a smile, hoping to lighten the moment a bit. "Like you, I had my own revelation at Inman Manor. It was peaceful there, and I was quite surprised how well I took to it. While I am shocked at no longer being a professor, perhaps you and I could make a go of it in a smaller town."

His uncle perched his spectacles on the bridge of his nose, gaze narrowing. "A go of what, exactly?"

"That is the question, is it not?"

A smile ghosted across his uncle's lips. "I suppose time will tell."

"Speaking of time, I have an errand to run." Bram strode toward the door. "I should be back shortly to help you cart your things down to the loading dock."

"It's a good thing we delivered Miss Inman's antiquities to the museum yesterday, for I daresay my books alone shall take up most of the wagon. Oh, where did you say you're off to?"

Bram paused on the threshold, hating what he was about to do. There was no other option . . . unless he called in a favor owed him by an old friend. But no. He would not provide for Eva with someone else's money.

He stepped into the corridor, calling over his shoulder, "The pawn shop."

His watch wouldn't bring a whole thirty pounds, but added to his meager savings, he ought to scrape up enough.

Hopefully.

These swollen eyes were familiar. The ache in her head. The weight on her shoulders. Eva knew the embrace of this old acquaintance all too well, for sorrow always visited with no invitation. She'd managed to keep her emotions tightly buttoned up until she'd returned home yesterday to pack her travel bag for her new position. But then she'd walked by Penny's empty room. She shouldn't have looked in, should never have gazed at the bed so tidily made, never to be slept in again by her sister. Breathing in the faint memory of rosemary soap lingering on the air had been a mistake as well, as had straining to listen for any remnants of Penny's sweet singing.

And she definitely should not have given in to that first sob, for she'd wept the day away and half the night.

Now, standing alone in the middle of her own bedroom, clutching the copy of *Good Wives* she'd forgotten to send along with Penny, the pressure to let loose another bout of tears was nearly too much to bear. How she wished she could turn back the hands of time, rewind the clock to the moments when laughter echoed through the halls of Inman Manor and Penny's infectious smile lit up the darkest corners of her heart. Knees weakening, she curled over the book like a prayer. Utterly abandoned by all.

Oh, poppet. How I long to hear your voice.

The novel slipped from her fingers, landing atop her bed like a corpse in a grave. Eva whirled, gasping for breath. What a failure she was! She didn't deserve God's smile. No wonder the mighty Creator punished her with such trials.

"If we confess our sins, He is faithful and just to forgive us our sins, as far as the east is from the west."

Quite unbidden, Bram's words floated back to her—misquotation and all. Her lips quivered, and she slapped her hand to her mouth. No doubt he would say she wasn't truly alone, for God was still here with her, even if no one else was . . . and that one singular thought hung like a lifeline. Dare she grasp it? Yet what was the alternative? Wallowing in what might or should have been had earned her nothing but a headache and burning eyes.

Slowly, a new determination began to take root. She would—she must—choose to believe God was not perpetually angry with her. That He had forgiven her for past mistakes, that there was grace for her in this nightmarish situation.

For that was the only way she'd survive.

With trembling hands, she pressed her fingertips to her eyes, pushing back tears until she caught her breath. Then she tossed back her shoulders and strode from her bedroom. There was much to do before leaving the day after tomorrow.

She swung into the office, intent on a final review of the accounts so that once the manor sold, she'd have an up-to-date list of creditors to be paid. She stopped just past the threshold. In the corner of the room, her steward perched on a ladder, applying plaster over the hole in the ceiling—a duty for a tradesman, not a man of his standing.

"Oh, Sinclair." She leaned against the desk, determination slowly leaking from her. "I hate to see you stooping to such a task."

"Not stooping at all, miss. I'm reaching, and I'm just about finished." With a grin, he spread on the final coat, then descended. When he landed, he scooped up the bucket and held it aloft. "I don't think you'll be needing this in here any time soon, unless the ol' ship springs another leak."

His humor was a balm. "Thank you. Such a task is far beyond what you should have to do."

"I don't mind, miss. It's better than having no task at all."

She clutched her arm to her belly, his words a direct hit. "About that, I should like a word with you." Retracing her steps, she shut the door.

"Must be serious," he rumbled.

"I am afraid it is." She faced him, fighting the need to nibble one of her nails. "As you know, taxes were due yesterday, and I was not able to pay the full amount. As such, I expect a possession order to arrive on Monday morning that will detail the eviction date. I am told it shall be soon, for the properties acquired this quarter are to be auctioned off at the beginning of the year."

His brows drew into a thick line. "You're losing the manor, then?"

She sucked in a deep breath. "I am."

"It's a sorry business, miss." Morning light streaming through the single window cast a shadow on half his face, his cheeks not nearly as rounded since Mrs. Pottinger's baking was now nonexistent. Little flecks of plaster rained from his hair as he shook his fist in the air. "Abominable business, if you ask me!"

"Yes, well, there is nothing we can do about it." She crossed to the desk and picked up a pen, giving her hands something to do. "I am packing up what belongings I have left and am taking a position on Monday as a lady's companion. I should be grateful if you would remain here and ready the house for auction. The larger the sale, the sooner the manor's debts will be paid off. And once those relics are purchased, I am hoping to provide you and the staff an extra stipend to get you by until you are situated elsewhere."

"It's very generous of you, miss, but . . ." His angular jaw worked a moment, a muscle rising and falling on the side of his neck. "What of yourself and Miss Penny?"

"I imagine we shall get on brilliantly. My sister is being well cared for by the generous sponsorship of Mrs. Mortimer, and I shall want for nothing as a companion to Mrs. Pempernill." How happy the words sounded, as if Penny were off on a grand tour, and she were a lady-in-waiting to the Queen. She rolled the pen between her fingers, warding off the urge to snap it in half. "It is you and the staff that concern me."

"Don't trouble yourself on our account, miss. Such is the life of those in service. Would you like me to tell them?"

His thoughtfulness stuck in her throat. "That is very kind of you, but no. It is my responsibility, and I shall do so tomorrow after Sunday morning service. Until then, I would appreciate it if you kept this information to yourself."

"As you wish."

"Thank you, Sinclair. I would never have made a go of it this long without you at my side."

A hefty sigh deflated him. "It were a hard hand you were dealt, yet you played it very nicely, miss. You can count on me to ready the house for sale. I know a man in Bedford who'll pay for a load of furniture."

She pursed her lips. Surely Sinclair knew she'd already sold everything that would bring in a coin or two. "There is no furniture of value remaining. What is left is worn beyond salability or in need of repair."

"He's a scrapper, miss." The steward shrugged, sending another good dusting of plaster bits to the floorboards. "He'll take anything. If I load up the wagon today, I can leave tomorrow and be there on Monday morning when he opens up."

"I see." Slowly, she nodded. "I guess this is good-bye, then." She set down the pen and offered her hand.

"Aye, miss. It's been a pleasure serving you and your family all these years." He gave her hand a hearty shake, the crow's-feet at the edges of his eyes knitting into tangled lines. His Adam's apple bobbed several times as he pulled away. "I'll see to any remaining paperwork and stay till the end."

"Once again, I thank you. You are a good man, Mr. Sinclair."

"May God bless you, miss." He grabbed his hat off the wall hook and strode to the door, where he hesitated. "Only, I can't help but wonder . . ."

She angled her head. "Yes?"

"Well . . . never mind. Weren't important. Good day."

He strode out the door, leaving her to ponder what he might have said, though deep in her heart, she suspected what he was thinking.

If she'd left the cursed acres alone, she'd have not met with such a foul end.

27

Eva had never enjoyed the Sunday morning shuffle down the aisle to shake the reverend's hand at the end of service. Mr. Blackwood's fingers were too cold. His stare too intense. And though for the one day a week he wasn't garbed head to toe in grey, the black frock coat, waistcoat, and trousers he replaced it with were as solemn as a crypt. Did the man never once wish for a burst of colour when he opened his wardrobe each morn?

"Miss Inman." Mr. Blackwood dipped his head as he collected her hand. "I trust today's message about God's sovereignty was nourishment to your soul."

"Yes, thank you." She pulled away lest lightning strike them both in one zap. It hadn't been a lie so much as an exaggeration, but surely that was just as bad. The truth was, she couldn't remember the first half of his sermon. She'd been too preoccupied glancing around every few minutes to see if Mrs. Mortimer had arrived.

Instead of bolting off as was her habit, Eva lingered in the vestibule. "I note that your sister was not in attendance today, Mr. Blackwood. I had hoped to ask her how things went dropping off my sister at the school for the blind on Friday. Did she happen to mention anything to you when she returned to the vicarage?"

"She did not. You are welcome to stop by the house and ask her yourself, but best not to do so until later in the week when she has recuperated. She is quite spent whenever she returns from one of her shopping excursions." His thin face darkened to match his suit. "A vice I have warned her against time and again."

Interesting. Mrs. Mortimer never mentioned shopping. Had she taken Penny for new things the girl might need at school? And if so, how would she repay the woman? Eva tugged her gloves on tighter to keep from biting a nail. "I thought Mrs. Mortimer went to London merely to escort my sister."

"Despite my biblical counsel, she can never resist an opportunity to indulge in new fancies for herself."

Ahh. So nothing for Penny, then. But did the woman truly need to go shopping for herself? Every time Eva saw her, Mrs. Mortimer sported a new gown and matching hat to go with it.

"Pardon my asking, Mr. Blackwood, and I mean no offense, but if your sister is so very well off, why does she not simply live in London instead of your small vicarage?"

"Appearances can be deceiving, Miss Inman. I daresay Mrs. Mortimer would not survive a fortnight on her own, which is why she moved in with me four years ago when her husband died. I'm afraid the fellow pampered her to a fault, and as such, her stewardship capabilities are lacking in my estimation."

Oh dear. If the woman did give in to such temptations, Penny would be ousted if the tuition was not met. Eva clutched her Bible with a death grip, not daring to think what that would mean if such a thing happened when she was off galivanting across the continent with Mrs. Pempernill.

"If that is true, Reverend, then what of my sister? Mrs. Mortimer assured me she would sponsor Penny for at least a year of education."

"I wouldn't agonize over it." He patted her shoulder mechanically. "Just like Elisha and the widow's oil, Mrs. Mortimer always seems to pour out more money when I least expect it. Now, if you don't mind . . ." He tipped his head to indicate the congregants piling up for their chance to shake his cadaverous hand.

"Good day, Mr. Blackwood." She bobbed a small curtsey.

"A holy Sabbath to you, Miss Inman."

Outside, December air crawled beneath her skirts as she unhitched Dusty and climbed into the pony cart. No snow covered the ground, but it surely felt as if winter had arrived in full. For the most part, she ignored the cold, still concerned about Penny. She would have to make it a point to stay in constant contact with the headmaster, a Mr. Hardknuckle, if she remembered correctly. If any tuition payments weren't made, she'd simply have him alert her at once. But what she'd do then . . . Eva sighed, a cloud of mist puffing from her mouth. She had no idea what she'd do if Penny had to leave school before she returned from Tuscany with Mrs. Pempernill, which could be at least a year. And yet did she not have enough worries to manage without inventing fresh woes?

She gently eased the left rein while pulling slightly on the right, directing Dusty onto the lane for Inman Manor. It would be no easy task to inform the staff of their dismissal today. Oh, Tom would likely land another position in the countryside easily enough. Landowners were always in want of more muscle. It was Mrs. Pottinger, Mary, and Dixon who concerned her most. Dixon and Mrs. Pottinger were up in age, making them less desirable, and Mary had two fingers missing on her left hand from a farm incident as a child. It didn't matter in the least concerning the maid's duties, but some households would frown upon such an impediment. Oh, how she wished she didn't have to part with such faithful staff!

She guided Dusty through the front gate, and an entirely new worry sprang up. An unfamiliar horse was tethered near the front steps. Had Mr. Buckle reneged on his word, serving the possession order today instead of Monday? If so, what a villain! Belly churning, she parked the pony cart and trotted up the stairs. She'd give the man the rough side of her tongue for such a desecration of the Sabbath.

Inside, she yanked her bonnet strings, the frayed ribbon harsh against her skin, and was nearly out of her coat when Dixon rounded the corner and strode into the hall.

An inscrutable smile arched the housekeeper's lips. "You've a visitor, miss."

"Thank you, Dixon." She hung her coat on the hall tree. "As soon as I am finished with my guest, would you call the staff together for a meeting?"

Dixon's smile vanished. "Of course."

"Tom too."

"I see." The housekeeper's lips pinched to a ripple. "Just ring the bell when you're finished, miss, and I'll direct everyone to the sitting room."

"Thank you." Eva stepped past her, refusing to think about the awful news she'd have to share with her staff in just a few moments. Instead, she collected every bit of fury she could find, jammed it all into a tight ball, and prepared to verbally lob it at Mr. Buckle.

She stopped dead in her tracks, just steps from the sitting room door. What was she doing? It wasn't that man's fault revenues had been raised and she hadn't the funds to pay them. He was only doing his job.

Oh, God, forgive me.

Smoothing her skirts, she prepared to calmly face whatever Mr. Buckle may have for her.

But nothing could have prepared her for who stood near the mantel in the sitting room.

The past twenty-four hours had been nothing short of grueling. Moving all of Uncle Pendleton's books, along with their office belongings, and then relocating Bram's entire household had been an exhausting ordeal. It was strange to be living with his uncle again instead of on campus. Although Bram didn't possess much, all that shifting and lifting had taken a toll. He pressed a fist to the ache in the small of his back, stifling a wince. Then again, it might not have been all the manual labour but the breakneck ride he'd taken from Cambridge to Inman Manor. A speed wholly unwarranted, save for the fact that he longed to see Eva again. At any rate, whatever the cause, the twinge in his back was a sinister reminder he wasn't getting any younger . . . and what had he to show for all his years? Here he stood unemployed, living with a relative, and currently in need of a good shave.

A shush of the sitting room door and following intake of air pulled him from his thoughts. He pivoted—and was struck afresh by the uncommon allure of the redheaded, blue-eyed enchantress standing wide-eyed at the door, for Eva was all that and more. Yet when he looked closer, he couldn't help but note her skin was far too pale, especially for one who'd recently come in from a December day. There was a puffiness about her eyes as if she'd wept away every moment since he'd last seen her. Alarm tightened his chest.

"Eva?" He stepped from the hearth. "Have you been unwell?"

"No, I am . . ." Her nose scrunched far too adorably. "I am just a little confused as to why you are here."

"A happy confused or an I'd-really-hoped-to-never-see-you-again sort of confused?"

"Most decidedly happy. Forgive my manners." She swept across the rug and grabbed his hands. "It is very good to see you."

"You as well." He pressed a light kiss to the crown of her head, inhaling the fresh scent of outdoors lingering on her hair.

She pulled away, one arm gesturing toward the sofa. "Please sit. You must be exhausted after such a ride."

"It was a good day for it. The sun is out, unlike our last venture back from Cambridge." He smiled at the memory—a smile that grew as he noted a pinkening on her cheeks. Did she remember it fondly, then? He waited for her to settle on a chair, then took the side of the sofa closest to her.

"But what are you doing here?" She angled her head, studying his face. "Is everything all right? I hope there is nothing wrong with your dear uncle."

"Nothing of the sort. I came to apologize in person for not having telegraphed you as I had promised and to give you something." He handed over a banknote from inside his coat pocket.

Eva frowned at the paper for a beat, perplexity wrinkling her brow until understanding dawned in her eyes. "This is the exact amount I was short on for the property taxes!"

"I know. I only regret I couldn't have gotten it to you on Friday. But no matter. Tomorrow you shall go to the revenue office and square away your tax debt."

She clutched the paper to her chest like a cherished babe. "You have no idea how much this means to me."

"I think I have an inkling."

"No, you do not." She shook her head. "My travel bag is packed even now for a position I did not really want, one that I was going to take tomorrow." She waved the banknote in the air with a little squeal. "For now, you have rescued me, Bram Webb!"

"That is a bit dramatic." He laughed. "But I am glad you will not have to leave your home."

"And neither will my staff. I look forward to telling them." She flounced against the cushion with a satisfied sigh. "So," she murmured, "the relics must have sold. I am grateful to you for arranging the purchase."

"They have not sold yet. I ran into an issue at the college." Oy. What an understatement. "I have since moved your antiquities to the Fitzwilliam Museum. The curator was quite interested."

"My, you have been busy. But how did you have time for all that?" She straightened, suspicion gleaming silver in her pale blue eyes. "What happened at your board meeting?"

"Yes, well . . ." He shifted uncomfortably on the sofa. He'd relived that trauma in his head more times than he cared to admit and wasn't particularly keen on revisiting it again. The jut of Eva's jaw, however, would be difficult to soften with anything other than the truth. "Suffice it to say that the meeting did not go as hoped. I am afraid there will be a different crew returning here next semester. Your dig shall now be led by Professor Grimwinkle."

"Grimwinkle? I should think he would be concerned about getting his garments dirty. Why can you not finish the job?"

And here it was. The moment he'd have to admit he was an unemployed vagabond. He inhaled deeply. "My uncle and I are no longer employed by Trinity College."

"What!" She gripped the arms of the chair, wrinkling the banknote. "Oh, Bram."

Pity he could take, was expected, even, but the empathy in the quiver of her lips nearly undid him. "Come, now. It is not like I am dying. I simply have time to figure out what next I shall do."

"What of the curator position in Royston? You must let Mr. Toffit know you are available right away."

Hah! Would that he'd known when he penned that rejection note that he'd be without a job now. Lacing his fingers together, he cracked his knuckles. "Shortly after Mr. Toffit sent me the offer, I wrote to decline it, so I do not feel like I can go crawling back."

"Of course you can. Besides"—she wagged her finger—"that smacks of pride, sir."

"Hubris has nothing to do with it. That is simply how business operates."

"Humph. Maybe." Languidly, she lifted her arm and nibbled on the nail of her index finger.

He pulled it away.

And when their eyes met, they shared a smile that felt intimately more passionate than it should have.

"Well then, Mr. Webb, since you are now a man of leisure—leastwise for the time being—I have a perfectly wonderful idea." She rose, a merry twinkle sparking in her gaze.

Which was wholly infectious. If she told him her notion was to go to the moon and back, he'd sweep her off her feet here and now and give it a go.

Instead, he settled for a simple cock of his head. "An idea, eh? Do tell."

She fairly bounced on her toes. "How would you like to escort me to London?"

28

London never slept, and neither had Eva. They'd gotten a late start on Monday after her stop at the tax office and her secret visit to Mr. Toffit. She and Bram arrived too late the previous evening to visit Penny, and though she ought to have been weary from the eight-hour drive, sleep had eluded her all night. Even now as she descended the stairs to the lobby of the Great Eastern Hotel, she still wasn't tired. Too much nervous energy bubbled inside her at the thought of seeing her sister, which was silly, really. Now that she'd declined Mrs. Pempernill's lady's companion position, she could visit her little sister any time. Mrs. Mortimer might frown upon it, as might the headmaster, but hang it all—she missed Penny, and she *would* see her, if only for a few minutes.

Eva descended the last stair, clutching her copy of *Good Wives* while scanning the busy entryway. An ornate chandelier cast a warm glow over the scene, each crystal shimmering with light. Plush velvet curtains framed the tall front windows, and though it was morning, not much light seeped in from the grey day outside. Several gents strolled out the door with newspapers curled beneath their arms. Some ladies huddled near the restaurant entrance, the clack of flatware against china plates drifting out.

Finally, her gaze snagged upon a familiar figure. Bram stood tall and resolute by the front desk, his presence commanding attention even amidst the bustle of other guests. His shaggy hair framed his face in a tousled halo, lending him a rugged charm she found endearing. Despite the grind of yesterday's journey, he appeared refreshed. He smelled as such, too, for when she drew close, she inhaled the crisp scent of sandalwood shaving tonic on his skin.

"There you are." He grinned down at her. "Would you like breakfast?"

"I could not eat a thing. I am too excited to see my sister."

"It has only been four days since you said good-bye to the little imp, but I expected as much. I had the pony cart brought round to the front." He offered his arm. "Shall we?"

Heart warmed by his intuitive thoughtfulness, she placed her gloved fingers on his sleeve. "Thank you."

They stepped into a December morn devoid of colour. Dusty stamped a hoof at their approach, tossing his head as if to say he'd had enough of this dirty city and its noise. Bram helped her to the seat, his fingers lingering a beat too long against hers after she sat. Her heart fluttered. An easy smile spread on his lips as if he knew. And when he leapt up to the driver's seat and his thigh brushed against hers, that flutter turned into a full-fledged gallop. Sweet heaven. It may as well be an August afternoon for all the warmth surging to her cheeks. She averted her face as he urged Dusty to walk on. Better to study the passing buildings than reveal what an effect he had on her, for no doubt he'd have something to say about it.

They drove in silence for some time, he directing the pony cart in a river of traffic and she trying to ignore the rhythmic press of Bram's body against her side as the cart bumped through ruts and potholes.

Tiring of watching the passing buildings, she turned to him. "How do you know where to go? Do you frequent London often?"

"I have been to the British Museum several times. Other than that, no."

"Ah, I see. Your sense of direction stems from an extra keen awareness, the kind that locates relics at a dig, eh?"

He cut her a sideways glance, one brow arching. "Would that impress you?"

Everything about the man impressed her. Not that he need know, however. She clutched the seat as they juddered along. "Were you wanting to impress me?"

"If I could be the one to turn your head, I would die a happy man." His lips broke into a charming smile. "But the truth is, I showed the address you gave me to the desk clerk at the hotel. He was very helpful with directions. We should be there shortly."

Her gaze drifted to the sooty buildings leaning against one another on each side of the road. They'd left behind the tidier streets, and now the tang of coal smoke was thick on the air. Neglect walked these grimy lanes, as thoroughly depressing as the somber-garbed labourers scrambling to their workplaces. "Are you sure we are going the right way?"

"I thought so." He produced a slip of paper from inside his coat and handed it over. "But maybe you had better check."

She glanced at the handwriting, then searched for the next street sign. Sure enough, *Woolpack Lane* stood out in white letters against a black background. "It says here Spindle Street is where you turn left."

"Which ought to be the upcoming crossroad."

Bram guided the horse around the corner. She stifled a moan. Factories loomed like titans of progress, sucking in human souls and spitting out commodities all crated and ready to ship. Her nose burned, a metallic tang of chemicals and machinery coating each breath like a filmy oil that couldn't be scrubbed off.

Inside each great beast they passed, pistons pounded and gears whirred, the drone climbing inside of her bones, shaking her from the core outward. It was surreal, this cheerless, hopeless, strangling district of commerce.

She scooted closer to Bram. "Why would a school be in this neighbourhood?"

He did not meet her gaze. "Cheap rent, I suppose."

Good thing she wore gloves, or her nails would be chewed to nubs, especially when Bram halted the pony cart in front of a monstrous building. The bricks were held together with grime and despair, a high bank of windows at the top cranked open, the glass opaque with a smoky pall. The placard above the wide front doors read *Greenwell's*, but this was no merry institution of higher learning or academic gleanings. This was a grotesque shell of horror.

"I—" Bram cleared his throat. "I am sure it is much more polished inside."

Hah. What a lie.

They stepped into a grinding, clacking, vast expanse filled with rows of tables and labourers, machinery and pulleys, and so much dust it coated the lungs. Dim light made it hard to see faces, giving the shadowed workers an eerie appearance, like ghosts in a graveyard. It smelled of linseed oil and sweat, the only fresh air leaking in from windows high on the walls. Just like all the other buildings they'd passed, this was a factory, and judging by the lint floating in the air and buzz of sewing machines, it was some sort of garment manufacturer.

A half-wall partition sectioned off a reception area of sorts, where a needle-nosed fellow perched on a stool behind a counter. Lint covered his suit like a late-winter snow, all grey and mottling into patches on his shoulders. He narrowed his eyes at them.

Rising to her toes, Eva spoke into Bram's ear to be heard above the noise of the place. "This cannot be right."

"Are you sure Mrs. Mortimer gave you the correct address?" he rumbled back.

"Oy! You two." The man at the counter aimed his pen at them, his voice as rough as the factory floor. "This ain't no gatherin' place. State yer business or be off."

Eva approached the counter, but even standing so close to him, she raised her voice. "We are looking for Greenwell's School for the Blind. Do you know where it is?"

A great guffaw rolled out of the fellow, his sharp-edged shoulders shaking with the force of his mirth. "Is that what this is now, eh? A blind school? Hah! What a corker, that one." He slapped his hand atop the counter, a puff of dust rising like smoke.

"Pardon us," Bram grumbled. "We are clearly in the wrong place." He guided Eva around with a touch to the small of her back. "Let's go. We will telegraph Mrs. Mortimer and sort this out."

Disappointment weighed like wet wool, dragging Eva's steps. She'd so hoped to see Penny this morning. Near the door, her foot slipped on some of the collecting lint, and when she flailed her arm, her fingers let loose of the book she'd meant to give Penny.

"Oh!" She dashed after the thing, swooping down to pick it up, but then she paused, her gaze locking on to a small rock. She picked it up along with the book, a mix of terror and fury rising like bile up to her throat. The pebble was smooth. Oval. Shiny where a finger had rubbed it, worn with a notch on one end.

And it had a reddish grain to it.

"Bram?" She glanced up at him, his name a shiver on her lips.

And yet somehow he heard. "What is it? You look as if you have seen a spirit."

She held up the rock on an open palm. "I think Penny may be here after all."

⚭

Bram tensed, recognition crawling beneath his skin like fire ants, leaving a hot trail of fury. Squaring his shoulders, he stomped to the front counter. "Where is Penny Inman?"

The clerk merely sucked on his teeth, making him look more like a ground squirrel than a man.

Bram slammed his palms against the wood, the sharp report of it louder than the machinery. "I asked you a question! Where does Penny Inman work?"

A great scowl carved deep lines into the man's brow. "There's no names 'ere. Just numbers. Once a body steps onto that floor"—he hitched his thumb over his shoulder—"they're part o' the machine. Ye'd have to ask ol' Greenwell himself what number she was assigned."

"She is a twelve-year-old girl, not a number!" Bram lunged over the counter and grabbed the man by the collar, hauling him to his feet. The smack of the stool cracked against the floorboards. "She has dark hair, darker eyes, and she is blind."

Beneath Bram's grip, the fellow's Adam's apple bobbed like a snake swallowing a rat. "Sh-she's in the piecing room, first door on the right. But you didn't hear it from me."

Bram dropped him like a filthy rag, then turned to Eva. "Stay here."

He wheeled about and rounded the corner of the wooden partition. Disgust added to his wrath. The people working here—mostly women and children—didn't make eye contact as he passed. How beat down must they be to live in such fear? Greenwell ought to be hung by his neck from the rafters of this place, and yet such a justice would be a mere drop in the bucket, for all the other factories they'd driven past must surely look the same behind their walls.

Lord, have mercy on these poor souls.

Sickened, he stalked toward the piecing room door.

Just as a brick wall of a man sidestepped into his path,

planting his feet for a fight. "Where do ye think yer goin'? Ye don't work here."

Bram flexed his fingers. A fight would feel good right about now. "I do not need to work here to find what I am looking for. Step aside."

"Ye think ye can waltz onto my floor and demand things of me? Turn yer pretty little self around"—he twirled his podgy finger in the air—"and get ye gone. This ain't no charity house, mate."

"I am not asking for charity, just for a twelve-year-old girl who has no business being here." Bram widened his stance. "Now move."

A sneer twisted the man's thick lips. "And if I don't?"

"Then you shall regret it, I promise you that."

"Ye don't scare me." The man spit out a linty glob, then swiped the back of his hand across his mouth. "I've dealt with twaddle like you before, and they all end up pretzeled out on the kerb."

Bram's hands curled into fists. He'd have to strike fast and hard, but brute force alone wouldn't be enough. He'd have to rely on speed, agility, and precision—a lesson he'd learned well as a feral lad.

"Bram?" Eva's voice shouted hoarse at his back. "Is Penny here?"

Blast. He couldn't fight with Eva standing so close—and judging by the sneering grin on the hulk in front of him, that man knew it as well. Gritting his teeth, Bram dug into his pocket and pulled out the pouch of his remaining coins. How he'd make it home was anybody's guess.

"Here." He thrust the leather pouch into the man's big hand. "Let us pass."

Testing the weight of the coins in his palm—and apparently satisfied—the bully shoved the money inside his coat and strolled away.

A great sigh heaved from Bram's lungs, then he faced Eva. "I told you to remain in the foyer."

"How could I when I fear Penny is in here somewhere?" Her jaw quivered.

And squeezed his heart. "All right but stay close."

He led her from the factory floor into the piecing room, which—though he couldn't believe it possible—was even more dismal and depressing. It was a cramped space, cluttered with piles of fabric and spools of thread. Dust hung in the air, clung to the body, coated the tongue. Long wooden tables lined each wall, the *snip-snip-snip* of scissors cutting harsh holes into the ear. Most children stood at their workstations, dressed in garments little better than rags. Those too short stood on crates. Those with bent legs or none at all sat on rickety stools.

Bram scanned for Penny's slight form, and when he spied her in the farthest corner, Eva must have as well, for she took off in a run.

"Penny!" Eva clung to her sister.

He wrapped his arms around the two of them, their weeping breaking off pieces of his heart until nothing but the need to leave this place pounded in his chest. "Come. I am taking you both home."

By then several other children had gathered around, one of whom tugged on Eva's skirts. "Mish Inman! Pleash. Take me home too."

Eva pulled away, bending toward a girl with a deformed lip, and as she stared at the child, she gasped. "Little Ginny? Can it be?"

"It can be because it is Ginny Novak," Penny cut in. "Andy Kitman and Lucy Watson are here too. Mrs. Mortimer didn't find them positions any more than she sent me to school. She sold us all to Mr. Greenwell, knowing we'd never make our way home from here."

Eva glanced wildly around, then snapped her pale face to

him. "She is right. There is Andy on that stool, the one with the clubfoot, and farther down is young Lucy, who cannot hear. Oh, Bram." She lifted a shaky hand to her mouth. "This is horrible."

No, this was criminal. And yet not a judge in the land would begrudge a profitable businessman his workers, no matter the age or impediment.

Shoving down a fresh burst of rage, Bram forced an even tone to his voice. "I will carry Andy, and you make a chain of the other children. We will take them all home."

"What about us?" Three more girls pulled on his sleeve, one of whom held Lucy's hand. "Can we come too?"

Oh, God. He glanced at the lint-coated rafters. *What am I to do?*

"We cannot leave them here, not if they wish to go." Eva's words may as well have been the voice of the Almighty, for deep in his heart, he knew he couldn't turn his back on such a plea.

"All right." He lifted his voice to be heard by all—which might be a mistake, but so be it. "Any who wish to return to their homes instead of working for Mr. Greenwell, clasp hands with the one in front of you and I shall lead you out."

Without waiting to see just how many would take him up on his offer, he strode over to a towheaded, clubfooted boy and swung him off the stool. "Are you Andy?"

"Aye, sir." Impossibly blue eyes gazed at him in awe. "Are you really taking me back to my mum?"

"God willing, young master." He hefted the boy up to his shoulder, then spoke under his breath, "Please be willing, Lord."

He strode past Eva. "Bring up the rear, if you will."

"Thank you." She beamed.

"Do not thank me yet. We have not made it out of here."

With a firm grip on Andy and not just a little trepidation, he stalked from the room. This time eyeballs did turn his way—and no wonder. What a circus he led. The workers closest to them stood idle, sewing machines forgotten, trouser legs left unsewn. Near the opening to the foyer, the big foreman stood with his arms folded, a smug tilt to his head. Bram swallowed hard. It would take a miracle to make it past that cully. He had no more money.

Surprisingly, though, the man let him pass with nothing but a smirk. That had been easy.

Too easy.

And as Bram neared the front door, he saw why.

Stationed in front of the entrance was a man in a black suit, flanked by henchmen. Greenwell. He'd bet on it.

Blast! Bram stopped in front of the man. "Mr. Greenwell, I presume?"

"Indeed." Greenwell's dark gaze swept over him, assessing him as he might a bolt of fabric to be purchased. "And you are?"

"Of no consequence. Allow us to leave, and that will be the end of it."

A smile lifted a wafer-thin moustache above the man's mouth. "You cannot take my workers. That is theft."

"Slavery was abolished fifty years ago, so there is no theft involved. These children are not your property."

"They are my legal charges. I purchased them." With a snap of Greenwell's fingers, the needle-nosed clerk came running and produced a portfolio of documents. "Would you care to see?"

"You may have some fancy paperwork, Mr. Greenwell, but it will not stand against what I intend to see published in the newspaper smearing your name." Bram sharpened his tone. "Unless, of course, you let us pass."

Red spread like a bruise up the man's neck. "That is blackmail."

"That"—Bram grinned—"is correct."

Sneering, the man stretched himself to full height. "Fine. Children are a penny a dozen. These will be easily replaced." His brows drew into an ominous line. "But tell Mrs. Mortimer I am finished with her."

"Oh, I assure you, I have a great many things to tell Mrs. Mortimer." Bram sidestepped the man, nerves on edge, but he reached the front door without any more fight. He shoved the scarred wood open with his fist and held it wide, silently counting as children filed by.

There were ten.

Ten young lives.

All in his care.

And he hadn't a penny left in his pocket.

29

This was probably a mistake. Even so, Bram rang the bell on the elegant Bath-stone town house, knowing full well the boy on his shoulder and gaggle of children huddled at his back didn't belong here in Mayfair. Not at the home of one of the wealthiest men in England. He'd always been welcome here, but now? With a collection of raggedy waifs? A sigh poured out of him. What other choice did he have?

The heavy oak door swung open to a perfectly liveried butler. He was a youngish fellow, not a grey lock daring a glint from his slicked-back hair—certainly not the same man Bram remembered from years ago when he'd visited this house.

"May I help you?" A kind enough question, but as the butler's gaze drifted from Bram to the disparate troop of children behind him, a distinct twitch near his left eye came to life.

Despite the weight of the boy he carried, Bram straightened his shoulders. "Is Mr. Price at home? I should like a word with him."

"Mr. Price donates to the Lowry Street Charity Home. I suggest you seek aid there. Good day." The door swung.

Bram shot out his foot, stopping it before it could shut. "I am not seeking charity. What I seek is my old friend Mr. Price. Please let him know Mr. Bram Webb is on his doorstep."

The man eyed him through the thin space between door and jamb—a look that could rival one of Grimwinkle's. "Very well," he said at length.

This time Bram allowed the door to close.

And as soon as it did, Eva stepped up beside him. "What are we doing here? We should be seeing about getting these children some food. It was a long walk here for those who did not fit in the pony cart, and the younger ones are tired."

"Soon. Very soon. Trust me."

The lines of her face softened, the blue of her eyes warming to a summer sky. "I do trust you."

Heat kindled in his chest, her words stirring something deep inside—a sense of purpose, responsibility, of being the protector she needed most in this unpredictable world. In that moment, surrounded by weary children he'd taken under his wing and the woman he loved with all his heart, he knew with absolute certainty he'd move mountains to ensure their safety and well-being.

He gave Eva's fingers a squeeze. "Thank you."

The door reopened—wide, this time. "Please come in." The butler stepped aside until they all gathered in the ornate front hall. "Follow me, if you will, but try not to touch anything." He strode off at a good clip.

Bram smirked. Either the man was in a hurry to attend some other task, or he thought such speed would deter the children from shoving candlesticks into their pockets.

They entered a spacious sitting room, all gold and green and smelling of beeswax. Bram set Andy down on one of the many sofas, glad to remove the burden. Though the boy was slight, he'd left a distinct cramp in Bram's bicep.

Eva ushered the rest of the children to various other seats. "Sit still, children, and make sure not to touch anything just as the gentleman asked."

Out of habit, Bram approached the mantel and lifted the lid of the humidor. The rich scent of Dominican tobacco wafted out, instantly easing some of the tightness in his neck. He reached to pocket a few of the cigars, but inches away from contact, shut the lid instead. Eva wouldn't appreciate him smelling of smoke.

"Kipes!" one of the children exclaimed. "This place is a palace."

"Miss Inman?" Another girl chimed in, wonder in her voice. "Are we going to live here?"

"No, Maggie. We are merely guests for a brief time."

Bram turned from the hearth as Eva drew close, a certain amount of awe in her own gaze. "I had no idea you rubbed elbows with the elite."

"You should never judge a book by its cover." He grinned.

Her lips slightly parted as she peered up at him. "I have been wrong about you in so many ways."

The admiration in her eyes went down deep, unpacked, and made a home in his heart. How had this woman come to be so much a part of him? Lightly, he ran his finger along the curve of her cheek. "I could get used to a look like that."

"Well, this is a surprise," a bass voice rumbled from the doorway.

Bram turned to see his old friend Edmund Price entering, a dark-haired beauty at his side. Both wore a golden glow to their skin, likely having returned from a recent dig in Egypt.

"You know me, Price. Just keeping you on your toes." He clapped the man on the back.

"That is my job now." Ami, Price's wife, gave her husband a sideways embrace, then held out her hand to Bram. "But it is good to see you again, and I note you have brought along a friend—or rather, I should say *friends*."

He pressed his lips to the top of Ami's hand, then urged Eva forward with a slight touch to her arm. "Indeed, I have. Ami Price, meet Miss Eva Inman. Eva, Mrs. Price."

Eva dipped a full curtsey. "I am pleased to meet you, Mrs. Price."

Ami laughed, the sound so merry that several of the children giggled along with her. "No need for such formality. Please call me Ami. And since this artful gentleman you have taken up with has neglected to introduce you to my husband, it is up to me to do the honour. Eva, this is Edmund Price."

Eva's jaw dropped. "*The* Edmund Price?"

Edmund chuckled. "The one and only—to which my wife would say was God's mercy." He winked at Ami.

His wife promptly batted his arm. "Scoundrel . . . but very true. I would say such a thing."

"Miss Inman?" a small voice called from one of the sofas. "My tummy is grumbly."

Before Eva could answer, Ami swooped over to the children and crouched to their level, her fine silk skirts billowing like a soft cloud around her. "But what is this? Has our friend Mr. Webb brought us a crew of adventurers with empty bellies? We cannot have such a tragedy. Come, let us go dig about the kitchen and see what relics we can unearth, hmm?" She swiped little Andy into her arms.

Eva's brows lifted, clearly astonished that a lady from an elegant home would stoop to such an act. Bram smirked. She had no idea Ami Price was a feisty Egyptologist at heart.

She didn't marvel for long, though. She advanced with her hands held out. "Children, you heard the lady. Form a chain and follow Mrs. Price just as you did Mr. Webb. Penny and I shall bring up the rear." She glanced back at Bram as if for permission.

Which was entirely endearing.

He nodded, and soon the room emptied to naught but him and his old friend.

Edmund strolled to the drink cart and poured from a carafe of water. "Looks like you have been caught in some sort of net this time—and with a school of fish to accompany you. I am certain there is intrigue involved." He waggled his eyebrows as he handed over a glass.

Bram chugged the drink, hoping the refreshment would somehow make words flow. There was so much to explain. "Remember that favor you said you owed me?"

"I do."

"I am calling it in, old friend."

"Are you?" Edmund sank into an overstuffed chair and stretched out his legs. "Perhaps you had better enlighten me, then, on exactly what terms I consented to without knowing the finer points of our agreement."

Bram paced a moment, rubbing furiously at the back of his neck. Where to begin? "It is a long story, but the shortened version is I accompanied Miss Inman to London to visit her sister at a school for the blind in which the girl had recently been enrolled. Turns out it was a sweatshop she had been sold to under false pretense—as were several other of the children. Deplorable conditions." Even now his hands curled into fists. "Of the ten children I rescued, four reside in Royston, and I will see them returned to their families." He stopped in front of Edmund. "As long as you can part with a carriage, that is."

"That is all? I am to get off with the simple lending of a coach?" His eyes narrowed. "What of the other six children?"

"Yes, well . . . that is where the actual favor comes in. Four of them are orphans, and the other two were sold by their families, so I do not think they will be a welcome sight should they be returned to their front stoop."

"And you expect me to do what with them?"

He shrugged. "You and that wife of yours are a resourceful team. I am sure you will think of something."

A great laugh pealed out of his friend. "Ami was just lamenting the other day how she longed for the pitter-patter of little feet; however, I do not think this was what she had in mind."

"So . . ." Bram lowered to an adjacent chair, setting his empty glass on a side table. "You will help me?"

"No." He stabbed his finger through the air. "You steal my cigars."

Bram shot up his hands "Frisk me if you like. You will not find a one in my pockets."

"The day is not over." Rising, Edmund collected both glasses and returned them to the cart, one of his brows lifting. "But I will help that lovely lady of yours. I am sure it has been trying enough for her to put up with you."

Bram sank against the cushion, blessed relief making breathing much easier. He hadn't realized just how uptight he'd been until now. "Thank you, Price. You always were a good sport."

"Amongst other things, you mean. Now then." All humor fled from his friend's face as Edmund leaned forward on his chair. "Though I never made it into Parliament, I have the ear of a good many politicians. There are rumblings of a new Factory and Workshop Act in the making, so tell me all about this sweatshop. I shall see what I can do about shutting it down."

Inman Manor was a respectable home—or at least it had been—but even in its glory days, the place was a scrap heap compared to this fine town house. The flickering glow of the hearth fire and overhead chandeliers cast a golden hue across the elegantly appointed drawing room. Velvet draperies and plush settees lined the walls, every table surface, baseboard, and mantel gleaming to polished perfection. Eva nibbled on her fingernail, marveling at the opulence and the kindness of the Prices for taking in such a menagerie she and Bram had brought to their door . . . which was a crisis of her own making. She never should have sent Penny away with that grasping, conniving Mrs. Mortimer! What a fool she'd been.

". . . you think, Eva?"

Ami's playful voice pulled her from her musings, and she shifted on the cushion to face the woman. "Forgive me." Eva smiled. "What did you say?"

"Oh, nothing of consequence, really. I merely commented on how delicious dinner was. I still can hardly believe I live in a home with a French chef. Good thing we have one, though. All I can cook is burned water." Ami picked up a rose-sprigged teapot and began pouring, one brow arched at Eva. "But something troubles you. I hope you are not worrying about the children. I daresay they shall all sleep like babes tonight."

"No doubt. I am grateful for the generosity of you and your husband. Truly. I do not deserve such a kindness. This whole thing could have been avoided had I not run ahead of God's timing."

Laughter bubbled out of the slight woman as she handed over a steaming cup of Earl Grey. "Then we are kindred spirits, my friend. If I had but a penny for every time I galloped off on my own, I daresay I would be wealthier than my husband." She resumed her seat with her own cup and saucer. "But tell me why you think such a thing, for sometimes we are harder on ourselves than need be—a truth I have fought like a wet cat this past year."

"I do not wish to burden you. I have already imposed on you enough as is."

"Bosh! It is the sharing of burdens that makes them lighter." She set the cup aside and leaned forward on her chair, sincerity gleaming in her eyes. "Please, if nothing else, I will know how to pray for you."

A smile twitched Eva's lip. This woman could tame a wild horse by sheer will alone. "All right." She fiddled with the handle of her teacup, taking care not to spill the hot liquid but grateful all the same to give her hands something to do. "The thing is, I never should have sent Penny away from home, for it was only two days later when Mr. Webb arrived with the tax money

I needed. I realize that does not make a lot of sense to you, not knowing my history and all, but suffice it to say I should have trusted God to provide instead of making things happen on my own."

"Then we are more than kindred spirits. We are twins separated at birth." A smirk twisted the lady's mouth. "Allow me a different perspective, Eva. The way I see it, if you had not sent your sister to that awful sweatshop, then you never would have discovered the other children, and they would not have been rescued. So do not assume it was not God's plan all along."

"But *I* am responsible for Penny, and she suffered because of me."

Ami wagged her finger. "You are not God. You cannot protect her from suffering."

She'd certainly heard that one before. "You sound like Mr. Webb."

"I shall take that as a compliment, for he is a good man." She reclaimed her teacup and took a few sips before murmuring so low, Eva had to strain to catch all her words. "Pain is a part of life on this earth, yet through it all, God is sovereign." Tears glistened in her eyes as she once again set the half-empty cup aside, this time apparently for good as she shoved it a distance away.

"It seems as if you speak as much to yourself as you do to me."

"I do." Lips pressed tightly together, she glanced away. "My . . . em, my father recently died, you see."

"Oh!" Eva's hand flew to her chest, her own heart squeezing for the woman's loss. "I am so sorry. I had no idea."

"No wonder on that account. I wore black for only a month. Dreadful colour. Made me even more gloomy." She retrieved a fire poker, then set about jabbing at the hearth coals. "I miss him dearly, of course, but at least he died doing what he loved. Edmund and I were on a dig with him in Egypt. My father had been struggling with sore joints for some time yet assured me he was getting better. He was not, and he hid how his affliction affected his mobility—or tried to. He fell from a ladder and hit his head, hence our return to London."

She jammed the poker back into the stand, then sat once again, her cheeks rosy from being so near the heat, or perhaps from emotion. "I haven't the heart right now to pursue another expedition, so speaking of God's timing, you happen to find me with nothing to do. Caring for the children you've brought me will be a welcome diversion."

Despite the sorrow lingering on the edge of the woman's voice, a glimmer of hope stirred in Eva's heart. Ami's resilience was a good reminder that even in the midst of hardship, there was always the possibility of finding solace and purpose in unexpected places, and most importantly, that God did not abandon one even in difficult times. "With all that you have been through, it is more than kind of you to take them in for now."

"Think nothing of it. I feel certain you would have done the same had Edmund and I shown up on your doorstep with a gaggle of young ones." She flounced back against the cushion, a sudden impish tilt to her head. "Now, on to happier topics. Tell me about you and Bram."

Eva shrugged. "We are old friends. I have known him since childhood."

"Come now, there is more to it than that. His gaze follows you around like a lost puppy. There is no mistaking he is a man in love, and you cannot deny you return that affection or your cheeks would not be blazing like those coals I just stirred."

Eva's palms flew to her face. Sure enough, her skin was hot to the touch. Her gaze met Ami's, and quite out of the blue, they both broke into laughter.

Eva sank against the back of her seat, completely relaxed in this sweet woman's presence. "Is it so very obvious?"

"To everyone but Bram, I suspect. I hope he comes to his senses quickly, though, for you are a gem he ought not let slip through his fingers. Men can be dolts when it comes to acting on their feelings, but if he doesn't, do not be afraid to act upon yours." Ami shoved a loosened lock of hair from her brow, her gaze burning into Eva's. "Love ought not languish for want of acknowledgment, for life is too short."

30

"Beware of Blackwoodsssss . . . hissss."

Her father's last words had woken Eva up in the middle of the night, sat next to her on the coach ride back to Royston all the next day, and now—standing next to Bram and Penny outside the vicarage on a cold December evening—those same words spread over her skin like a stinging rash. How wrong she had been! All this time she'd been wary of Mr. Blackwood when her father had been trying to warn her of his sister . . . but how had he known?

Penny tugged on her coat sleeve, pulling her from the unanswered question. "They've been in there for quite some time now. How long do you think it will take?"

Eva stared at the front door of the small cottage from where she stood on the driveway with Bram and several other Royston citizens. She'd had no idea when they returned Ginny, Lucy, and Andy that their families would follow along to the police station and then to the vicarage. It made perfect sense, though. Why wouldn't they wish to see justice played out as much as she did?

She squeezed Penny's shoulder. "Shouldn't be much longer

now. The constables ought to be bringing out Mrs. Mortimer very soon."

"I hope so. I cannot wait to tell that woman what I think and—"

"You shall do no such thing." Her words puffed out on a cloud of steam. "You will remain silent, or I shall have the professor take you back to the coach. Is that understood?"

A magnificent scowl carved into her sister's brow.

Bram leaned aside, his breath warm against Eva's ear. "I could say the same to you, you know. The constables warned us all to keep our distance. They will not abide a mob."

Eva glanced at the other families gathered near the police wagon, anger and resentment present in the folded arms, the wide stances, the grim jawlines. Her own fingers curled beneath her gloves. "I think it safe to say we all just wish to see justice carried out."

"And so it begins." He gestured toward the house, where Mrs. Mortimer strode between two constables, Mr. Blackwood at the rear.

"There she is. Vile woman!" one lady called.

"A jail cell's too good for the likes o' her. She ought to be made to work in a sweatshop like my little Ginny," another harsh voice cried out.

"She should be strung up, that's what," someone else called out.

"Back off, all of you," the lead constable growled as he swung the wagon's rear door open.

Reverend Blackwood frowned at the gathering. "Come, now. Let us behave in a godly fashion while this matter is sorted out."

"Tell that to yer sister." One of the men shook his fist in the air. "She's the one what sold our little ones!"

Mrs. Mortimer tossed her head. "And you were all glad to part with them. Not one of you put up a fuss . . . save for you."

She speared Eva with a malignant gaze. "This was your doing, was it not?"

It was strange to see the woman without her feathered hat or string of pearls, her hair frizzled about her shoulders, her skin paler than the moonlight without her thickly painted cosmetics. She looked like a bizarre sketch waiting to be painted.

"No, Mrs. Mortimer. You brought this on yourself." Eva faced the reverend. "How could you let your sister get away with such fraud? You are a man of God."

His head dipped slightly. "I had no idea what she was involved with," he murmured.

"Of course you didn't," his sister snapped. "Your nose is stuck in your holy books from dawn till dusk."

He jerked his face toward Mrs. Mortimer. "That is no crime."

"Neither does it smack of the brotherly love and duty you preach on Sunday mornings. And where has all your talk gotten you? A tiny house in a nowhere town without a friend to call upon. You will die a lonely, bitter old man, Ebenezer. Quite a legacy for a vicar."

The constable rattled his keys but made no move to gather Mrs. Mortimer into the wagon. Instead, his gaze shot to Mr. Blackwood as if this were a game of cricket to be observed.

Eva stared as well. The stoic reverend—the intense, commanding deliverer of brimstone and hellfire—aged in front of them like the turning of time's pages. His blue eyes faded, a haunted mask carving lines on his face. He was speechless. Helpless. Hopeless? It appeared so, for his hands twisted together as if he were grappling with demons too formidable to conquer. Eva got the distinct impression that if one were to touch him ever so slightly, he'd shatter into a million pieces right there on the drive. She'd never seen the man so broken.

And the sight—quite surprisingly—broke her heart.

She immediately stepped up beside him and faced his sister.

"You are wrong, Mrs. Mortimer. I call myself a friend of Mr. Blackwood. I daresay many others would as well."

A sharp intake of air from the reverend cut a hole in the sudden quiet.

"You're no saint, Miss Inman," Mrs. Mortimer sneered. "And neither was your father. He knew all along what I was doing, caught me in the act the very first time I snatched that orphan boy off the streets—and he took my money to keep quiet about it. I can only say it was a good thing your father died when he did, for I'd have not allowed him to continue to bleed me."

Eva's hand flew to her throat, the truth of the woman's words stealing her breath. He'd known! *She'd* been the source of her father's unexplained revenue. No wonder he'd tried to warn her against the woman.

Eva's knees weakened and were it not for Bram's strong arm shoring her up as he stepped beside her, she'd have collapsed on the spot. Her father had taken money—for a vulnerable child, no less! What a betrayal. What a . . .

Her breath caught as a new revelation hit her sideways.

Her father hadn't just been trying to give her a warning. That's why he'd not allowed her to profess her secret. He'd been trying to breathe his own guilt through lungs that no longer worked. A cry strangled in her throat.

Oh, Papa!

"It is all right, Eva. I am here. I have you," Bram whispered in her ear.

Or was it God speaking to her soul?

Either way, the words ignited a fire within her—a determination to seek justice and redemption where he had not. Slowly yet surely, strength seeped into the weak cracks of her soul. She pulled away from Bram as Mrs. Mortimer was loaded into the police wagon.

"My father's actions do not define me, Mrs. Mortimer, nor will they absolve you of your sins. Justice will prevail. I shall see to it." Eva cast a glance around at the jutted jaws and eyes burning around her. "We all shall see to it."

It was a solemn ride home. Understandable on Penny's behalf. She was stretched out on the carriage seat, head leaning hard against Eva's shoulder, the rhythmic sway of the coach having rocked her to sleep. A smile tugged at Bram's lips. The girl looked so peaceful now, but when awake, she was a regular firebrand.

Directly across from him, Eva stared out at the night, silent as a gravestone. Were she not wearing gloves, no doubt her fingernails would be chewed to nubs. But even agitated, never had a woman captivated him more.

"Hey," he said softly. "Do not be overly tough on yourself—or on your father. Mrs. Mortimer bears the weight of guilt in this matter."

Her gaze shot to him, and even in the spare moonlight whispering through the window, sparks flared in her pale blue eyes. "My father should have gone to the authorities. He never should have taken that woman's money."

"And tell me, how was that budget once you took over the reins of the family estate?"

She looked away, backbone rigid, shoulders set. The next rut in the road could snap her in half. She had every right to feel betrayed, yet he'd learned long ago that though truth might be absolute, discerning the right course of action when living that truth was often anything but obvious. Like guiding stars, the light offered direction but did not clear the path one had to walk.

"Eva." He rested a light touch on her knee, as if the contact might lessen some of her anguish. "Your father loved you and your sister. He would have done anything to provide for his daughters and save the family estate, and by the looks of it, he did. I am not saying it was right. I merely suggest his intentions were not solely self-serving. He was a man caught in a desperate situation, willing to sacrifice his integrity to ensure the well-being of his family. It is easy to judge from the outside, but we can never truly understand the burdens others carry or the choices they feel forced to make. We are all fallen creatures."

She stared at his hand for a long while. Good. Hopefully he'd offered some sort of comfort to her tortured thoughts.

As the coach rolled through the gates of Inman Manor, she lifted her face. Sweet mercy, but she was beautiful in the shadowy confines of this coach.

"How did you become so wise?" she murmured.

He pulled back, a chuckle rumbling in his throat. "Years of practice in making awful decisions."

The carriage eased to a stop. He opened the door—Edmund having provided only a driver, not a footman—and once his feet hit gravel, he immediately offered his hand.

Penny yawned her way out. "Are we home?"

Home. The word did strange things to his gut. Would he ever be settled in a house of his own instead of relying on his uncle's good graces? Have a wife? A family?

"You are, indeed, my girl." He righted Penny, then clasped Eva's hand to help her down.

Once inside the manor, Dixon bustled to the front hall and ushered Penny upstairs. Bram had turned to Eva to wish her good night when the thud of footsteps pounded down the corridor. Who would be in such a clip at this late hour?

Mr. Sinclair appeared, hat in hand, coat over his arm as if he'd either rushed to get here or was in a hurry to leave.

"I've been waiting for you two. Come see." He wheeled about and retraced his steps, leaving Bram to arch a brow at Eva.

She merely shrugged and followed the man.

Sinclair swung into the breakfast room that yet faintly smelled of old artifacts. Bram inhaled the musty scent, taking comfort in the familiarity of it. The steward led them to the far end of the table, where a canvas had been laid out. Atop it sat a stone box the size of one of Price's humidors.

Bram swooped over to the relic, pulse racing. The heavy lid appeared to be fused shut with the passage of time and a thick line of wax. He glanced at the steward. "Where did you find this?"

"Tom and I were filling up that sinkhole Miss Inman told me about when I took a misstep and landed my leg in the chasm. Took some work to get me out, which made the opening larger—and that's when we saw the corner of this box. It was too perfect to be a simple rock. Thought I'd wait till your return to see what's inside. Didn't wish to bring a curse down on my head."

"Oh, Sinclair." Eva shook her head. "You and your superstitions."

Bram's fingers itched for tools he didn't have. "Can you get me a wooden mallet and a chisel?"

"Straightaway, Professor."

In the meantime, Bram flipped open his pocketknife and bent to scale away the wax seal bit by bit.

"What do you suppose is inside?" Eva's question curled over his shoulder.

"No idea."

"What is your best guess?"

"Anxious, are you?" He grinned up at her. "Coins, most like. Or jewelry. Maybe even a religious item or documents, something that whoever sealed this did not want ruined by water or air."

"I wish your uncle could be here to see this."

His heart panged. "Me too."

Moments later, Sinclair returned with the requested items. Once the wax was removed, Bram set down his knife, then ever so carefully placed the tip of the chisel into the opening crevice.

Even more gently, he tapped the handle with the mallet's flat head. Little by little, the lid gave, until finally he dropped the tools and lifted with a great heave. Centuries of dust crumbled to the canvas. Stone ground against stone.

And then he stared into a darkened, miniature tomb. "Light, please."

Eva brought a lamp close, illuminating rectangular wax tablets.

Bram raised one reverently, completely forgetting to breathe as his eyes scanned the Latin.

"Well." Eva huffed her disappointment. "Certainly not the treasure I had hoped for."

She had no idea.

Bram jerked his head up, gaze seeking Sinclair's. "Ready my horse at once."

Willing his hands not to tremble, he gently laid the tablet back in the box with all the care of a newborn babe.

"Where are you going at such an hour?"

He straightened, hardly able to stand for the thrill coursing through his veins. "I must return to Cambridge immediately. This is exactly what my uncle and I had hoped to find."

Her brows knitted. "But that is not the Holy Grail."

"It does not need to be. These tablets are a covenant for the members of Caelum Academia—indisputable proof there was a Roman settlement here, serving as both an intellectual refuge for artists and a secret place of Christian worship during a time of religious persecution. Just as my uncle said!" He grabbed hold of her shoulders, grin wide. "Do you understand what this means, Eva? My uncle will be vindicated. His pension, his position, both restored. It is a miracle!"

She smiled. "How wonderful!" But then her smile faltered. "I, em, I suppose you shall be reinstated as well?"

"Likely, but what really matters is my uncle's career will no longer end in shame."

"You are right. I am very happy for him—and for you. Though I cannot say I am pleased about you riding all the way to Cambridge in the dark. Please be careful."

"Don't burden yourself on my account. I generally land on my feet." He reset the lid, then wrapped the canvas tightly around the box and tucked it all beneath his arm.

"I guess this is good-bye, then." Her voice rang surprisingly hollow.

He faced her, searching her gaze for the cause of such a strained tone—but her eyes were still waters, unwilling to give their secrets. "It is good-bye, though I am sure Penny shall have something to say about me leaving without any parting words to her."

"She will survive." Eva turned away, words traveling under her breath. "Though I am not sure I will."

He cocked his head, turning her around with a firm grasp to her arm. "What was that?"

A battle waged on her face, her jaw shifting as if she chewed on something too large for her to swallow. What on earth troubled her so?

Alarm churned in his belly. "Eva? What is it?"

She inhaled so deeply, the rise of her chest pressed hard against her coat buttons. And when she blew it out, she tipped her chin defiantly. "If this is good-bye, then you should know you take my heart with you—just as you did when you left all those years ago. Whether I like it or not, you are part of me, Bram Webb, and I am a better person for it. I wish you all the best and brightest."

Flinging her arms around his neck, she lifted to her toes, her lips meeting his with an abandon he'd never known. He'd kissed plenty of women in his day, but none had given themselves to him so earnestly, so pure and raw that the touch ached in his soul.

And then she was gone. Before he could pull her into his

embrace. Before he could kiss her back with all the passion inside him begging to be released. He should follow her. Chase her down. Profess the love that beat with each pound of his heart and tell her he would return as soon as humanly possible.

But the box beneath his arm weighed heavy. If they were to have any kind of future, he must see to this now.

Duty called. God help him.

Duty called.

31

Trinity College was a veritable crypt. Not even the headmaster's clerk was at his desk this morning. Standing in the empty office, Bram reached for his pocket watch, his fingers coming up empty. Blast. How he missed that timepiece. Still, lamenting the loss or even waiting around here would do no good. He'd simply have to come back later and hope—and pray—Sir George Gabriel Stokes hadn't left Trinity altogether to make merry elsewhere for Christmas.

For there was no way he'd present this precious antiquity to Grimwinkle.

Clutching the canvas-wrapped box, Bram strode from administration, cold air nipping his cheeks as he passed through the front entry. He welcomed the brisk slap in the face chasing away the fatigue that dogged him after his midnight reunion with his uncle.

His footsteps clapped unchallenged on the stone walk that eventually spilled onto Trinity Street—where a tall man in a black coat was about to ascend into a lacquered carriage.

Of all the providence!

Bram dashed ahead. "Sir George, a moment, if you please."

A face with a sharp nose and even sharper eyes turned his way, and as recognition dawned, the headmaster shook his head. "You are wasting your time, Mr. Webb. I will not rescind Professor Grimwinkle's decision. Good day." He grabbed hold of the coach handle and alighted the step.

"But you will, sir, once you lay eyes on this—a discovery sure to win awards and bring acclaim to Trinity." Bram held up the wrapped relic.

Sir George didn't so much as turn around. "Whatever you have, bring it to the attention of Professor Grimwinkle. I do not have the time for this right now. I should have been in London last evening."

Bram advanced. If he had to grab hold of the horses' bridles to stop the man, he'd do so. "Please, sir. Two more minutes will not make a difference. I hold history in my hands. Do not turn your back on it."

The fabric between the headmaster's shoulder blades stretched taut before he stepped down to the pavement with a frown. "Two minutes, Webb. That is all."

Quickly yet carefully, Bram unwrapped the canvas to reveal the stone. "This is not the ideal place to present such a treasure, but if you would not mind lifting the lid, sir?"

Bram held the box steady on his arms while the headmaster removed the cover, and as soon as the man did so, he glanced at the wax tablets, then back up at Bram. "What am I looking at?"

"The covenant of Caelum Academia, proof of the much-debated Roman settlement just outside of Royston—a find no one thought possible. This is evidence the place was more than just a fictional Atlantis."

Sir George bent over the box, his gaze drifting across the inscriptions carved into the wax coating on the topmost wooden tablet. "*Nos exsules Romani, hoc firmo atque inviolabili foedere ac nova Academia Caeli foedere firmato, a nobis posthac fides, obses, pactum.*"

"'We, exiles of Rome,'" Bram murmured, still hardly believing he held such a treasure in his hands, "'herewith bind ourselves in this strong and inviolable pact as the new settlement of Caelum Academia. Stated henceforth are our beliefs, our pledge, and our covenant.'"

"Yes, I can obviously read Latin." Irritation ran thick in the headmaster's tone as he restored the cover to the box. "Am I to understand you discovered this at the dig you were conducting in Royston?"

"Yes, sir."

"Hmm." The man slapped his gloves against the palm of his hand, silent for a moment. "Where are the rest of the relics?"

"What we have uncovered thus far are here in Cambridge. I offered them to the history department, but Professor Grimwinkle failed to act on the purchase. When I returned last night, word was waiting for me that the Fitzwilliam Museum is proposing a fair price for the lot."

The skin of the headmaster's concave cheeks rode tight against his bones. "You mean to say you presented the professor with antiquities never before seen, and he turned them down?"

"Like I said, Sir George, this one piece"—he lifted the box higher—"is enough to bring acclaim to the college, but included with the rest of the finds, well, I should say the collection would have given Trinity's Roman history department no competition in the whole of England—and all because of the determined belief of former Regius Professor Sebastian Pendleton. Once word of this find gets out, I daresay he will be a most sought-after speaker."

Bram sucked in a lungful of cold air. That was it! He had been right. If Grimwinkle had successfully gotten him and his uncle out of the picture and finished the dig himself, then Grimwinkle would've been the one to receive all the acclaim, which was prime motivation for him to have hired Trestwell to end the dig, or at least scare or frustrate him and his uncle away.

"Your uncle will indeed be a most sought-after speaker—but as a representative of Trinity College." The headmaster's voice bounced off the college stone walls. "Tell Professor Pendleton he is fully reinstated to his position. As are you. I shall send word to my clerk to draw up the paperwork. And whatever the Fitzwilliam is offering, I will see it doubled. Here." He pulled out a thick wad of banknotes from his wallet and handed them over. "This is a retainer of good faith, so you know I mean my word. Now, if you will excuse me, I really must be off."

Bram gaped. This was better than he'd hoped for! "Godspeed, Sir George. Until the new year."

"Professor." The imposing man tipped his black hat, then disappeared into his fancy coach.

As the horses' hooves clip-clopped over the cobbles, Bram carefully rewrapped the canvas around the box. His mission had been accomplished—more than accomplished. He'd vindicated his uncle and restored the man's pension. He'd collect more money than Eva would know what to do with. And he even had his old job back.

So why the empty hole in his chest?

Tucking the box beneath his arm, he hailed a cab, trying hard to ignore the truth he'd been denying ever since Eva had kissed him. She'd been wrong. Terribly wrong. He hadn't taken her heart with him here to Cambridge.

He'd left his with her.

In order that we may start afresh and go to Meg's wedding with free minds, it will be well to begin with a little gossip about the Marches. And here let me premise that if any of the elders think there is too much "lovering" in the story, as I fear they may (I'm not afraid the young folks will make that objection), I can only say with Mrs. March, "What can

you expect when I have four gay girls in the house, and a dashing young neighbor over the way?"

"I wish we had a dashing young neighbour."

Eva glanced up from the opening of *Good Wives* and arched a brow at her sister. They sat curled up in the window seat of Penny's bedroom, late-morning sun lighting glossy highlights in her sister's hair and a surprisingly wistful tilt to her chin. "What is this? My little poppet pining for a boy, of all things?"

"Not just any boy." Penny leaned her head against the thick sill. "A dashing one who doesn't mind getting his fingernails dirty and has an interest in digging up relics. I liked my time as an archaeologist. I wish the professors and their crew were still here."

"I thought you liked reading."

"I do, but I also like . . ."

Penny continued on, but Eva didn't hear a word the girl said. She couldn't. She was too interested in the man riding down the front drive on a chestnut cob.

Closing the book, she dashed to the door. "That is enough reading for now."

"But you've only just begun!"

"Later, I promise," she called over her shoulder as she dropped the book onto a side table.

Grabbing hold of her skirt hem, she tore down the stairs, ran across the front hall, and yanked open the door. The cold December air didn't stand a chance at chilling her, so fervently did her heart beat in her chest. Was this truly happening? "You have returned!"

"I have." Bram grinned as he dismounted, hair wild beneath his hat, skin ruddy from the ride, so handsome it hurt to look at him.

A welcome sight, but wholly unexpected. "Why have you come?"

335

"Several reasons." He climbed the stairs and stopped in front of her, smelling of winter air and horseflesh. "Do you wish to hear of them out here or inside?"

"La! Some hostess I am. Please, come in."

The second they crossed the threshold, Penny hurled herself at Bram.

"I knew you'd come back." She wrapped her arms around Bram's waist.

"Penny!" Eva slapped her hand against her chest, mortified. "Such manners. You are no better than Jo March."

Bram merely laughed as he peeled the girl from him and stooped to her level. "Despite what your sister says, I am happy to receive such a welcome." He straightened, his gaze seeking Eva's. "I wonder if I might have a word with you?"

"Of course. Penny, how about you see if Mrs. Pottinger would bring us some tea?"

"All right." The girl bounded down the passage, waving her hand behind her back. "But don't leave without saying good-bye this time, Professor."

"I promise." He grinned.

Eva led him to the sitting room, where Bram pulled off his hat and ran his fingers through his hair. "By the by"—he peered at her with a mysterious gleam in his eyes—"Mr. Toffit sends his regards."

She immediately turned lest he see the giveaway smile on her face and gestured to the sofa, rising hope making it hard for her to even think of sitting—and yet she did. It was even harder to keep her tone dulcet instead of all-out giddy. "What were you doing at Mr. Toffit's?"

"I shall get to that, but first I have something for you." He handed over several banknotes. "This is merely a good faith deposit for the purchase of your antiquities. The first payment of many to come. In the new year you shall have nine thousand pounds in total."

Eva blinked. Surely she wasn't hearing properly. Nine thousand pounds? Nine *thousand*? She stared at Bram, mouth agape.

Leaning near, he closed her lips with a light touch to her jaw. "It is all yours. With the proper investment of that sum and the additional sales when the excavation continues next term, not only will Inman Manor be restored but you and Penny are set for life. Your sister can attend any school she wishes, and you will no longer be bent over a ledger that will not balance."

She shook her head, hardly daring to believe this could be true. "Such an amount! You told me the antiquities would fetch a fair sum, but this I can hardly believe." She rubbed her fingers over the paper, supremely happy and yet also a bit confused. "Wait a minute. The *first* payment? What about the thirty pounds you gave me to pay the tax bill? I thought that was from the sale of the relics—or at least from the sale of the ring. Where did you get that money?"

"Pah! You know. Here and there." He clapped his hands together, then gave them a brisk rub. "Now then, I have more good news. My—"

"Hold it right there, sir." She held up her own hand as if stopping a wild horse. "You always change the subject when a topic does not suit. You are hiding something. Where did you get the funds for my tax bill? And do not think of spinning some fanciful tale to put me off, for I will not have it."

"I, em . . ." He tugged at the muffler around his neck, taking his time to unwind it before coiling it at his side on the sofa. "If you must know, I pawned my watch, but—"

"Your cherished pocket watch?" She collapsed against the chairback. Bram was a man of many secrets, but this one . . . "Had I known you did such a thing, I never would have accepted your money."

"Which is why I did not tell you."

"Oh, Bram." Her heart sank as she thought of the many times he'd pulled out that flash of silver and flipped open the lid, of the loving tone in his voice when he'd told her of his uncle's sweet gifting.

And he'd done it all for her sake.

Tears welled, turning the sitting room into a blur of colour and light.

"Hey," he rumbled. "Only smiles today."

"But—"

"Tut-tut." He wagged his finger. "Smiles, or I will not tell you what else I have come to say."

She tried to push her lips into a curve—though it probably looked more like a grimace. She would make things right for him. With this banknote in her hands, the first thing she'd do would be to track down that timepiece and redeem it for this thoughtful man.

"A little weak, but a good effort." He brushed his thumb across her mouth.

Which tickled—and she couldn't help but smile.

"That is better. Now, what I was trying to tell you is that those wax tablets paid off exactly as I had hoped. The headmaster reinstated my uncle's position *and* his pension."

Her smile spread into a full-fledged grin. "That is wonderful! I am so happy for him."

"My job was reinstated as well."

"Oh, I . . ." She worked her jaw, willing congratulatory words to her tongue. None came. In fact, every single word she ever knew flew from her head. He'd go back to his world now. For good. Live in Cambridge. Take up his old life and forget all about her. A banknote fluttered from her lax fingers, slowly flapping to the floor.

Bram retrieved it, his brows cinching as he laid it on the tea table. "But this is good news. I shall be returning to finish the dig here, and once the semester ends, why, apparently the curator position for the new Royston Museum has not yet been filled. Someone whispered to Mr. Toffit that he ought to keep the job open for me to claim at the end of the school year. I do not suppose you know anything about that, do you?"

She shot to her feet, palms slapping against her heart. "You mean . . . ?"

"I thought as much." He grinned like a pirate as he rose, all swagger and bluster. "Once my uncle retires and I officially resign from Trinity in May, you will be looking at the new curator. My uncle shall be a paid consultant, leveraging his expertise to provide guidance on exhibits, acquisitions, and research projects, all where I can still keep an eye on him."

"How perfect!"

"And you are to have new neighbours, that is if you do not mind letting out the cottage to Uncle Pendleton and I until the building for the museum is outfitted with living quarters."

A dashing young neighbor over the way.

Well, well. Penny would be over the moon with this news . . . as was she. First an exorbitant amount of money, now the man she loved most in the world was to live in her own backyard? Eva grinned in full. "Of course I do not mind, but . . ." Once again her smile faltered. "I still do not understand. Why would you leave an esteemed academic position for a small-town museum?"

"The salary is good. The work is a dream, plus I will be close enough to continue working on your dig if you will allow it. Both my uncle and I are weary of academic politics, and most importantly . . ." He collected both her hands, his skin feverishly warm against hers.

"What?" she breathed—barely.

His gaze burned into hers, the grey in his eyes liquid silver. "I could not very well leave you without a heart—that is, if your sentiments have not changed."

"They have not," she whispered.

"Neither have mine."

His lips touched hers with the heat of a thousand suns, making her, breaking her, filling her with a love so pure, the world didn't exist. There was only this man, this moment, this beautiful joining of two hearts into a new thing, a bold thing. Something she never wanted to end.

And yet he pulled away and cupped her face with his hand that smelled of leather and horse and so many promises of gentle cherishing. "I have loved you since you were a girl, Eva Inman. No, longer than that, for somehow you have always been a part of me. I see you when I close my eyes. I breathe you in the night. I hear your voice in the wind and feel your touch on my cheek." With his free hand, he guided her palm to his face. "I have loved none but you—nor ever shall. I do not know how I ever lived so long and so far away from you, and I find I can do it no more. Would you be my wife?"

"Oh, Bram." Her throat closed, but that didn't stop her from furiously nodding her head.

"Is that a yes?" He laughed.

She grinned. "It is. And you were right."

"About what?" He angled his head, curiosity rife in the lift of his brows.

"This is a day for smiling!"

32

Six months later, Eva beamed wider than ever as she stood before the new museum alongside her husband, his uncle—who was now hers too—and the members of the historical society. Ahead, a vibrant red ribbon stretched across the entrance, drawing the gazes of eager onlookers. Though Mr. Toffit delivered a meticulously prepared speech, capturing the crowd's attention, Eva's thoughts were consumed by the handsome man beside her and his selfless dedication to his role as curator. Silently, she prayed for God to richly bless her husband.

For He had surely blessed her. Life with a man she loved. All her valuables redeemed from the pawn shop. Penny thriving in a respected school. How could life get any better?

"And so it is my great pleasure—"Mr. Toffit stretched to his full height, his tall hat compensating for what he lacked—"to declare the Royston Historical Museum is now officially open to the public, with many exhibits and more to come—featuring none other than some local finds from Inman Manor. Now then, Mr. Webb, if you please." With a flourish, he handed Bram a pair of large shears, their silver blades gleaming in the June sunshine.

"Thank you, Mr. Toffit, but I should like to defer the honour to Professor Emeritus Sebastian Pendleton." Bram pressed the scissors into his uncle's grip with a wink and a smile.

As Uncle Pendleton approached the ribbon, Eva whispered in her husband's ear. "I can still hardly believe Sir George granted your uncle not only his pension but a new title as well."

"I yet smile when I think of it," Bram whispered back. "Though I doubt if Grimwinkle does."

"He deserved to be dismissed! His thievery of your uncle's notes should have been brought to light decades before this, not to mention his paying off Mr. Trestwell to hinder your dig."

A sly grin spread on her husband's lips. "Have you not yet learned, wife, that all transpires in God's timing, not yours?"

Apparently not, though she was loath to admit it aloud.

The ribbon fell. Applause thundered. Mr. Toffit opened the door wide and stationed himself at the head of the receiving line.

Bram pulled out his silver pocket watch, and after a glance at the glass face, tucked it away. "Right on time, though I should have expected nothing less. Are you ready to receive our first patrons?"

"I am." She smiled as Bram guided her to their designated spot near the open door. Guests ascended the stairs, excited chatter filling the air. Truly, it was a lovely day in all respects— save one.

She glanced up at Bram. "How I wish Penny were here. She would have loved such excitement."

Bram reached for her hand, giving her fingers a reassuring squeeze. "Your sister is devoted to her studies."

True enough. Though a bit hesitant to enroll at first, after encouragement from Bram and her, Penny had found pure contentment at the Royal Normal College and Academy of Music for the Blind, for she'd said as much in her most recent correspondence. She'd joined the choir, excelled in mastering Braille, and had even discovered a knack for piano. Gratitude swelled in Eva's chest. The windfall from the antiquities of the cursed acres had been a godsend, affording her sister the opportunity to thrive in the finest institution England had to offer—something Eva had never dreamed could happen.

"Eva!" Lottie squealed.

She barely opened her arms before her friend swooped in for an embrace. "Congratulations! This is quite an event for Royston." She kissed each of Eva's cheeks.

"Thank you." She grinned as she looked past Lottie, one brow arching. "But where is your mother? She adores gatherings such as this."

"She has taken to her bed again. A summer cold, of all things." Lottie rolled her eyes. "You'd think the woman suffered the plague, with all her moaning and groaning."

"At least she has not got you tied up watching the younger ones."

"She does, actually, but I bribed Freddie to keep them busy for a while. I couldn't miss this event." Lottie sidestepped to Bram. "If you see any available gents, I wouldn't mind an introduction."

"I shall keep an eye open." He laughed.

"Ho ho!" Mr. Finebridge approached as Lottie moved on to greet Mr. Toffit. "A lovely morning and a fine ceremony. I heard there were to be refreshments, and I can only hope they are of the spirited kind." He waggled his thick eyebrows, the odour of rum wafting about him.

Eva tried hard not to wrinkle her nose. "There is tea, Mr. Finebridge, as is proper for so early in the day."

"It's never too early for a merry spirit, my dear." He flapped his elbows, then sidled over to Bram. "Say, Webb, did you hear about your old friend Trestwell?"

Eva stiffened.

Bram scowled. "He is no friend of mine, Mr. Finebridge."

"Exactly as I thought, which should please you to know the

fellow is currently laid up in the county jail for disturbing the peace."

Eva gasped, though truly she ought not be surprised. Richard Trestwell's brutish ways were destined to catch up with him sometime. "What has he done this time?"

"The usual, scrapped a fight with the wrong man down at the Old Bull." Mr. Finebridge scratched his side whiskers, a sardonic twist to his lips. "I daresay he'll be eating mashed potatoes for quite some time. That jaw of his is pretty busted up."

Bram humphed. "What happened to the other man?"

"That's the best part. Seems the barkeep had a sudden lapse of memory when it came to identifying the other party. Ol' Trestwell will bear the brunt of the blame for the broken tables and chairs. Ho ho!" He cuffed Bram on the arm good-naturedly. "Best of luck on your museum and all. Being there's no refreshments of my sort, I suppose I shall find other enterprises for the morning. Good day to you both."

Eva dipped her head. "Good day, Mr. Finebridge."

The moment he was out of hearing, Bram murmured, "That man's liver is going to swim away before he realizes it is gone."

"You, sir, are a scoundrel." Eva batted his sleeve, laughing. "But likely very correct. The man is—"

Bram's gaze drifted past her, a subtle shake of his head accompanying his silent observation.

She turned to face the Reverend Mr. Blackwood, dressed from head to toe in his usual grey, though since becoming headmaster at the newly founded Haven Academy, he'd added a sprig of colour to his monotone garments: a badge of red with the school's insignia on his lapel.

"Mr. and Mrs. Webb." He tipped his hat.

"Mr. Blackwood. Thank you for coming." Eva folded her hands, posture at once straightening. Though the man had admittedly softened these past months, her old habit was hard to break. "I am surprised you took time away from your students this morning."

"Classes are cancelled due to personal business. It is my monthly prison visit to see my sister, but I thought to first stop by here and offer my congratulations."

"Very thoughtful of you." Eva's brows gathered. "How is Mrs. Mortimer holding up?"

"As profitably as she can possibly make of her situation. She sells contraband to the other inmates, and though I've informed the staff, they have yet to catch her in the act. Needless to say, I pray daily for her soul."

"I shall join you in that prayer, Mr. Blackwood."

"Thank you." He moved on to Bram. "When you have a moment, Mr. Webb, I should like to speak with you in reference to a workshop or two for my students."

"I will meet you inside shortly."

"Very good."

Mr. Blackwood moved on, Eva's gaze following him. Other than the splash of red on his frock coat, he didn't look any differently on the outside, but inwardly he'd been transformed. "His sister's conviction surely did alter that man," she murmured.

"Bearing the weight of tragedy can reshape a person's perspective on what truly matters." Bram glanced down at her, empathy shining in his eyes. "Adversity has a way of reshuffling one's priorities in life."

"Yes, but to open a school for vulnerable children? I would say that is quite a miracle."

"Turns out a heart does beat beneath that grey coat of his after all, eh?"

"Mrs. Webb." Mrs. Muggins stepped up to her next, offering neither a hand of greeting nor a smile.

"Mrs. Muggins." Eva dipped a small curtsey, for though the woman refused to play by her own rules, the old widow still held others to more formal acknowledgments. "Thank you for visiting the museum on opening day."

"It is my civic duty, though it remains to be seen if it is a waste of my time." She passed by Bram without a word.

Bram leaned aside. "If there were a profession for skeptics, that woman would win the highest acclaim."

And so went the next half hour, until finally the last patron paused in front of Eva and Bram, the woman's greeting as trilling as a nearby skylark singing in a tree. "Congratulations, Mr. and Mrs. Webb. This museum is a fine addition to Royston. Just what we needed!"

"Mrs. Quibble, how lovely to see you." Eva lightly squeezed the woman's arm.

"I knew it would be a grand event with you at the helm." Her gaze shot to Bram. "No offense, Mr. Webb."

"None taken, Mrs. Quibble."

Eva gestured toward the door, where merry conversation drifted out. "There are refreshments inside. I think you will especially find the lemon fingers to your liking."

"No doubt I shall." She patted her gloved hand against her stomach, then stepped closer. "However, I purposely held back to have a private word with you, Eva. I've put off asking you to return full time to the relief society being you're newly married and all, but it's been nearly half a year since your wedding, and I feel confident you are settled in your matrimonial role. In light of such, when can I expect your service to resume? It is never too early for you to start planning the next fundraising gala, you know."

"That is very true, Mrs. Quibble, and I am happy to help with preliminary arrangements, but I am afraid I will not be able to attend the December event."

"I . . . I don't understand." Mrs. Quibble faltered, her voice losing its chirpy quality as she blinked. "You have already filled in your diary six months out?"

"I have indeed." She beamed. The woman—and Bram—could have no idea just how busy her schedule would be. "However, you can put me down for the following year."

"I am at sixes and sevens to hear such dire tidings." Mrs. Quibble fanned herself with a lace handkerchief, looking for all the world as if she'd just heard the Queen herself had perished. "I suppose there is nothing for me to do but hold you to your promise, unless . . ." Her tiny black eyes darted about Eva's face as if looking for a place to perch. "Is there anything I can say to persuade you otherwise?"

"I am sorry, Mrs. Quibble, but no. There is nothing under the sun that could induce me to change my mind."

"Well then." A huge sigh deflated the woman as she tucked away her handkerchief. "I suppose I shall have to inquire with Miss Barker."

"You will find her inside. Please enjoy the spread of pastries and selections of tea."

Mrs. Quibble stepped past them to Mr. Toffit. "Would you mind escorting me inside, sir? I'm feeling a bit faint."

"Oh dear. We cannot have that." At once, he shored the lady up with a strong arm and guided her inside the new museum.

The moment they disappeared, Bram turned to her with a look that never failed to flutter her heart. "I was not aware of any engagements on our December calendar."

She straightened his collar, savoring the final moments of her precious secret. "That is because I have not told you yet."

He pulled her close, a shrewd gleam in his eyes. "Told me what exactly?"

"I think you already know, sir." She grinned.

"Are you . . . ?" His hand slid to her belly, his touch sending shivers down her spine. Wonder sparked in his eyes. "You are! I am right, am I not?" Excitement rumbled in his tone.

Her grin grew. "You are."

Tossing back his head, he laughed—and she couldn't help

but join in. Ah, how wonderful it was to share such joy, such life, such unbridled oneness.

He ran his fingers along her arms, love radiating off him. "Remember that day you agreed to be my wife?"

"I shall never forget it."

"I did not think life could get any better than that," he mused. "Turns out I was very wrong. Every day with you is a gift."

Indeed.

Every day *was* a gift.

"You know, husband, I used to wonder when God would smile on me." She captured his face in her hands, heart so full she could hardly stand it. "And it turns out He has been all along."

HISTORICAL NOTES

Vindolanda

The fictional dig in this story, Caelum Academia, is inspired by a real historical excavation in Northumberland, one that is still being explored by archaeologists today. Vindolanda is an ancient Roman fort that was one of the most important military sites on the northern-most tip of the Roman Empire. It was established in AD 85 and was continuously occupied for over three hundred years. Today it is known for the discovery of a collection of wooden writing tablets dating from the first and second centuries that contained a wealth of information about daily life at the fort. That's where I got the idea for the tablets that are uncovered at Inman Manor.

Guy Fawkes Day

This British holiday is sometimes called Bonfire Night, and it is still celebrated today. The roots of this event go back to what is known as the Gunpowder Plot. Guy Fawkes was part of a group of men who conspired to blow up Parliament and kill King James I, because they were angry about unfair policies and the persecution of Catholics. Effigies of Guy Fawkes are often paraded through the streets before being burned on the bonfire, symbolizing the punishment of the plotters. A large fire is lit at night to commemorate the foiled attempt to burn down the House of Lords, often accompanied by fireworks to add to the festivities.

Spotted Dick

This dessert—which is still commonly served with a traditional Sunday roast—gained popularity during the Victorian era. It is a British pudding consisting of a moist suet-based sponge cake that is loaded with dried fruit (usually currants or raisins). It is often served warm with a custard sauce or whipped cream. The name strikes Americans as hilarious, but it simply came about because of the spots, which are the fruit, and *dick* possibly being a colloquial term for pudding.

Glebe

A glebe is a piece of land, often attached to a church, that is used for various purposes, such as providing income to support the clergy and maintain the church property, or serving as a residence. It can include fields, gardens, and other areas used for cultivation or pastoral activities.

Little Women and *Good Wives*

While Louisa May Alcott is an American author, Brits loved her classic novels. Originally, *Little Women* was the title of the first part of the book we know today—chapters 1–23—and was published in 1868. So many readers wanted to read more that Alcott wrote a sequel entitled *Good Wives* in 1869. That book was eventually added to the first as chapters 24–47 instead of being a stand-alone read.

Sweatshops

The Industrial Revolution changed the world in good ways and in bad. Sweatshops were definitely part of the bad. The term implies harsh and exploitative labor practices, and unfortunately, London had its fair share of them, particularly in the garment, textile, and shoemaking industries. These awful places were characterized by poor working conditions, long hours, low pay, and often employed children as young as five years old. Employees were subjected to verbal and physical abuse and were expected to work for extended hours without breaks. Conditions were cramped and unsanitary, with inadequate ventilation and lighting. Accidents, injuries, and health issues were common. During the late nineteenth century, legislative reforms were passed to outlaw such abuses.

Royal Normal College and Academy of Music for the Blind

The school Penny eventually attends is still in operation today, though the name has changed to simply the Royal National College for the Blind. Since its opening in 1872, this institution has been well-known for providing educational and vocational training for blind and visually impaired individuals.

DISCUSSION QUESTIONS

1. Eva struggles with feeling abandoned after her parents die. Think about a time when you felt abandoned or isolated. What were the circumstances surrounding that event? How did it impact you emotionally? What methods did you use to cope with that situation?

2. Eva believed she caused her mother's death by leaving a window open, though that was not true. Do you have any childhood misconceptions that still impact your thoughts and emotions? Eventually, Eva found relief when she confided in Bram. How does sharing struggles contribute to your emotional growth?

3. Uncle Pendleton is in the early stages of dementia. What do you know about dementia symptoms, the progression of the illness, and the impact on the person and their loved ones? Is there anyone in your life who suffers from this? If so, what are your struggles in your relationship with that person? How can you provide

support to the person suffering and to the caregivers involved?

4. Penny is blind, yet she shows remarkable resilience and
determination. What factors have contributed to her
positive attitude and her refusal to let her blindness hinder her? How does Penny's attitude toward her lack of
sight influence the way others perceive and interact with
her? What lesson can we learn from her example?

5. Have you ever heard of Guy Fawkes Day? What is
something you celebrate that others in different parts of
the world might consider odd? What are the origins and
significance of this celebration? How does it reflect the
values and beliefs of your community?

6. Bram tells Eva that an anchor is an ancient symbol of
hope and faith. Reflecting on your own beliefs and
experiences, what symbols represent faith and hope to
you?

7. Bram tells Eva the very first time she asked God to
pardon her, God did. He infers that is what grace is all
about. What is your understanding of grace? Why do
you think Eva had such a hard time believing God for-
gave her? Do you ever struggle to accept God can forgive whatever you've done?

8. Who do you think was the bigger scoundrel: Richard
Trestwell or Professor Grimwinkle? Why?

9. Which character did you identify with the most and
why?

10. Eva has a great love of Heffer's bookstore in Cambridge, which is still there today. Do you have a favorite bookstore? What do you like about it?

ACKNOWLEDGMENTS

Some say it takes a village to raise a child and to write a book. I say it takes a lot of mango kombucha and cashews mixed with chocolate chips . . . which may be why my jeans are always so much tighter by the time I type *The End*.

But it also takes awesome publishing experts. Thanks to my editors at Bethany: Rochelle Gloege and Kate Deppe (and a shoutout to Raela just because she's always game to chat all things movie, Netflix, and book related). And kudos to Wendy Lawton over at Books & Such Literary Management, who encouraged me to give Bethany a whirl in the first place.

A huge amount of gratitude and combat pay to my long-suffering critique buddies: Tara Johnson, Julie Klassen, Shannon McNear, Ane Mulligan, MaryLu Tyndall, and Erica Vetsch. A special badge of award goes to Chawna Schroeder, who has the most story-detailed mind a girl could have, and to Dani Snyder, first reader.

I have so many awesome readers that there's just not space in the universe to list them all, but I do like to mention a few at the back of every book. So thank-yous this time go to Patti

Palusis, Rachel Warren Ratliff, Connie Porter Saunders, and Lisamarie Whiting.

And as usual, a round of applause for my husband, Mark, who is always up for a romp through England and plotting in a pub.

BIBLIOGRAPHY

The Archaeology of Roman Britain. R.G. Collingwood and Ian Richmond. 1969. W&J Mackay & Co. Ltd., Chatham, Kent.

A Country House at Work, Three Centuries of Dunham Massey. Pamela Sambrook. 2003. National Trust Enterprises Ltd., London.

Children's Work and Welfare, 1780–1890. Pamela Horn. 1994. The Press Syndicate of the University of Cambridge.

Le Morte d'Arthur. Sir Thomas Malory. 1999. Modern Library, New York.

Life and Letters on the Roman Frontier. Alan K. Bowman. 1994. British Museum Pub. Ltd., London.

Love in the Time of Victoria. Francoise Barret-Ducrocq. 1989. Penguin Books USA Inc., New York.

Remember, Remember: A Cultural History of Guy Fawkes Day. James Sharpe. 2005. Harvard University Press, Cambridge, Massachusetts.

Roman Britain and Where to Find It. Denise Allen and Mike Bryan. 2020. Amberley Publishing, Gloucestershire.

Vindolanda, A Roman Frontier Fort on Hadrian's Wall. Robin Birley. 2009. Amberley Publishing, Gloucestershire.

Coming Soon

A VICTORIAN CHRISTMAS NOVELLA

AVAILABLE FALL 2026

When Isabelle Beaumont inherits an orphanage, she determines to make the most of it and give the children of Haven House the best Christmas ever. Little does she realize just how daunting a task that will be with the building damaged by fire and the ledgers woefully unbalanced.

Barrister Rafe Munro would like nothing more than to comfort his mourning mother, and what better time than at Christmas? In search of a special gift for her, he discovers his recently deceased sister may have birthed a son out of wedlock and left the child at the orphanage where she volunteered. But the new director of Haven House hasn't a clue where to find the proof.

As Isabelle and Rafe join forces to sort things out while bringing joy to the children and his mother, they are met with unforeseen challenges. It's all too much for Isabelle. When faced with a tempting offer to sell Haven House, she must decide if the orphanage will remain in operation. And when Rafe's search proves fruitful, his mother has a most unexpected reaction. Can Christmas be redeemed, or is the memorable holiday they've both worked so hard for better forgotten?

Michelle Griep has been writing since she first discovered blank wall space and Crayola. She is a Christy Award–winning author of historical romances that both intrigue and evoke a smile. She's an Anglophile at heart, and you'll most often find her partaking of a proper cream tea while scheming up her next novel . . . but it's probably easier to find her at MichelleGriep.com or on Facebook, Instagram, and Pinterest.

Sign Up for Michelle's Newsletter

Keep up to date with Michelle's latest news on book releases and events by signing up for her email list at the link below.

MichelleGriep.com

FOLLOW MICHELLE ON SOCIAL MEDIA

Michelle Griep   @MichelleGriep   @MichelleGriep

You Are Invited!

Join like-minded fans in the **Inspirational Regency Readers** group on Facebook.

From book news from popular Regency authors like Kristi Ann Hunter, Michelle Griep, Erica Vetsch, Julie Klassen, and many others, to games and giveaways, to discussions of favorite Regency reads and adaptations new and old, to places we long to travel, you will find plenty of fun and friendship within this growing community.

Free and easy to join, simply search for "Inspirational Regency Readers" on Facebook.

We look forward to seeing you there!

BETHANYHOUSE